MW01125329

STRAIGHT FROM THE HEART—
SHANNON DRAKE

"SHANNON DRAKE CONTINUES TO PRODUCE
ADDICTING ROMANCES"
Publishers Weekly

KNIGHT OF FIRE

"EXCELLENT!"
Rendezvous

"STUNNING STORYTELLING! . . .
A shining love story that entrances readers
with its hypnotic power"
Romantic Times

BRIDE OF THE WIND

"*Bride of the Wind* fires the imagination"
Affaire de Coeur

DAMSEL IN DISTRESS

"WOW! . . . SUPERB!"
Rendezvous

"WONDERFULLY ROMANTIC,
EXCITING AND SENSUAL . . .
Carries you away to a world of
love, adventure, and the stuff legends are made of"
Romantic Times

Other Avon Books by
Shannon Drake

BRIDE OF THE WIND
DAMSEL IN DISTRESS
KNIGHT OF FIRE

Avon Books are available at special quantity discounts for bulk purchases for sales promotions, premiums, fund raising or educational use. Special books, or book excerpts, can also be created to fit specific needs.

For details write or telephone the office of the Director of Special Markets, Avon Books, Dept. FP, 1350 Avenue of the Americas, New York, New York 10019, 1-800-238-0658.

SHANNON DRAKE

BRANDED HEARTS

AVON BOOKS ◆ NEW YORK

If you purchased this book without a cover, you should be aware that this book is stolen property. It was reported as ''unsold and destroyed'' to the publisher, and neither the author nor the publisher has received any payment for this ''stripped book.''

BRANDED HEARTS is an original publication of Avon Books. This work has never before appeared in book form. This work is a novel. Any similarity to actual persons or events is purely coincidental.

AVON BOOKS
A division of
The Hearst Corporation
1350 Avenue of the Americas
New York, New York 10019

Copyright © 1994 by Heather Graham Pozzessere
Author photograph by Lewis Feldman
Published by arrangement with the author
Library of Congress Catalog Card Number: 94-96255
ISBN: 0-380-77170-5

All rights reserved, which includes the right to reproduce this book or portions thereof in any form whatsoever except as provided by the U.S. Copyright Law. For information address Acton and Dystel, Inc., 928 Broadway, New York, New York 10010.

First Avon Books Special Printing: November 1994
First Avon Books Printing: February 1995

AVON TRADEMARK REG. U.S. PAT. OFF. AND IN OTHER COUNTRIES, MARCA REGISTRADA, HECHO EN U.S.A.

Printed in the U.S.A.

RA   10   9   8   7   6   5   4   3   2   1

With lots of love and thanks
to Nan Ryan and Lori Copeland,
two of the very best "ex-best friends" possible

One

Coopersville
Colorado Territory

*T*he saloon on the east side of Main Street seemed an impressive enough establishment, Ian McShane decided. He observed the place more carefully as he tied his horse at the hitching post in front of it. Then he crossed the planked-wood sidewalks that bordered most of the businesses in the town, pushed open the double wood-slatted doors, and stepped inside. For a moment he stood there, letting his eyes adjust to the dim interior, and observed the place.

Music played, not too loudly or wildly. Encompassed in some of the smoke that filled the room, a talented young man played a piano, seemingly oblivious to everything around him, except the pleasant sound of his music. A young woman, half hidden from Ian's view, sang to the man's piano tune with a soft and lovely soprano, a sound that seemed plaintive and out of place here, no matter how "respectable" the establishment, for in the midst of more earthly masculine pursuits such as playing cards, drinking, and bawdy, bartered gratification, she seemed to weave silken, haunting

1

dreams that curled around a man's heart and soul. Perhaps it was her choice of song that created that illusion—a ballad from the recently ended war between the states. The words were sad but the feminine beauty of her voice made them poignant. Or perhaps it was the mystery of the songstress herself, for her back was turned to him and his view of her was partially blocked by a support beam. The rise of smoke from the patrons near the piano might have rivaled that on a battlefield, but through its haze he could see that she was slim, darkly clad, and blond. Worth investigating later, he determined. Not now. No matter how intriguing she might prove to be.

He stiffened his shoulders and willed himself to forget the pianist and the songstress, since such a business needed much more than just a talented pair of entertainers in order to survive. He studied the saloon once again. The tables and chairs looked sturdy—obviously meant to survive a barroom brawl or two—but were handsomely carved. The bar was beautifully carved as well; etched glass mirrors rose behind it. A long winding staircase led to the second floor, and though McCastle's was billed as a "gentlemen's bar," this was a frontier town, built by cattlemen and gold seekers, and few of them were gentlemen. McCastle's provided every kind of pleasure, he had heard. Wine, women, and song could all be found, here the wine and song in public view, the women more discreetly in the rooms at the top of the beautifully crafted staircase.

He found himself wondering if the blond nightingale was part and parcel of the entertainment McCastle's offered upstairs, then he again reminded himself that, for the moment, he had to be more amused than intrigued by the prospect of such entertainment. He'd come to town with a purpose, a purpose that had simmered in him for an eternity it seemed at times, always aglow, like the flicker of a small flame, burning within him. Sometimes, though, the flame rose. To something like a brush-fire, wild, and so hot it singed everything around it. Memory could make him forget hunger, taste, touch, or desire. Any woman, any need. Memory could bring back the past in vivid pain and color, and he would swallow hard and fight the pain and assure himself that he would have his revenge. His time would come. He would make it come. He had dedicated his life to it. He had waited a long time to reach this point.

And he was close now. So close, here in Coopersville. And at McCastle's. By chance, he had happened upon the information and good fortune to come here, right where he could get a firm foothold to begin.

There had been a change at McCastle's recently. One he was going to be able to use well to his own advantage.

He stepped up to the bar, adjusted his hat, and stared at the denizens of the place. There were cowhands stretched out alongside of him to his left, most of them still clad in chaps and dust, spurred boots and wide-brimmed hats. Some of the town's leading businessmen seemed to be gathered at his other side, upright fellows in black gentlemen's suits, crisp white shirts, fresh-shined shoes, and slicked-down hair. Mixed in among them all were some of the town merchants with their vests and timepieces and rolled-up sleeves.

At the gaming tables, the cowmen and the businessmen seemed to mix; there were at least four poker games going on at various tables, two of them run by the house, and two of them undertaken by clientele alone, dealer's choice games, both of them sporting large amounts of cash upon the table.

"What'll it be, sir?"

The bartender had curling gray hair and whiskers, intelligent eyes, and a pleasant manner. His crisp striped shirt spoke of the establishment's respectability, which was remarkable in a dust-covered new town etched out on the border of Indian territory.

For a moment he thought back to a time, a life, he had known briefly. A time with cool breezes and soft, sweet scents, the whisper of a river and the fresh feel of morning dew on rich, thick grasses. A lemonade would have been nice.

He looked around at the mixed crew of customers in the saloon.

"I'd better make it whiskey," he told the bartender, tossing down a gold coin. The bartender grinned good-naturedly and handed Ian a bottle and a shot glass. Ian surveyed the room for a moment. He wanted information. It never hurt to play for a little money.

He strode to one of the tables at the back of the saloon. An old-timer sunk low into his chair with his hat pulled down over his eyes appeared to be dozing through the proceedings. A small pile of coins sat in front of him, but he wasn't paying the least heed to the cards being played. It didn't matter. He was being assisted by the two young fellows who sat on either side of him. They were identical twins, about twenty years old with shaggy brown hair cut the same length, the same brown eyes that glinted with the innocence of youth, and the same wide white-toothed smiles.

The other two players were something else. Dealing was a rough-looking gent with a scar down his left cheek, sallow features slim and taut, eyes so light a brown they appeared snake-yellow, and hair so dust covered it was difficult to discern its true color.

Across from him sat his very antithesis—a man dressed in an immaculate black frock coat and breeches, and wearing a crimson brocaded vest complete with an elegant gold pocket watch. His features were lean and thin as well, his eyes were a faded blue, and his smoothly combed hair was snow-white. His gaze had held steadily on the rough-hewn man dealing the cards but as Ian stood by the table, his light blue eyes traveled upward with mild interest and he studied Ian.

"You got money, stranger?" he inquired.

Ian drew a handful of coins from an inner pocket of his long black duster, setting them down before him on the table. One of the twins immediately stood up, supplying him with a chair. He was barely seated before he inhaled the sweet scent of perfume. He arched a brow as he looked to his right. A sweet young thing—perhaps not-so-sweet and maybe even not-so-young—was perched on the edge of his chair. She wore a vivid, royal blue dress but seemed to be spilling out of it, she was so spectacularly endowed. Her hair was dark, her eyes were a bright green, and her smile was wide and warm and seemingly sincere.

He nodded to her, smiling wryly. He was oddly disappointed. He'd been hoping for the songstress. He shrugged to himself and tossed in his ante. "Deal me in, cowhand," he said softly.

The scar-cheeked cowhand did so. "Where you hail from, stranger?" he inquired casually, the cards falling as he spoke.

"Here and there," Ian replied casually, watching the cards fall.

"Where 'here' and where 'there'?" asked the smooth player in black. "And what are you doing out in this 'here' now?"

"It's a free country, last I heard," Ian said, glancing at the man, then watching the cards fall again. The old-timer didn't look at his cards. "Is he playing?" Ian asked one of the twins.

"Sure. Old man Turner dozes off now and then but me and Jimmy check his cards for him. He's been doing okay tonight. He usually plays his best when he sleeps through half the game. Jimmy and I ain't doing so well. Neither is Scar there," he added, indicating the cowhand. He waved a hand toward the man in black. "It seems to be Johnny Durango's night tonight."

"Gentlemen," said the man who had been referred to as Johnny Durango, studying his hand then. "There is a fine art to poker. You've yet to learn it."

"Ah, yes! There is an art!" Ian murmured, meeting Durango's eyes. Ian started to pour himself a whiskey. The buxom brunette at his side with the golden smile reached past him and poured for him. He nodded, picked up his glass. He lifted it to her. Her smile deepened.

"Thanks," he said.

"My pleasure. I'm Dulcie," she told him with a wonderful husky voice.

"You bet you are!" he murmured softly, studying his cards. He adjusted his hand, looking at the twin who had spoken to him.

"You boys regulars here?" he asked.

"Sure thing, we work for the place. Well, we came for the gold, but there weren't no gold in our claim, and so we're here."

"We worked for the old man!" his twin said softly.

"And now the old man is dead," volunteered the scar-cheeked cowhand with a shrug.

"We've worked for his partner as well, and his partner is boss *and* tough as nails," one of the twins said earnestly.

"Yeah, tough as nails," the other agreed. His voice was oddly a mixture of conviction and doubt.

"You're dealing, cowboy," Johnny Durango said sharply.

"Bet's to you, Jimmy," Scar announced.

"Five dollars. And old man Turner will see me."

The second twin followed suit; Ian threw in. Johnny Durango threw in a five, and another five. "I raise you, gentlemen. Scar, ten to you to stay."

The betting finished out, all of them remaining in the hand. Ian held three kings. He lost to Johnny Durango's three aces.

The game continued. Turner won a hand; the deal shifted around—skipping Turner, who continued to doze, the only man at the table other than Johnny Durango to take a pot.

Ian hadn't been playing long when he discovered that his buxom beauty was giving away his cards. He managed to send her away and won a hand. When she returned, he kept his eyes on the man with the colorless blue eyes who had mastered the fine "art" of playing.

The art was in his sleeves. Watching him closely during several games, Ian saw that a pair of aces was easily—and often—being shifted in and out of play from the man's shirt. When the play ended on the next game, Ian rose to take the pot.

"I beg your pardon?" Johnny Durango said coolly.

"My full house beats the three kings you had on the table," Ian said flatly.

"Why, how dare you, sir, how dare you!"

"Why I dare, Durango, because you've been cheating us blind!" Ian told him simply.

The man leapt up, drawing his pistol. Ian struck out swiftly, knocking the gun from the man's hand. Durango then leapt across the table, fists flying. Ian ducked and dived, catching his opponent in the gut, and crashed hard with him to the floor, where they rolled, entangled, toward the bar.

Ian had a good grip on his opponent's shoulder and was ready to drag Durango up with him when a searing pain burst across the top of his head as a bottle was cracked hard atop it. The earth began to spin and blacken. He fought the threat of losing consciousness, turning to stare at a man who had been drinking at a table near them, a younger fellow than Durango, dressed in the neat, pristine clothing of a banker. Some banker. When Dulcie hadn't been there to give away Ian's cards, this fellow had probably been doing his best from his own table.

Ian didn't pass out. The fellow reached for another bottle, alarm rising in his eyes. Ian strode swiftly forward and punched him hard in the stomach. The man doubled over with a gasp, then quickly stood, a placating hand before him. He worked his jaw but didn't speak. His hand still out to ward off another blow, he stumbled from the saloon.

"What in God's name—!" began a melodic but firm feminine voice.

Ian spun on Durango again, toward the sound of the voice.

"Stop! Damn you, just stop where you are!" Durango rasped out.

Ian did stop, a brow raised. The man had seized hold of a woman.

The songstress.

"Durango, you ridiculous bastard!" she gasped out.

She was being held hard to Durango's side, half smothered by him, so it seemed, and turned slightly away from Ian. But she was still so obviously . . . female. Delicate tendrils of hair covered her face and Ian could still see so little of her. Still he felt that same tug of emotion that he had felt when he had heard her sing. She was shadowed by Durango's body and the darkness forming in the saloon with twilight's coming, and she might have had the face of a musk ox, but at that moment, Ian didn't care. Durango was welcome to die quickly if he didn't let her go.

"Durango, you eager to go to hell?" he asked quietly.

Durango replied by slipping a very small pistol out of his sleeve—the same sleeve that had held the aces—and leveling it against the back of the woman's head.

"Damn you, let her go!" Ian grated out.

"Tough man, the stranger who rides into town!" Durango said. "Kill me, I kill her."

"You'll be dead before your finger can move on the trigger!" Ian warned softly.

"Do you dare take the chance?" Durango asked.

"All right, no more!" the woman suddenly cried. "Durango, you slimy bastard!" she shouted, suddenly slamming a backward kick into Durango that caused him to explode with a groan, releasing her. Ian made good use of the opportunity, and fired.

He hit Durango's hand, shattering bone. Durango screeched in rage and pain, but he was helpless. It was his gun hand that had been shattered, and his little pistol was on the floor.

Suddenly there was chaos. Durango's cohort who had wielded the liquor bottle against Ian's head was stumbling as quickly as he could out the door. The twins were on their feet—hell, half the saloon's patrons were now up and on their feet and cheering Ian on.

Everybody loves a winner, he thought a bit wearily.

Except the loser.

"You damned ass of a loser Reb!" Durango was

shouting at him, holding his bloodied hand. "You should have killed me, you should have finished it between us. You've signed your death warrant!"

"I've signed lots of them, so I've been told," Ian said casually. He turned to the twins. "Get the money he cheated off all of us, and get him out of here. And get me the damned manager—no, the owner. What the hell kind of a place is this anyway?"

The buxom brunette sidled up behind him, giggling softly as she whispered, "Why, honey, it's a house of ill repute. A whorehouse. A damned nice one at that!"

"Are you paid to help white trash like that cheat honest men?" he asked her in return.

"I've yet to meet an honest man," Dulcie told him gravely. "You honest, stranger?" she asked sweetly.

"I should have your ass fired," he warned her, his voice still very low.

Dulcie smiled. "Honey, if I owe you, you should simply have my ass." She slipped on by him, all innocence, and he couldn't help but be amused. Still, this was business. He'd be damned if he'd let himself be amused. "I want to see the owner! Now!" Ian announced, his words a sharp command.

The blond songstress who had so recently been in the hustler's grasp suddenly came forward. The crowd that had gathered around the twins as they dragged out Durango gave way instantly for her.

She was out of the shadow.

She didn't have the face of an ox at all. She stood in front of him, watching him, assessing him, dead still and silent, her chin held high with absolute dignity. She seemed angry. He had just saved her from the surefire promise of an early grave, and she seemed irritated. As if he had somehow ruined her day.

She was dressed in black, an exquisite beaded black dress which rose chastely to the column of her neck, almost as if she were in mourning. Nothing could be more concealing in style, yet the garment hugged her breasts and torso, and despite the circumstances surrounding his meeting with her, he felt a swift, sharp stab of desire . . . and something deeper that tugged at his soul, as her song had done.

She was of medium height, and against the stark black of her gown, her hair was a startling shade of deep sun blond, worn in a severe chignon. Her eyes were bluer than the sky on the clearest, most radiant day. He couldn't quite determine her age, but he thought that she was over twenty and under thirty. She was beautiful, slim, graceful in her every movement, small-boned, delicate, and yet with a look of wisdom and maturity in her eyes. She seemed to enchant him instantly. In fact, for long seconds he found himself speechless, then he became annoyed with himself for letting her unsettle him.

"A thank-you might be in order," he told her.

Imperiously she arched an elegant golden brow. "For what, sir? I could have handled myself quite well alone against Johnny Durango—without causing half this travesty!"

"Durango was cheating. And he was holding a gun to your head."

"He wouldn't have pulled the trigger."

"Why not? Are you in league with him?"

"Of course not!"

"Half the place is, so it seems. The sheriff can look into it. I take it there is a sheriff in this armpit of a town."

"You don't need the sheriff," she said, her tone changing slightly.

"I don't? Well, then, I've asked to see the owner of this wretched whorehouse!" he stated harshly.

"So you have," she replied coolly, smoothing back a strand of sun-colored hair that had escaped from her chignon. "I am Ann McCastle, the owner of this fine establishment!"

She wasn't what he had been expecting. Not in the least. And damn her, she had him again. His surprise must have shown in his face. She smiled mirthlessly. "I am Ann McCastle, sir, and I repeat, you do not need to draw the sheriff into this."

"Oh?" he inquired, smiling himself. She didn't want the law in. *Had* she been in league with Durango? What else might it be? But how strange, he had the upper hand here suddenly. She was still irritated—no, downright furious. But she was going to have to do the right thing.

Grovel.

"Well, Ann McCastle," he said, leaning against the bar as he addressed her, his voice very low again since it seemed they still had an audience—everyone else in the saloon, "this place is billed as a proper establishment for law-abiding citizens. I was cheated and attacked. Seems to me something should be done about it."

"Seems to me you know how to take care of yourself!" she murmured irritably.

"Seems to me I shouldn't have to."

"It's a nasty old world, sir. And you're in a damned rough part of it."

"Honest folk are entitled—"

"Honest folk aren't usually quite so adept with guns."

"There's been a war on recently, hadn't you heard? And, lady, there isn't a single law in the land against a man being able to take care of himself, but I'm sure there are any number of laws against gambling establishments being on the take and hustling their customers. Then again, if you can't understand things from my view, I am willing to take my complaints to the sheriff or a marshal—"

"There's no need," she said smoothly, but again, there was that almost indiscernible note of unease in her voice. She didn't want the law around.

Why not?

It didn't matter right now. All that mattered was that she didn't like to talk about the sheriff. And it was something that he could use.

"No need of the law . . . " he murmured.

"Aaron!" she called, her voice rising as she addressed the handsome young piano player. "Give us a tune again, please. Gentlemen, return to your games!"

There was a slight grumbling from the men—cowhands, merchants, and businessmen alike—who had been trying to catch bits and pieces of their conversation.

"Gentlemen . . . " she repeated. There was something about the way she said the word . . . as if she were a princess and they were knights sworn to do her bidding. The tone of her voice could move mountains, so it seemed.

Ian gave himself fair warning that Ann McCastle certainly did wield a power all her own.

The piano began to play.

Disgruntled, the men went back to their games.

Ann McCastle directed her attention now to Ian exclusively. She didn't exactly grovel, but despite the acidity in her voice as she spoke, she said the proper words for the situation.

"We are, of course, deeply disturbed that you've had such a displeasing experience. We will be delighted to provide a night's lodging for you as our guest, and, of course, invite you to eat and drink at our expense as well. And I know that any of our young ladies—"

"Whores?" he inquired, unable to resist the temptation to lean close to her and whisper the word softly in her ear, despite the music that now played and the conversation that filled the bar again. After all, despite her elegance and eloquence, McCastle's was a western saloon, and no amount of silk was going to change that.

She exhaled with a patient but oh so weary, patronizing, sigh. "Any *lady* here, sir," she emphasized, "will be glad to help make up for the experience you have suffered here this afternoon." She turned from him, calling to the bartender, "Harold, a cool beer for this gentleman, please!"

Harold was the very soul of propriety, just winking slightly as he set down the beer and then ambled along back behind the bar.

Ian sipped the beer, adjusted the rim of his hat, and stared at Ann McCastle.

"Sir—" she began anew with impatience.

"All right," he said.

"Then—"

"I'll accept a night's lodging, and . . . "

"And?"

"I assume you've got a decent cook."

"Of course. Henri is the best."

"French?" he inquired with dry humor.

"Yes."

"Out here?" he said skeptically. "In the wild, wicked west?"

"Yes!" she snapped. "So then things are settled—"

"Almost," Ian said, then leaned comfortably against the bar, watching her as he took another sip of the beer.

"What now?" she asked, her blue eyes narrowing.

"You offered me the companionship of a . . . lady."

"Yes. You've met Dulcie. You can meet the others—"

"I know who I want."

"Dulcie will be pleased—"

"I don't want Dulcie."

"Then—"

"I want you."

Her blue eyes widened. She was startled, and perhaps just a little bit alarmed. For a second, he had her.

Quickly she regained her composure. Her lashes swept cheeks, her chin tilted higher. "You don't seem to understand. I am the owner."

"Definitely a lady of the house."

"But—"

"You mean to tell me you came to own such an establishment as this by spending your life in a nunnery?"

Her eyes flashed with anger and narrowed again. "I mean that I do whatever the hell I choose to do—sir!"

He smiled, lifted his beer, took a long sip of it, and set the glass back down on the bar.

"Then, Ann McCastle, I think that you should choose to be with me tonight," he told her. "Excuse me, I think I'll just see to my horse for the night."

He started to walk out of the saloon, a half smile curving his lip. She was going to follow him; he was certain.

She did follow him. He had just come out and was loosening the girth on his bay, Joe, when he heard her pause behind him. His smile deepened. He didn't turn. He waited.

She lashed out in a whisper. "I don't really owe you anything! You should be grateful for what you're being offered. It was a poker game, for God's

sake. I'm not in control of the way men choose to
play—"

"Really?" he said, pausing at last and turning to
her. "I think a male owner might have known what
kind of shark was frequenting his establishment."

"Lots of sharks frequent lots of similar establishments!" she returned angrily.

He shrugged. "Maybe. But you see, I was cheated
at *your* place. And I am willing to bring a complaint
about it to the law."

She paled.

"I can actually pay you—"

"What? You mean you aren't in the saloon business for the money yourself, Mrs. McCastle? It is
Mrs. McCastle, isn't it?"

Without responding to his question, she continued, "In fact, I'd be willing to pay a lot if you'd just
go away!"

Now he was all the more intrigued. Not that it
mattered. He was not going away. Not for love or
money or any other force on earth. Especially not
now. Not since he had met Ann McCastle and sized
up the situation within the saloon. He was exactly
where he wanted to be.

"It's not going to happen," he told her. "I'm in
town for a while. Definitely for the night. I wouldn't
miss the night to come at McCastle's for all the
money on earth."

"What if I really could give you a lot of money?"

"I'd still be looking forward to my night with you,
Ann McCastle."

"What makes you think I'd be worth it?" she exploded.

He shrugged and allowed his gaze to roam up and
down the black-clad length of her. She would be
worth it. She was like a rose growing alone on a
parched plain of dry dust. Elegant and golden, yet

seeming to burn with a wild inner fire. He was definitely intrigued by the thought of trying to break
through her barriers to get at that inner fire. In fact,
it seemed now that his own dead-set purpose was
cast along an incredibly fascinating course.

There was no need, however, to let Ann McCastle
know just how compelling he found her. She'd already informed him she did what she chose. She was
a confident and determined woman, as well as a
strikingly beautiful one. She could probably seduce
heart, soul, and mind from most men—not to mention their hard-earned cash.

"I don't know that you're worth a wooden nickel,
ma'am," he told her casually, "but I am the adventurous type and—"

"How dare you—" she began, her voice low and
furious, her eyes flashing like sapphires.

"And I am extremely determined and tenacious,"
he finished, as if she hadn't interrupted.

"And you can go straight to hell!" she informed
him as she turned to walk away from him.

He hadn't intended to follow her, but he did. He
caught her arm before she could step up to the
planked-wood sidewalk in front of McCastle's and
swung her around to face him.

"In time," he told her, "I might just oblige you
and wind up in the devil's domain. But it won't be
soon enough for your purposes. And you should be
glad I am not a man who is easily offended. My
pride could have been sadly bruised by such a 'lady'
as yourself refusing my heartfelt attentions!"

"There isn't one damned heartfelt thing about
you!" she assured him.

She didn't try to wrench free of him. He could feel
the wealth of fury that seemed to pulse all around
her, and he was startled to realize that what had
begun as an entertaining game with her was sud-

denly so much more. His roads had often been long and hard, but he suddenly couldn't remember wanting a woman more than he wanted her now.

He needed this one, he reminded himself. She was a step in the direction he wanted to go.

"Why are you so afraid of the law?" he demanded of her suddenly.

"I'm not!"

"You are."

"I'm telling you—"

"And you're lying, and on top of that, you're not doing half as well as you think you are. What happened in there today shouldn't ever have occurred."

"Men fight in saloons all the time—"

"Out in the streets, if the saloon is worth its whiskey. And they fight—they don't cheat!"

"Oh! So it's proper and legal when they blow holes in one another but when someone loses five dollars in a poker game—"

"The law can step in one way or the other!"

She fell silent, staring at him, furious.

He lowered his voice. "You need help, lady, and you need it fast."

Now she did jerk back from him, and put her hands on her hips. "You shot a gun from a man's hand—"

"And saved your life."

"Johnny never would have shot me."

"Because you're involved in the fleecing of your customers with him and your girls?"

"My girls are not—"

"Oh, sweet Jesu!" he swore. "At least one of your girls damned well was in on it!"

"So I had a little bit of trouble this afternoon. And you seem to think I need a dozen men about to—"

"I didn't say anything about your needing a

dozen men. You need one man. One good man."

"And you're suggesting that should be you?" she inquired with amused disdain.

"Damned right, Ann McCastle. Damned right!" he told her. He turned around, heading for his horse again. She hadn't moved. She was staring after him. He knew it.

He loosed Joe's reins from the hitching post and smiled back at her. "But then, Ann McCastle, you can make up your own mind about that after tonight. You *will* be seeing me tonight."

"Not in your wildest dreams, cowboy!"

He laughed softly, indicating a building up the street. "That's the sheriff's office up there?"

She swore furiously beneath her breath and spun around.

"See you later, Annie!" he called softly.

She went still and stiff, then turned back to him, a guarded expression on her face.

"Sir, I'm telling you, you won't be seeing me! And I don't wish to leave things as they are—"

"You know, neither do I. McCastle's does have a certain reputation to maintain. I should go to the law right now to guard that reputation. Or else you're just going to have to listen to me. I'll have your word right now that you will be seeing me later, or I'll walk right to the sheriff's office. Maybe McCastle's is in need of a thorough investigation."

She would have hit him if she'd been close enough, he thought.

"Fine!" she spat out. "You've got my word. But what if my word isn't any good?"

"It will be good," he promised her. "I'll see to it that it's good. By the way, my name's McShane. Ian McShane. And it's a name you are going to know very well."

"You think so?"

"I know so," he assured her. He tipped his hat to her and turned about, leading Joe toward the public stables down the street.

He was aware that she watched him all the way.

He smiled grimly as he walked. It had all gone damned well, incredibly well. He had struck up a relationship—as it was—with Ann McCastle, and it had been easier than he'd ever imagined, thanks to the fool card hustler. He had exactly what he'd come for and more. He was well on his way.

And yet . . .

Just what was behind the cool exterior of the perfect little golden goddess who now ran the place? Why did she fear the law; what lay behind the sky-blue beauty of those haunting eyes . . . ?

Sweet Jesus, did it matter? He had his own purpose here. He kept the secrets of his past; she was welcome to hers. Her fear of the law had served him very well.

It didn't matter.

Yet suddenly, something did matter.

The night.

All the fires of hell and damnation seemed to be burning within him. Wickedly hot, yearning, hungry. He closed his eyes, and saw her face. Paused, and still seemed to feel her heat. He could even hear the echo of her voice, the song that had reached out to him when he'd first entered the saloon.

It was all just a means to an end, he reminded himself impatiently.

McCastle's was a means to an end.

And she . . .

Ann McCastle, willing or not, was miraculously aligned just where he needed her to be as well, a means to an end.

No such sweet logic worked with him now. The fires continued to burn.

Yes, something mattered.

The night . . .

He could hardly wait for the darkness to come.

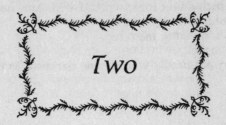

Two

As the owner of a saloon, Ann had had both the opportunity and the misfortune to study men. She and Eddie had bought the place nearly four years ago, and though she'd met her share of the best and worst of humanity before then, the saloon had given her a chance to study more males than she'd ever imagined. She had come across all manner of the gender. White men, red men, wild men, tame men, black men, cowboys, gunslingers, bankers. Bitter ex-Rebs, worn-out cattlemen and rustlers. She'd known those with a glint of cruelty in their eyes—she even thought she knew full well the face of true evil—but she'd also seen the kindness and the goodness that could be found in some.

Men had often caused a fair amount of trouble in her life. She'd never given a damn about the slings and arrows cast her way by many members of her own fair sex over the fact that she owned the saloon—she owned the saloon for her own reasons and they were all that mattered. But on occasion owning the saloon had set her up for the unwanted determinations of some of the clientele. There were those who just couldn't believe that a "little woman" could manage such a place, and at times, it had been damned hard. There were those who wanted to challenge her simply for being a "little woman." So far she had prevailed. Partly because she had spent half her life learning how to shoot a gun, and partly through willpower alone. Life had taught her bitter lessons at an early age and she had sworn she wouldn't be waylaid in her pursuits by friends or enemies. She didn't need to blink when challenged. She would prevail—or accept death. It was that simple.

Of course, until two weeks ago, she'd had another edge of protection. Eddie had been with her. By the simple virtue of being a man, Eddie had protected her.

But in all of her days, she'd never met anybody quite like this stranger Ian McShane, who had entered her life today so aggressively.

She'd seen him when he had arrived. Seen him like a dark, defined presence when he'd first pushed open the doors and stood there, silhouetted with the sun at his back. She hadn't seen his face then, but she'd sensed trouble. Big trouble. He was a tall man and dressed in a black railway duster; he had seemed even taller with the red falling sun at his back. And he certainly was big enough, she thought, though because of his height he gave the appearance of being lean. He was all muscle, lean and wiry like a cougar, more graceful than broad, yet she was quite certain that he could bring down many a man with a heavier build, perhaps more than one at the same time.

There was something about his eyes that fascinated her. That flicker of amusement within their dark depths when he challenged her, and the fire that burned deeply within them. He'd been around, she thought. Yet he didn't seem wearied by his experience; rather, he seemed sharper for it. Stronger. And she'd probably only witnessed a fraction of his skill in handling the pistols that hung from his gun belt. He wanted something out of life, and he was determined to get it. He wanted something out of her as well, and to her great distress, she realized that he meant to get that, too.

Tonight.

She felt a wave of something akin to panic seize her and she stiffened her spine, furious with herself. Still, she felt like running back into the saloon and tossing back a glass of whiskey in order to steady her nerves.

She had no intention of keeping any promises to the man! Yet . . . what would happen when she didn't? She swore violently to herself. He was ruggedly good-looking, harsh yet seductive, a man of mystery with more than a hint of danger about him. She was sure he had had no trouble finding women who were more than willing to be at his side. Why was he so determined to have her? She sensed that his interest in her was much deeper than a traveler's desire for a night's entertainment, and that frightened her.

She forced herself to walk sedately back into the saloon and to the bar, but once she reached it—and wonderful, dependable old Harold reached her—she did lean against the fine mahogany for support. "Whiskey!" she said urgently.

One of Harold's salt-and-pepper brows flew up in surprise, but he quickly set a shot glass in front of her and poured out a few fingers of the house's finest. He watched her as she took it down with a single swallow, shuddered, then gasped, and finally set the glass back on the bar. He remained before her in sympathetic silence.

"That stuff is awful," Ann said, shuddering again. "And you should go easy on it."

"Why?" she asked wryly. "It isn't a ladies' drink?"

"It isn't your drink," he observed quietly. "Ann, why are you letting this stranger get under your skin?"

She opened her mouth, then realized that Harold didn't know what the stranger had asked of her. She shook her head. "I'm just nervous, I guess," she lied. She smiled at him, aware as always that when she was in the saloon, she was being watched. And she never betrayed what she was feeling. She never let anyone goad her temper.

Until today.

She kept her voice very low, smiling as she spoke, determined to prove that she was poised—and made of iron. She had come too far to lose this place now.

"Ever since Eddie died, I've felt the stares—and nearly the teeth—of the sharks!" she said. "There are at least half a dozen men in the vicinity waiting for me to falter, and then they'll swim in for the kill!"

Harold shrugged, leaning back as he dried a glass. "Annie, you were in trouble here today."

"Durango wouldn't have hurt me—"

"Not under usual circumstances. Now, he'll be ready to slit your throat."

"Great. I can thank McShane for that as well."

"McShane?" Harold said, frowning.

She nodded, watching Harold. "That's what the stranger said. You know the name?"

Harold shrugged, shaking his head. "No . . . ah, no. He's sure a good shot, though."

"That he is," she agreed.

"Intriguing fellow," Harold commented.

"Yes, and I wonder what he's doing in town."

"The war has been over a few years now, Annie. Lots of fellows are coming out west; they ain't got anything left back east. You don't question every traveler who comes this way."

"Yes, well, this man isn't just a traveler who happened to come this way. He isn't just drifting west."

Harold leaned his elbows on the bar, his smile ironic. "Annie, we've had two-bit hustlers in here, downright outlaws, a lawman or two, Africans, Indians, showmen, gold diggers, farmers, and ranchers. Why should this fellow be any better—or worse?"

She shook her head uneasily. "He wants something."

"Everybody wants something."

"He wants something out of McCastle's."

Harold shrugged again. "Maybe it's something that McCastle's is ready to give."

"McCastle's isn't ready to give a damned thing," Ann told him. "Not a single damned thing. Maybe I should have another drink."

He leaned closer to her. "Maybe you shouldn't. Cocoa and Dulcie are both upstairs with one of the Weatherly boys."

Ann arched a brow sharply and nodded, managing to put the appearance of the stranger in town to the back of her mind.

"I'm going to my room," she told Harold. "Send them to me the minute they're back down and Weatherly is gone. Did anyone else slip in from the Circle Z?"

He shook his head. "Just young Joe Weatherly."

Her eyes lit up with a sparkle. "Just young Joe. Good." She smiled and started to turn away from the bar. She was startled when Harold's hand landed on hers.

"Annie, you've got to be careful."

"Harold, I am careful—and good."

Harold shook his head sadly. "Annie, you are

good. That's the problem. I don't mean good at what you do. You're good inside, and you shouldn't—"

"Oh, God, Harold!" she exclaimed softly, pausing long enough to set her free hand over his and squeeze gently. "Harold, they left me empty inside those many years ago—"

"Wrong, Annie! You should be some fine man's wife, raising fine sons and daughters to go to good schools. You should be singing to a husband in an elegant drawing room instead of a saloon—"

"Harold, I live here among good friends and some of the best people in the world, and it doesn't matter to me that life has cast them into roles where they have to make their money in hard ways. I'm careful, Harold, and I'm good. And I love you because you're an old dear, but you aren't going to change my mind about what I have to do."

"You just have to take care, Annie. I forgot to let you know, there's a letter from Ralph Reninger in your room that he brought by earlier today."

"Oh, no!" she murmured, then shook her head ruefully. "I think I had an appointment with him yesterday and I forgot all about it when the folks from that traveling theater made a sudden appearance for lunch." She felt exceptionally guilty. She didn't know Ralph well, but he was an earnest young man who had handled Eddie's affairs since the war had ended. After Eddie's death, he had told her he needed to see her, and of course she understood that she did need to see him and be advised if there was anything special she needed to do to put the saloon into her name alone. She'd never worried that Eddie might have left any of his property elsewhere—they'd been each other's only family, very close, and his death had hurt her terribly; she still couldn't believe that he was really gone.

Ralph had realized how much pain she had been

in; that was why he had told her they needed to talk in the very near future, just as soon as she could handle it. Well, of course, she was stronger now. She just hadn't had the time to stop by Ralph's office.

"Eddie's been buried these two weeks now, and legal affairs have to be set right. You'd best make sure you look through that letter good and see that young Mr. Reninger and watch out for your own interests. Annie, I tell you and tell you—"

"To take care!" she finished for him. "And I do! Don't worry, I'll get to the letter. But for the moment, don't forget to send the girls to me the minute they're free!"

Impulsively, she kissed his cheek. Then she hurried away from the bar and up the stairway to her room. There she closed the door.

The letter Harold had mentioned was on her bed, an impressive white envelope with white embossing. It was addressed to her in an elegant script. She plucked it up and tapped it against her lips but didn't open it at the moment. Agitated, she tossed it down on her dressing table. Maybe she'd get a chance to run over and see Ralph this afternoon. Probably not. Not with this irritating stranger now breathing down her neck!

She paced the room for a few moments, then sat in the old rocker by the doors to the balcony that overlooked Main Street. Her fingers curled over the carved wood arms of the chair. She loved the chair. She'd bought it from a woman who was returning east. The woman's husband had been the one with the dreams of a new life on the western frontier, but he had been killed by the Apache. The woman had wanted only to return home with her family, and Ann had felt her suffering. She'd loved the chair because it had reminded her of the one her mother had packed so lovingly when they'd left Missouri and begun their trip west. She had bought more furniture from the woman, paying outrageous sums so that the poor woman could get back home. Most of the furnishings she had put here in her own room, including the cherrywood four-poster bed and the draperies at the window, delicate lace sheers beneath a heavier fall of velvet.

It was a beautiful room, she thought. Her private haven. It was large and spacious with the bed as the room's centerpiece, the chair facing the balcony doors, a matching wardrobe and handsomely carved dressing table, and a daybed across from the chair, facing the balcony doors as well. A Persian rug lay on the gleaming hardwood floor, a silk Chinese dressing screen stood to the side of her wardrobe, and another of her personal treasures, a hip tub with fine gilt fixtures, sat in a little alcove next to the fireplace. Even Eddie had laughed at the hip tub.

"A bath just ain't something a body needs that often," he'd told her, scratching his old grizzled head in confusion. "Like gents, ladies can visit the bathhouse out back a couple times a year! Why, think of all the water that's got to be fetched and hauled and dragged up the stairs for such silliness, Annie!"

"Eddie," she'd told him in return, patting his whiskered chin, "there's no greater luxury in the world than a steaming bath next to a crackling fire in absolute and total privacy, I swear it!"

"You prune too much in water, you stay pruned!" Eddie had warned her. But he'd always seen to it that she'd had plenty of water. And he'd even taken to going to the bathhouse himself once a week, since she'd convinced him that he looked absolutely charming when dressed up handsomely in a frock coat and vest each evening, his silver hair slicked down and combed back.

Well, Eddie was gone. She'd loved him dearly,

and now she missed him. Sometimes she didn't believe that he was gone. He'd known her better than anyone else ever had. He had known what drove her, he'd understood her. He'd known about her nocturnal activities, and though he'd tried often enough to dissuade her from them, he had never gotten in her way. He had given her his complete confidence, he'd known she could create and run an establishment like McCastle's. He'd never interfered, he'd just been there with his huge bulk of a frontiersman's body and his authority had somehow never been questioned.

When Eddie had been around, she'd never experienced the trouble she'd had today. If he'd been there, Durango wouldn't have tried to fleece anyone, and she'd never have been put in such a wretched position with a man like the dangerous stranger who'd threatened to come her way tonight.

She bit into her lower lip worriedly. She hadn't entirely forgotten the stranger in the last few minutes. He would be trouble tonight. Maybe more trouble than she had expected.

But for the moment . . .

She couldn't worry about him. She had more pressing concerns.

She rose from the rocking chair and drew back the sheer white lace curtains that fluttered over the glass-paned balcony doors.

A few matrons ambled along the sidewalk toward the dry goods store. A merchant stepped from the bank, the barber stepped from his shop to inspect one of his razors against the setting sun.

And the stranger was coming back. Impossibly tall in his long black duster and low-brimmed hat, he moved smoothly along the street. He looked up suddenly, almost as if he had known someone might be looking down at him.

She stepped back quickly, dropping the curtain as if the white lace were flame, burning her fingers.

His face seemed etched in her memory. Large, deep, dark eyes of mahogany brown, brows even darker, hair so deep it was almost a sleek black, falling nearly dead straight to the top of his shoulders. High broad cheekbones, hard-squared chin, generous, cleanly defined mouth, lips quick to curl into a sardonic, sensual grin. Indian, she thought suddenly. There was Indian blood in him. She didn't know what kind or how much, but she'd seen that straight black hair before, known the power and ruthlessness of eyes so dark. *Why was he here? Just what in God's name was he after? How did she keep from being used in his pursuits?*

Or strung up by them?

"Annie!"

She heard her name called along with a quick tapping on her door. She spun swiftly around and hurried to the door, throwing it open. Dulcie swept by her, followed by Cocoa, a tall, elegant woman who was shaped like Venus and whose skin was as ebony as that of a Nubian princess. These women were not just her employees. They were her friends.

And her cohorts in crime.

Except that anything done against Cash Weatherly of the Circle Z ranch was not a crime. Because Cash deserved whatever happened to him. He deserved death by drawing and quartering.

Ann had thought often enough about riding straight to the ranch, fluttering her eyelashes in order to gain entry, and shooting the man straight through the heart. But she might not make it. She didn't mind dying herself—and she most certainly would be hanged for the deed—but she might be stopped.

And he wouldn't suffer enough.

No ...

Her plan was to destroy him entirely, and when she did kill him, she wanted him to know exactly why he was dying.

Dulcie perched on the foot of Ann's bed, while Cocoa stretched out languorously on the daybed looking like a well-satisfied cat who had just consumed a canary.

"Well?" Ann demanded, looking from one of them to the other. "Did you learn anything, did—"

"Did we learn anything, sugar!" Cocoa exclaimed, her voice deep and husky, just like a purr.

"The poor boy!" Dulcie added with a soft laugh. "He was entirely out of his league."

"He was all but singing every single family secret he had a clue to!" Cocoa said delightedly.

"His dad has four to six hired guns living at the ranch at all times," Dulcie provided.

"We knew he hired gun power," Ann said, "but—"

"And did you know the old man has a thing for you? A *serious* thing. He's been to see old Eddie's lawyer to find out if there isn't a way to get to you through this place! Joey says that what his father found out made him madder than hell, and more determined. He says that Cash goes through women, chewing them up and spitting them out, the way other men go through chewing tobacco, but that he has a hankering for you that just won't go away, no matter how many others he can grasp, ladies or whores."

Ann paused at that, startled. She'd been careful and distant any time Cash had been in the saloon. She didn't want him discovering in any way who she was, not by the slightest mistake or slip on her part. She hadn't realized that he was interested in her.

But then, until recently, she'd had Eddie to hide behind any time she had chosen.

"Fine. Let him hanker," she murmured. But she felt a momentary chill, and another moment's anger with herself. She had let things slide dangerously! Cash had managed to find the time to talk with Eddie's lawyer! But then, Cash hadn't felt the pain, the sorrow, or the loneliness she had endured at Eddie's death. He was a scheming, cruel man, and wouldn't have given a wooden nickel for Eddie's life. For a moment she wondered if there might have been some strange stipulation in Eddie's will that a man like Cash could use against her, but she quickly dismissed the idea. Even if she had been lamentably slow in arranging to see Ralph in order to go through legal matters with him, Eddie had never been a fool. He would never have left her at the mercy of Cash Weatherly! Sometime tonight, when she had time alone, she'd read through the letter, backwards and forwards, and tomorrow, come hell or high water, she would make a point of seeing Ralph and becoming certain of all her legal rights.

First things first.

"What about the gold shipment? Did you find out anything about that?"

Cocoa and Dulcie looked at one another.

"Well?" Ann demanded.

Cocoa grinned like a cat again. Dulcie smirked.

"Will one of you—"

"It's five thousand dollars in gold coins, Annie! Five thousand!" Dulcie said excitedly.

"The Nebraska cattlemen gave it to Cash in his office just this morning," Cocoa added.

"And they're moving the money out—"

"Tonight!" Cocoa announced triumphantly.

"Tonight!" Ann gasped, dropping to sit at the foot

of her bed herself. "My God, I'm going to have to move—"

"Fast!" Dulcie advised.

"What arrangements?" Anne asked.

"This is the best part," Dulcie told her. "Cash is such an arrogant fool. He's convinced no one would dare challenge him in any way, so he's having it transported in a wagon into town with only two men on guard duty."

"Which two men?" Ann asked quickly.

Cocoa's enthusiasm seemed to dampen a bit. "Well, maybe it's not quite as good as it sounded at first. The men are Ross Reynolds and Hugh Phiffer."

Ann knew them both. Meaner than snakes. Crack shots. They were supposedly legitimate, law-abiding citizens now, who were in Cash's employ, but few people were fooled. They were killers, pure and simple. She wouldn't be up against any fools if she was up against them.

"You know, Ann, Dulcie and I were just so darned pleased with ourselves, we weren't thinking. You can't possibly believe that you can—"

"Where is Joey now?" Ann asked.

"Sleeping like a babe in Dulcie's room," Cocoa told her.

"He has enough whiskey in him to be out around the clock," Dulcie said.

"Good, good," Ann murmured. She started to pace from the door to the bed, then swung on Dulcie suddenly. "Just what were you up to this afternoon?" she demanded angrily.

"What?" Dulcie gasped with a squeak.

"Cheating with Durango?" Ann asked.

"Well, I—he promised me—I—"

"Dulcie! This is a legitimate establishment!" Ann said.

Cocoa laughed huskily. "When you're not playing outlaw, it is!" she said flatly.

"Cocoa, you know what this is all about!" Ann reminded her quietly.

Both girls were silent. Ann inhaled and exhaled on a long sigh.

"You've just got to remember that we're all trying to come out of this alive and—"

"Personally, I am enamored of the idea of rich as well," Dulcie admitted.

"Dulcie, we've got to be smart!" Ann insisted.

Dulcie looked down at her beautifully manicured hands.

"Admit it," Ann said, "if Eddie had been alive today, you wouldn't have done what you did."

"Well, of course not, Eddie would have—" Dulcie began, and then broke off, horrified. "Oh, Annie, I am so sorry!"

Ann shook her head. "It's done. It's just that you picked the wrong man to cheat—"

"And, sugar, you should have known better!" Cocoa admonished. "One look at that fellow, and you should have known not to fool with him."

Ann looked at Cocoa, startled. "You're aware of what happened?"

"Honey, I was aware of him the minute he walked in. You have bought yourself some trouble."

"Yes, well, he's back already. And I've got to get out of here. Cocoa—"

"It will be my pleasure, honey," Cocoa assured her, rising from the daybed. She strolled to the door with her luxurious walk and then looked back, all business. "You take care tonight, d'you hear, Annie McCastle?"

Dulcie was up. "I'll keep your cowboy entertained as well," she assured Ann, "but Cocoa is right. You've got to promise—"

"I'll keep my distance!" Ann promised.

The two of them left her. When they were gone, Ann carefully closed her door and headed for her wardrobe, changing her clothing hastily behind the silk Chinese screen. When she was dressed, she swept her hair into a bandanna and hid that beneath a large, wide-brimmed hat. Then she reached beneath the laced pantalettes in the left drawer of her dressing table and drew out her guns.

They were Colt revolvers, six-shooters. She slid them into the tight gun belt that clung to her hips.

From the back of her wardrobe she pulled out a dun-colored caped duster and threw it around her shoulders. She slipped out of her room through the hidden door behind the wardrobe and crept down the back stairway and out to the stables.

To her dismay, she discovered that her hands were shaking as she saddled her horse. Tonight, of all nights, she needed a stout heart and a steady hand. She'd never been so nervous. It was all because of that damned stranger.

She'd have to worry about him later.

There was nothing to be done about it. Nothing at all.

Except . . .

Even as she mounted her bay and slipped out by the cover of darkness, she knew that she was going to come back to trouble.

If she managed to come back.

Oh, God, Dulcie and Cocoa and Harold were right. She was going to have to be very careful. So very careful.

For some reason, he'd expected to see Ann Mc-Castle the second he walked into the saloon. She'd been so determined and defiant, not in the least afraid of him—only afraid of the prospect that he might bring in the law.

The same bartender was still serving and Ian asked him for another beer, sipping it slowly as he looked around the place again. Not much had changed, but some of the saloon's patrons were now supping and the aromas of their meals reminded him that he was hungry. Just when he was about to ask the bartender about getting a good steak, a woman appeared at his side.

She was startling in her beauty, thin, lithe and graceful, like an exotic jungle cat. She might have been sculpted by a gifted artist from a single stand of ebony. Her eyes were enormous, her cologne was light and haunting and exotic as well.

"Mr. McShane," she said, slipping an arm through his. "Ann McCastle sends her regrets—she will be with you later in the evening, but for now, well, we are here to provide for your comfort and entertainment. Henri has one of the juiciest steaks you could imagine just waiting to be seared to your desire. You're welcome to dine here in the dining room, or I can take you some place more private if you prefer. . . ."

It was probably the most sensual dinner invitation he'd ever received, except that, of course, he was being offered so much more than a steak.

He watched her, appreciating her rare beauty.

"Beer?" she murmured, taking a sip from his glass. She set it down. "Sir, we have some of the finest whiskey available in all the West."

Ian smiled, nodding her way. "I've had some, and it was fine."

"But you haven't had what we reserve for special guests!" she said huskily.

Oh, she was right. He hadn't. Not yet. And he wasn't intended to, he realized, more intrigued than ever by Annie McCastle. He was supposed to be sprawled out cold in a whiskey-induced sleep by the time she arrived. And this lady would help him along into such a state so that he'd collapse with a smile on his face.

"The beer will be fine," he said.

"And the steak?"

"Rare."

"I'll have it served in my room," she offered, starting to turn.

He caught her arm. "A table down here will be just fine."

To his surprise, she appeared hurt.

"Mr. McShane, if you'd prefer a woman of a different variety—"

"I wouldn't," he told her, a spark of appreciation in his eyes. "You're probably the most stunning woman I've come across in all my life. But I think I have a bit of a score to settle now. And I've got one shot. I'll wait for Ann McCastle."

"She may be some time."

"I'll wait till hell freezes over."

She lowered her head, sweeping long lashes covering her eyes, then she looked back at him again. She was smiling. She knew he wasn't going to be budged, and she seemed to like him for it. He liked her. A lot.

"I wouldn't mind some company while I eat my steak," he said.

"I'd be honored to sit with you. Just let me see to your meal."

"Take your time," he told her. "I'm in no rush, and I enjoy watching the goings-on in this place."

He realized that his words didn't exactly put her at ease, but she smiled again and headed around the bar for a single swinging door that led to the kitchen. When she was gone, he took a careful glance around.

Harold was busy pouring beers; the twins were playing cards again with another pair of cowboys and old man Turner, and Dulcie was laughing away in the arms of a handsomely clad mustachioed man who looked as if he might have just stepped off a riverboat.

He headed for the stairs, quickly slipping up them.

There wasn't much activity at the moment. Opening doors in quiet haste, he came upon a young fellow who was buck naked, spread-eagled, and passed out cold. The next two rooms were empty, then he came upon a redhead "entertaining" a bewhiskered little bald man.

The next room was empty too, but it gave him pause. There was something different about it. The furniture was exceptionally fine. There was something very personal about the room, as if its owner cherished privacy.

Ann McCastle's room, he thought.

He stepped in, closed the door. Thrown over her dressing screen he found the black dress she had worn earlier. He fingered the material and drew the gown to his face. Breathed in her scent absently.

He set the gown back where it had been and started to leave the room.

Then he paused, noting something unusual behind the screen.

His eyes narrowed as he stared at the wall there.

He stepped closer. Took a better look at what he had barely seen at first. He ran his fingers over the wall and the framework for what had been so cleverly and all but invisibly crafted into it.

A door.

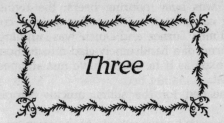

Three

She knew exactly where she needed to be for what she needed to do.

The butte rose at a low level just over the trail and she reached it in plenty of time. She dismounted from her bay, leaving him hidden among the dark shadows of a copse of trees, and squatted low, then ran to the very edge of the butte, and lay there, flat against the ground.

She waited.

A long time. Too long. She began to worry about what might be happening at the saloon. She became irritated with herself, telling herself that Ian McShane had no sway over her. Let him bring lawmen to the place. No one could prove anything about her. So there had been a problem with a little card hustling. It was over. She'd handled it, and she'd convince anyone who wanted to challenge her that she could handle anything that did come up.

But it could be argued that Ian McShane had handled the problem.

Well, Ian McShane was definitely part of the problem itself now. Of course, he couldn't make her do anything. But he wouldn't go away. And his eyes were sharp. Sharp enough to catch Durango slipping aces up his sleeve. If he stayed around too long, he just might become too interested in her activities.

Time was ticking by now. He would be looking for her. No, Cocoa was smooth. She would keep him entertained. Ian McShane might already be passed out cold somewhere. Cocoa could outdrink any man in the West, mainly because she was as clever as a whip and could appear to be drinking herself while seeing that the entire contents of a whiskey bottle went down her companion's throat.

She glanced up above her. The moon was riding high. It was growing so late.

She knew the importance of patience in any quest but she grew restless anyway. She worried about McShane in her place. She worried about the warnings Dulcie and Cocoa had given her about Cash Weatherly. There was nothing that he could do. Cash wasn't just pretending to be an upright citizen these days, he was turning into a politician. He might be able to hire a thug easily enough to commit murder in an alley, but to seize a business from someone, he would have to have the right cards to play. He would never be able to touch her.

Damn, why hadn't she forced herself to find time for Ralph Reninger?

Because Eddie had died. Because she'd *hurt.* Because there had been so much to keep together at the saloon.

But now . . .

Dear God, finally!

She heard hoofbeats, a rumbling against the ground. She flattened herself against the ledge.

In the moonlight, she could see the wagon coming. It was a buckboard with two men in the front, the boxes that contained the gold in the back. Flattened down against the earth, she watched the wagon approach, barely breathing. She waited, then she took careful aim . . .

And fired.

The man riding on the right side of the wagon clutched his shoulder and went flying from the wagon. The man to his left started to reach for his gun.

Too late.

Ann fired again, catching him in the shoulder as well. She heard his cry of fury and pain, and felt a trickle of guilt seep along her spine.

She'd let them both live! Even though they'd have killed her without blinking!

But wasn't she becoming just a little bit like them?

She shook her head. God forgive her, so far, she hadn't killed anyone. She hadn't even injured anyone who hadn't been guilty of hurting others. Who didn't deserve some pain.

What was she, judge and jury? she mocked herself. But she hadn't managed to be in the same place as justice in a long time.

There was no time to reflect on her life at the moment. She couldn't dwell on any of it. She quickly let off another two shots into the air so that the horses would keep on running with the wagon and its contents. Then she leapt up and spun around, ready to take flight. She heard the men shouting behind her.

"Fool! Cash Weatherly will see that you die for this, and slowly!" cried one of the men.

"Shoot the bastard, you've got a clear shot!" she heard his companion reply.

Her heart hammered in her chest. She had thought their wounds would have immobilized them, that she would have been safe to run. Instead, they were ready to fight back. She was a clear, clean target right now and she had left them both not just alive—but each with a good arm with which to shoot her!

Wildly she spun back around to take aim and fire

before she could be cut down. Even as she turned, a shot whistled by her ear. She gasped, choking back a scream, raising a pistol to fire. Dear God, it would be too late. The man was still standing, clutching his injured shoulder with one hand, aiming his pistol at her heart with the other.

She froze, sucking in air, envisioning her own bloody death as she heard the loud retort of gunfire. But she didn't die; no crimson stain of death spread out against her chest. Instead, the man who had been about to shoot her through the heart was spinning in the dust. He fell.

She looked around, her heart in her throat. Instinctively she fell to the earth, peering out over the edge of the butte again. She could see no one except Weatherly's two men in the dust below! The horses had drawn the wagon away into the night as she had intended, but it was so far gone now that she couldn't even hear the sound of it careening down the trail. There was just the groaning to be heard on the wind from the one man below who was still alive. He seemed to be staring up at her.

Who had shot the man who'd been about to kill her? Why?

And would he be coming after her now?

She rose cautiously. She wondered if the eyes of the living man below were upon her. If so, all that he could see was the shadow of a figure in a duster beneath the moonlight.

Still, he might fire at that figure. . . .

Thank God! He seemed to have passed out!

She turned again and ran, hurrying to her bay. Maybe she would manage to disappear just as cleanly as whoever had shot Weatherly's man. She needed to get back to the saloon.

She needed to find the wagon.

Or did she?

Most of all, she just needed to ride. She couldn't be taken here by surprise.

She leapt atop her bay, then paused, swinging her horse around in the night to try to see on all sides of her into the darkness.

Someone else had been there. Someone might have saved her life. She never made mistakes. Tonight she had. She'd always thought that once she did make a mistake, she'd pay the ultimate price.

Somehow, it hadn't happened.

Quit panicking! Think, she commanded herself.

The gold was gone. She needed to follow the wagon, find it.

She wasn't in this for the gold. All she wanted was to destroy Cash Weatherly. But if she didn't get the gold, it could wind up back in Cash's hands.

Take it slowly, Annie. Slowly and intelligently! she warned herself.

She rode carefully into the night, in the direction the wagon had gone. Even though it was dark, she could make out the tracks the heavy wagon had left in the dusty trail, and she followed them, riding hard. Then about a mile outside of town, the trail split, and the wagon tracks disappeared. The wagon must have careened off the trail into the scrub. Ann jumped off her horse and carefully picked through the brush, trying to determine in which direction the horses had dragged the wagon. But she found no sign. She stayed in the junction of north and south, east and west, a little while longer, listening closely, but all she heard were nature's night noises. Damn! She'd lost the wagon! She couldn't spend all night riding in ten different directions looking for it. She had no choice but to remount and head back to the saloon.

She rode through the darkness down the back streets of town and to the rear of the saloon, where

she dismounted. She slipped her bay into the corral
between the house and the stables. Like a shadow
in the night she moved toward the back of the saloon, carefully watching the movement within. Certain no one was watching back, she hurried to the
cellar door and down the steps until she reached the
secret stairway that led back to her room. Panting,
shaking, exhausted, she climbed the steps. She
opened the door to her room, ready to plunge inside
with a loud, relieved sigh.

She froze instead.

She could hear *noise* coming from within the
chamber.

The hidden door that opened into her room from
the secret stairway was behind her dressing screen,
shielding her from the view of anyone in the center
to the rear of her room. She paused behind the dressing screen and listened, barely daring to breathe. She
heard a . . . splash. Yes, definitely a splash. Then another one.

And then words in a deep, masculine voice.

"Who's there? Ann McCastle? Are you in here?"

Her throat seemed to tighten as if it had been
clamped.

He was in here. That bastard McShane. He was in
her room, in her tub. Invading her privacy, her life.
He'd just come right up here and made himself at
home.

And he'd heard her come in. Damn!

Oh, God, she had known that he was going to be
trouble.

"Ann McCastle, show yourself, or I'll come looking for you. I've waited long enough, ma'am, and I
won't be playing any more games with you."

The hallway door to her room suddenly burst
open. Cocoa stood there. Because of the angle of the
dressing screen, Ann could see her clearly as she

stood in the doorway, just as Cocoa could see Ann. McShane wouldn't be able to see her, unless she stood on tiptoe looking over the screen.

Cocoa gazed from McShane to Anne and back to McShane again. "You're—here! Where have you been for the past few hours?" Cocoa gasped at him. Then she turned to Ann with a wild expression in her eyes. "We—we lost him, Annie!" she said desperately. Her eyes widened in dismay as she stared at Ann. She motioned desperately up and down her own body to remind Ann about the telltale outfit she was wearing.

The last thing they needed was for a man like McShane to realize that Ann had ridden out earlier that night in cowboy garb.

Ann inhaled sharply, ducking lower behind the screen. She came to life, doffing the duster, guns, boots, trousers, and shirt. Cocoa made a beeline across the room to her and grabbed half the paraphernalia from her.

"Maybe we should throw it in the stairway," Cocoa mouthed.

Ann shook her head. No. The stairway had been there when she and Eddie had bought the place. Someone else might know about it, and it could be discovered at any time. It was better to have her things safely stuffed into her wardrobe, where they could be hidden beneath cotton chemises, silk stockings, and the like.

"In there!" she mouthed back, pointing to the bottom drawer.

Cocoa nodded, and thrust the clothing deep into the bottom drawer of Ann's wardrobe.

Ann was clad in only slim pantalettes and a chemise when she suddenly heard a voice so close behind her she jumped, hugging her breasts as she spun around.

He had come from the tub. She was grateful that he'd wrapped a towel around his waist, but she still just stared at him over the top of the dressing screen anyway. His skin was bronze, almost copper, and he was so tautly muscled that he seemed to gleam in the candlelight. He was handsome despite the ruggedness of his features and the jagged scars that stretched here and there, one on his left shoulder, one on his right side, one down his left calf.

"Were you planning on joining me? It would help to make amends for your having eluded me all evening."

"Join you!" she gasped.

"Well, you are in the act of stripping, aren't you?"

She gasped again, then wanted to kick herself. She ran a house of ill repute, for God's sake, and this man was making her blush and stutter.

She glanced at Cocoa. She needed some time. She didn't much care how, but she had to buy herself a few minutes to gather her wits about her.

"No, I, uh—spilled something. I was just changing. I have to finish some business. I—" She broke off, suddenly furious. "What are you doing in my room?" she demanded.

"Waiting."

"For what?"

"A night's lodging, a good meal—and the lady of my choice."

"I told you—"

"You tell me anything you want to tell me. You and I have to talk."

She didn't like the sound of his voice. It was too commanding. Confident. *Arrogant.* Even worse, it was determined.

And she was still half naked. She wrenched a simple calico dress from the wardrobe and pulled it over her head. "I'll give you a moment of my time when I'm ready!" she announced.

Cocoa was still standing there in dead silence, staring from Ann to Ian. He turned away from them both, walked to the center of the room, his back to them, dropped the towel, and reached for his breeches.

Cocoa choked and gasped. Ann flashed her a furious glance. Surely, Cocoa had seen dozens of naked male buttocks. But Cocoa and she were staring just the same. He was just so compact and muscular. Everything about him was intense and striking.

His trousers on, he turned back to them both. They were still just gaping like a pair of schoolgirls. He arched a brow, but other than that didn't seem to notice. He was suddenly very serious.

"Ann McCastle, I'm telling you now," he said, reaching for his shirt, "you're talking to me tonight. There's a situation here and you've got to come to terms with it. Cocoa, would you mind leaving us?"

"No! Of course not, I'm on my way, I'm gone—" Cocoa began.

"Don't be absurd! He can't tell you what to do or not do here!" Ann said indignantly.

"Cocoa?" he inquired politely.

"Cocoa, you stay right there!"

"Annie, you've got to handle this one on your own," Cocoa murmured, and managed to flee before Ann could make any other attempt to stop her.

"To begin with, we made a deal," McShane said angrily.

"No! You made a few demands. I didn't make any deals."

"I made damned plain what I wanted."

To her amazement, she felt a surge of panic again. "You've been offered what compensation I can give. I'm busy. I'm—"

"A busy little bee, indeed. Just where have you been all night?" he inquired coolly.

"With a customer!" she snapped.

He seemed so in control! Casual, almost. She realized that he might be in control, but he wasn't in the least casual. His jaw was tight, his lips were set in a grim expression.

"I have to go downstairs now!" she announced.

"You don't!"

"But I do!" she insisted.

He took a step toward her and she felt as if the blood were sizzling inside of her.

"Mrs. McCastle, I'm going to try to give you a chance to keep our relationship cordial. I've been trying to arrange to speak with you alone and uninterrupted. You don't seem to understand. You have to spend time with me."

What was he talking about? She still felt as if she were on fire, and her head was spinning. She couldn't stay. She absolutely couldn't talk to him now.

She knotted her fingers into fists at her sides. "I will talk with you, Mr. McShane, when I have finished with my customer!" She turned away from him. She did so with dignity. She walked the first few steps into the hallway.

Then she raced down the stairs and quickly looked around.

It was so late!

No, she corrected herself, it was so early. The night was over; the dawn was coming.

She could hear movement from beyond the bar in the kitchen where some of the help were still cleaning, but the saloon itself was empty.

Except for old man Turner.

Bless him!

He was still in his poker seat and there was a half-empty bottle of whiskey on the table. Ann shrugged. Turner had drunk too much and passed out. Well, that was all right with her. It suited her purposes just fine.

She hurried across the room, drew out the chair to his right, and slid into it.

Ann leaned forward, resting her elbows on the table, smiling away as if she were listening intently to something old man Turner was saying. She laughed, clinked her glass against that half-empty bottle in front of him, and laughed again. She leaned back then, and feigned surprise at the sight of Ian McShane as he came down the stairs and into the near-empty saloon.

Her heart seemed to skip a beat and then thunder as he strode toward her, dead-set determined. His tone was low and level though as he inquired, "You had to come back down to be with Turner?"

"He's one of the best customers in the place," she told him sweetly.

"Charming, right?"

"He keeps me laughing," Ann agreed uneasily. "He's far more pleasant than you are."

McShane smiled without humor. He reached over and plucked up old man Turner's hat. Turner remained sunk down in his chair, his chin in his chest.

"A laugh a minute, right?" McShane said.

She frowned uneasily, stiffening as he pulled out the chair opposite her, next to Turner. He sat, staring at her hard.

"I do find him amusing. Sweet. An absolute joy to be with."

McShane leaned back. "Well then, this fellow is far more extraordinary than he appears. And you are one incredible little liar."

"And you are obnoxious!" she flared. "I do find Mr. Turner quite extraordinary—"

"And quite dead."

"What?" Ann gasped.

"Dead."

"Dead!"

McShane smiled, his arms crossed over his chest as he shook his head. "Dead, Ann. Stiff, stone-cold dead. The old fellow must have passed on early in the day, winning hands against Durango because he never picked up his cards for others to see. Maybe you could call someone to see that the poor old fellow gets laid out all nice and properly."

He leaned forward suddenly. "Then, Ann McCastle, you had best tell me the truth about just what the hell you were up to tonight." He stood, nearly knocking his chair over with the sudden vehemence of his motion. "I'll be up in your room. May I suggest that you join me there quickly?"

With that he turned around and strode toward the stairway.

Stunned, Ann looked from his retreating back to old man Turner.

His head had fallen back now.

Damned if it didn't look like the old corpse was grinning at her.

And the joke was on her.

She shook her head sadly, then leaned over to press the old man's eyes closed. She'd call someone from the kitchen to lay him out on one of the tables with a blanket tonight, then Gus, the town's mortician, could take him from there. Maybe they could have a fine Irish wake for him, right in the saloon, tomorrow night.

She rose, closing her own eyes, rubbing her temples. Her mind seemed so numb! She heard footsteps coming back down the stairs and her eyes flew open in alarm. Him again. McShane. Damn it, but the man just didn't go away!

She backed away from the table; he came around it.

"What—" she began.

"I'm not taking any chances," he told her. Before she could protest, he had reached for her hands. She was drawn toward him with the power and speed of lightning, and suddenly hiked gut down over his shoulder.

"Damn you!" she sputtered, slamming her fists against his back. "You can't just do this, you can't just walk around like you own the place—"

"Yes, I can," he said flatly. He was walking toward the stairs again. Swiftly and gracefully despite her weight.

She pushed up against his back, struggling to free herself, trying to reason with him.

"We can't just leave Turner—"

"Why? He isn't going anywhere."

"But he's dead!"

"He's been dead all day!"

And they were halfway up the stairs.

"You've got to let me down."

"You made a promise."

"I won't keep it, I can't keep it—"

"Ah, but I told you I'd see to it that you did go by your word, Mrs. McCastle."

He held her firmly. She could have twisted, struck and squirmed until her energy failed, and he wouldn't have released her.

But his determined ascent of the stairway was suddenly halted when the doors to the saloon burst open. He spun around, moving with an uncanny speed. She crawled up against his back again to look over his other shoulder.

She barely managed to suppress a sharp gasp.

It was Cash Weatherly himself.

A tall man, with broad, powerful shoulders, he

stood very straight just inside the doorway. His hands were on his hips as he stared at the scene before him, looking oddly startled by it. He'd come alone. A low-brimmed hat was pulled over his face, shadowing his hard, curiously ageless features.

"Ann McCastle?" he said, his voice a mixture of inquiry and surprise.

Ian McShane lowered her to her feet on the step right below him.

Ann hadn't seen Weatherly since the day of Eddie's funeral, and she had managed to keep her distance from him on that cool, rainy day.

"What are you doing here at dawn?" Ann demanded, the hair at her nape seeming to stand on end. She wondered where Harold was, but then she hoped that he wasn't too close. Harold was no gunfighter. She had to watch her tone and tread carefully for the moment. She was totally defenseless by herself.

What was he doing here?

"Me and my boys are out looking for thieves," he said, stepping farther into the saloon and staring boldly up at her and Ian McShane. "One of my wagons was held up tonight. One man wounded, another dead. You seen anyone come running in here like he was hiding out?"

"No," Ann said. She cleared her throat. "No. I can talk with my help later—"

"Well, that will be fine. You talk to your help." His stare, cool blue and hostile, had fixed upon Ian McShane. "You seen anything, stranger?"

"Nope. Can't say that I have," Ian said smoothly.

"Those thieves took off with the payment in gold for my herd this year. My boys and I are awful upset. When we find out who robbed us blind, I'm afraid the wretched outlaw might not even make the sheriff's place for a decent hanging. And if anyone was to know something and hold back about the robbery, why, the boys might just be mad enough to make life a living hell for that poor soul. You listening to me, stranger?"

Ann didn't turn to look at McShane, who was standing behind her. She just looked straight down at Weatherly. Dangerous, deadly, staring up at McShane. He was a striking man; she could see his features clearly now. They were handsome, clean-cut. His hair was a wavy silver, his eyes were that riveting, cool blue, his clothing was impeccably tailored, and he wore it with a flair. He was a rancher, a rich man, a respectable man, and he played the role well. But just like his ranch hands, he had a talent for drawing his guns, and he had a strangely compelling way of making most people see things his way. Men who hadn't planned on selling their land had turned over huge tracts to Weatherly. He made loans, and they were repaid with many different kinds of interest.

"My name is McShane," Ian said quietly. "And I hear you clear as a bell."

"And you don't know anything about a wagon load full of gold."

"Not a thing."

"You just passing through town, boy?"

The question startled Ann. She would never have thought to have called Ian McShane "boy" under any circumstances. She wondered at his age. Thirty? A little younger? A little older? Sometimes, when he stared at her, she felt that he had lived forever.

McShane didn't seem to take offense at the term. She glanced up at him and saw his lips twisted into a tight smile of grim amusement and a spark of fire in his eyes. "Actually, I intend to stay for a while."

"Well, bear in mind, the West can be a dangerous place for those who don't know it."

"I know the West," Ian told him.

"This can be a tough town. Tougher for some than others."

"I've got an adventurous nature," Ian said.

Cash seemed to grow impatient with the conversation. "Suit yourself, stranger." He stared at Ann. "Since I'm here, Ann McCastle, I think we need to have a talk. I didn't want to make things too hard on you right after Eddie's death, but there are some things you may as well know right soon."

Talk? What was going on? Ann wondered. Suddenly everyone wanted to talk with her.

"The lady is busy," Ian McShane announced firmly.

Cash lifted his head slightly to study McShane again. "You don't seem to understand the situation in this town, son. I have serious business with Ann. Ann, surely you can call down another lady for the stranger," Cash suggested.

"No other lady," McShane said, his voice husky and low and brooking no opposition, "Ann is busy."

In a thousand years, she never would have imagined herself feeling glad that McShane was standing behind her, claiming her. But she was. She hated Cash. Hated him more than she could ever fear McShane.

"Ann," Cash began furiously, "I came to advise you, as Eddie's old friend, that you might be in a serious and awkward situation. If you'll just listen to me, and accept a few of my proposals, you'll come out of it all right. I've got a proposition for you that will keep you in satins and lace all your life. Now, McShane, if you'll just step aside, we'll keep the situation peaceful—"

"What in God's name are you talking about?" Ann cried out.

Cash stared at her, arching a brow at her in surprise. He smiled as he answered her. "Eddie was a gambler, Ann, you know that."

"What?" Ann started down the stairs, frantically assuring herself that Eddie would never have left her in debt to Cash!

"Eddie's attorney, that young Mr. Ralph Reninger, has been trying to put me off, Ann, but I am a power in this territory, and I can make things happen. I know that Eddie was up to his eyes in debt when he died. Debts have to be settled. You and Eddie owned this place in shares, Annie, free and clear of one another. Eddie's shares will have to be sold to pay off his debts. Eddie's debts could drag you down, Annie. Make you lose this place, everything you have. But I intend to correct Eddie's mistakes— for you, Ann. I have the power to take this place, because I have the money and the power to settle Eddie's debts. And I don't want you involved in a saloon anymore. I've got more private intentions for the use of your time."

The world was spinning, swaying. She'd been using this place to support her forays against him, to bring about his ultimate destruction.

And now . . .

Now he thought that he could use McCastle's against her because Eddie had gambled himself into debt. Was it true? She and Eddie had owned the place in shares, and what was making her feel very weak now was the fact that they had actually owned it on a sixty-forty basis, sixty percent of their shares in his name because she had insisted it was only fair, they'd bought the saloon with money he had made fur trapping.

For at least the tenth time that day, she mentally berated herself for not forcing herself to have had a better business sense when Ralph had tried to talk to her, no matter how deeply she had grieved for Eddie.

She would rather die than let Cash take control of the saloon. She wanted to speak, to lash out. To rail against God. But she couldn't move.

Cash was still smiling, damned aware he had taken her completely by surprise. He started walking across the room, coming closer and closer to her. No . . .

What the hell was the matter with her? He was just throwing out some kind of veiled threat. She didn't need to be afraid of him. She needed to move! Get away from him. If he touched her, she would perish.

He never reached her. It seemed a sweep of fire brushed past her. The hard-muscled body of Ian McShane separated her from Cash.

"Sorry, Weatherly," Ian said smoothly.

"Damn you, boy, this isn't any of your concern," Cash snapped angrily. "We've got a history here in this town; you're no part of it. Don't go making me angry!" he warned. But he studied McShane again carefully, noting the man's strong, supple build. "Like I said, there are other women here."

"But this is the lady I want," McShane insisted.

"Ann, I don't want any trouble. Do something. Take care of this boy. You and me, we need to talk and I think it ought to be now!" Cash insisted.

"Weatherly, you got something to say to her, you've got to come back at a more opportune time," McShane said flatly.

Ann let out a shrill, involuntary cry; Cash was going for his gun.

Except that, quick as he was, he paused in the act. Ann swung around.

McShane had already drawn his gun. It was aimed point-blank at Weatherly's heart. He smiled, swung the gun in his hand, and returned it to his holster. "We certainly don't want any trouble here, Weatherly, do we?" Ian asked politely. "Not among good, law-abiding citizens."

At that moment, Dulcie suddenly came running out on the landing. In the kitchen doorway, Harold appeared with Jimmy at his side.

Weatherly's eyes continued to burn their cold blue fury. "Any of you find out what's happened to my gold, I want to know," he grated out. "And Ann McCastle, I hope you don't live to regret this night. There's a lot you need to learn. And McShane, as for you . . ."

"You threatening me, Weatherly?" McShane asked.

"Giving you fair warning. Hell, you could have worked for me. You still can. I'll give you a chance. Follow me out of here right now."

"I'm busy. And I work for myself," McShane said. He didn't seem to mind any of his audience; he didn't even seem to notice the arrival of others. Suddenly he swept Ann back up into his arms before facing Cash once again.

"McShane!" Ann cried with sudden alarm. "You've got to stop! He doesn't bluff. I've got to know what he's saying, I do have to talk—"

"I think I should do the talking," McShane said. For a moment, his dark eyes fell upon her, still looking enigmatic. They rose to Cash.

"I've already bought Eddie McCastle's shares in the place, Weatherly. They were for sale before Eddie died. When Mr. McCastle knew the extent of the trouble he was in, he began to look for a buyer. You can verify what I'm saying with Ralph Reninger, or with Sheriff Bickford, who has been informed of all the legal situations regarding the late Mr. McCastle's estate as well. Now, sir, as it stands, you have no more business here, so we will bid you good-night."

He turned his back on Cash Weatherly and started up the stairs again with Ann in his arms.

Cash, it seemed, was too stunned to reply.

As Ann was herself. She couldn't seem to part her lips to speak. She couldn't begin to move in protest.

"Excuse me," McShane said politely to Dulcie, striding past her. Like Harold and Jimmy, Dulcie just stood there with her mouth open and watched him walk by.

Staring up at McShane's hard features and dark eyes, Ann couldn't even seem to manage to blink.

And so it was, until he entered her room.

And she heard the door close behind them.

And she was forced to move because he dropped her down upon her bed.

And stood towering over her.

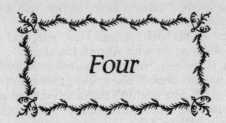

Four

She scrambled to sit, smoothing down her skirts, but he had turned from her almost as quickly as he had set her down. She leapt up as he walked back out into the hall and moved to follow him, filled with outraged and frantic questions. But just as she reached the door, he came back through it, his dark eyes flashing with annoyance when they lit upon her. "Weatherly is gone," he told her, watching her, waiting for her reaction.

So Cash had left, she mused. He'd come alone—looking for the thieves who had stolen his gold and certain that he could manage to deal with her on his own. But he'd come across Ian McShane—who was making his own claim on her and the saloon. She felt like breaking into hysterical laughter.

It seemed so impossible. Eddie had been in so much debt that he'd felt it necessary to sell his shares, *and he'd never told her!* She had chided him on his gambling, she had warned him that he loved a game of cards too dearly. She could have helped him but his pride had probably kept him from telling her the truth.

Sweet Jesu, how could he have done this to her? Could it all be the truth?

Cash Weatherly was a scheming, conniving liar—

among other things. Cash's existence was a lie, a scheme, a treacherous game of chance at all times.

But Cash was gone now.

Ian McShane was not.

This wretched, domineering stranger seemed no better than Cash, ready to seize what he wanted in life, and damn the consequences.

"You bastard!" she whispered, so exhausted and furious that she didn't pause to judge the man, or the tenseness that constricted his lean, hard form.

"If you'd rather that Weatherly owned the place, then I'm just damned sorry for you. It isn't going to happen. Was this 'history' that he referred to between himself and McCastle's important? Was there something going on between the two of you? If so, it's over."

She wanted to kill him. How anyone could possibly think that she would dream of breathing the same air as Weatherly!

She slammed a fist furiously against McShane's chest. The action seemed like fuel to the fire of her anger. She pounded him a second time, and tried for a third. He caught her wrists, shoving her back into the room again. She was startled herself at the fight within her when she bent down and bit one of the hands constraining her. He swore beneath his breath and she gasped as the air was knocked out of her as he lifted her by the waist and tossed her back down on the bed. Before she could move, he had crawled on top of her, catching her wrists once again and holding them tautly atop her rib cage as he balanced back on his haunches above her hips. She was effectively pinned down, yet he kept his weight off her, which seemed to matter little at the moment. She still couldn't believe what she had heard. Eddie had gambled away his money—and her livelihood! She had trusted him so, and in the end he had betrayed

her. He hadn't meant to betray her, she was certain.
Not Eddie. She lowered her lashes and bit lightly
into her lower lip, thinking of the day he had died.
There'd been an accident just outside of town. He'd
probably been jumping old Peterson, his sorrel gelding, again. When Annie had reached him, he'd been
still on the ground, unconscious, she had thought.
She'd talked to him, whispered to him, begged him
to hang on, the doctor was coming. His eyes had
opened. He had said her name, looking into her
eyes. Annie. He'd tried to say more; she had shushed
him, told him to save his strength.

"You have to know . . . "

"Shush!"

"Annie!"

His eyes had glazed over again. He had died, his
fingers entwined with hers. She still hadn't gotten
over the pain of losing him. But dear God! Now she
knew. He had known that he was dying, he'd been
trying to tell her what he had done, to prepare her.

Eddie! she thought. He must have thought he was
selling to someone from whom he could buy the
shares back as soon as he'd gotten ahead a bit again.
But how could he have done it to her? The saloon
had been her idea. His investment, her planning and
very hard work. She could remember how he had
doubted at first that she had the ability to put it all
together, but she had convinced him that as long as
he could put up a tough front to the world, they
could manage well enough.

"I don't believe this!" she cried out suddenly,
wriggling, squirming, anything to keep fighting. She
refused to believe it! "McCastle's is mine, I was the
one—"

"Calm down!" he ordered, his voice ringing with
an authority that brooked no opposition. "Damn it,
woman, calm down. You're like a fine Arabian mare,

lightning and fire to be free, racing herself to death!"

She realized that she was fighting herself. His position atop her was secure. He would never budge his hold on her; he was lean but all muscle, stronger than she had ever imagined, ruthless now in his determination to make her listen. "Eddie McCastle was in debt badly, just like Cash was saying—"

Ann started to swear.

"Wait—"

"No! He could have come to me, I was co-owner. Ralph should have given me the chance—"

"Listen to me, damn you! Eddie was in debt, and *alive*! He wanted a deal where his shares would have to be sold back to him before they could be offered to another bidder, except, of course, in the event of his death—"

"I don't believe you!" she cried out. "I don't believe any of this, I can't believe any of it!"

"I've been trying to tell you all day—"

"It can't be, I don't believe you!" She swallowed hard, suddenly feeling too keenly the force of the man straddling her, hot muscle beneath the roughness of fabric, subtle, fluid movement.

"It can. Apparently Eddie was human," he said flatly. "Look," he added impatiently, "I never met Eddie; this was all done via wires to Ralph, who apparently assured Eddie that I'd sell back, just as he assured me the saloon was good and Eddie was a decent fellow with a decent partner. I didn't even know anything about you, except for that. And if it didn't work out for you, I'm sorry. What was the plan, anyway?" he asked casually. "Marry the old fellow and keep him happy a few years and make out like a bandit when he died?"

Marry the old fellow?

She stared at him, blinked, then cried out in rage, so furious that she escaped the somewhat relaxed hold he'd had on her to strike wildly at his face.

He recaptured her wrists just in time to save his sight. She still struggled savagely against him and in the tussle he wound up with more than half of his body on top of hers. He'd pinned her arms around her back so that her breasts were flush to his chest. His thigh lay over her hip. His eyes were just inches from her own when she at last lay still again, silent but seething, and suddenly afraid. She didn't think that he was going to hurt her. If he'd wanted to, he would have done so by now. But she was oddly unnerved by him. Maybe it was the force, maybe it was simply his no-quarter-given strength. Maybe it was because he filled her world; she breathed in his clean but very masculine scent, a combination of leather, brandy, tobacco, and man. She was encompassed by the raw strength and heat that seemed to leap so vividly from his form to her own.

And what was worse, she was so afraid she was going to burst into tears. Something she'd never do in front of this stranger. And the most horrible thing was that she was so tired she *wanted* to cry out. She couldn't fight anymore, but the wildness still seemed alive within her. Something about him created strange liquid fires in her bones, and as much as she wanted to wrench free from him and escape, she wanted to rest her head against his chest, touch his face, study his hard, sculpted features, and learn the texture of his bronzed skin. He was an intriguing man, compelling with his thick, straight, near-ebony hair and piercing dark eyes. Sometimes, when he just looked at her, she felt as if his gaze seared right through her, touched inside of her. Even the feel of him was intriguing, making her want to reach out even while she battled to escape him.

After the way he had treated her, the things that

he had said! she roared silently to herself. Where was her sense of pride?

"Bastard!" she hissed, but forced herself to remain still, determined not to dignify his accusations with another futile struggle.

"Listen—"

"You've no right to judge—"

"Will you listen to me? I'm not trying to judge you, I'm trying to reason with you. I own half this place. Actually, I own more than half of it, but I don't really wish to dislodge you. If you don't want to believe me, I'm sorry, but you'll have to face the truth sooner or later. Ralph will explain anything to you that you don't fully understand. Now pay attention, please, so that we don't have to go through this again. I need this place. Plain and simple. And we're going to make a go of it, you and me. We can make it easy on one another, or you can try to make it hard, but you do that and I will make life hell for you. I'm not letting go. Not for a minute. And you're going to be an angel in the days ahead, otherwise I'll make it a point to find out exactly what is going on in all aspects of this place, because you're not going to ruin my plans with whatever illegal little activities you've been running."

"I haven't been running any little illegal activities!" she lashed out.

He arched a brow at her. She gritted her teeth, watching his dark, enigmatic eyes, so uncomfortably close to her own.

She was so tired. She'd been awake for more than twenty-four hours now and she was simply exhausted. It was all still absolutely unbelievable. She'd been living her life with one purpose for so long now, and this man thought that he could come in and take over with a sweep of his hand, threatening everything.

And she didn't even know how to fight him right now. She felt as if she had barely managed to survive the day.

And another one was already dawning.

He sighed suddenly. His hold on her eased slightly again. Not in the same way it had eased before. She thought he'd never be unprepared for an attack from her again.

"Damn you, Ann McCastle. Can't you see? You need help here. If Eddie had left you everything free and clear, you'd still have been in trouble. Every Cash Weatherly from across the territory would have swept in to see what the pickings were with a woman alone trying to run this place and survive. They'll be coming anyway, just like Cash did, except you won't be vulnerable because I'll be here."

"I don't believe any of this!"

"Go see Ralph Reninger tomorrow. The only reason Cash Weatherly isn't here right now instead of me is that Reninger happened to be my attorney as well as Eddie McCastle's, and he'd known I was looking for interests in this area when Eddie came to him because he was in trouble. If Eddie had died without settling his debts, you might have been in worse trouble."

She blinked back tears. "He didn't tell me!" she grated out.

"Maybe he meant to. See Ralph or the sheriff and ask them any questions you might have. Except— you don't much like the sheriff, do you?"

"I like him just fine."

"As long as he doesn't snoop around here."

"I said I like him just fine!"

"Be careful if you're shielding someone, Ann."

"I'm not shielding anyone. And I don't believe—"

"Yes, you do," he said quietly.

She clenched her teeth together hard, feeling pained and confused. But McShane was right. Eddie had done this to her. It must be true. She had heard it from McShane—and Cash Weatherly. And now that she thought about it, it seemed like something Eddie would do. He probably had thought he could get himself out of trouble without ever having to tell her just how much trouble he had been in. She didn't understand McShane, or what he wanted with the saloon, but somehow, he must have convinced Eddie that he would eventually sell the shares back to him.

And she had to admit, Eddie had been a gambler, an Irishman who always believed a four-leaf clover would come his way at the right time. He hadn't had two cents to his name when he'd first found her, but that hadn't mattered. Eddie had known how to make money when he needed it. He had taken her in, and he'd quickly done some fur trapping to keep them both in food and clothing. She'd taken care of him, and she'd loved him, in return. He'd known right away that she was resilient, determined, and capable, and though he had needed some convincing to open the saloon, he'd been quick to tell her she was as smart as a whip, and where she led, he'd be happy to follow. He hadn't been a worrier. He had always been confident that things would work out. He'd always had a smile and a funny story for her. A tale about the leprechauns or banshees. He had loved a good bottle of Irish whiskey, fiddle music, a warm fire—and a game of poker. And after the Irish whiskey he had so enjoyed, he hadn't played the game of poker very well.

Still staring warily at McShane, Ann allowed her head to ease onto the pillow.

"I'm exhausted!" she whispered.

"Good!" he said. "Remind me not to try to engage

in battle with you, ma'am, when you're feeling more energetic."

"Go to hell," she snapped back quickly, causing him to laugh huskily.

"You've already made the suggestion."

"I repeat it strongly."

"Eventually, I will surely oblige."

"Can you let go of me now, please? You are about to break my arms."

"No, Annie, I'm not about to break your arms. But I am incredibly annoyed."

"Will you—"

"What was that? Did I hear you say please? Or is that the word you're choking on."

"Get off of me!"

He arched a brow, sat back stubbornly on his haunches, still keeping his weight on hers. "Battle of wills, Ann? I don't think I'm quite so tired as you are."

"Will you please get off of me?"

"I don't know—" he began.

"Half-breed bastard!" she hissed, squirming wildly again.

"Quarter Sioux, Ann—and rather proud of it," he added, his hold tightening upon her so that she went dead still, seething as she stared up at him. "I don't know if I *dare* get off of you, I was about to say, because of you. Are you going to fly at me again?"

She inhaled deeply; she counted to ten and then beyond, staring at him. Finally she managed to tell him, "Not tonight."

He eased his hold. She drew back from him, hugging her arms to her chest.

"Could you . . . get off my bed?" she inquired.

"Give me a pillow for the daybed."

"There are other rooms."

"We're going to put up a united front here, Ann,

whether you like it or not. Your friend Cash just walked away now not just because I was faster on the draw but because he's no fool and he wasn't going to murder either of us in front of witnesses. But he wasn't happy. In fact, he was seething, just itching to put a bullet through my head. And he just might want to come back and see if you've become available.''

She closed her eyes. ''Then just . . . keep your distance!''

''Come to think of it, you did promise me the night.''

''You came here under false pretenses.''

''You never asked if I owned part of the place.''

''Will you go to hell, will you *please* go to hell?''

''In due time. Throw me a pillow. Unless you want me to get back in with you?''

She threw him a pillow quickly. She really was too tired to do otherwise. She was grateful to have managed to put some distance between them; she definitely lacked the strength to evict him from her room right now.

She lay back down, hugging her own pillow, feeling her eyes begin to close. She watched him toss the pillow she had given him onto the daybed.

This was a miracle, she reminded herself. He'd tormented her through half the day and night, carried her into this room, and staked all his claims—and then walked away, demanding nothing but his place here.

He'd kept her from Cash, or Cash from her.

She bit into her lower lip, exhaling with relief and, oddly enough, just a shade of disappointment. The scent of him seemed to linger about her. There was so much sleek energy in his every movement, so much heat emanating from his body, something vital and compelling that made her long to reach out and touch him. What a strange man. Arresting, striking, ruggedly evocative, and more powerful than even she'd imagined.

And probably more dangerous, she reminded herself.

He walked to the balcony doors, staring out to where the sun was now beginning to pour its light through the paned glass windows and the sheer fall of lace. Her heart skipped a beat as she watched him. He was so different from any other man she had ever met. Tall, wickedly supple in his hard-muscled form. His features were so intriguing, ruggedly hewn and defined, his eyes so dark, so very much like coal fires.

He dropped the velvet draperies into place, casting the room into darkness and shadow.

She heard him unbuckling his gun belt and stretching out on the daybed—his guns at his side.

He was the enemy, she told herself. He was threatening her existence.

Her very reason for being.

She trembled suddenly. At least he was at a distance for the time being. She desperately needed to get some rest if she was going to deal with him at all.

She closed her eyes. She wondered if he was as tired. If he would sleep so easily . . .

He was tired. Dead exhausted. But his very weariness made his sleep restless. Filled with dreams.

He could see . . .

The cloud of dust. Gathering. Growing.

They came like a storm. The horses running at full speed and appearing, from a distance, almost like mythical beasts, like creatures racing across clouds. But they didn't ride on clouds, they created that misted field in which they ran, their mighty hooves kicking up earth and dust and sending it all spiraling into the sky around them. With the setting sun at their backs, they created so extraordinary a picture that the boy paused in mid-stride, mesmerized by the image.

They moved closer. The boy realized that there weren't so many men on horseback, maybe ten. But the small number wasn't reassuring as the men's faces began to appear more clearly. They were grim faces. Some bearded, some clean-shaven. Some young, some aging. Some of the men's eyes appeared near dead, some were blazing. Some men just looked weary, as if they were about to do a job that had to be done.

Some actually smiled.

Back east passionate men were spouting passionate phrases about abolishing slavery.

But out here along the Kansas/Missouri border an ugly, hateful war was being waged. A war with no honor, and no ethics.

What was holding him so damned still? The war had come to him and his family now, no matter that the politicians in Washington hadn't yet officially declared it a war. He was sixteen. He'd known he'd be just the right age when they finally called this hatred and violence between slave states and free states what it truly was—war.

But his fight was here, now—earlier than it should have been. And it wasn't going to take place on any battlefield. It was going to rage against women and children as well as men.

"Pa!" he shouted, dropping the water bucket he carried, racing for the back of his folks' wagon. "Pa!"

His father had heard the riders. He came leaping down from the rear of the wagon. He didn't tell his son to take cover—he just hesitated, anguish in his eyes for a brief moment before he tossed his boy the extra rifle he carried. "Make your shots count, my

boy!'' he said, and he tried to offer an encouraging
smile before shouting loud and hard to the other
settlers nearing the land they had so recently purchased with such excitement and so many dreams.
"No time for defensive positions, they're almost
upon us!''

It wasn't much of a party of settlers. Just the four
wagons he and his folks had originally set out with,
and a small group with two wagons that had asked
his father if they could join on last night. The boy
hadn't even met the families in those wagons yet so
he couldn't judge how many good fighting guns
they could provide. They'd joined up with the other
wagons for safety. How damned ironic. But it
seemed that it was a time for fanatics. The slaveholders were killing folks, the abolitionists were killing folks, and sometimes it didn't matter what
people did, who they were, or what they believed,
they were a part of the fight just because of where
they came from. His father had wanted to escape the
fanatics who didn't care what they did to others in
order to achieve their goals. And then again, some
men weren't so pure in their goals, they just loved
to fight and kill and say it was for a cause. Their
own cause. Sometimes power, sometimes whatever
booty they could steal.

All that mattered now was that these abolitionists
meant to mow them down because they had hailed
from southern states. And there were maybe eight
men who could shoot, a handful of children, a handful of women. Death was coming, injustice was
sweeping down upon them, and they could all see
that there was nothing they could do about it—except to die fighting and maybe bring a few of their
attackers along to face judgment with them.

No attempt was made to arrange the wagons.
There was no time. Men, women, and children were

suddenly everywhere, crying, shouting as they milled in confusion.

"Find your cover!" the boy's father commanded.

The confusion began to abate, with so little time. A husband yelled at his pregnant wife to get back down on the floor of their wagon. A mother shouted at her daughter to crawl down behind the horses, while taking aim herself. A dog barked, a baby cried.

Too late for anything else.

The riders were upon them. The dust cloud began to choke them. It became a storm. The ground trembled. The horses that raced so hard cast off droplets of sweat while foam worked around their bits.

The first shot was fired.

It came from their leader.

His hair was iron gray, his features were weathered and hard, his eyes were a cool blue. It was an oddly striking face, chilling, somehow compelling, strangely ageless. He was one of those who smiled as he rode. Smiled as he took aim and fired.

A shriek of agony rent the air. A burst of gunfire followed, attackers and defenders taking aim, firing.

The boy took his own first shot. The rifle kicked back but he held it steady. He'd been buffalo hunting often enough.

He'd just never aimed his rifle at a man before. But then, he'd never had men aiming their rifles at him and his family before either.

He caught a fellow in the shoulder. Sent that man screaming from his saddle like a maddened goshawk.

Horses reared; horses fell; men, women, and children tried to take cover behind them. The dust was stirred up so that the air tasted of it along with the acrid smell of gunpowder. The same black powder hung in the air, hurting his lungs when he tried to inhale. Nothing that could be seen seemed real anymore, the day was so filled with powder and dust.

Hooves pounded near him. He reloaded his rifle, powder and shot, tamped it down, tried to take aim. He did so just in time to see a rider fire from a revolving pistol.

He saw the blood expanding across his father's shirt. Saw him clutch his chest, saw him fall.

He started to scream himself. His scream froze as he saw his mother racing to his sprawled pa. She was a beautiful woman. Everyone had always said so. Slim and always laughing, with the face of an angel. One second she was running.

And the next she was dead.

The boy fell to his knees, shrieking in agony, aiming at the rider. Firing. Finding little solace as the man was blown clean from his horse. The boy jumped up and raced to his parents, shouting to them, crying their names, holding them, shaking them, heedless of the blood that stained his hands. Grief maddened him. He wouldn't accept death, couldn't believe that it could come this way, riding hard across the plain on a cool, sunlit day.

"Git down, boy, get back out of the path!"

It was old Rufus Megee yelling out. Old Rufus with his wild Indian tales, funny, mile-long whiskers, and rheumy green eyes. The boy saw the rider coming behind Rufus and instinct sprang to life within him. He took aim, fired, watched the rider fall. But Rufus went down, too, and even as he stared in horror at old Rufus, he looked across the field and saw a young girl running. One of the riders came up close behind her, reaching for her, laughing.

"Little young!" one of the riders called out with a derisive snort.

"He likes 'em that way!" called out another.

The girl turned. To the astonishment of the riders,

the little caped creature was carrying a pistol. She took aim and fired. She missed, but just barely. She nicked her attacker's ear. Blood spurted from it as the man howled out in pain.

The boy saw what was going to happen next. He just couldn't stop it. He screamed and screamed as he watched, but he couldn't do anything at all. He made it to his feet, but he hadn't even begun to run when the furious rider turned on her, swinging the stock of his rifle hard across the girl's hooded head.

The boy heard the impact. Watched her crumple. He shrieked and screamed and started to run, his rifle empty now, but swinging nonetheless. He leapt over the fallen bodies of horses and humans, knowing full well that he was going to die and determined that these monsters would die with him.

He plowed into a horse, falling back. He rose, and saw the leader of the death party staring down at him. The man smiled, leveled his pistol at the boy.

The boy let out a howl like a wounded wolf, pitting himself at the man. The smooth smile momentarily left the man's face.

His gun fired.

The boy felt the explosion with all of his being. He thought, So this is what it is like to die! As the world faded and went to black around him, he was aware of no pain. He could only feel the sticky red of his blood burgeoning from his temple and down his face. He could taste the gunpowder, and then the dirt. As he fell the dust and powder covered him, and the sounds of war faded away. Guns were fired. He didn't hear the cracking of them.

He closed his eyes.

But he didn't die.

When he opened his eyes, he could still taste dirt and blood. Instinct kept him still. He realized after a moment that there were horses near him, very near

him, almost trampling his head. And the men were
talking.

"That's it, the sorry lot of them!" someone said,
and spat into the dust.

"That may be it, Rudy, and it may be not," came
another voice, and damn, it was near the boy, so
very near him! It was their leader, the boy thought.
The man with the iron gray hair and cool blue eyes.
The voice was full of confidence and authority. "You
all go around them, one by one. We can't think
they're all gone on to hell and damnation; we've got
to know for sure that they're all stone-cold dead."

"Like we ain't got a right to do what we've done
to the lot of these kind!" a gruff voice exploded.

"Some folks don't quite see our rights the way we
do," said the leader, speaking again, and this time
with just a trace of amusement in his voice. "See that
they're dead!"

"We've got company," said the gruff-voiced man.
"Look up on those hills far yonder."

"Injuns!" someone supplied. Rudy's voice, the boy
thought.

"Pawnee warriors, so it appears," the leader murmured. "Let's finish here and move on."

The boy very carefully half opened an eye.

"Hell, Captain!" One of the five remaining
mounted men exploded. "You make sure they're all
dead! That is a Pawnee war party on the hill and I
ain't ready to take them all on!"

It was the one called Rudy who was being can-
tankerous, the boy saw. Rudy spoke dismissively.
He spun his horse around.

The captain smiled mirthlessly, lifted his pistol,
took aim, clicked back the trigger, and fired. He hit
Rudy straight in the back of the head. Rudy probably never knew he was dead till his soul landed in
hell.

"I'll get right on it, Captain," a short, fat, bewhiskered little man—the one with the gruff voice—said, starting to leap down from his horse.

"Never mind," the captain told him, wiping his pistol lovingly with a silk scarf he drew from his pocket, then returning the pistol to its holster and the scarf to his pocket. He sat calmly, staring up at the ridge of the small dirt hill where the Indians waited. He drew a slim silver case from his inner pocket and selected a thin cigarillo from it, then struck a match against his boot to light the smoke. He watched the warriors, gauging the distance between their position and that of the Indians. He drew in on his cigarillo, puffed out a cloud of smoke, then flicked the still-burning cigarillo down to the dirt. The smoke rose before the boy's half-closed eyes, entered his lungs. He nearly coughed. By the grace of God, he did not.

"These firebrands of hell are dead and gone, it does appear. And gentlemen, I'm not actually in a mood to wrestle with Pawnees myself. Be quick, men. Gather up the horses, livestock, and what valuables you can seize quickly. We ride on out." He started ahead, then reined back, turning to look at the horsemen behind him with one hand rested on his mount's rump. "Just you remember. No one, no one, tells me no. You ride with me, boys, and I'm like God. Just like God, your damned god, you got that fellows? It's a pact." He stopped and laughed suddenly. "Why, you're just like a little grouping of the Lord's demons and it's my guess we're all straight out of hell ourselves, doing the work we do. Want to keep away from the fires for a while, boys, you listen to me. You shoot when I say. You ride when I say. You take what I tell you to take." He waved his gun around the bloody scene. "And you leave the corpses to the Pawnees when I say!"

He turned and started to ride. Hard. The others, only three left now, the gruff fellow and two quiet, younger men, followed swiftly behind him.

The boy tried to move. Pawnees coming. The dead ones were the lucky ones, he knew that well enough.

And if these men had failed to kill others among the settlers . . . ?

Well, they would probably be dead soon enough.

He had to move, had to move, do something . . .

But he couldn't move, and the fragile grasp he'd had on consciousness escaped him. The gray smoke from the burning cigarillo seemed to envelop him and turn to black. He had to fight. There had to be a way to do battle, dear God, all of the innocents there to suffer so horribly!

He twisted, struggling against the darkness; he groaned, praying for strength. . . .

Five

Ann bolted up, furiously blinking the sleep from her eyes, wondering at the commotion within her room. Confused for a moment, she caught her breath, and then realized that it was McShane.

He was murmuring in his sleep, twisting this way and that.

She leapt up and walked gingerly toward the day-bed, watching him incredulously. His handsome face was tautly drawn and sleek with sweat. His fingers knotted into the pillow as if he waged some war with it. The length of his body twisted as if he were in pain, struggling. His shirt had come open. She could see the ripple and bulge of muscles within his chest and shoulders as he fought a nightmare battle. Her breath seemed to catch as she watched; she drew her hand to her mouth and bit down to keep from crying out. He was suffering.

Maybe he deserved to suffer.

But as angry as she had been with him, a gut-deep instinct seemed to tear at her heart, and she knew that she couldn't leave him, that she couldn't let him fight this battle again. She came closer to him, sitting carefully by his side. He thrashed, and she inched back, thinking that if he were to strike her in his sleep, he might well break her jaw.

"McShane!" she whispered, touching his shoulder, feeling the wire-taut constriction of his muscles. "McShane!" she repeated more urgently, trying now to shake him awake.

In the midst of blackness and billowing smoke, Ian heard her voice. He fought the blanket of sleep that lay upon him. Good God, sleep, he had slept too deeply, he had learned to hear the snap of a twig in the forest and now . . .

His eyes flew open. Instinctively he reached for the pistol he'd placed by his pillow and he bolted up.

Ann McCastle was seated beside him, stiffening as he reached for his pistol. He grated his teeth and let his gun lie where it had been. He ran his fingers through his thick shock of dark hair, smoothing it back from his face.

He met her crystal blue eyes, startled to see that there was no ice or fury within them. What he saw there was a striking innocence and empathy, but a guarded expression quickly seemed to replace them as he stared at her.

"I thought I should wake you. You were tossing, you—seemed to be in pain."

He nodded, rueing the fact that she had seen such a weakness in him.

"Yeah. Well, thanks. Sorry I woke you."

"It seemed as if you were having a terrible dream."

"Yeah."

"Do you have it often?"

He shook his head. "No," he said quietly. "I haven't had it in years." He stared at her sharply.

"I was hard to wake? Damn, but I can usually hear a shift in the breeze!"

"Perhaps you were very, very tired."

"I've been tired before," he muttered, gripping his hands together tightly. "I can't let it happen again," he muttered.

"I don't think we can stop ourselves from dreaming," she said.

"I will!" he swore vehemently. He reached out, caught her slim hand. Startled by the softness of it, he turned it in his own. Her fingers were elegantly long and slim, her nails were neatly trimmed. "I will!" he repeated.

She withdrew her hand, then stood quickly, as if suddenly aware of just how close she had come to him. He had touched her again, he realized, awake now, angry with himself, but fascinated by her.

She was still clad in the simple calico. Her hair had come loose. In sun-gold waves it streamed around her shoulders and down her back. She seemed very young, ridiculously pure, and more desirable than he had even imagined before. All the same, he just wanted to reach out and touch her face.

She backed away from him. "We should probably try to get a little more sleep."

He knew she was right but watching her he suddenly didn't feel quite so tired. He felt the same swift, strange roil of emotion that he'd felt when he had heard her singing, before he had ever seen her face. Now he knew its striking elegance and beauty as well, just as he was coming to know the sweep of the passions—anger and determination—that raged so hotly within her, regardless of the cool demeanor she presented to the world. How damned ironic.

He ran his fingers through his hair and pressed his hands to his temples as he sat on the daybed, watching her.

For most of his life, whatever he had wanted from women had been his for the taking. His relationships had been casual. The women he had wanted had wanted him as well. He'd never stayed long in one place. When he had been very young, injured in body and spirit, he had stayed with his grandfather's people. His grandfather, Blue Winged Crow, had given him the help he had needed to heal. White Eagle Woman, the young widow of a warrior killed several years before, had shed her mourning by teaching him that they had both needed to care again. She had taught him the art of lovemaking, and he had learned both tenderness and passion. She had always known that he would leave, just as he had always known she would one day choose another Sioux warrior for a new husband, now that she had broken her mourning.

When he'd recovered and left his grandfather's people, the war had kept him moving. And he'd known throughout every long bloody year of battle that if he survived the bitter struggle between North and South, it would just mean that he had at last reached the beginning of his own private war. Sometimes, he was certain that he had survived just because he knew that somehow he was going to fight again. But that hadn't really mattered at the time. The war had made whatever brief moments of warmth he could find precious. Men—and women—seized those moments, and went onward when they were over. Still, for one of the scouts of John Hunt Morgan's famous cavalry, desire was something easily gratified; hungers could be quickly sated. They lived rough, hard, dangerous lives. Their passions could be very much the same.

Strange, the war already seemed as if it had been a long time ago.

Now, he'd bought into a saloon that hosted a

high-class, well-run brothel as well, where anything he wanted should have been available for the going price of the day. He'd come with one purpose in mind, and he'd never imagined such a distraction. He owned the damned place!

Yet the one thing he wanted he didn't seem to be able to buy or command.

She was still watching him, appearing both very wary and very worried. He stared at her in return, smiling grimly. He'd come here because of Cash Weatherly. Well, she'd brought Cash Weatherly right into the doors of the place. Cash Weatherly wanted what he owned.

Weatherly wanted her, as well. He probably wanted her badly enough to kill in order to get her.

Ian was startled by the violent anger that seized him at the thought. This place was a brothel, he reminded himself mockingly. No matter what her relationship had been to Eddie McCastle, she might well have taken on customers as well.

He wished he had been able to spend time with Ralph today. It had been damned difficult, doing this transaction by wire and mail. All he'd really known about Ann McCastle was that she'd been Eddie's partner, and a partner with the same last name usually meant a wife. She might have been a daughter, but not many men went into a business that included a brothel with their daughters. When he'd called her Mrs. McCastle, she'd accepted that as the proper form of address, and Eddie had needed assurances from Ralph that Ian would have both the financial and the physical strength and the willpower to keep others from trying to take the saloon over from her. Still, no matter how protective Eddie had been of Ann McCastle, they'd held their shares in the place separately, probably because Eddie had known he was one bad businessman—or poker player—himself. Eddie McCastle must have cared for her very deeply. Ian could well understand how the old man had been swept up in her charms—he was falling prey to Annie McCastle himself. Enough to feel anger, frustration, and a surge of pure *possessiveness* that was making this all the harder. She might have entertained plenty of customers.

Cash Weatherly might have had her a dozen times already.

In fact, Annie had assured Ian yesterday that she had been with a customer when she should have been with him. Had she been lying?

He was certain that she had been lying, he just felt in his gut, but still, the idea that she might have been with Cash was enough to make him feel like ripping up leather with his teeth.

Cash wanted her. . . .

There was no damned way Cash was going to get her! he determined suddenly. Ever. In any way.

He paused for one moment, wondering if he was about to do what he was going to do because he hated Cash Weatherly so much that he didn't intend to give him a single chance to take something he wanted so badly—or just because Ian wanted that same thing so badly himself.

It was the only thing to do. He owned the largest percentage of the saloon, but it was impossible to own a woman.

He couldn't own her. He had to have her in the next best way.

He leapt up with such speed that she let out a startled cry, darting back, staring at him again with the wariness she might have reserved for a lunatic.

But he didn't touch her then. He walked past her to the pitcher and ewer on the washstand. He filled the bowl with water and soaked his face. He dried it and turned back to her.

"You need to get dressed and ready."

"I am dressed. I haven't been undressed," she reminded him.

He nodded. "Something a little fancier, but decent, of course. No black. And nothing too revealing. None of those outfits you might wear in the saloon. Or to entertain. And hurry. Let's get this over with. Never mind; I'll help you find the right dress."

"What?" she gasped, her eyes wide.

"A dress. I'll help you find the right one."

"Wait!" she cried, leaping forward to stop him from striding toward her wardrobe. She stood unwavering as if she were a stone statue, and no longer looked wary. She didn't seem to think he was a lunatic anymore, she seemed to know it for a fact. "I can choose my own clothing, thank you. But the right dress for what?"

"A wedding."

"Whose wedding?"

"Your wedding."

"My wedding?" she said incredulously.

"Our wedding," he said impatiently. He set his hands on her waist and lifted her cleanly and simply out of his way. He started toward her wardrobe again.

She caught his arm. Clung to it, rather, with her full weight. He paused, looking down at her. Her eyes looked wild against the tousled gold of her hair.

"We are not having a wedding today!"

"Why not?"

"Because—because—I don't even know you!"

"Ian McShane, ma'am," he said politely.

"Fine! I know you. That doesn't mean that I like you."

"You don't need to like me."

"This makes no sense—"

"It makes a hell of a lot of sense."

"It makes no sense at all!" she cried. She stared at her hands, clutching his arm. She released him instantly and backed off warily again. "What is the matter with you? Who do you think you are? You can't just come in here demanding things, expecting everything to be your way."

"I do own most of the place," he reminded her.

"I don't even know if that's true—" she began, but broke off when he snatched Reninger's letter from her dresser—where he had seen it lying unopened the night before—and pressed it into her hands. She held it, unwilling to open it. He took it back from her and ripped it open. " 'From the offices of Reninger and Bowling—Dear Ann, I remain heartily sorry for Eddie's death and in the deepest sympathy with you for your loss, but matters grow urgent and I must see you at your earliest convenience. It distresses me to give you this information in a letter, but you must be advised that Eddie had sold his shares in the saloon just before his death, and you must be made aware of your own legal rights as now regards the ownership of McCastle's. Please be advised that a Mr. Ian McShane'—"

"Stop!" she cried out, her face ashen. For a moment, her guard was down. Her eyes were liquid and shimmering, and she seemed entirely vulnerable. He wanted to reach out for her, a swift wave of tenderness washing over him. He wanted to draw her near, hold her, promise her that everything would work out fine. It was almost a saintly emotion, he told himself wryly, except that at the same time, he was stricken with a painful tightening in his loins. He wanted to hold her, all right, he mocked himself. He just wanted to do a hell of a lot more at the same time. Well, he intended to marry her. And maybe, once he'd accomplished all he'd come to do, he could return her property to her, take that stricken look from her face.

"You see, I really do own the controlling shares in the saloon," he told her quietly.

"But you don't own me!" she cried. "You don't own me!" She waved a hand in the air. "Oh, my God, you do have your nerve! Threatening me all day yesterday that you'd go to the law, making bargains when you weren't going to cause trouble for the place, hell, no! You were just going to seize the whole thing—"

"You did promise me the night," he reminded her.

"That promise meant nothing because everything about you is a lie!"

"Nothing is a lie," he warned. "In fact, I still think it might not be a bad idea to have the sheriff look into things before I take over. I wouldn't want my ownership tainted with the sins of the past."

She was silent again, her lips set in a tight expression, her blue eyes glittering.

"You bastard!" she grated out.

"Is there any reason why we shouldn't marry?"

"There are a million reasons—"

"No. This is business. Because I told you the truth last night. You'll have a dozen Cash Weatherlys sneaking around here, and you'll have the man himself back, determined to get you one way or another. Are you blind? He covets you. It was in his eyes last night. He would have liked to have killed me then and there, and if I hadn't been in his way, he would have just taken what he wanted, most probably. It appeared to me that Cash had been just waiting for Eddie to be out of the way so that he could come and sweep up both you and the saloon."

She stood silently staring at him then, feeling a

chill in her blood. What *would* have happened if McShane hadn't been there last night?

"I can fight Cash on my own," she said. She was dismayed to hear the weakness in her own voice.

She could fight Cash. She had been fighting Cash. But Cash Weatherly hadn't been determined to get his hands on the saloon or *her* before. It seemed that Ian McShane was right about a number of things. By the look in Cash's eyes last night, he had been waiting for Eddie to be out of the way. Because Eddie knew her, and knew Cash, and he would have died before he let Cash get anywhere near her.

He arched a brow. "If you really want to fight him, and more—*if you really want some protection from him*—and if you want to win, listen to me. Do what I'm asking."

"Demanding," she corrected icily.

"I don't intend to let him have you, and I guarantee you, I know *him*—I know his type of man. He'll be back for you. And I can wage a number of gun battles, come out of most of them just fine, but maybe a lot of innocent men will die in the streets as well. I can shower the streets with bullets, but none of them will be as powerful in helping to fight him as a wedding certificate, my legal claim to you. He'll be raring to spill blood once he hears about this; it will be like a knife twisting hard right inside him. He hates to be turned down. He hates to lose anything that he wants. But if you're legally married to me, he'll know he'll have a fight to the finish with me before he'll ever be able to force himself on you."

She blinked suddenly; her eyes lowered. "Marrying you would hurt him?" she inquired pensively.

"Hell, yes. Don't you understand what I'm saying? Not getting what he wants is hell to a man like that."

"What about a man like you?"

"I pursue what I want," he assured her in a low tone, "until I get it. So, shall we do it?"

Ian expected a fight from her. He was ready for it. He'd talk until he made her see where they stood.

She stared at him intently, twisting her lower lip suddenly, gnawing into it lightly.

"Why do you want to hurt Cash Weatherly?"

"I've my reasons."

"But why—"

"Why do you want to hurt him?" he countered.

"It's none of your damned business," she assured him.

"Likewise. So will you marry me?"

"This is still insane—"

"It's not insane. Sweet Jesu, I am telling you that he will be back here after you. And I hand it to you that you are tough and full of fight, but it appears that Cash Weatherly is one ruthless man."

"Why are you so determined on marriage?" she asked cautiously.

"Because it just makes so damned much sense. I'll not only own the majority of the place, but I'll be married to the icon running it," he drawled. "I'll not only be able to keep Cash Weatherly at bay and irritate the hell out of him, but I'll have some real control over any other poor fellows who come panting around the place after you."

"You are so complimentary to me!" she murmured with sweet sarcasm.

"Well?"

"All right," she said suddenly, determinedly. "Maybe this is the right business move. But first, let's establish just a few rules—"

"Rules?"

"Agreements, between us. You aren't to question me, and I won't question you. We're both after something, obviously. We'll lead separate lives and—"

"I'll question anyone—including you—when I please," he said, crossing his arms over his chest, "and no separate lives."

"Wait a minute—"

"No, I'm not waiting a minute. You can't get a much simpler agreement going. You get protection—and whether you want to admit it or not, you need it. I get a nice room at night—and a warm female body within it."

"I won't do it then!"

"Yes, you will. You've already agreed."

"I cannot believe that I have just agreed to marry such an arrogant bastard!" she said, her voice grating as she stared at him.

He arched a brow. "Well, honey, it was a damned surprise to me to find myself proposing to a whore."

She moved like lightning, striking with a force that carried quite a wallop. He felt the fire on his face where she slapped him, he could even feel the imprint of her fingers forming on his cheek.

His reaction was half anger with himself—that he hadn't been quick enough to stop her—and half a weak semblance of control as his temper spiraled.

He caught her by the arms, drawing her so roughly against him that her head fell back and her eyes, still blazing a furious and defiant blue, met his.

"If I had hurt you, I'd have had that coming. But I call a spade a spade, Ann McCastle, just the way I see it, and I'll be damned if I'll let you take a hand against me for saying it like it is."

"Then let me say it like it is! You're just a grasping, arrogant, greedy, self-righteous, opportunistic son of a bitch, no better than any other lowlife I've met out here, and maybe a hell of a lot worse."

He let that sink in, his fingers tightening on her arms.

"Well, then," he said after a moment, "now that we've exchanged our vows of undying devotion, let's get on with finding a justice and seeing this through. Because you are going to marry me."

"Am I?" she asked, her eyes mocking and quizzical now. "Why? Just because I've agreed doesn't mean that the deed is done. You want a *marriage*. I should marry you because you were instantly enamored of my charms?" she demanded tauntingly.

"No. You're going to do it because I'm not giving you much of a damned choice," he replied flatly.

"No," she told him, wrenching free from his hold. "You're wrong. I'll always have a choice, McShane. I am doing just exactly what I damned well choose."

"Well, then, if I'm such an arrogant bastard—and a lowlife—why have you chosen to agree?" he couldn't help but inquire.

"I don't agree anymore. It seemed to make good business sense to do this until you started behaving so irrationally—"

"I am not behaving irrationally. I'm being honest with you."

"Well, I'll be honest with you. I don't want a . . . personal involvement."

His dark eyes were suddenly fierce and enigmatic. "Then don't get involved. Just behave the way a wife should and be in the right bed at night."

"Damn you! I will not make any promises."

"I'll make them for you. I promise I'll see to it that you're a good wife and that you're in the right bed at night."

She could feel a suffusion of blood creeping into her cheeks. "I should tell you to go right to hell!" she hissed to him.

"Should you?"

"Yes! Go to hell!"

He shook his head slowly. "You don't mean it, because you may not like me very much, but you know damned well that I'm better than what could happen to you if you don't become my wife. So, what shall we do? Do you *choose* to marry me?"

She was dying to strike out at him again, but she forced herself to remain still—for the moment. He did have a few good points. The last thing in the world she wanted was for Cash to find any kind of an excuse to come too close to the goings-on at the saloon—or come too close to her! McShane could be the most maddening, arrogant, irritating man in the world, but there was something strangely *honest* about him, despite the mystery surrounding him. And there was something about him as well that challenged and even excited her, made her feel just a little bit breathless. If Cash Weatherly ever really touched her, she'd want to die. With McShane . . .

He could say what he wanted to say, but she still had her wits and her wiles and she *would* have her way. And although he had barged into the saloon so confidently, he wasn't infallible, and he didn't know everything. He'd stepped into a business arrangement, and he'd apparently planned and plotted a great deal—except that he'd made a few assumptions about her that he either hadn't had time to check out or hadn't realized could be wrong. She wasn't about to enlighten him. The less he knew about her the better. She was going to marry him, and keep her distance from him.

And buy herself some protection from Cash Weatherly while she proceeded on her own to bring him down.

Very quietly, she said, "I'll marry you."

"No rules or regulations!" he reminded her in a soft taunt.

"No rules."

He shrugged. "Fine then. And I'm certain that upon occasion I'll be glad to be able to remind you that you did *choose* to marry me. Now, let's find a dress—"

"No!" she cried. "I'll find a dress."

"A proper dress."

"You met me when I was clad in black from head to toe! How much more proper could I possibly be?" she exclaimed.

"No more black. No mourning for Eddie."

"Please!" she implored. "Just—just leave me be. Go on down. I'll come right after you."

He sighed. "You won't show, you'll disappear—"

"I won't disappear."

"Give me your word. And don't break it, I warn you."

She wanted to fight.

But she didn't. She fought her own inner battle instead, and then gave him the promise he had demanded. "My word. I swear to you! Ten minutes, I'll be ready and downstairs and I'll be properly dressed."

She was actually entreating him, Ian thought. Did he dare trust her?

She returned his stare, the expression in her eyes inscrutable.

"Your turn, McShane. You've given me your business reason, but why is it that you choose to marry a . . . whore?"

The tables were turned. Did he dare tell her the truth?

That he'd have wed Medusa to keep a really stern hand on the saloon and hurt Cash Weatherly in any way possible. His shares in the place gave him a base from which to observe Weatherly and plan his revenge. But marrying Ann McCastle would make it all so much sweeter. Taking what Cash wanted did mean a lot to him. Marrying Ann McCastle gave him a husband's rights, and that included the right to defend his wife.

All of that was the truth. But only half of the truth.

"Well, Ann McCastle, you are quite an extraordinary whore, aren't you?" He couldn't quite determine her reaction to his words. Her beautiful blue eyes were glittering and he couldn't begin to read the emotion within them. "I don't seem to be able to buy or command you—so I'm resorting to marriage," he said, and offered her a sweeping bow. "Besides, there is one thing about marrying a beautiful whore."

"Oh? Pray tell, what is that?" she asked.

"She becomes a beautiful woman, a whore no more," he said smoothly. "Ten minutes," he told her, starting for the hallway door. But once there, he paused and turned back. "That is one thing to remember."

"What is?" she asked coolly.

"Once you've *chosen* to marry me, you will be my wife."

"And what exactly do you mean by that?"

"Only that marriage will limit a few of your choices, Ann. And I will see to it that they are limited. I certainly don't think you'll be entertaining any more customers. Or behaving in too friendly a manner to the cowhands downstairs."

"Really?" she threw back.

"Oh, yeah. Really."

"You still won't own me!" she warned him. "And you just go ahead and try to limit whatever you wish."

His lips curved into a smile. "Try?"

"Indeed, you can try."

"Oh, I will," he promised her solemnly. "You

can bet on it, Ann McCastle. I will. Try—and prevail.''

He stepped out of the room, closing the door behind him. He heard her swear vociferously, kick the
wardrobe, cry out softly.

And swear again.

She was calling him absolutely every evil word he
had ever heard, and doing so with a vengeance.

Still, a sudden smile curved his lips as he started
down the hallway to the stairs, but then his smile
faded and he frowned as he walked into the main
saloon.

Why had she really agreed to marry him? She
didn't seem to be all that much afraid of Weatherly—she simply seemed to hate the man.

He was suddenly determined to find out just what
was going on in the clever little mind behind the
glorious sky-blue eyes.

Damned determined.

She'd lost her mind, completely, Ann told herself,
staring after Ian McShane as he walked out of her
room, closing the door behind him. But he seemed
to have a talent for making her do so because he
infuriated her to no end!

She hurried to her wardrobe, throwing open the
door. Her holster and guns had been thrown down
quickly, along with her duster, trousers, and shirt.
She made quick work of folding the clothing and
burying it in the single bottom drawer of the wardrobe. She hesitated. The guns she had always kept
in her dressing table drawer, but she decided to bury
them beneath the clothing.

She stepped back and stared at the clothes hanging before her. She was supposed to be finding a
wedding dress.

She still couldn't believe that she had agreed to

this madness. She hesitated, closing her eyes, shivering. She had time to back out. She was marrying a man who was quite convinced he knew what there was to know about her, one who had a set opinion of her, and one who was more than a little mysterious and definitely dangerous.

But whatever he was, he would stand between her and Cash. He had already proved that he would do so. And whatever he was, wasn't he better than even the possibility she could fall prey to Cash? It wasn't that she had suddenly lost faith in herself. She was confident, strong in her convictions and determinations, competent—and a damned good shot. But she was also aware that she played on dangerous ground with ruthless men, some of them damned good shots as well—and most of them bigger than she was. No matter what happened with McShane, it would be better than taking her chances with Cash. She had already argued this out with herself.

Yet what of McShane?

She would have to deal with him step by step, she told herself. Make him keep his distance by convincing him she was still in deep mourning for Eddie. But then she remembered the lie she'd told McShane the night before—that she had been with a customer. "Oh, God," she groaned. What kind of mourning was that?

She felt a trembling begin inside of her again. She didn't dare let him too close!

Surely she could bargain with him. He was welcome to manage the saloon, his new acquisition. She would have more time for her other work. And if he started to become too curious about her activities . . .

She had inside help. She'd just have to see to it that he was kept occupied with the business.

Hastily then she reached for a dress. She had told him she would be just a few minutes. But if she was going to go ahead with this marriage, she wanted to make sure everything he had told her about his ownership of the saloon was true. She flew into action, dressing more quickly than she had in all her life. She gave her hair nothing more than a few quick strokes of her brush and started to tear out her bedroom door, then hesitated, and went racing down the secret stairway instead.

She rushed down the main street, staring at the signs above the shops and businesses until she found the one she wanted. She hurried in, startling a young man who sat at the front desk.

"May I help you—" he began.

Ann walked right past him, having seen the name "Mr. Reninger" on a door behind him.

She didn't know Ralph Reninger well. He had been in the saloon a few times since he'd first come to Coopersville about six months ago. She'd heard some of the cattlemen say he was an ex-Reb adjusting to civilian life in the West, like so many others. He was always polite to her, and at Eddie's funeral he had been unerringly courteous and sympathetic.

Still, when she burst in on him as he was giving directions to a clerk, he certainly appeared indignant.

"Mr. Reninger—"

Before she could say more, the young man who sat outside his office rushed in behind her.

"I tried to stop this woman, sir, but—"

Reninger rose. "It's all right. You two may excuse us."

The young man and the clerk glanced at one another, then exited the room. They didn't close the door securely. Ann snapped it completely shut, then stared accusingly at the handsome young attorney.

"Is all this true?" she demanded angrily.

"If you're referring to Eddie having sold his shares to Ian McShane, yes, it's true."

"Why didn't you tell me?" she demanded.

"Ann, I tried to tell you. I couldn't try to explain all this the day he died, you were in tears. Then there was the wake, and the funeral, and then I kept trying to set up a time to see you, but *you* kept sending me your regrets that something had come up. I brought that letter over because I had no choice."

There was a chair in front of his desk. She sank into it. For a moment, she felt defeated. Then she stared at him hard, trying to pin him.

"What do you know about this man?" she demanded.

"He's an ex-officer, and I promise you, a decent—"

"How can you speak about decency?" She felt as if she was choking. "Eddie was selling the place out from beneath my nose and you—"

"I was Eddie's attorney. It was his right to keep whatever he did with his property confidential. I told him he needed to speak with you time and time again, but I couldn't force him to do so!" He was silent for a moment, then he lifted a hand in a helpless gesture. "Ann, he thought he'd be able to buy the shares back in just a little bit of time. I don't believe that Ian intends to stay in town very long, and he would have been pleased to sell back."

She leaned forward. "Why? What's he doing here?"

"Ann, I'm an attorney, and I'm bound to keep the confidences of my clients. I can't tell you about his affairs, I—"

"Damn you!" she said, standing.

He stood as well, unhappily silent.

"You can't tell me anything."

"No."

"I'm about to marry the bastard and you can't tell me anything?"

"You're going to marry him?" Ralph said. "But he just came into town. I've barely seen him—"

"And I've barely met him! Thanks so much for your help!" she said angrily, swinging around and starting for the door. She'd glanced at her watch. The ten minutes Ian had given her had been up about five minutes ago. She couldn't believe it, but she was determined to be where she was supposed to be as quickly as possible. She had given her word.

She had already opened his office door to leave when he called her back. "Ann, please!"

"What?" she demanded, turning back.

He stood tall, a proud man. "I haven't told him anything about you at all, either. He knows you were Eddie's partner, and that's it."

She hesitated. "If I ask you not to divulge anything you know about me now, will you offer me the same confidentiality that you gave him and Eddie?"

"Yes, Ann. I will offer you that."

"Thank you," she told him.

She left the office with dignity. Then she all but ran down the street, hurried to the back of the saloon, slipped up the stairway into her room, and leaned against the wall to gasp for air. She had at least two seconds left in which she dared to catch her breath before hurrying down the front staircase to join the man she was about to marry.

Six

It was a little past noon when Ian went downstairs. Despite the time of day, candles were burning in the saloon. The scent of them filled the air, and a cloud of smoke sat low over the room. Black crepe had been hung over the doors and windows.

Little else was different from yesterday; men sat around the tables playing cards. Others stood at the bar.

Harold served drinks in a black frock coat today. Ian quickly realized it was in honor of old man Turner, who had finally been taken from his chair at the poker table and had been laid out properly in a rough wood coffin. The coffin remained opened, set on tables arranged in the center of the saloon. His hands had been crossed over his chest; his last poker hand remained clasped in his fingers. Upon occasion, a player in the room, slightly more somber for the occasion, would raise a glass toward the coffin. "Gentlemen, I raise the bet, in memory of old man Turner!"

A "Here, here!" would sound, heads would lift and eyes rise to the coffin, and the play would begin again.

"Did you know he was dead?" Harold asked quietly as Ian came to the bar.

Ian nodded. "Last night, yes. You've done well, laying him out here."

"It seemed the right thing to do, being as how he was such a good customer and all. And seeing as how he played his last cards here, drank his last drink here." Harold shrugged and lowered his voice. "I think he had his last, er—well, his last *poke* right upstairs, too, you know what I mean, but they say that was back in 1855, before my time as barkeep here."

Ian nodded, a half smile curving his lip. "It seems fitting that his wake take place in the saloon."

Harold looked at him curiously. "Well, I knew Annie would have seen it that way, but from what I heard early this morning, it seems you're the man who has the right to see things his way. Is that true?"

"I imagine I'll spend some time proving it to certain folks, but yes, that's right."

Harold shrugged, keeping a steady eye on Ian. "I had a feeling Eddie had been gambling too much. He'd taken off for days at a time now and then. You planning on keeping on the same staff?"

Ian nodded. "Far as I can see, the place does well."

"It has a touch of class. Annie sees to that. Is she coming down? Reverend Eldridge has come to say a few words over poor old Turner. At first he thought we ought to move the body over to the church for a proper service, but then as he's a fair to middling logical man of God, he seemed to think it was fitting to hold the old man's funeral service here. He's, uh, refreshing himself at the moment, but I imagine he'll be ready to get started in a few minutes."

"The *Reverend* Eldridge is here?" Ian asked.

"Sure," Harold said, puzzled.

"A bonafide minister?"

"Yessir, right over from our own Church of Saint Agnes just down off Main Street."

"Where is he now?"

Harold pointed over the bar to one of the round tables. One of the skinniest men Ian had ever seen was seated there, delightedly consuming a plate brimming with beef, potatoes, and gravy.

"How such a little guy can put away so much food is beyond me!" Harold murmured, shaking his head. "Good thing most of our customers expire elsewhere. I don't think we could afford to feed the Reverend on a regular basis."

"Maybe not," Ian agreed with a grin, watching the thin little blond man relish another bite of food. In his vocational black, he looked like a snub-nosed Ichabod Crane, the poor beleagered schoolmaster terrified of the Headless Horseman in Washington Irving's *The Legend of Sleepy Hollow*.

"Anyway, I'm glad to see him today," Ian murmured. "Think he'd mind sticking around after the funeral service?"

"For what?"

"A wedding."

"Wedding?" Harold said blankly.

"I'd appreciate it if you'd stand up for me; Dulcie or Cocoa can do the same for Ann."

"For Ann?" Harold repeated, staring at Ian blankly.

Ian grinned and walked on over to meet the Reverend Eldridge. The slim man, who was balding and looked older than Ian had thought at first glance, offered Ian a broad smile, pausing in his eating to stand up and reach out a hand. "Heard tell there was a new man in town. Welcome to Coopersville, sir. And I hope I'll be seeing you in the church come Sunday."

"Thanks," Ian said.

"You mustn't be bashful. Why, even the girls come to see me on Sundays," Eldridge said. "Lord knows, they're lost little souls, but good ones nonetheless, I do believe. The Lord loves all of his children, lost though they might be." He glanced over at Turner's coffin and crossed himself. "There's a lost lamb returned to the fold! But I say, sir, it's a good day when we set those beneath the ground taken by the good Lord's natural will, and not through the gunfire of others! Glad I am to be saying the words over such a death, and not a killing!"

"Well, Reverend, I'd like to make your day a little gladder. Think you can add a wedding to your day's work as well?"

"A—a wedding, sir?" He swallowed with surprise, his Adam's apple rising and falling in his skinny throat. "A wedding? Why, sir, a wedding needs time, thought, and careful consideration."

"I can give you about fifteen minutes."

"Not on my part, sir, but rather on yours!"

"I've given it thought and consideration."

"And time?"

"Yes—at least fifteen minutes."

"Mr. McShane—"

"Reverend, will you or won't you perform a marriage ceremony for me?"

"I—er, of course, sir, if you're determined on marriage, I will bless your union before God's eyes, most certainly. Who's to be the bride?"

"Ann McCastle."

The Reverend's furry, white-blond brow shot up. "Annie?"

Ian shrugged. "Eddie McCastle hasn't been dead long, I'll admit." He moved closer, lowering his voice in a conspiratorial way. "Reverend, I think she may be a bit more temptation than some men can withstand, alone the way she is now. What do you say?"

"I say—" he began, then paused, reflecting on the situation. He lifted his hands. "I say congratulations, sir. Congratulations. Shall I read the funeral ceremony first, or do we go for the nuptials beforehand?"

They were both startled by the sound of an exasperated sigh behind them and turned quickly.

"Let's have Mr. Turner buried first, shall we?" Ann suggested, her voice both soft and wry. She was dressed in an elegant ivory gown, lace over satin. The bodice was tight and form-fitting, dipping just low enough to be enticing rather than indecent. She looked as pure as a saint, her golden hair still free and curling down her back in rich, thick waves, her large blue eyes brilliant.

"Annie!" said Reverend Eldridge with pleasure, capturing her hand and patting it affectionately. He seemed genuinely happy. "I'm glad to see this, Annie, that I am! Now if I can just see the other young ladies happy in a state of marital bliss . . . !"

"Ah, yes! Marital bliss!" Ian murmured.

"Married!" came a gasp.

They all turned to see Cocoa gaping at Ann. Ann shrugged, Ian noted, with a small warning shake to her head. Cocoa still squeaked out the word again. "Married?" she repeated, and stood gaping.

Ian turned to Cocoa, giving her a slight tap on the jaw to close her mouth. "Careful, now. It seems you're giving something away," he whispered.

"But, but—" Cocoa gasped.

"Can we please bury Mr. Turner now?" Ann insisted.

"Yes, let's please do!" Ian agreed. "Dulcie, Cocoa,

one of you will need to stand witness for Ann."

Cocoa still couldn't speak. Dulcie seemed just as surprised, but more in control. She nudged Cocoa in the ribs. "Maybe I'd best do the witnessing," she murmured.

"We have to have Mr. Turner's funeral first."

"Maybe we should have the wedding first," Dulcie said, staring at Ann.

But Ann shivered slightly, shaking her head, and surprising Ian.

"I'm not—I'm not getting married with a corpse as a witness, no matter how much I liked the old fellow when he was alive. It would be like a bad omen." She must have felt Ian staring at her curiously because she suddenly became impatient again. "Can we please get on with this?"

"Reverend?" Ian said.

"Gentlemen! And ladies!" Reverend Eldridge said, his voice amazingly loud and powerful for so small a man. He drew the attention of every card player and drinker in the saloon, all of them turning to him. He cleared his throat.

"Shall we gather 'round our dear departed brother, Charles Turner?"

Every man in the place, dandy to drifter, rose and came forward, his head slightly bowed.

"Would anyone like to speak for Mr. Turner. Mr. McShane?" Eldridge suggested.

"Reverend, I played cards with the gentleman only after he had already departed this world. It would be more fitting if a friend was to speak for him."

Scar came forward, out of the crowd. "Can I say a few words, Reverend?"

"Scar, you go right ahead," the Reverend agreed.

"Charlie was a fine fellow!" Scar said, clutching his dusty hat to his chest. "Didn't bathe too much, and didn't smell too good, but he didn't cheat at no cards, neither, and he never did shoot a friend in the back. Me and the Yeagher boys used his winnings from when he was playing dead to buy him this here coffin, and we want to wish him so long. Charlie," he went on, addressing the corpse, "we sure hope you're heading to heaven, since you didn't cheat none and you've been too old for too much fornicating now for a long time, but if you don't make heaven, well then, half of us poor bastards will surely be meeting up with you in hell one day!"

"Scar!" the Reverend protested. "We're supposed to be praying that his soul will pass through the pearly gates, not inviting the devil up to meet him!"

"Sorry, Reverend!"

"No talk of hell and damnation. Scar, now you'll step back, we'll just read the words from the Good Book's pages," Eldridge said.

Eldridge pulled a pair of small gold-rimmed spectacles from his pocket and began reading from his small Bible. His voice was melodious and compelling. Amazingly, the room remained still while he read the funeral service. Ashes to ashes. Dust to dust.

Ian watched Ann McCastle as the words were read. She seemed pale and completely immersed in the ceremony, her head bowed as the Reverend spoke, a somber expression on her beautiful features.

The six gamblers from the table nearest the coffin were asked to carry it out. Everyone followed the coffin down the street to the cemetery. Turner was laid in the hole that had been dug out for him that morning. Eldridge said a few more words and tossed a handful of dirt on the coffin. "May he rest in peace," he said, and looked sadly and solemnly into the hole. He looked up. "Now, folks, who's for the wedding?" he asked with a broad grin.

"Back to the saloon!" Scar cried cheerfully.

"No, I think not," Reverend Eldridge said, shaking his head. Ian arched a brow at him. Ann looked at him curiously as well. "The church isn't much farther than the saloon. I could see the reason for holding a wake for Charlie Turner in the place where he died so fine and quiet, but a marriage is a holy bond done in God's name. Aaron, you here?" he asked, looking about the crowd.

The handsome young man who played piano at the saloon stepped forward.

"Here, Reverend."

"Crank up the organ then, son. Let's do this as proper as we can."

"Sure, Reverend."

The crowd started forward, following Aaron.

Only Ann remained behind. Ian paused, waiting for her. "What is it?" he asked impatiently.

She glanced at him, and he found himself wondering again at the haunting purity of her beauty. He told himself it was because she was so fair, a natural golden blond with a flawless ivory complexion and innocent, sky-blue eyes. Still, the way she looked in the gown she wore, he felt as if he were sweeping a young innocent out of a convent in order to make her his wife.

"I didn't plan on being married in church."

"It is the customary place to get married."

"But this isn't a customary marriage."

"Wherever we marry, I intend for the ceremony to be legal."

"Yes, legal, but . . . " Her voice trailed away. "This makes it more . . . real."

He took her arm, noting that the others were now far ahead of them.

"It's real one way or the other!" he announced, starting forward with her. As they walked, he looked straight ahead. He was almost dragging her forward. "Look, either you're in this or you're not."

"You know that I had rather not be in!"

"You've got five seconds to back out," he offered.

"Oh, just walk!" she grumbled.

When they reached the church, Dulcie met them at the back. "Mr. McShane, you go on up and stand next to Harold. Annie, we've picked a few flowers here—a bouquet." She stuffed the flowers into Ann's hand. "Oh, my God! I just don't believe this!" she said.

"Neither do I," Ann murmured.

"Get down there, Mr. McShane, right in front of the altar. Annie, I'll walk ahead of you. Doc Dylan is going to give you away."

Ian walked down the aisle at Dulcie's urging. Looking back, he saw an older man with shining silver hair smile happily at Ann and take her arm. The organ was playing. Dulcie, thoroughly immersed in her role as bridesmaid now, began to walk down the aisle. Ann walked behind her, looking very pale.

She came to the altar; the distinguished gentleman gave her up to Ian for marriage. Reverend Eldridge read the words and asked for their vows. Ian's mind had been made up, pure and simple. He spoke his vows loudly enough to be heard throughout the church.

Ann whispered hers so low that she had to be asked twice to repeat herself. But it didn't matter in the end. She did manage to speak the right words, even if her lips trembled as she did so. Ian wore a small topaz ring on his little finger which fitted loosely over Ann's ring finger. They were proclaimed man and wife, and Ian was given permission to kiss his bride.

He took her into his arms. It felt good. Damned

good, he thought. She was lithe and slim, she was beautifully curved as well. He kissed her lips, and was startled by the warmth that filled him, by the hunger such a simple thing as a groom's first kiss for his bride might evoke. She didn't respond; but rather clamped her mouth tightly against him. Thus challenged, he held her still, sweeping her more firmly against him until she was all but flush to the entire length of his body. He parted her lips, kissed her more deeply, hungrily, demanding a response. Her fingers dug into his arms, her mouth parted to his onslaught, and she ceased to fight here in front of so many others because she could not win. When she gave in, he meant to leave her be.

Yet he did not. He held her. Explored the sweet depths of her mouth. Tasted the pleasant, subtle freshness of the mint leaves she had probably chewed after caring for her teeth. Tasted . . .

The woman he had married. The remarkable woman, the remarkable *whore*, he taunted himself. But the saloon was his, she was his, and vengeance would soon be his as well.

A roaring came to his ears at last—from the saloon crowd who had come to the church to watch them wed.

"Ahem!" Eldridge said, clearing his throat.

Ian released his bride at last. Her eyes were blue daggers she cast upon him as she steadied herself, pressing the back of her hand to her lips as she stared at him. The hand was shaking, he noted.

"We've some papers to sign, good people," Eldridge began. "And then—"

"Then a wedding toast!" Scar announced.

Ann's signature wavered, Ian noticed, as they set their hands to the certificate Eldridge quickly prepared for them. She still seemed to be trembling as she watched him make the entry into the church journal. Eldridge smiled broadly at her. "Congratulations, my dear!"

She nodded. "Thank you" was all she could manage in reply.

"Let's return to the saloon then, shall we?" Eldridge said happily. "Ceremonies do work up my appetite!"

Eldridge linked arms with Ann, escorting her out of the church, back to the dusty road, and down Main Street toward the saloon. Ian followed, walking more slowly, pausing as they passed the cemetery. Old man Turner's grave had been filled in. A crude wooden cross marked the spot.

Flowers lay over a grave nearby, one that was probably no more than two weeks old. Knowing what he would find, Ian walked over to the grave anyway.

A heavy wooden cross had been fixed into the ground. Words had been deeply etched into the horizontal plank. "Edward J. McCastle, Eddie, deeply beloved, sleeps with the angels now, may they tend to his care." Simple, sweet. Wild violets lay scattered over the mound of earth.

Ian was surprised to realize that he wished he might have met the old gentleman.

He shook himself, wondering if his new bride missed him. She had spoken of him as if she had known him well, very well, as a wife should have known him. And like a wife, she had wanted to deny his faults. Maybe she had cared for the poor old bastard.

She might have cared for him—but she had still been furious to discover that she had been sold out by him. He paused by the graveyard. He felt as if soft, invisible ties were snaking around him. What did it matter to him, what Eddie McCastle had been like? Except that Ian was wondering about Ann's relationship with the man. And what did that matter? Ian told himself he had to keep in mind why he had come to town, why he had watched and waited so carefully before he'd set a foot inside Coopersville. But he couldn't help wondering about Eddie because of his new bride, whom he found so incredibly compelling and beguiling. The poor old fellow was gone, resting here beside Charles Turner, whose great accomplishment seemed to have been that he could play poker better dead than alive.

What a strange day, Ian thought. And what a strange day for a wedding. He looked up at the sky. Storm clouds were gathering. Billowing in great gray sheets across the sky, seeming to collide and do battle with one another, as if they prophesied a day of reckoning.

The reckoning was coming, he told himself grimly.

Then, for a moment, he paused again. He had just dragged Ann McCastle into that reckoning. No help for it, he thought, and still . . .

He'd see that she came out of it all right!

Was that going to be enough?

He could hear the sound of piano music coming from the saloon. He squared his shoulders and walked forward.

"Ann! Fair Ann, beautiful, beautiful Ann!"

She was greeted the minute she came into the saloon by a lean, tall young man with a handsome face, pale blue eyes, and a shock of almost white-blond hair. As much as she detested Cash Weatherly, she hadn't managed to let that emotion color her feelings for his youngest son. Joe was simply all smiles and charm. He was well liked by the respectable citizens of the town, and popular with cowhands, kitchen help, the "ladies" of the saloon—rich

men, poor men, workers, and the elite all seemed to
be fond of Joe Weatherly.

He had his father's coloring, but Ann assumed he
resembled his mother in all other aspects because he
had a gentleness about him that was endearing. He
could shoot, and he knew how to drive cattle, but
he loved to go east, or follow whatever traveling the-
atrical troop was in the near vicinity. He quoted
Shakespeare and Defoe, and dreamed of visiting the
great art capitals of Europe. Ann even felt a twinge
of guilt when she had the girls draw family secrets
from him, because she liked him so much. But so
far, Cash Weatherly hadn't seemed to realize that his
youngest son had helped bring about some of his
difficulties.

"You're married, Annie!" Joey said, catching her
hands, holding her at arm's length, shaking his head.
"I awaken alone in the grips of a hammering hang-
over only to discover that the girl of my dreams, no,
the woman of my every fantasy, has gone off and
married another!" He pulled her close and chastely
kissed her forehead. "Actually, I admit," he said
softly for her ears alone, "I feared my father's wrath
should I lay my heart at your feet. I'm happy for
you, Annie. You'll be a good wife. Who is this lucky
bastard who's come to take over the saloon and
sweep you away?"

"The saloon really remains mine," she informed
him. Well, she meant for it to remain hers as much
as possible. Then she nearly jumped a mile high. She
had been unaware that Ian had come in and stood
directly behind her until he stretched out an arm
around her, shaking Joe Weatherly's hand. "Ian
McShane, sir. And you're . . . ?"

"Weatherly. Joe Weatherly. There are a few of us
Weatherlys around in these parts."

"You're kin to Cash?"

"He's my father. I've brothers, Carl and Jenson, and a sister, Meg. My mother . . . died a few years ago. We've a ranch outside of town." He shrugged. "We've lots of property outside of town. Some of that ownership is contested by the Indians, but the white men just seem to leave us alone. Might be because we seem to have so many cowhands, and every one of them talented with a gun. What do you say, Annie?"

"I say your family has powerful holdings," she replied nonchalantly.

"More and more of them daily," he agreed pleasantly, "though I hear tell my father came in here this morning breathing fire because someone held up his wagon with the gold he'd just been paid for this year's cattle."

Joey didn't seem to be tremendously concerned.

"One of his men was killed, or so he said," Ann told Joey.

Joey shrugged, and lowered his voice. "Ever heard that saying, Annie? 'He who lives by the sword dies by the sword!' My father hires gunfighters. You win a gunfight, you usually take a life. You lose a gunfight, you often forfeit a life. His men know what they're up against. And he pays them well. Anyway, he must be laid out at my house and there must be some kind of a vigil going on there. I should be getting back, but then they think I've traveled on over to the new mining town that's springing up just south of here, looking into some property I bought on my own. Besides, I've got to drink to Annie's happiness—and of course yours, Mr. McShane."

"Of course," Ian agreed wryly.

"You won't be missed?" Ann asked.

"Oh, I don't imagine. I've never had the hard head for business, that thirst for power, that has driven my family. I'm afraid I'm rather a disappointment. I think I shall remain a while at McCastle's. Home will not be enjoyable. Not only is my father missing his gold, but Grainger Bennington refused to sell him some land he's been hankering after for a long time. Shall I get you some champagne, Ann, Mr. McShane?" Joe asked.

Ann stood still for a minute, staring at Joe, feeling as if a cool breeze was wafting over her. *Grainger Bennington had refused to sell land to Weatherly. Weatherly would be in a wretchedly foul mood now, and Grainger . . .*

Grainger lived alone. All alone, an hour's ride out of town, with no one near him.

"No, no, you two gentlemen sit," Ann said sweetly. She even managed a tremulous smile for her new husband, who arched a brow at her, his dark eyes as unfathomable as ever. "I'll see to the champagne. And if you'll excuse me for just a few minutes, I should see to a few other things. Business, you know."

She slipped past them gracefully, skirting around the bar to ask Harold to take several bottles of their best champagne to the table. Harold agreed with a frown. Their regulars were lifting their glasses to her each time she took a step. She had to stop, smile, and then escape as quickly as she could each time.

In the kitchen she found Dulcie perched on a worktable, tasting small pastries Henri had just laid out by her side, a champagne glass in her free hand.

"Dulcie, you've got to get out there for me, quickly!" Ann said.

Dulcie frowned at her sternly. "What is in your head now, Ann McCastle?" She giggled suddenly, making Ann wonder how much champagne she'd already managed to imbibe. She pointed a finger at

Ann. "You married him. *Married!* What was in your head, Annie?"

"He was heading for my wardrobe!" Ann whispered.

"You married him rather than let him see your clothing?" Dulcie demanded incredulously.

"No! I listened to his *proposal* because he was going to go into my wardrobe. Dulcie, think of what I keep there! But that's not the reason I married him. It's complicated. I married him to keep Cash away."

"I'll bet you married him because he just doesn't take no for an answer," Dulcie advised her, giggling again. "He wants something, Annie. All right, well, he wants you, but he wants more. I know men!"

"Dulcie, yes, you know men, and I haven't time for this discussion."

Henri, a huge man, well over six feet tall and at least three hundred pounds, went strolling by her, swearing in his native French. *"Mon Dieu!"* He, too, wagged a finger at Ann. *"Ma chèrie*, you must warn us next time you wish to marry a stranger!"

"Henri," she said with a sigh, "it shouldn't be a common occurrence! Please, please, just do your best today. Give anyone whatever they want, and keep it all on the house. I think I can still afford such a thing—never mind, *he* can afford such a thing. And Dulcie!"

She spoke with sharp determination. Dulcie set down her champagne and leapt from the table.

"Get out there, please! Keep him occupied."

"You're going to disappear again?" Dulcie said incredulously.

"I have to!" Ann whispered back.

"And we're supposed to keep him occupied?" she demanded. "Like I said, Ann, you just *married* him!"

"Please! Find Cocoa. And find Ginger. Have her play the piano, I'll be taking Aaron with me."

"You had best be willing to accept the consequences when you get back!" Dulcie warned her.

"Dulcie, keep him from finding out that I've gone!" Ann said. She couldn't argue any longer. She was wasting precious time. She slipped silently from the kitchen and whispered to Aaron at the piano. He nodded and kept playing.

Ann slipped back through the kitchen again and outside, reaching her own room through the cellar to keep from being seen going up the front staircase.

Guilt assailed her as she hurried to change. Grainger Bennington was an honorable man. A stubborn one, a man who apparently couldn't be bought. She wasn't sure why she was feeling quite so desperate, but she was. Weatherly had made Bennington the offer months ago about buying his place, and Bennington had kept putting him off. But now Bennington had told Weatherly no, just as Weatherly was suffering other disappointments. Ann was scared. She'd been watching Cash a long time now. When he was angry, he could strike swiftly. He'd be in a mean mood now, eager for revenge.

She had played her cards too long, perhaps. Maybe she shouldn't have played them at all. Maybe she should have found a way to walk right up to Weatherly and shoot him through the heart because she was afraid for Grainger Bennington. He was a good man. A lonely one who came in to the saloon maybe twice a month. He paid the girls, but as often as not he asked for nothing but a little conversation. Eddie and Ann had both bought him drinks often enough, and they had both listened to him declare that Cash Weatherly, no matter how powerful and wealthy a man he might be, didn't have the right to force folks out. No man had that right.

Her fingers shook as she finished dressing and belted on her guns. It was madness for her to leave

the saloon now, in the middle of her wedding celebration. But it didn't matter. Not when a good man's
life was at stake. She slipped through the hidden
door and hurried out back to the stables. The sun
was about to set and the air was heavy with the
promise of a storm.

"Annie!"

Aaron whispered to her from inside the stables.
He was saddling their horses. She hurried to help
him. "We've got to get out to the Bennington place."

"Why? What's happened?"

"Grainger has point-blank refused one of Cash
Weatherly's generous offers."

"Ann, Weatherly may not strike now. He may not
strike at all."

"And Cash may have already sent someone out
there to do Grainger in. And if not, you're going to
have to convince Grainger that he either needs to
come in to town for a while or hire a gun of his own.
No matter what happens, Grainger can't see me."

"All right, Annie. We'll ride. But what's going to
happen when your groom discovers you gone?"

"He won't find out."

"He will," Aaron warned. "I can go alone."

She shook her head. She was the best shot; she
could pick off asassins from a long way off. She
couldn't risk Aaron's life if Grainger was under attack already.

Grainger could be dead already.

"Aaron, let's ride. Dulcie will take care of Mc-
Shane."

Aaron was shaking his head, staring at her gravely. "Annie, why'd you go and *marry* the man?"

She sighed deeply. "Aaron!"

He chuckled. "You can use that tone with me,
cousin, but is McShane going to be happy when he
discovers that his brand-new bride has disappeared

from her own wedding reception? Somehow, I don't
think so."

"Aaron, please, Grainger may be—"

"Dead or in danger. I know. Fine. If you insist,
we'll both go. Take your time, Annie. Your saddle
girth looks too loose. Maybe you should get another
saddle. Then we'll go. And pray for Dulcie."

"Dulcie will be just fine," Ann said stubbornly.
She couldn't take her time. Too much time had
passed while she was changing. It ticked away now
as they saddled their horses. . . .

Dulcie wasn't fine. In fact, Dulcie decided, if Ann
didn't start to manage this confusion better, she was
going to start coming down with the damned va-
pors. She did feel like passing out, fainting dead
away, just like a delicate plantation belle.

She had the finest champagne for McShane, she
had a story all concocted about Ann's being busy in
the liquor vault down in the cellar. She'd have to
keep coming up with new stories, of course, but for
the moment—and under the circumstances!—she
had thought she was in control of the situation.
Cocoa had given her a little bit of laudanum to slip
into the champagne. She'd have both McShane and
Joey Weatherly sleeping on the table in no time. All
men needed a little rest.

Except that Ian McShane wasn't going to get any
rest. Because he wasn't there for her to watch!

"Gentlemen . . . " she had begun, coming up behind Joey at the table and slipping around him to
join the two. Only the second man at the table wasn't
McShane, it was Doc. "Thanks, Dulcie!" he said, taking the champagne and the glasses.

Dulcie stared at Joey. "Where's McShane?"

"Gone."

"Gone where?"

"Why, that lawyer fellow, you know—Eddie's young lawyer from back east who just opened the office here a while back—"

"Reninger, fellow's name is Reninger," Doc supplied.

"Yeah," Joey agreed. "He came in a while ago. He didn't seem too surprised to hear about the wedding, but he needed to talk to McShane nonetheless."

"So where did they go?" Dulcie asked, reaching for one of the glasses of champagne Doc had just poured. She emptied it in a single swallow. "Where is McShane?" she insisted.

"Don't know now," Joey said, and grinned. "But he's been gone a while now, too. He and Ralph rode out of here fast. He does throw a fine wedding party, doesn't he?"

Dulcie swallowed more champagne.

Too late, she remembered the laudanum.

She never made it from the table. When she started to fall, Joey plucked her up.

"Strange, Dulcie can usually drink any man under the table. Is she all right?" he asked Doc.

Doc looked at Dulcie's eyes carefully, and felt for her pulse. He nodded. "She's going to be fine." He frowned, and sniffed the bottle of champagne thoughtfully.

"Why don't you take her upstairs to bed? I'll get us some whiskey instead of this bubbly French stuff, what do you say?"

Joey agreed, and carried Dulcie off to bed. Frowning, Doc walked slowly to the bar, asking Harold for a bottle of whiskey.

Doc sat back down. Things were getting stranger and stranger in town.

They had been getting strange and then . . .

McShane had arrived.

Doc tossed back some whiskey. He suddenly had the feeling that all hell was about to break loose, that the town just might light up as if a massive cannon had exploded.

McShane was going to be the catalyst, the man to touch that spark of fire to the fuse.

Doc would be damned if he could see just who was going to get burned by the fire, but it was coming, yes indeed. It was all going to burn . . .

He sipped his whiskey thoughtfully. Just who in the hell was this McShane?

Did Cash Weatherly know?

Seven

*R*alph Reninger had already made his
way through law school when the war had started.
Because of his family connections and a stint at a
military academy in Virginia, he'd been appointed
Ian's first lieutenant in the thirty-man cavalry unit
Ian had led, scouting out Union positions throughout the war.

Ralph had spent many a night explaining the fine
points of the law to Ian and passionately assuring
him that the Constitution had given the southern
states the right to secede.

There had been many nights when Ian had lain
awake, amused, listening to Ralph. The law had as
yet to stand him very well. As he had pointed out
to Ralph upon many an occasion, the law was only
as strong as the power that rested behind it. But
Ralph had proved to be an invaluable aide, smart
and quick to judge any situation. Throughout the
war, Ralph had known what he would do once the
conflict ended—he would go west, out to the wild,
wicked towns and territories, and he'd bring the law
with him. His determination had amused Ian at first,
but Ian himself had still been dealing with the U.S.
government and its war records when Ralph had
found out just where Ian's nemesis had gone. And

Ralph had finally convinced Ian of the real beauty of the law when he had furnished him with a way to come into the very heart of Weatherly's town as a businessman.

Now, Ralph, who was still the perfect aide-de-camp, even though the war had ended nearly three years before, had more information for him.

They had stepped outside of the saloon to make sure that no one would overhear their conversation. Ian noted that his friend, who was slim with sandy hair and clear hazel eyes, was dressing like a lawyer these days. His shirt was immaculately white, his vest a somber shade of dark green, his frock coat a dark brown.

"You're married?" Ralph said, his voice tinged with amusement. But his amusement faded quickly. "You married Annie McCastle? I know how important all of this is to you, Ian, but haven't you taken it just a bit far?"

"I think it's a good arrangement between Mrs. McCastle and myself."

"Mrs. McCastle?" Ralph said, confused. He looked at his friend, but Ian was staring moodily at the dusty boards of the wooden sidewalk as he leaned against the outer wall of the saloon. He'd been busy with legal matters, with all the fine points of the law. It had never occurred to him before that his friend had assumed that Ann McCastle, Eddie's partner, was Eddie's widow. He opened his mouth to correct Ian, but then he closed it again. He had done his work ethically and honestly, but he still felt a twinge of guilt where Ann was concerned. If he'd only known her a bit better, it might have been easier to force her into a meeting more quickly. But she had been so devastated by Eddie's death, and then she had been busy running the saloon, keeping a tight grasp on things. Ralph hadn't expected Ian for another few days; he'd thought he had a little more time in which to explain the situation to Ann.

He lowered his head, exhaling. Ann had apparently chosen not to inform Ian about her relationship with Eddie. He'd keep quiet himself. Maybe he owed her that much. If he didn't owe it to her, he was going to give it to her anyway.

He looked at Ian again. "Married," he repeated. "Not that I don't envy you. There's not a man in this town—including Weatherly—who wouldn't take a chance at having Annie McCastle for a wife. Even those who assure their wives that their tongues don't lie in the dust for a woman who does something so disreputable as run a saloon. Not that I know her very well, though—" he added, brightening. "I have spent a night or two with the charming and lovely Miss Dulcie. But marrying Annie, Ian! Was that right? Even in a quest for justice—"

"She'll get her saloon back when I've finished with Weatherly. I'll return it to her legally—you can see to that, right?"

"Sure. You've just married her—legally. What will you do about that when you're done with Weatherly?"

"Well, you can free her from marriage legally too, right?"

"Ian—"

"She'll get whatever she wants, Ralph. And that wouldn't have been the case if someone else had come in on Eddie McCastle's debt situation."

"But Ian—"

"I don't know if it was right or wrong, but I'm in no mood for a lecture, my friend. You came—"

"I came," Ralph said quickly, "because I think there's going to be trouble."

"Why?" Ian demanded intently.

"Weatherly has been buying up the town, you

know. Somehow he's persuaded half the cowmen in the area to sell their ranches, and he's pressured a number of the miners into selling their claim grants as well. The cowmen have had trouble with their cattle; sicknesses, losses in the night. The gold seekers who have capitulated seem to have had their share of trouble as well—before they capitulated. Little things. Mules running off with supplies. Shafts seemingly strong by day collapsing when no one is around. That sort of thing."

"Why in particular do you expect trouble today—and for whom?"

"A man named Grainger Bennington. He's got a small farm a short ride out of town. He was in to see me last week because he's been receiving what he called 'frighteningly persuasive' offers for his property from your old friend, Weatherly. He wanted to know if there was anything Weatherly could do to legally budge him from his property. I told him no, that no one could demand he sell his holdings, unless he fell into a position where he couldn't pay his debts. Grainger is a fine, stubborn fellow, but he's kind of a loner, though he has been known to frequent McCastle's upon occasion. He listened very gravely to everything that I had to say, then he told me that a few of his old friends had sold out—Weatherly had made offers they'd decided to accept. They'd been having all manner of mishaps, as I explained earlier. Anyway, word is out that Grainger Bennington gave Cash Weatherly a definite no on the sale of his property this morning. And we'll assume—since word does seem to travel faster than a bullet in these parts—that Weatherly's heard about your marriage about now. If what we all suspect about the man but can't prove is true, I imagine some harm is about to befall Mr. Bennington. What do you say?"

"Tell me how to get out there."

"Just get your horse. I'm riding with you."

"Ralph, the war is over. You're a lawyer."

"And I'm a damned good shot and I take orders well," Ralph said, then added with an amused and curious smile and soft voice, "You do have a bride in that saloon somewhere. Are you going to just ride out?"

"I have a bride who's already trying to hide from me, but she seems quite fond of keeping her hands on her property. She'll be here when I get back," Ian said with assurance.

Ann and Aaron rode swiftly to the sweeping rise of dusty, sagebrush-covered land that overlooked the dip of valley where the Bennington farm lay. Ann gasped, stricken, covering her mouth with the back of her hand as she stared down at the place.

She had smelled the smoke long before they had come to the rise; she had feared the worst, and she had found it. Grainger Bennington's handsome wooden farmhouse had been burned to the ground. The corrals had been opened; the barn had burned as well. Stray chickens, pecking here and there, surrounded the place. She could see no other horses, none of the cattle. No life stirred. . . .

There was no sign of Grainger Bennington.

"Oh, my God, Aaron!" she cried out in dismay, feeling the prick of tears behind her eyes. Had Grainger perished in the flames? Had Weatherly had the decency to shoot him first, then leave the body to burn in the inferno? The ruins still smoked. Dusk had come, and it seemed as if an eerie mist rose against the red-streaked sky and the sunken crescent of sun that just barely arched into the horizon.

"Annie, don't panic on me!" Aaron pleaded softly. "Maybe Grainger got out—"

"Weatherly wouldn't have let him out!" she wailed. Kicking her horse, she raced down the outcropping to the valley, through the smoldering pieces of house and barn that had fallen when the burned structures had collapsed, and to the front of the house. She dismounted, coughing and choking from the smoke, trying to walk into the ruins. Aaron caught up with her.

"Annie, what do you think you're doing?"

"Looking for Grainger."

"Annie, you'll burn yourself! Touch any of this debris now and you'll burn your skin right off your bones. If Grainger is in there, you won't be able to help him anymore. Annie—" He broke off, pausing, listening. "Annie, we've got to get out of here. Someone is coming. You can't help Grainger and you could hurt yourself."

He gripped her by her arm, leading her back to her horse. She knew there was nothing she could do. She leaped atop her mount and followed Aaron as he raced hard for the outcropping.

"Aaron, wait!" she cried to him as they reached the top. She dismounted quickly, urged her horse to move forward, and motioned Aaron to dismount and join her on her stomach on the crest, looking down upon what had been the Bennington farm, watching the riders who were coming down the trail.

There were five of them. To Ann's vast relief, she saw that Grainger Bennington was one of them; the sheriff, his deputy, and two other local ranchers completed the party.

She turned and lay back on the earth, relieved. "Grainger made it out!" she whispered.

"Grainger made it out—and you'd better make it back!" Aaron warned her. "It's your wedding day, remember?"

She hadn't. She started to bolt up, then realized she'd be in clear view of the men if she did so. She rolled down the slope toward the horses, then inched up and hurried carefully toward her mount, Aaron following closely behind her.

"Grainger made it out, Ann. Why are you so quiet?"

"Aaron, Grainger knew something was going to happen. But he's stubborn. He wouldn't have just left his place for Weatherly and his men to move in and burn it down."

"Maybe someone else went out ahead of us to see what was going on."

"Who?" Ann demanded. "When I first brought up to the sheriff the possibility that Cash Weatherly was a murdering thief, he nearly laughed me out of his office, assuring me that Weatherly would make one fine senator once the territory acquired statehood!"

"Someone else. Ann!" Aaron said lightly. "Grainger is alive—isn't that the important thing? And we'll have a barn raising for him when the place cools off. He's alive, and he can make another stand."

"Yes, you're right. It's just—" She paused, shaking her head. "Aaron, I haven't had a chance to tell you what happened last night."

"What happened?" he demanded sharply.

She hesitated, almost wishing she hadn't spoken. Aaron was going to be angry with her for taking on Weatherly's men without him, and he was going to be concerned and worried.

"What happened?" he insisted.

She told him about the close call she'd had with Weatherly's gunmen. "But when I might have been shot, Ian, someone else gunned down Weatherly's man. And—and stole the gold."

"Thank God!"

"I tried to find the gold."

"Thank God you're alive, Ann!" he snapped.

"I know, Aaron, I know."

"Were you seen or possibly recognized?"

She shook her head vehemently. "No, I'm certain I wasn't. It's just that this is all so strange. Last night another thief came after *my* stolen goods. And now today, Grainger had been warned."

"Annie, it's hardly likely that a gunfighter who slipped away with stolen gold last night would become a vigilante out to uphold justice for Grainger today!"

"I know, I know."

"We're going to have to be exceptionally careful," he mused. "Other thieves in the area could put us in grave jeopardy."

"I know," she murmured. "And I just don't understand what happened with Grainger—"

"Ann, we didn't get there in time. Whether Grainger knew to get out himself, battled down the arsonists single-handedly, or was warned by someone else, it was a damned good thing. We wouldn't have been one bit of help to him."

"Because of that stupid wedding!" Ann grated.

"May I remind you that you have a bridegroom waiting, who is not in the least bit stupid? You'd better be worrying about how to get back in there!" Aaron warned.

She cast him an evil glare.

"Annie, I was there. You walked down the aisle of your own free will. You chose to do it."

She swore at him and nudged her horse, racing the mare back toward town. She slowed when they reached the saloon, silently letting Aaron take her horse. She slipped inside, racing up to her room. She was breathless when she got there, but she barely dared take the time for a few extra breaths. She shed her masculine garb, redonned her wedding apparel, and then paused as she brushed out her hair, wondering at her irritation. She was delighted that Grainger was alive and well. It was wonderful that he was in one piece, unharmed. But . . .

But she had gone through a great deal of trouble and risk to help him, and he hadn't needed her help.

She set the brush down nervously. She had to sweep back down into the saloon and pretend that she'd never left it, even when she'd been gone for hours. She had to face the problem that didn't seem to go away.

McShane.

As she raced back down the stairs, she wondered if she smelled like smoke. A bath would be in order. As soon as she slipped down into the main room itself, she whispered to Harold to see to it that the kitchen help brought fresh hot water to the tub for her. "Where's Dulcie and McShane?" she asked nervously. She looked around. She didn't see either of them. To her amazement, she suddenly felt as if a wolf's canines had torn into her stomach. *They hadn't gone upstairs, had they?* She felt faint and ill. She had asked Dulcie to keep him out of the way, to keep him entertained. Last night she had wanted one of the girls to seduce him. . . .

But not now! she thought. They were married! He couldn't go off with another woman! Even though she had asked the girls to keep him occupied, she didn't want him going upstairs . . .

Oh, God! Why not? she cried to herself, wondering why the thought of him with another woman made her feel sick, furious.

"Dulcie's in bed," Harold told her.

"With . . . McShane?" She could barely breathe out the question.

"With McShane? The man you married earlier?"

Harold said. He looked at her, frowning, shaking his head. "She's—had some strange kind of reaction to the champagne. She's sleeping. She'll be fine."

Ann didn't know whether to be relieved or frightened.

"Then where is McShane?" she asked.

"I'm not rightly sure. He was out talking to a friend, last I heard. Haven't seen him in a while."

Ann nodded, feeling relieved that McShane wasn't around. She gazed around the saloon again. Joe Weatherly was just finishing up what must have been a very friendly card game; the three other players—a businessman and two cowboys—were rising, shaking hands with one another. As they walked away, Ann came to life, walking into their midst, shaking hands with them all, accepting congratulations on her marriage. Before Joey could rise, she sank down beside him. "Good day?" she asked.

"You should get married more often, Annie. It was very good luck for me."

"I think we're going to have to find you a room in the saloon if you don't go home soon," she said.

He made a face. "Yeah, well, I suppose I do have to ride on back to the ranch, eh, Annie? Face up to the old man." He shook his head, then lifted the shot glass of whiskey in front of him. "To my old man— the biggest bastard in the territory!"

"Shh!" Ann warned him. "Lots of folks here respect your father. You want them telling tales on you?"

"What's he going to do? Plug his own son? The great war hero? The outstanding citizen? You're right, Annie. Some folks are fooled by him. But you're not, are you?"

"Joey—"

"You don't like him. I've seen it. And that just makes me like you all the more, Annie."

She sighed. "I hear that Dulcie has had a turn of some sort and that she's sleeping. Go up and just crawl in and sleep with her."

"She'll think I owe her in the morning."

"You will owe her. You need to get some sleep. Now isn't it the time for you to go home?"

He leaned across the table and caught her chin, then kissed her cheek lightly. "I love you, Annie. Did you know that?"

She blushed uneasily, unprepared for the statement. "Joey, please—"

"That's right, you married a stranger today." He shrugged. "Seems a right fellow. Seems things have hopped—since he's come to town. He'll look after you, Annie. You mark my words. He's got the power to do it."

"I don't need to be looked after—"

"We all need to be looked after, Annie. All of us. Do you smell smoke?"

"We're in a saloon!" she reminded him.

He shrugged again. "Seems to me I smell a different kind of smoke . . . oh, well." He stood, reaching for her hand, helping her to her feet. He kissed her hand. "Kind lady, all the best wishes in the world. I will take you up on your generous offer. Annie, aren't there a few extra rooms? I don't want Dulcie to throttle me."

There was an extra room. She was still hoping McShane might want to use it.

"Dulcie will be delighted to find you with her."

He started for the stairway and Ann looked uneasily around the saloon. Still no sign of McShane. Damn the bastard! Well, fine. Maybe he would stay away all night. She hurried up the stairs and into her room. Her bath awaited, the water steaming, rising temptingly above the tub in a compelling mist. She stepped behind her screen and hastily shed her clothing, then hurried for the tub and stepped in. She nearly screeched at the heat of the water, then savored it as she sank slowly into it. The water rushed around her. Heaven, she thought as she leaned back and closed her eyes.

She should hurry. Get out of the tub and dressed before McShane reappeared. But the hot water felt so good. The clean fresh scent of the soap was so delicious.

She sat there in sweet luxury. . . .

Ian tilted back his hat, staring at the stairway, shaking his head.

When he'd stepped up to the doorway of the saloon, his new wife had been busy. Talking earnestly with Joe Weatherly. She hadn't seen Ian. If she'd asked about him earlier, she would have been told that he had left the saloon. Was she delighted with the good fortune that her groom had disappeared?

He pulled his hat low for another minute, reminding himself that he should be grateful for the way things had turned out today. He and Ralph had arrived at the Bennington place just in time to see two riders hightailing it away. He'd gotten off a shot that had hit one of the arsonists, wounded him, but how badly Ian didn't know. And there'd been no way to pursue the men at that time; the fires around the house had already been rising and he and Ralph were just able to pull an unconsious Grainger Bennington from the flames licking their way greedily over what had been his home.

Grainger had proved to be a good fellow: smart, stubborn, and not afraid, not even after all that had happened. He told them that he'd been sitting there with his rifle, expecting trouble, but still, he'd never known what hit him. He'd been knocked out from behind while sitting in the rocker in his parlor, waiting. He was grateful to be alive, and determined to go back out to his place with the sheriff. Ian and Ralph had given what statements they could to the lawmen, but when Ralph had told the sheriff they'd been expecting trouble because Grainger had turned down Cash Weatherly's offer to buy his place, the sheriff had shaken his head in sorrow and disgust. "Gentlemen, the man is rich and powerful, but that ain't no crime, not even in the West. Don't go throwing around accusations without proof or you'll find yourselves hanging by threads in a court of law getting your pants sued off you. Now Ralph, you know that, and your friend here seems a mighty intelligent fellow. We'll do what we can."

"Sheriff—" Ralph had begun.

Ian had interceded at that point. "Ralph, the sheriff's right. You're the lawyer. You know you need some proof against a man in order to hold him for a crime. Let the sheriff get on with his business."

They hadn't been going to prove anything then and Ralph had realized it. He'd shut his mouth; they'd gone back to his office. Ralph had given him a rundown of every sorry event in the territory that might have been associated with Weatherly. They'd gone over legal forms until his eyes had ached and he had remembered that he actually had a wife to go home to. The wife probably wasn't waiting up for him, but . . .

Ian exhaled on a long sigh, trying to control the rise of his temper.

No, she wasn't up waiting for him. She was up flirting with Joe Weatherly and being kissed by him.

He had nothing against Joe Weatherly. He'd seen the young man for the first time today, and he'd been startled to discover that he liked him. Joe Weatherly was young, of course, somewhere in his very early twenties, though that didn't seem all that young really, not anymore. Not since the war. Boys without beards had carried rifles, fired them, killed the enemy, died at the hands of the enemy.

But despite having been raised by an evil bastard like Cash, Joe had managed to retain some of his innate goodness—he had the ability to laugh at himself, showed appreciation for others, and had a broad, sincere smile. There'd been a time when Ian had thought he'd hate a horse if Cash Weatherly had ridden it, but the years, if they hadn't dimmed his desperate desire for justice, had tempered his emotions. He could honestly say that he didn't hold a thing against young Joe.

Until now.

He wanted to throttle the boy.

No.

He stretched his fingers out, knotted them into fists, stretched them out again. It was Ann. It was seeing her laugh with Joe, it was seeing her head bent so intimately toward his. It was seeing her smile, and it was seeing the affection in her eyes as she spoke with the young man. Then she had left him. And gone upstairs.

His wife. Who hadn't seemed to know or care that he had disappeared from the saloon. Who was probably expecting him to be gone all night.

He rose suddenly, with such a force that his chair toppled over.

And he started up the stairway, after his wife.

Eight

When Ian entered the room, he wasn't intentionally quiet. In fact, he'd felt like slamming the door so hard that it would shudder against the wall. But he hadn't done that, and when he first stepped into the room, she didn't even realize that he had come in, and he paused, staring at her with narrowed eyes, his anger simmering and growing steadily as he did so.

She was his wife, but she seemed to have forgotten that because she'd spent a good part of her evening flirting with Joe Weatherly.

It was your idea to marry her, McShane! he cautioned himself.

But he still felt his blood boil as he watched her.

She was in the hip tub, her head leaning against the section of planking that was raised at the back of the tub for just such a purpose. Massive tendrils of golden hair had been piled on top of her head. Her knees were slightly tucked up, her fingers dangled casually over the gilded edge of the tub. The water still steamed, sending a seductive scent of lavender into the air around her.

He felt his own pulse ticking at his throat, felt it grow louder. Then it was like a thunder that invaded the length of him, tensing the muscles in his limbs, neck, and shoulders. He was torn between a tangle of emotions. He was certainly a grown man with a great deal of control over his desires, and a tremendous amount of carefully cultivated discipline. He had wanted her last night, yet he had been quite capable of turning away from her. But now she was his *wife*. And despite his warning, she had spent some part of the evening with Joe Weatherly. Had she reckoned an hour in the tub would cleanse away her activities? Or did she give a damn? Had she been planning on his spending another night on the daybed?

Not tonight, he determined. And he slammed the door hard behind him, staring at her as she jumped with alarm, nearly bolting from the tub before falling back into the cover of the water.

"I thought you were—gone!" she gasped with dismay.

"Yeah, you must have," he drawled huskily. His eyes on her, he stepped into the room, slipped off his duster and cast it over a chair. He unbuckled his gun belt, strode across the room, and set the belt on the bedside table. A lamp glittered there, bathing the room in its soft glow.

"You—you did disappear," she whispered uneasily.

He smiled, arms crossed over his chest. "I've been back a while."

"What?" she demanded. She was trying to sink lower in the tub. There was only so far she was going to be able to go. He was still mesmerized by her. By her golden hair, twisted into a knot on top of her head to keep it from the water. By the rise of her breasts over the water's edge, the nipples just beneath the water, hardened by her nervousness perhaps.

"I've been back."

"How long?" she demanded in a voice that sounded angry and worried at the same time.

"Long enough."

"For what?" she asked warily.

"To watch you with Joe."

She closed her eyes, seeming to be relieved. "Well," she said lightly. "You did leave."

"But I'm back."

"So you are." Ann *was* relieved. So relieved! He didn't realize she had been out at dusk herself. But now . . .

How had she let herself stay in this bathtub so long that he could come and find her here? She was in an absolute panic, and determined that he would not realize it. He was watching her as if he were a wolf eyeing his wounded prey, his dark eyes enigmatic as they raked over her. She felt a shiver sweep over her, along with a startling warmth, and it was all caused by the fires within his eyes. Part of her was afraid, part of her was ready to fight, and oddly enough, part of her was excited. She needed to look away from his eyes. She felt as if she was being touched, when he still stood nowhere near her. She wanted to bolt up and run, yet she certainly could not, she thought.

She'd married him. She'd agreed, and she'd gone through with it, and he'd warned her from the start that there would be no rules or agreements. But now she wanted an armistice, a truce, some time. She didn't know if she was more afraid of him or of the way that he made her feel.

"You were gone—" she began again.

"Never so far gone, Mrs. McShane, that I would miss this night with my wife," he assured her.

And then he moved. He had been standing so still that he startled her, striding so swiftly, suddenly, and purposefully for the tub.

She was trying to reason with him! Ian realized as he neared her. Reason with him, send him away because he had been gone earlier.

She stared at him, her eyes huge and brilliantly blue against the pale beauty of her face, watching almost stunned as he came upon her. Then she started to rise as if in a panic as he neared her, reaching blindly for the towel that lay on a chair near the tub.

He didn't know if it was his anger that drove him so or simple frustration that she had probably bedded half the cowboys in the region yet seemed to think of him as some monster. Maybe it was neither of those emotions, maybe it was just the simple fact that she was so incredibly, erotically desirable that he could see no reason for discipline or control. She was his wife. Whatever else she had been was in the past. He had made that determination. She wasn't going to spend time with Joe Weatherly or any other man again, not while he lived. The sooner she spent time with him, the sooner she'd realize that she was married in every sense of the word. And that he'd rip any other lover of hers—paying or not—to shreds if he caught her forgetting the fact that she was married to him now, and not to some old-timer who let her do whatever the hell she chose just so long as she cast him the crumbs of one of her smiles now and then. The sooner she understood, the sooner this awful, haunting hunger he felt would be appeased and his agony would end.

He reached her before she could grasp the towel, sweeping his arms around her and lifting her from the tub even as she gasped out with startled dismay at his action.

"Wait!" she cried, "I'm soaking."

"I like wet women," he informed her.

She blushed furiously, straining against his chest.

"I was in the middle of a bath," she said indignantly. "You were supposed to be gone—"

"And you're married now. What the hell were you doing with Joe Weatherly?"

"I—" she began, then broke off, suddenly very pale. "I was talking—"

"Good. You can talk to me now. And if I catch you with the customers again, I'll tan your hide."

"How dare you—"

"How dare you!" he all but roared to her, amazed that she could be so defiant. He dropped her on the bed. She was trying to leap away even as he lowered himself over her. She struggled against his now damp chest but he didn't allow her to budge him an inch. He pressed her down into the softness of the bed with his weight, giving no quarter, brooking no resistance. He'd thought from the moment he'd seen her in the tub that he'd wanted to touch her. Feel the silky softness of her flesh at leisure, caress the fullness of her breasts, taste the pebbled, dusty rose nipples that so seduced him. He'd wanted to savor all of her—with his eyes, his fingertips, his kiss and caress. But it wasn't to be. She was wildfire beneath him. In pinning her he found he'd wedged her limbs apart. In pressing her down he'd found his lips a breath from hers. In holding her he found his mouth atop hers, fevered, passionate. The drumbeat of his pulse continued to shudder through her. Her nipples pressed through the fabric of his shirt. His tongue parted her lips, savaged her mouth, tasted, and hungered anew. A whimper sounded from her throat, but no more. Her fingers gripped his shirt at his shoulders. He kept her mouth imprisoned as he stroked a hand down her body, his fingers sweeping over her breast and her hip. They ran over the soft blond triangle between her thighs before tearing at the buttons of his trousers and easing them down.

Hard and engorged, his sex lay against her. His lips parted from hers. She gasped wildly for breath, staring up at him, golden blond hair like a billowing, silken mane about them both, the soft teasing tendrils seeming to fan the blinding ache of desire with him.

"Wait!" she gasped out.

"Wait!" he lashed back, frustrated, agonized. "What?" he mocked. "Whores don't bed the men they marry?"

"Bastard!" she snapped out furiously. "Go ahead! Just do it, do what you must!"

"Go ahead, do what you must?" he repeated, shaking himself. What was she doing to him? She'd probably charged half the territory for her favors. He'd *married* her, for God's sake. "How incredibly erotic, Mrs. McShane. Such titillating words must have created immediate success in any fine brothel, bringing the customers back by the score!"

She didn't seem to find his words amusing. She was staring at him, her eyes twin blazing sapphires. Even though she held herself stiffly beneath him, her body was vividly alive. A tiny pulse at her throat pounded furiously, a gentle trembling seared through the length of her, her flesh, sweetly smelling of lavender soap, radiated a blazing heat.

"By the score!" she hissed. "Do it!"

Enough. He could bear no more.

He sank into her. In such sweet agony by then that although he instantly realized her innocence, an excruciating hunger swept him into her again and again before he could accept the realization, and by then the best he could do was garner control, slow his movements, whisper some ridiculous assurance.

She half choked rather than let any protest or cry escape her then. Yet by that point, he had wanted her with such urgency and passion that despite the circumstances, he came quickly to an explosive climax, burying himself deep inside her with one final thrust and remaining there while his head spun with amazement, realization, guilt—and with it, a new explosion of anger that he had been taken by such deep and startling surprise. He had hurt her, obviously. He had to be responsible for his own actions, but damn her!

A slight sound, almost like a sob, came from her. She was pressing hard against his chest with her palms once again, trying to dislodge him from her. He pulled out, rolling away from her to sit at the foot of the bed, running his fingers through his hair. Damn her, and damn her again. What was this life she was leading? Why hadn't she said something to him?

He stood, swearing as his open trousers started to slide farther down his hips. Still swearing, he sat again and wrenched off his boots and socks and pants, heedless of whether his shirttails concealed any of him—it was too late to worry about whatever sensibilities she may or may not have had.

Scowling, he turned back to face her, to demand a few answers.

She had scooted up against the bedstead, her back to it. She had wrenched up the bedcovers and pulled them to her. She was hugging her knees to her chest, her hair was an angelic fall of gold about her. She looked young. Unbelievably young, fair, beautiful, innocent, vulnerable.

He felt as if he deserved just about every derogatory term she had cast his way. "Lowlife bastard" for sure. But it was an absolutely unbelievable situation.

He threw up his hands, shaking his head. He felt as if he should apologize, yet he was angry that he should feel like just such a lowlife. He wanted to

touch her again, comfort her, stroke her, but he
knew she didn't want him to touch her, didn't want
his comfort.

"Ann, for Christ's sake, how in hell could I have
known?"

"Known what?" she whispered.

"Oh, for God's sake, what kind of an idiot do you
think I am?"

"An arrogant one!" she retorted quickly, looking
away.

"You didn't have to be hurt!" he snapped back.
"But you didn't say anything, you were married to
Eddie—"

"Oh!" she gasped out in anger. "Who ever told
you I was married to Eddie? Ralph?" she demanded
incredulously.

"No, damn it, Ralph never told me you *were* married to Eddie, and he never told me you weren't. *You*
never told me that you weren't! Your name *is* Ann
McCastle."

"You assumed I'd marry him for money or profit
or just to own this place."

"And you knew it and didn't correct me."

"You were judging—"

"I was assuming, and I wasn't judging you. But I
think it's time you do let me in on the truth. Just
what the hell was going on here?"

"Eddie took me in when I was in need. He was
my adoptive father!" she strangled out.

He stood, walking around to her.

"Father?" he said.

"Father! Just that, nothing more."

"Yeah, well, obviously," he said ruefully.

She wouldn't look at him. He sat at her side,
reaching for her chin. She tried ardently to escape
him, managing only to lose her hold on the covers.
A strangled sob slipped from her lips, and she

lashed out wildly at him again. He swore softly, grappling with her until he straddled her. She went still, her cheeks burning as she remembered her state of complete nakedness, and felt his half-naked body pressed against hers. She met his gaze at last—only because she was determinedly refusing to look at the rest of his hard, muscular body.

And damn if he didn't feel the absolute sear of desire and heat knife into him again, watching her, feeling her. He kept his own eyes on hers, aware of the tensing and hardening of his body against the compelling softness of hers, aware that she felt each nuance of change taking place in him.

"You knew I thought you had been his wife. You knew it from the beginning, and you could have— should have—told me the truth!"

"Maybe you were just so damned sure of yourself that I didn't think it was possible to correct your mistaken assumptions!"

"If you didn't want this—any of this!—you could have told me the truth about yourself!" he said angrily.

"You came in making judgments; I didn't owe you any explanations."

"They were logical judgments!"

"You probably wouldn't have believed anything I had to tell you," she informed him with icy dignity.

"You didn't give me a chance," he reminded her.

"You didn't give *me* a chance!" she cried. "You'd made your logical judgments."

"Well, forgive me! You are running a brothel here, a *whorehouse!*"

Strange how the fact of it didn't seem to bother her, but the way that he'd said the word did. Her eyes were blue fire again as she raised her arm to swing at him. He caught her wrist before she could touch him, and her lashes fell, sweeping gold against her cheeks.

"Well, rest assured. I'm considering not running a brothel anymore," she told him, "I can't believe I have these poor girls doing *this* for a living."

"They make good money."

"They can't possibly make enough money to compensate them for doing what we just did."

"Thanks," he told her dryly. "What a testimonial to my abilities with the fairer sex."

"I never realized what they went through, how they suffered!"

"Ann, it isn't so bad."

"Bad? No, it's horrible, it's agony, it's—"

"It didn't have to be!" he insisted.

"But—"

He was never going to shut her up with words. He pinned her hands above her head, leaned low, and caught her lips with his own. He could taste her tears. She had cried, but in silence. Now he definitely had something to prove to her. He was achingly sorry to have hurt someone so badly, yet his anger had faded with another thought. In a way, he was glad. She'd somehow snared him from the beginning. He'd been willing enough to marry her believing she had been a whore. Because she'd been a part of this place, a means to an end. But he never would have married her for that reason alone, he realized. He never would have wanted her for that reason alone. And now he was, perversely enough, pleased. Tough guy, he mocked himself, wanting a woman who is all your own. But he did want her, now, again. He wanted to make love to her the right way this time, he wanted to make her come alive.

"This won't help!" she whispered, as his lips parted from hers. But she hadn't fought the kiss.

Maybe she had just realized that she couldn't fight him and win, not in bed.

"Give me a chance."

Her eyes widened in alarm. "But you've already—"

"You haven't," he interrupted.

"I was right here!" she protested.

He shook his head, a smile curving his lips. "All right, well, you have, but you haven't."

"Haven't—?" she began, but broke off because he had shifted. The time had come for everything that he had wanted. A brush of his lips against her breast, so lush, ripe. The stroke of his fingers down the length of her flesh. It was silk and ivory, so perfect in so many ways. The softness seduced and titillated, every gasp and involuntary movement she made against him was evocative. Simply by her breathing, her gasping and moving here and there beneath him, she aroused him incredibly again. Slow, he counseled himself, rubbing his palm over her hip, brushing his face against her abdomen, gently pressing kisses upon her flesh, sliding the bulk of his body lower against her. He stroked a finger tantalizingly down the length of her inner thigh, teased and hovered with delicate strokes against the golden triangle of her mound. She tensed, twisting.

"Are you in pain?" he taunted.

"Pain?" she gasped in a whisper. "No, not pain, but you mustn't—"

He chuckled hoarsely. "My love, lie still!" he counseled, and was pleased to see that she couldn't quite manage to do so.

He pressed his lips more intimately against her flesh, stroked delicately with his tongue. Her fingers suddenly laced into his hair, the entire and exquisite length of her body went as taut as piano wire. No mercy, no quarter given, he commanded himself, stroking, touching, and yet finding in the sweet taste and scent of her that her slightest twist, sigh, breath, or touch brought an agony of longing streaking back through his own body. He rose above her. Her eyes were closed; her breath came in short pants. He enveloped her into his arms; she clung to him in turn, holding tight when he swept deep into her, holding again, trying with the greatest attempt at discipline to go slowly, to arouse with each thrust and stroke. The world seemed to hold erotically still; no sound but their breath, no movement but that of his hips, no sensation but that of her liquid warmth. Then it seemed that she rocked ever so slightly with him, and it seemed that the sound of their breathing had become that of a tempest, the room was rocked with frenzied movement, and sensation was the small death of exploding deeply within her. Yet even as his climax peaked, and he gripped himself in aftermath, he felt something within her. Something small, yet something sweet. Some little tensing . . .

He pressed his lips against the dampness of her throat. Balanced his weight upon his hands so that he could rise and look down into her eyes.

"Ann."

"What?"

"Open your eyes."

"Will you please—"

"I'll leave you be and let you go to sleep as soon as you open your eyes and look at me."

Her eyes flew open.

"Was there any improvement?" he asked politely.

"Yes, there was a definite improvement. I didn't think that I was actually going to die of the agony," she informed him, her chin rising. But her lips trembled slightly, and there was a strange clouded beauty to her sapphire eyes. He could feel her heart, slowing now, yet the pulse still so very fierce.

Carefully he rolled off of her and then lay back,

starting to laugh. "Well, I'm glad, very glad," he told her. "I wouldn't want you in awful anguish *every* time. And just think," he pointed out politely, "they say that it actually improves with each experience. By the end of the week, you may actually be telling me that I'm tolerable!"

She muttered a soft curse and rolled away from him, wrenching up the sheets and drawing them around her.

He turned his back on her, partially exasperated, partially amused—and even just a little bit pleased. Because she had been lying. Things hadn't been quite that terrible. He had felt just the slightest quickening in her body.

And if she hadn't experienced the earth's greatest passion, well . . . she was on the road to discovery. And she remained soft, sleek, beautiful and warm beside him.

His wife. He smiled.

In time, he turned back to her again. She was half asleep, barely aware. Sweetly pliant. He slipped his arms around her and held her tight. Her hair softly teased his face. A tenderness stirred in his soul. She was such a fighter! Fighting him, fighting herself. So delicate, so strong, so determined. She could wage war on so many fronts!

Just how many, he didn't really know as yet, he reminded himself ironically.

She nudged against him, naturally curling into the curve of his body as she slept. He pulled her even closer. She was in danger, of that he was certain. As much from her own reckless spirit as she was from outside forces. He was going to have to tie her in, slowly, carefully.

With her in his arms, he slept. No nightmares plagued him. When he dreamed, it was of the musky scent of silken, feminine flesh. Of being entangled in

soft waves of sunshine, tendrils of hair that fell in
soft seduction over his shoulders and chest.

He woke, hard with hunger. Her buttocks were
pressed to his groin, his chest was flush against her
back, his arms lay around her. She remained half
asleep. He stroked her thigh, slipped two fingers
within her. She awoke with a small gasp, her shoulders stiffening. He pressed his lips to her neck, her
shoulders, her spine, stroking within her all the
while. The seduction of his fingers was replaced by
that of his erection. His hand slid from inside her to
her breast, his palm moving over her nipple, then
his hand caressing the fullness of the mound. He
moved slowly, tortuously slowly, until the pulse
against his temple seemed like thunder, sweat
beaded upon his skin, and the hunger and desire
within him demanded surcease. Moving within her,
touching her, breathing her scent . . . he raced toward climax, braced himself, stroked her, exploded
within her. His heart hammering, his breath a gasp,
he felt the slight shuddering within her, heard the
gasp that escaped her lips, then felt her shuddering
again . . . and again. He smiled. She wasn't going to
give him anything. She was never going to admit to
anything that he didn't drag out of her.

But he didn't say anything. He held her close,
lightly stroking her, leisurely appreciating the perfect rise of her hip, the softness of her flesh.

She caught his hand where it lay upon her breast.
"We should—get up."

"We're newlyweds. We should sleep a while
longer."

She didn't seem willing to fight him, and instead
eased by his side.

A while later, Ian was halfway dozing himself
when he became aware that she had turned. He lay

on his back; her head rested on his chest. Her elegant fingers rested upon his abdomen.

He stroked her hair.

"Ian," she said, her head still upon his chest, not looking at him.

"Yes."

She hesitated. "You are tolerable."

"I'm—what?"

"Tolerable."

"Just tolerable?"

"And just barely!" she added with an aggravated sigh.

He grinned broadly, staring up at the ceiling. "Thanks," he told her lightly, "I'll try not to let that eloquent rush of approval increase my arrogance."

"See that you don't," she murmured against his chest.

He didn't respond, but the smile remained on his lips as he stared up at the ceiling, feeling oddly at peace. His fingers continued to move gently over the tresses that lay in wild, soft waves atop him.

Then his smile faded.

For it was just then he realized that there was another scent about her other than the evocative lavender of her soap and the musk of their bodies.

Smoke.

There was the slight—but unmistakable—scent of smoke in her hair.

Nine

"*A*nnie!"

It was Dulcie, catching her just outside her door as she tried to hurry along the hallway.

"What?" Ann asked nervously, looking back. *He* was probably awake. She had tried to slip away, and he had let her do so, but she'd had the feeling that a smile had curved his lips all the while, and that he had told her the truth that first night when he had awakened from the depths of his nightmare—he usually awakened with the slightest shift in a breeze.

"What?" Dulcie repeated incredulously. "What? How can you ask that? What happened yesterday?"

"What happened? You were certainly no help!" Ann assured her.

Dulcie sighed with a shake of her head. "I was trying to drug him into a deep, long sleep—"

"And wound up passed out yourself?"

Dulcie nodded, then frowned. "Joey Weatherly is in my room."

"Is he?" Ann inquired with wicked innocence.

"I don't remember . . . but, at least it's Joey. Ann! You've got to tell me what happened. You disappeared, and McShane disappeared, at almost exactly the same time."

"The same time?" Ann asked. She looked nervously back at her door again. "I don't want to talk here. Let's go to your room."

"Joey is there!"

"Cocoa's room," Ann said, pushing Dulcie forward along the hallway. She knocked quickly and heard a muffled "Come in." At the invitation, she opened the door, pressed Dulcie ahead of her, and followed quickly herself, perching on one side of the foot of Cocoa's bed while Dulcie sat upon the other.

Cocoa was just sitting up, rubbing her eyes. She had been sleeping in the buff, and was completely unconcerned with her lack of apparel.

"You all might have let me get some sleep today— since I held down this fort entirely by myself when trouble reigned!" she said indignantly, rising to stride across the room to the armchair where she'd tossed her robe. She moved with a slow, fluid grace, her body a length of sheer ebony perfection and disdain.

"You held down the fort—" Ann began, arching a brow.

"You were out saving the world and Dulcie was out cold," Cocoa informed her, slipping into a silk robe that was as sensual as the woman herself. It was blood red and looked striking on her.

"Dulcie, how could you?" Ann asked.

"Not on purpose!"

"But McShane was out somewhere doing something and not one of us has the least idea of what!" Ann reminded them.

"Your husband, Annie, was Dulcie's responsibility yesterday. I didn't lose the man."

"He was gone before I could lose him!" Dulcie said indignantly.

"And he did come back," Cocoa reminded them softly. Ann colored then as they both stared at her.

"Well?" Dulcie demanded breathlessly. Ann

found herself inching against the bedpost while Dulcie turned and leaned closely toward her and Cocoa began a slow walk back, pinning Ann with the questions in her dark eyes.

"Well?" Ann murmured in return.

"Oh, come on, Annie, tell us about him!" Cocoa urged her.

"There's nothing to tell—"

"Nothing to tell!" Dulcie moaned.

"Now that's an outright lie, sugar," Cocoa said, chuckling softly.

"There's nothing to tell!" Ann insisted, her voice just a bit strangled.

"You think about it, Dulcie," Cocoa said, laughter still in her voice. "Does that half-breed look like the type of man who's going to marry a woman he thinks is a whore and lie chastely alone on his marital bed?"

"He's a quarter Sioux," Ann murmured.

"She's just not going to get to the good parts, is she, Dulcie?" Cocoa said, shaking her head. "But I think our lovely leader, our elegant little ice queen, has come into her own."

"Annie!" Dulcie wailed. "Was he wonderful?"

"Please—" Ann protested.

"She probably didn't even know what she was getting," Dulcie said disgustedly to Cocoa.

"Ah, what a waste of good muscle tone and hard, hot flesh!" Cocoa agreed with a sigh.

"If you two don't mind—"

"But we do. We're dying for details!" Dulcie said.

"What is she supposed to do?" an amused, male voice suddenly drawled from the doorway. "Draw pictures?"

McShane! Ann saw with dismay. Looking perfectly comfortable and well entertained as he leaned against the door frame to the room, while she sat in complete discomfort, her cheeks on fire.

She leapt up, heading quickly for the door, but when she would have passed by he caught her arm. He spun her around so quickly that she was taken by complete surprise when he drew her into his arms, holding her upon her toes, sweeping her into a kiss that scalded, plundered, and invaded. Furious at first, she clenched her fists against him. But even here, even now, he had the ability to seduce, to bring a staggering warmth to her with the invasion of his lips, teeth, and tongue. Her heart thundered mercilessly, she couldn't breathe. When he set her down at last she would have fallen had he not continued to hold her, his dark eyes staring sharply into hers as if he demanded something from her still which he hadn't quite gotten.

Her feet steadied beneath her. "McShane—" she began, tensing to wrench from his grasp, angry now that she could think and reason again. "Let—"

But he had already turned from her. "She was wonderful. Just wonderful!" he told the two, and winked. "But as for the details, well, they just keep improving!"

Ann pressed her palms against him, pushing from him to rush for the stairway.

She hurried down to the kitchen, slamming cabinets as she searched for a coffee cup. "Here, here, *ma chèrie!*" Henri said, coming forward, taking a cup from her hand and approaching the pot on the stove. "You will break the crockery, then what profit for McCastle's, eh?"

When there was coffee in the cup, he handed it back to her. She sipped it, grateful for the delicious brew. Then she realized that Henri was watching her, everyone seemed to be watching her. Well, Dulcie and Cocoa she could understand, she supposed, they did know everything about her, everything about her life. But as for the rest of them . . .

"Good morning, Henri!" Ian said, striding into the kitchen. He pulled out a chair at the large, butcher-block table in the center of the room where Henri did much of his food preparation and the employees usually ate. He smiled politely, folding his fingers together before him. He had washed; his black hair was slicked back, he wore a clean, simply tailored, crisp white shirt, and against it, his dark good looks were nearly diabolical. "My love, how about some coffee?" he inquired of Ann.

"I'd be delighted to give you coffee," she said. Perhaps the tone of her voice somehow frightened Henri. Perhaps it even told Henri that McShane would have received his coffee either down his back or on his lap. For whatever reason, Henri spoke up quickly, determined to deter any coffee crises.

"Annie, sit with your new man. I'll bring coffee. And a wedding breakfast—a repast!—to rival all else. Delicate crepes, tender omelets, delicious ham, my special croissants!" He urged Ann into the chair that faced Ian. Ian smiled at her innocently, raising a brow to her. She wanted to kick him. He must have known that she longed to wring his neck. His smile carried a warning—maybe even a dare.

Dignity, she reminded herself, staring him down while she sipped her coffee.

"What will you do with your saloon, Monsieur McShane?" Henri asked, rattling pans and procuring the ingredients for their breakfast.

"Explore the place," he said blandly.

Ann drank a big sip of coffee that nearly scalded her throat. "Is there a problem, my love?" Ian asked politely.

She shook her head. "What is there to explore, McShane? This is a saloon. We have the kitchen, the bar, and the main room, the wine cellar and storage, and the rooms above."

Ian leaned forward, sipping his coffee, tasting it, savoring it. He replied so slowly that she longed to kick him again.

"I intend to keep McCastle's up to the highest standards, of course. Upon occasion, I worked with the engineers in the war. I'm going to make sure that our building is secure, my love. It's our livelihood."

"It's in excellent shape," she assured him. "I'm quite certain that your job should be the public room, McShane. Keep your eye on the poker games, prevent problems. Make sure the whiskey we're delivered is what we've purchased and not watered-down rotgut."

"But, my love," he argued, leaning closer to her, an ebony fire alight in his eyes, "you do seem to manage the domestics of this operation with skill and knowledge. I wouldn't intrude where I'm not needed. I wouldn't attempt to fix what is not broken."

"The building isn't broken!" she snapped.

"Croissants!" Henri said with enthusiasm, setting a plate of the fluffy pastries before them. Ann had reason to be grateful. Ian did seem to be amazed by the accomplishments of their saloon cook. Chef, rather. Henri did rate the title.

Ian broke apart a soft, oven-warmed croissant, breathed in the scent of it, and took a bite. He looked over at Henri. "Monsieur, you could be running a restaurant anywhere in the world you chose!"

Henri shrugged, smiling with pride. "*Merci, merci,* monsieur. I am pleased to be where I am, working for Mademoiselle Annie—Madame Annie!" he corrected himself, moving on with pleasure.

"Just who all does work for Madame Annie?" Ian asked, watching his bride.

"Well, people do come and go—" she began.

"Who's working for you now?"

"Dulcie, Cocoa, and the pretty young blond, Ginger, work the saloon. Ginger has a lovely voice as well and Dulcie and Cocoa—"

"I'm well aware of their talents. Go on."

"Aaron plays piano."

"The handsome young musician. Go on."

"Harold tends the bar, and he has an assistant, a fellow named Mark Engle. Here in the kitchen, Henri has Betty and Louella to assist him. Sammy-Jane is the upstairs maid, and the Yeagher twins have been with us—more or less—to keep fair play going."

"Umm," Ian said wryly.

She ignored his comment. "Oh, and we've two professional dealers, Michael Tyler and Treat Williamson. Perhaps tonight you can watch their play. It's a Saturday; it should be quite busy. A lot of the cowhands collect their pay today."

"And what have been your duties?" he asked her, sipping his coffee, the question deceptively lazy.

She stared at him for a moment. "I do the ordering. I oversee everything."

"A convenient job."

"Meaning?"

"Ah, most often it isn't necessary that you be in one particular place at one particular time."

She shrugged. "I work very hard."

"I'm sure you do," he told her, "it's just what you work at that still concerns me."

"Whiskey, wine, gambling—and the comforts of men," she said lightly, and stood, hurrying to the coffeepot, determined not to let him see that she was worried.

What was she going to do now that he was here? She didn't know why, but he wasn't fond of Cash Weatherly.

But that didn't mean that he would actually condone her nocturnal activities.

Maybe it didn't even mean that he wouldn't want to see her hanged for a few of her deeds.

"I'd love more coffee," Ian said politely. Ann turned from the stove with the pot in one hand. Henri slipped the pot from her grasp as she started back to the table.

"Madame, allow me!" he said with a flourish.

To Ann's relief, Henri then went on to carry the conversation for her that morning, setting before them a magnificent breakfast that surpassed all of his promises. Ann had thought that she could eat nothing, but discovered instead that she was famished. It was only while she was finishing the last of Henri's delicate crepes that she caught Ian's eyes on her and noted the amusement in them. She set her fork down, wondering if there was some fault with her manners, staring at him in return.

"Henri really is an excellent chef," she said defensively.

He leaned close to her. "My love, it is to be expected that you might have a keen appetite this morning."

"Oh," she groaned, her teeth grating. She leapt up. "You will excuse me, since I do run the *domestics* of this place so well." She fled from the kitchen into the saloon. Aaron was at the piano. He glanced up at her as she came in, a question in his eyes. She strode over to him, listening to the melody he played as she assured him that their secrets were still well kept—for the time being at least.

"Did your groom miss you?" he asked.

"My groom seems to have been gone as well," she told him. "But I've got to find somewhere else to keep my clothing and guns. And he means to inspect the place for structural faults. What if he finds the stairway?"

"Then you may be one pretty bird that has wound up caged, cousin!" he told her softly. His eyes, a dark brooding hazel, touched hers. He smiled. "I never did care for this life you've been leading."

"Aaron, you know—"

"I know that your death, your arrest, or your hanging can't change anything that happened in the past. Annie, if you could just learn to live in the present, that would be the greatest victory you could achieve."

"I wish I could," she whispered.

Aaron looked up at her again. "He's in the room now, talking to Harold," he warned her. "Want to sing something? Does he know that we're related, by the way, or do I need to fear for my life in case he thinks you're flirting with me?"

"You don't need to fear for your life," she told him.

"He doesn't know we're related."

"Play 'Lorena,'" she told him, her stubborn refusal to answer becoming an answer in itself.

But Aaron sighed and played, and she sang the beautiful war ballad, caught up in the beauty of the music right along with him as she did so. She really did have quite a remarkable place here, she thought. Aaron was exceptionally talented. He made music live, he gave it personality, he touched the heart when he played. Henri could prepare the greatest delicacies on earth. And the girls . . .

Every one of them was her friend. They knew one another's lives, each other's strengths and weaknesses. They had stood by her, worked with her. She couldn't betray any of them, but then, they weren't actually guilty of anything. If she had dragged anyone into danger with her, it was Aaron. But he had made his choices as well.

The song ended. Instead of the sweet sweep of the music, she heard the noise within the saloon. The clink of glass, the shuffle of cards, laughter, conversation. They were slipping into the afternoon, and it was a Saturday.

The doors to the saloon swung inward with a sudden force. Ann blinked against the daylight that streamed in, then tensed.

Sheriff Bickford came striding in, his hat pulled low over his eyes, looking this way and that as he headed for the bar. "Afternoon, Annie," he called to her. "Afternoon—Mrs. McShane, so I hear. Congratulations."

"Thank you," she murmured, striding to the bar to join him. He was a large, heavyset man with silver-gray hair and the long, sad face of a hound. His eyes were dark—and sharp. He was a kind and intelligent man who had a tremendous respect for the law. He saw his job very simply, quoting the Constitution upon occasion. The law must be upheld. He was the sheriff, he didn't make the laws, he didn't even agree with all the laws, but he could see to it that laws were upheld and that criminals themselves were held securely until a judge and jury could decide their fate.

Ann liked him. And though he could be slow and thorough and even naive at times, he was no fool. She was very careful around him.

"Harold, give Sheriff Bickford a tall beer, will you, please?"

She turned back to the sheriff, smiling as Harold placed the beer in front of him.

"Thanks, Annie."

She nodded, silent, waiting.

"Annie, have you seen any strangers hanging around town?"

She arched a brow. *Only the one I married!* she might have replied. But she didn't. "Not really, no. There were several people through with the stage on Wednesday; I'm sure there will be several more this week. But no one has stayed on."

Bickford shook his head with disgust.

"I just don't get it, I just don't get it. First, Cash Weatherly's gold is stolen from two of his sharpest hands, one man is left dead, the other wounded. And the survivor knows nothing—all he saw was the silhouette of a man on a cliff, and the gold has disappeared entirely. Then, yesterday, a good God-fearing man like Grainger Bennington loses his whole place and he claims that he was knocked out and the fire set on purpose, though when we were out there, I couldn't find a damn thing, except a few empty paint cans, and Grainger admitted he'd just painted his barn and that they were his cans. So what's going on, Annie? What's going on? I heard tell things go lunatic during the full moon, but the moon ain't even full yet. Why would anybody want to burn out Grainger? Did he set the fire himself, knocking over a candle or lamp? All that I know is that we need to thank the good Lord for that husband of yours, Annie."

"Thank the Lord for—my husband?" she repeated.

"McShane," Sheriff Bickford said, taking down a long swallow of beer.

Whenever his name was mentioned, he seemed to be near.

"Sheriff, there isn't any question," Ian stated flatly, "Ralph and I both saw riders leaving the Bennington place. We fired, and I'm sure I hit one. Find yourself an injured man and you'll find who set that fire."

Ann didn't realize she had ceased to breathe until she audibly sucked in a gulp of air. Thank God, they were staring at one another with hostile expressions; neither one seemed to notice her in the least.

The sheriff's eyes dropped first. He shook his head. "You can't go casting accusations at the good people in this town without proof!"

Ian had walked to the bar. He motioned to Harold and Harold brought him a beer as well. He finally realized that Ann was staring at him, gaping. He gently tapped her mouth closed, but he frowned still and his frown was for the sheriff. "Sheriff, you've got to be willing to look where you don't want to look."

"Now, sir, you did mighty fine by Grainger yesterday. He's a good man and he's told me that you risked your own life getting him out of that house before it was charred to cinders. But you'd best take heed. You're the new fellow in town, and it's already rumored that you're faster with a gun than any man ought rightly to be."

Ian arched a brow, a wry smile in place. "Sheriff, no man alive in these parts could possibly be too fast with a gun."

"These parts are dangerous, McShane, but we keep a tight watch on our town and the ranches and folks in my jurisdiction. I can handle things!"

"Sheriff, no one has ever doubted your ability to handle things, or your commitment to your job, or what a fine man you are at that."

"You've got to let me do my job, McShane," he said, drinking another swallow of his beer. "When I need help, I'll call on you. Lord knows, we do get enough riffraff in here, drifters, outlaws preying on the pay wagons and the like. Lord almighty! It seems a few people around here are down on Cash Weatherly, a man providing work for half the territory upon occasion, when most of the time it seems he's the victim of scoundrels and thieves. And Mr. McShane, I don't want to argue, sir. I came in here to tell you what fine work you did saving my old friend Grainger. Come next Saturday, we're going to gather the community around, do a barn raising for Grainger, try to help him get some of his stock back. Mr. Weatherly has offered cattle from his own herds to supplement what Grainger's got left. We'll put Grainger back on his feet right quick and proper, and you'll see the truth in what I'm telling you— whatever evil falls on this town comes from outside of it!" He lifted his beer to them both, finished the last sip of it, and set the glass back down upon the bar. "Much obliged to you both now, and best wishes to you both. Maybe you'll want to be building your own house, setting up ranching now that you're married. That would be fine, Annie."

She smiled. "I do enjoy running the saloon, Sheriff Bickford."

"But you might want to be making a real lady out of Annie, now that she's your wife, Mr. McShane."

"Sheriff," Ann repeated, feeling her cheeks grow warm, "I believe that my girls are ladies, and I do enjoy their company."

"But what about little ones, Annie? You want them growing up in a saloon?"

"Sheriff, we don't have any little ones," Ann said, trying very hard to control the tone of her voice. She might be fooling the sheriff but she wasn't fooling McShane. A tight smile stretched across his lips as he leaned lazily against the bar.

"Sheriff, you do have a point. Ann should have a fine house—and a passel of little ones to keep her busy."

"But I'm very busy now!" she snapped.

At last the sheriff shrugged, apparently pleased that he had given Ian the idea of bringing respectability into her life. "Again, my best to you both." He lifted his hat. Some of the cowboys raised a hand in acknowledgment as he departed the saloon.

Ann swung on Ian.

"It's my saloon," she informed him.

He shrugged, watching her. "Well, Annie, that is debatable. I do own sixty percent. But then, I always meant to share and share alike."

"Well, you don't need to share in the burden," she said, her pride causing her to forget that she had *wanted* him busy with the saloon. "I can manage this place. I've been doing just fine, you said that yourself when we were talking earlier, why fix what isn't broken—"

"Eddie McCastle hasn't been dead a full two weeks, has he? The saloon hasn't been under your management for very long."

"I managed the place before Eddie died!"

He arched a brow. "This is a tale that grows more and more intriguing." He moved closer to her, suddenly reminding her of every intimacy they had shared. "How did my magnificent, innocent little bride ever become such a talented manager of a den of gamblers, liars, whores, and thieves?"

"None of your damned business," she told him, and shoving angrily at his chest, she started to turn away. He caught her wrists, drawing her quickly back against him.

"A united front, remember, my love?" he asked her softly.

She started to wrench away, then remembered just why the sheriff had been in the saloon. She searched out his eyes. "What were you doing out at the Bennington place yesterday?" she demanded.

"A friend came by, worried about Grainger Bennington. I rode out with him."

"Oh, a friend. Ralph? The attorney who seems to be twisting everything out of my fingers?"

"Yeah, Ralph."

"And you just ran right out on your wedding day."

"Somehow, I didn't think you'd miss me. And remember, I did come back. Besides, as you just heard from the sheriff, we saved the fellow's life. Doesn't that please you? Or is Grainger an enemy of yours?"

"No, I like Grainger. He's a gentleman. Courteous. Polite. Charming—"

"And he's probably had his tongue on the floor for you since he first saw your face and was always willing to admire you from afar—unlike present company?"

She wasn't going to take the bait. She replied with complete dignity. "I am quite delighted that Grainger Bennington is alive and well. I am just somewhat amazed that you came in here like some kind of bat out of hell, insisting on marriage—only to ride off with a friend."

"I'll try to remember how much you'll miss me next time I receive an invitation," he promised.

"You needn't—the matter is quite curious, and that is all," she informed him quickly. "You may run off and play with your attorney friend Ralph whenever you choose—in fact, the more often, the better. Now, will you please let me go? I do have work to do. I mean, that is if you want a united front. I do acquiesce that I most probably couldn't break your hold, but I can manage to present much less than a united front."

He arched a brow. "Go ahead."

"What?"

"Scream, squawk, fight—go ahead. Do your worst."

"Why are you doing this?" Ann hissed.

"Because I don't like being threatened."

"I don't like being held against my will. And mocked and tormented!"

To Ann's amazement, her simple statements gave her the freedom she had craved. His hold upon her eased instantly, though it still seemed as if his dark eyes were piercing through her. Once free, however, she found herself still staring at him.

"You don't seem to like much that isn't your own dictate," he said casually, sipping his beer.

"The same could definitely be said about you."

His smile had a sardonic twist. "Maybe. And maybe that means you should be forewarned."

"About what?"

"When it comes down to a choice between your dictates and mine, Annie *McShane*, my dictates are going to win out. I like things run a certain way—"

"The saloon runs fine—"

"Maybe. Maybe not."

"You've no right to interfere—"

"I've every right. I own more than half the place. What are you afraid I'll do—or find out—Ann?" he demanded suddenly.

"Nothing!" she snapped quickly. "Nothing. I have been doing things my way, I am independent in my decisions, in my thinking—"

"Too independent."

"No," she insisted, shaking her head. "No, I cannot be too independent. I have done well here, I have created a business worth enough so that Eddie could gamble with his holdings as collateral. I—"

"You," he interrupted very firmly, "are in over your head. I don't yet know about everything that is going on here, but I give you fair warning—I don't know what you've been doing, but it had best cease. Because I'll stop you. I'll pull you out of this place faster than lightning, if it kills us both. I'll see to it that motherhood does set you out quietly on a ranch or a pretty little gingerbread house right here in town. Out of harm's way."

"Out of your way!" she accused him.

"Maybe," he said softly. "But then I watched you with the sheriff, Annie. You're all charm, sweet smiles, and wide-eyed innocence when he talks. It makes me even more curious to discover what's going on here."

"There's nothing going on here!" she cried with aggravation. "Maybe you should just leave things alone!" she insisted.

She started to swing around but he caught hold of her arm again. "And maybe I'd just like to see you live to be a ripe old age. Maybe I'm worried about you."

"You barely know me!"

"But I married you. And damn you, Ann, I won't let you get yourself into trouble, do you understand?"

"If you're finding trouble anywhere," she assured him, "it's simply because you were determined to have it!"

"Don't push me, Annie," he warned her.

Suddenly, she was free again.

She wasn't going to win any arguments with him, Ann realized, and she was just aggravating herself by trying to do so.

She longed to slosh the beer he was drinking over his head and walk away.

Instead she just walked away, hurrying from the main room and back into the kitchen.

She managed to get some work done, to her own

surprise, taking inventory of supplies, making lists with Henri for the mercantile store.

What remained of the afternoon slipped by. Then evening came, and with it the sounds of revelry from the main room. She was congratulating herself for having avoided Ian for so long when she realized that because she hadn't seen him, she didn't know what he had been up to.

She raced from the kitchen and up the stairs. She rushed into her room, closing the door behind her. Sammy-Jane had been in to clean; her bed had fresh sheets and the quilt and pillows were plumped invitingly upon it. The sudsy remains of her bath were gone from the hip tub and fresh water had been set into her washing ewer. She strode quickly to her wardrobe and wrenched it open. She dug through the clothes in it, then sat back, breathing a sigh of relief. He hadn't been in her wardrobe. Yet. Did she dare keep her things here? Did she dare move anything?

She piled shawls and petticoats on top of her guns, pants, and duster, then slipped behind her wardrobe screen to the all but invisible door set so perfectly into the wall. She opened and closed it, biting into her lower lip.

She hurried back downstairs, greeting customers, slipping over to the piano where Aaron was playing—a stepped-up version of Chopin most of their regulars would never begin to recognize.

"Have you seen McShane?" she asked him.

"Lost your husband again, cousin?" he inquired, never missing a beat of the music.

"I can't knock you in the head in front of so many people!" she told him sweetly. "Aaron, help me!"

"He was in here, in the main room for a while. Joey came down, and he had a drink with Joey. He told Harold he'd be gone for a few hours and he left."

"He's still gone?"

"To the best of my knowledge. I am good, but it is sometimes difficult to play and see what is going on behind my back. My sweet Annie, you are going to have to begin to watch the man yourself."

He was laughing at her and she longed to douse him with a beer as well.

She refrained, remembering that she was trying to keep a grip on her dignity for as long as she could. But she couldn't stay in the main room, she was both exhausted and nervous. She ran back up the stairs and into her own room. She paced for a while, and looked out the window at the quiet street.

It had grown late. A half-moon was high in the sky. She strode back to the rocker and sat. This battle of wills that she was waging with McShane was wearing her out. She closed her eyes as she thought of her new husband.

He was going to destroy everything. And when he found out what was actually going on . . . what then? He seemed to be engaged in a strange rivalry with Cash Weatherly. An intense one. He had married her because of it. Now she was discovering just how thoroughly she had jumped from the frying pan into the fire.

And yet . . .

He challenged her, he excited her. She was ready to dump something—anything!—on his head most of the time, and still, she felt that inexorable draw to him. Even in the night, after the first . . . shock of him, she had liked certain things. The taut, hard feel of his muscles, the slick fire of his flesh. Just remembering what they had done the night before sent something stirring within her; she couldn't erase the intimate memories of his hands upon her body, the feel of his lips against her ... and, of course, his shock when he had realized that his harlot wife was as pure as the driven snow, knowledgeable about men only because of what she had heard rather than what she had done.

She might have told him. He might have even listened. She had known that he'd assumed that she'd been married to Eddie McCastle. And she was running a saloon that offered female companionship— so she really hadn't had much right to be so angry that he'd thought her a whore. But her life was such a long story. One she didn't share easily, certainly not with a stranger.

But he wasn't a stranger anymore, she reminded herself. She was such a liar, determined to deny him just because she couldn't allow him to get close to her. Just thinking of him brought forth a strange, wild surge of trembling within her. She wanted to be held, to taste his lips, to feel the vital heat of his body against her.

She had to keep her distance somehow. And he was even more curious about her now.

Her wedding night might have been so very different! she thought suddenly. *Her very life would have been so different, if Cloud Walker hadn't been the extraordinary savage he had proved to be.*

Ten

She had known, from the time she opened her eyes and met a pair of pitch-dark ones, saw *his* face, that she had been taken by the Indians. Pure terror had overwhelmed her when she saw his bronze, painted face, and instantly she knew that all the awful tales she had heard about them must be true; she could hear screams close by, anguished screams, shrieks that rose on the air, the sounds of sobbing. She longed to scream herself, but she was in too much pain to do so. But then the Indian's face was gone; he had left her to join his companions. They had moved on from the awful scene where they had found her and were now raiding a small settlement on the river, she realized.

When she tried to move, her head began to spin again, but she realized that she was tied to a travois drawn by a roan pony. She had been left to wait and watch while the Indians fell upon the poor settlers here. She could see fire leaping to the skies, men falling as shots tore into them. Not fifty feet from her, some of the bucks had taken a woman captive. Her cries were terrible; she fought with a vengeance. Her clothing was ripped to shreds, bits of calico seemed to rain in the sky against the orange and gold lights of the fires from the buildings. When the bucks were done, ten or twelve of them, the woman screamed no more. She lay like a naked white heap upon the earth until the bucks returned.

Ann started to scream to warn the woman when one brave reached down and grabbed a handful of her hair, ready to rip off the woman's scalp regardless of whether she was actually dead or still clinging to life. The brave paused in the act, and looked Ann's way. As he did so, the Indian warrior Ann had first seen came riding up hard, saying something to the other. The brave shrugged and dropped the woman's head, stared down at her, and swept her up over his shoulder, then proceeded to toss her like a saddlebag over his horse's haunches. Ann saw that much and shuddered with vast relief, but then, even as the one woman found life, Ann saw a white man running in front of her, saw a brave catch up with him and smash a tomahawk through his head.

Mercifully, at that point, Ann fainted.

Because she'd had a fever, her next impressions were mixed and confused. Someone gave her water to drink, bathed her, cooled her. She could hear them speaking in their strange tongue, and sometimes she knew where she was. Sometimes, when she slept, she could do the impossible and go back to a time before the Pawnee had come, and before the bad white men had come before them. Small snatches of her past seemed to float before her, and if she didn't try to cling too tightly to them with her mind, they remained. She could see her mother, flashing her a quick smile as she prepared coffee over an open fire, singing some kind of a sweet ballad. Her mother had been great with child at the end. Ann had been an only child for a very long time and the entire family had been so excited about the baby to come. Her parents had never been happier. They'd both wanted to come west. Even though both of her parents were Southerners, neither of their families had owned slaves—her father had been the seventh child of a plantation owner of modest means who hadn't been able to afford slaves. Ann's father had told her a number of times that although his family argued that slavery took place often enough in the Bible, he didn't quite see how it could be right itself. Still, both her mother and her father wanted to travel west because although they couldn't turn their backs on their own people in the debates that were growing more heated daily in 1858, they didn't want to be a part of the war that seemed certain to erupt. They were both adventurous. Her father wanted either to practice law or to teach it somewhere out on the frontier. They'd buy a small plot of land, and her mother could raise chickens and Ann could collect the eggs. Life was going to be good. Simple and good.

Yes, it should have been! She could close her eyes and see her father's handsome face, his magnificent golden beard, his twinkling blue eyes. The memory was sweet. But then it was destroyed, as ruthlessly and cruelly in her mind's eye as it had been in life. He was calling to her, shouting her name. She was trying to reach him, running, but even as she neared him, a gunshot exploded in her ears, a crimson flood demolished his face. He was falling and she was screaming . . .

And awakening.

Cool hands were on her again. A soft, singsong voice crooned to her, tried to soothe her. She cried. She prayed to lose consciousness, to forget all that she had seen, the pain done to others by both white men and Indians.

Even though she didn't want to heal, she did. She was young, and God had decided she would live. As she grew stronger, she quickly learned to deci-

pher emotions within the Indians' voices. She knew
when they were angry with one another, when
someone pleaded, when someone commanded. She
began to recognize different people.

Sometimes they took her outside, and she became
aware that she lived in one of their large villages.
There were many lodges within it, and each lodge
slept many people. The lodge where she was kept
was a very large circular structure, built with heavy
log frames and timber rafters, warmed and insulated
with prairie sod. A massive fire burned in the center
of the structure, the smoke escaping through a hole
in the top.

They lived so close together that each night she
could hear everything that went on.

Husbands and wives, warriors and captives. She
could hear the protests, the cries, as warriors claimed
their prizes. When her dizziness subsided and she
regained her strength, she grew more afraid. She
quickly realized that she was property; she belonged
to the man she had first seen. He was a young warrior called Cloud Walker, and he could give commands because he was the son of the great war chief
He Who Thinks, and he had proved himself many
times in battle. He could ride as if he were part of
his horse, yet on foot he was nearly as fleet, not even
seeming to touch the ground. He had bested the enemy many times this way.

All of this Ann learned from Brown Sparrow,
Cloud Walker's sister. She had recently lost her husband in a battle, and Cloud Walker's wife had been
killed by American soldiers who had destroyed one
of their villages, making their father want to kill all
of the white men, which is why they had been on
the warpath when she had been taken. Many women
and children had been lost in the raid. Brown Sparrow had lost her own daughter, a girl near Ann's

own age, thirteen. Brown Sparrow spoke some English, and gradually taught Ann some of her own language. Brown Sparrow told her brother in whispers at night that Ann was still too weak to do the work of a captive—or to be treated as such in any way.

As time passed and Ann grew stronger, she learned about her captors, the Pawnee, and she lived on edge.

During the long nights, she thought of the vicious slaughter she had witnessed, how she had watched the braves repeatedly rape the woman she had seen so near her, and nearly murder her as well. Once, she relived all that had happened in her dream, and she had awakened screaming only to discover Cloud Walker over her, slapping her very hard. She'd clenched her teeth when he'd left her, tears spilling from her eyes, determined she would endure her captivity no longer.

In the morning, when everyone seemed very busy, she slipped out, desperate to find some way to escape. She was found within an hour by Cloud Walker. He tied her wrists tightly together, leapt up atop his horse and left her standing, then started to canter back to the village. She'd had to run or be dragged. She was left lying in the dirt when they returned, and Brown Sparrow tended to her once again. Cloud Walker was furious that night, and she hated him with a passion. But he was apparently done with his vengeance.

"Are you trying to make me kill you?" he demanded. She shook her head. She wanted to live.

That night, she realized that he had left her with the will to live.

Brown Sparrow saw to it that she was given tasks to perform such as cleaning skins, weaving mats, and working skins into doeskin to make beautiful dresses, slippers, jackets, and boots. She worked hard and carefully and she seemed to please Brown Sparrow, Cloud Walker and He Who Thinks. She was seldom able to talk with the other captives, since she was always brought out of the lodge with a raw-hide rope upon her ankle, which kept her close to Brown Sparrow. She saw what happened to others, though. The woman who had been taken from the burning village once dropped a dish of food. One of the braves slapped her to her knees for the action. The woman wasn't easily beaten, though, for she stood and slapped the brave back, and cries went up through the village, laughter from men and women. Ann barely dared to breathe, praying for the woman's life.

The brave drew his knife. He began to berate the woman, walking around her, promising her a slow death.

Brown Sparrow held the rawhide that bound Ann, but Ann didn't think she could bear to see the woman brutally murdered for her act of defiance. She wrenched free of Brown Sparrow's hold upon her and ran for the lodge where Cloud Walker was cleaning his rifle. She entreated him to his feet, and led him back to the work circle. The brave had lifted his knife high and was about to plunge it into the woman's heart. Cloud Walker stepped in, speaking calming words to the brave, then struck the woman again and yelled savagely at her. She landed on her knees before him, but did not rise again. The woman seemed to have realized she had risked her life.

That night, Ann found Cloud Walker out alone by the river. Brokenly, with words from his language and her own, she thanked him for the woman's life. He nodded gravely to her. "She deserves to live," he said simply. "She endures what falls her way, hates those who hurt her, and plays with the children during the day, knowing their innocence. She will kill Running Elk if she is ever given the chance, yet she is able, at times, to laugh while she works, and she works well. Come back to the lodge now."

"May I stay by the river?"

"No, because you are a pretty bird with golden wings, and will fly when you can. Go back."

She obeyed him.

Time passed without incident. She learned that the Indians lived a life filled with ceremony and ritual. They planted corn and crops in May and then in June, when the stalks were strong enough to withstand predators, they left for their first buffalo hunt. Everyone hunted the buffalo. Only infants and ancients were left behind at the lodges. Tipis were packed along with clothing and belongings and the tribe split into many bands, each band consisting of about twenty-five people.

On the buffalo hunt, Cloud Walker led one of the bands. Ann, his captive, naturally rode with him. Brown Sparrow was there to watch her, but Ann knew there was no way to escape. They lived closely together on the buffalo hunt. The tipis seemed very small compared to the lodges, and at night she kept very still, knowing that Cloud Walker watched her constantly.

On horseback the braves found the herds, shooting down the buffalo with their rifles and arrows. The women and children moved in when the great beasts were down. Nothing was left to waste. The hides were made into clothing for the long winter, the sinew was used for thread, the meat was feasted upon and dried for later use, even the hooves were used as gourds, or made into rattles for the children, or used in some ceremonial way.

In August they returned to the village and the crops were harvested. The corn was shucked, shelled, and stored, and the women gathered nuts and wild plums and berries. The men continued to hunt deer and antelope.

In October, they split into bands again, for the last buffalo hunt before winter set in. It was the most important hunt; they had to prepare themselves for the bitter cold to come.

Ann had been with them for more than a year when she discovered what might have been her own fate.

One of the braves sleeping within her lodge, Buffalo, a half brother of Cloud Walker, came in one morning with tears in his eyes, seeking out one of the priests. She watched with curiosity as the shaman listened to him gravely, then cried as well. The two men consoled one another and went to He Who Thinks, and grave discussion took place between them.

The braves left that night, Cloud Walker among them. They left with painted faces and with articles from one of their sacred bundles, a carefully sewn and prepared hide that contained religious relics, pipes, tobacco, animal skins, rawhide—a human scalp.

They returned with a young Indian girl taken from a village far south along the river. She was young and pretty, and was treated like a queen, fed well, and carefully tended. Men and women spoke with her almost reverently. She wore the softest doeskin, she was given the most tender morsels of buffalo and deer meat. She lived among them for a while, and during that time, the priest went out each morning and sat, staring at the sky.

"What is he doing?" Ann asked Brown Sparrow at last. She assumed that the girl might well be a bride for one of the important young warriors, perhaps Cloud Walker, or his brother, Buffalo. She was about Ann's own age, slim, with a swift smile and a pleasant manner.

"Watching for the morning star," Brown Sparrow told her, shaking her head sadly, and would say no more. "Keep quiet, and keep away."

The priest came in at last one morning, having seen the morning star.

A ritual began. There was constant singing, a mournful litany. It went on for three days while the men prepared a scaffold.

Just before sunrise on the fourth day, the young maiden, so very well treated as a captive that she was just now beginning to grow wary, was entreated to the scaffold, and tied there, facing east.

Again, the Indians watched for the morning star. When it rose, one of the braves rushed forward . . . And shot an arrow through the maiden's heart.

Ann, crying out in disbelief, sank down, barely aware of what followed. A second brave cut open the maiden's breast and dabbed her blood on his face. Dried buffalo meat was laid out beneath the girl, to soak up whatever blood fell.

Then every warrior in the village shot an arrow into the battered body of the pitiful young creature, mothers shooting for little boys who could not shoot themselves. In the end, four men carried the torn and bloodied body out onto the prairie. Stomach down, the girl's corpse faced the morning star. They sang again, telling her that she had become a part of the earth.

The burial party returned for the feasting and dancing that lasted through the night. Men wore elaborate costumes; the shaman of the tribe danced with a buffalo head atop his own.

Ill, Ann retreated to the lodge—and realized her own predicament. Because she lived untouched, she might well be the next to die.

Brown Sparrow found her there. "It is the ritual of the morning star. It causes great sorrow to us all, but when a dreamer sees the star in his vision and arises to see it coming up on the eastern horizon, then we must sacrifice a maiden of about thirteen years. It is not a yearly ritual, it is not something we must do often, but earth demands her sacrifices so that the harvest may feed us all, so that the buffalo may continue to run."

Brown Sparrow left Ann, and she realized that if a dreamer in another band awoke to see the morning star, it was well known she was a captive here, taken young. It was necessary for the sacrificed girl to be an innocent one. They would know that she would be the perfect sacrifice when the time came. Maybe she had even been kept for that reason, perhaps to save the other village maidens. That was why Cloud Walker was gentle to her, but kept his distance from her.

She kept her own counsel, but grew evermore afraid, praying that some help might come. But the Indians were gleeful; soldiers were not so plentiful on the plains anymore. They were preparing to enter a great war, and they were being called back east.

Yet a few nights later she woke with alarm, her fears curiously allayed. She was not alone in her pallet on the floor; Cloud Walker had come to her. His dark face hovered tensely over hers; his gleaming body hard and muscular. She started to cry out, then stopped herself, shaking. This was life and death. If he raped her, she would live.

He shook his head, looking down at her. "The time will come, Little Dove." He stroked her cheek with his knuckles. "The time will come when you will trust and want me, when the pain of what you have seen in the past will fade, and though you will remain as gold as the sun, you will be one of us.

Then you will be my wife. I will not let them have you before then, but for now, rest easy."

He lay down beside her, taking her into his arms. In the very early morning, when he awoke and others still slept, he pressed his knife against his inner thigh, a place on him others could not readily see, and let several drops of blood stain the pallet.

He fought with his father that day. There was a council of the elders. He spoke eloquently for himself, passionately. She was his captive; he would do what he would with her. Ann didn't see what happened because the men were in the council alone, but the Indians loved legend and stories, and he was described as a very great man and warrior when the stories were told.

One night, he did not come to lie with Ann, just holding her close to his heart.

In the morning she realized that he had chosen to lie with the other white captive, the woman whose life had been twice saved. She was free now because Running Elk had been killed in the last buffalo hunt. Having fallen from his horse, he had been trampled to death. Ann had not seen what had happened, but she couldn't feel sorrow for so cruel a man. It had been a fitting end for him, she thought. And she was glad that the woman would have a kinder master; she was glad that Cloud Walker would not be alone. But she feared losing his protection.

Life was so strange. She could remember the terror and the hatred she had felt; she could remember laughing upon occasion, she could remember Cloud Walker as the man who had viciously led attacks and slain dozens of white settlers, and she could remember him as the man who had spoken so tenderly and played such a gentle deception to save her life. She could sometimes remember that first awakening among them, opening her eyes with fear and

horror filling her body when she looked into those
black ones . . .

"Ann?" a voice asked softly.

She opened her eyes.

And they were there again. Oh, God, it was real!
Coal-black eyes in a hard, bronzed face. Ink-dark
hair framing that face. She could almost hear the
cries, see the fires burning, the tomahawk falling to
cleave a man's head in two . . .

She started to scream.

"Ann!"

She was drawn up, shaken. Then suddenly enveloped in warmth. "Ann, Ann!"

The terror slipped away. He held her in his arms
as gently as a babe, sitting on the edge of her bed.
Their bed. She had married him. He owned the saloon. His English was as perfect as that of any student from Harvard or Yale, and though she was
certain that the fire which simmered in his heart was
as savage as that of any of his ancestors, she was no
longer in an Indian village and her life was not in
danger. Not from him, not at the moment. Perhaps
there were other things at risk, but . . .

Her cheeks colored as the fear that had gripped
her in her memories faded into the darkness around
them. The lamp by her bedside was unlit; only the
glow from a dying fire and the soft, pale moonlight
illuminated the room.

"Sweet Jesu, Annie, what did you think? That
some monster had come to claim you? Or are you
convinced that I *am* a monster?"

She shook her head. "It was—nothing."

"It was enough to make you scream loud enough
to wake the dead. I'm amazed we haven't had company; there must be a great deal of noise downstairs,
or else they'd think I was murdering you here."

"I—must have dozed off."

It was nice in his arms. Warm, secure. She was already discovering that she loved the subtle scent of him and the ripple of his muscles each time he moved. But she had secrets to keep. She couldn't let him question her, couldn't let him *in*, couldn't let him close.

"I'm fine, I'm sorry," she murmured, pressing against his chest to free herself.

His hold on her eased. She stood, quickly putting a few feet between them before turning to face him again. Even in the shadowed light that surrounded them, she could see a twist in his jaw as he stood as well, a telltale sign of anger. She couldn't help it; there was nothing she could do. If he were to discover all that there was to know about her, he would be much angrier.

And she might not be able to finish all that she had set out to do.

"So we both dream," he murmured suddenly, then shrugged. "It's late. Let's go to bed." He covered the few feet between them, spinning her so that her back faced him before she could protest and starting to unbutton her dress.

"I can manage," she told him breathlessly.

"Umm. You'll manage to find a way to slip back downstairs."

He had half the buttons undone. She could feel the tips of his fingers against her flesh. Each touch sent a shiver down her spine.

She spun away from him, talking in a rush. "What if I really was to protest. What if I screamed?"

He arched a brow. "They'd think downstairs that you were really having one hell of a good time."

A blush flooded her cheeks. "You just said that I'd screamed loud enough to wake the dead already, that I'd be alarming people."

"I lied. I was trying to ease your tension. Get back here."

He pulled her back again and continued the unbuttoning.

"I am very tense," she informed him uneasily.

His voice, his whisper, warm and evocative, brushed her ear. "I intend to keep easing the situation."

"The situation is what's making me tense."

"Last night should have made you tense."

"My life is making me tense."

"Then you should start behaving, and start sleeping with a clean conscience."

"My conscience is spotless."

"How intriguing. And I had marked you as a branded woman."

The last button was free. He pulled the voluminous yards of cotton, embroidery, and lace over her head, letting it fall where it would, and started on the ribbons of her petticoat. "Quite frankly," he said with irritation, "I am amazed that more women don't die innocent, considering how difficult it is to undress them."

"Perhaps it is not so difficult when a woman sheds her clothes more willingly," Ann retorted.

"Oh, that does it!"

She heard the tearing of fabric and turned in his arms just as her petticoat fell, ripped, from her form. She started to protest, but a cry was already on his lips. "More! More clothing. This torment is beyond reason."

She wasn't wearing that much more clothing, just a corset and pantalettes, and she wasn't sure whether to laugh or hit him. A smile teased his lips; there was a warmth deep in his ebony eyes, a strange tenderness to his voice. She almost felt like laughing herself. But the urge fled from her because he decided to give up on her clothing and pull her into his arms, flush against him, his lips seizing hers with force and coercion. His tongue plundered her mouth, pressing seductively deep, teasing, sweeping, filling her. His fingers worked over her hair, freeing it from pins which went falling across the room with delicate little sounds of which she was scarcely aware, since she could hear the pounding of her heart so loudly.

Perhaps she was seduced; perhaps she ran out of breath. She could barely stand, yet she was keenly aware of the movement of his hands upon her, down her back, over her buttocks, pulling her close. Her breasts were crushed against him, her hips likewise taut to his, and in the most intimate of places, she could feel the growth of his arousal.

She was amazed at the sensations that simple touch created within her, as if liquid sunlight streamed from that center of her, rushed like a sea of mercury throughout her, into her limbs, to her breasts, back to that center which suddenly seemed to ache with a strange, compelling void. His hands . . .

His hands had made very short work of the clothing he had previously found so annoying. A tug on strings sent her corset to the floor, another caused her pantalettes to slip down her legs. She stood in shoes, stockings, and garters, but those did not seem to cause him any displeasure, for he stepped back briefly, his eyes sweeping over her in an ebony inferno, then he came forward and swept her from the frothy pile of underclothing to carry her to the bed.

Perhaps he did find her shoes offensive, because he tossed them away next.

But then he stood again, staring down at her with such fire in his eyes that she nearly cried out from the feel of that alone against her flesh. Her gaze was caught with his as he shed his clothing, boots, socks, shirt, trousers, so easily strewn, in a matter of seconds. Yet when he stood there briefly still, she wondered momentarily deep within her heart if she did not look at him as he looked at her, for no matter what her protest might have been, she found him appealing—ruggedly, masculinely beautiful; rockhard from head to toe; fluidly, gracefully muscular; bronzed, honed, his shoulders broad, his body lean; his face expertly, proudly sculpted; his straight black hair a perfect frame for it; his ebony eyes a power within it. She could not look away, and when he strode the few feet to the bed to touch her, she felt again the swirl of mercury within her, felt as if he touched her before he actually did, *anticipated* his coming.

He climbed on top of her, straddling her, then laced his fingers with hers and held them as he lowered his face to kiss her lips again.

"May I just go ahead and do it again?" he inquired politely, his lips just a breath from hers.

"Will you never cease to torment me?" she cried softly.

"No, lady! Will you never cease to torment me!" he whispered. His palms caressed her cheeks, his fingers brushed her lips. She could feel his sex, engorged, against the flesh of her belly, yet he seemed in no hurry. "You, my lovely wife, are the cause of the greatest torment! First your voice . . . haunts and compels, enters into a man's soul, and he is then tangled within it. Your smile, your laughter, your frown, your rigid, impeccable dignity, all tease the senses. Then . . . there is touching you. The feel of you, the scent of you invading mind and memory. Like the sweet taste of clear water to drink, you draw one back again and again. You are the torment, my wild, sweet wife. One I had not expected to face."

"You insisted on marriage—" she began breathlessly.

"Indeed, I did. Perhaps I did so for all the wrong reasons. Yet I am greatly rewarded."

His dark eyes impaled her. He kissed her lips again. Parted them. His tongue slid sensually within, stroking slowly, darting, the movement more intense, hungrier, consuming more, demanding more. Soon she was so seduced by the play of his tongue that it took her long seconds to realize the shift of his body, the brush of his hands upon her, so light, feather light, her flesh seemed to burn just as the stroke had gone, to long for it again as it moved on, taunting, teasing, the sweetest torment. He pulled his lips from hers, but his mouth remained just inches above hers, his dark eyes upon her again. His palm rubbed the peak of her breast. He shifted his weight, and the stroke of his palm was replaced by the searing caress of his lips, gently, then more forcefully as his mouth closed around her, tugging, and sucking, tasting and teasing . . . all the while arousing her. Tears stung her eyes; she bit into her lip, trying not to allow the sensations to sweep her away; she didn't want to fight him, she had learned she couldn't fight him. He had made her furious, had made her smile, had awakened her so quickly and given flight in her heart and imagination to emotions she had never dreamed of. Perhaps it was the very speed that scared her so, for suddenly he was not just a part of her life but the very driving force of her life, demanding from her in an instant that she surrender so much of herself to him. He wanted more and more from her, a touch, a whisper, her home, her body, her very soul. Yet she had sold her soul so very long ago. . . .

He was heedless of it. She writhed against him, trying to escape the hot, wet touch that created such fire in her blood. His caress inched down her body, a stroke of his fingers, a brush of his tongue. His fingers threaded through the golden triangle at the base of her thighs, to the most intimate petals of her flesh. Stroked, parted, played, slipped within her. She closed her eyes, grating her teeth together, tossing her head upon the pillow. She would not cry out, not give what he sought.

But he was a ruthless lover, demanding what she would not offer, taking what she would not give. He twisted and turned her, bathing her flesh where he would with the fire of his lips and tongue, erotically brushing his kiss down the length of her spine, stroking into her, deeper . . . deeper. Twisting her anew, hot, wet strokes of his tongue invading everywhere, where his fingers had touched, brushed, parted.

She cried out at last, her fingers digging into his shoulders in an effort to stop the excruciatingly sensual and intimate play upon her. He was suddenly on top of her, his black eyes glittering with the height of his own passion.

"Tolerable?" he murmured.

She would not meet his eyes, writhing as if she might escape him still, curl into the fire of sensation that engulfed her.

He caught her chin between his thumb and forefinger, lowered his lips to hers and molded them there, breathing more fire into her, bringing the salty, sweet taste of their lovemaking to her even as his body firmly wedged hers to his will. His face rose above her again. The tormenting whisper caressed her lips once again.

"Tolerable?"

"Leave me be!" she cried softly.

A groan of frustration and anger escaped him and he was suddenly easing down the length of her body again, his touch and stroke fevered, missing nothing of her flesh, his lips creating a path of fire that inflamed her. He parted her thighs firmly, his stroke between them now as fevered, erotic as the fullness of his heady sweep down her body. A touch again, and at last she cried out, shuddering vehemently, certain that she would die, or explode, if he did not cease and desist, the aching, burning hunger inside of her was so desperate. "Tolerable!" she gasped. "Please, I . . . "

He was atop her. "More than tolerable?" he suggested.

"Please . . . !" she gasped.

"Please what?"

"I . . . want . . . I . . . "

"Me?" he suggested huskily.

"You," she breathed, her eyes closed.

He asked no more.

And all that she wanted, she received. He was within her. A firestorm of hunger, speed, power, and longing. There was no gentleness here now, no subtle play, no slow seduction. He moved within her, each thrust hard, harder, a rhythm that swept her up, brought her higher when she could fly no higher, and finally brought her to the explosion she had somehow ached for, longed for, when she had not even known it existed. It was so startling, so sweet, that she seemed to hover within the smoke and fire and mist of it, satiated, appeased, amazed, slick, wet, falling back down, and barely, just barely, aware of his tight convulsions, the searing heat of him that then seemed to enter her, the weight of his body again, the air which seemed to move within the room again.

She kept her eyes closed, listening as the slam of

her heart slowly quieted, desperately sweeping in breath after breath. She waited for him to tease her, to torment her, to offer her some arrogant form of masculine triumph.

But he did not. His lips brushed her forehead and he pulled her gently against him, his chest and hips curved against her back and buttocks, his hand smoothing down her hair.

That soft stroke of movement upon her was tender, subtle, lulling. She dared to open her eyes, saw his bronzed hand where it lay over her then, resting upon the sheets, dark against the whiteness of them.

"Don't begin to think—" she started to whisper brokenly.

"That you have surrendered anything?" he interrupted softly. "Annie, I would never begin to assume so!" he assured her, yet drew her closer. His lips brushed the top of her head. "Good night, Mrs. McShane," he said softly.

"But you don't understand, you can't—"

"Go to sleep, Annie," he commanded firmly.

Despite his words, she lay awake a while. Then she closed her eyes again and dared to feel the comfort of him there, the naked warmth and strength of him.

Then, at last, she did what he had commanded.

And slept. Deeply, with no dreams and no memories to plague her.

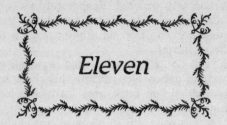

Eleven

*F*or a man who was actually quite pleased with his marriage—if it was possible to be pleased and frustrated at the same time—Ian Mc-Shane thought he was spending his Friday evening in a strange way.

Sitting in the dark, thoughtfully taking a sip now and then of the house's best brandy straight from the bottle.

There was just so damned much going on here that he couldn't quite understand.

The door, for instance.

The secret door that led from his bedroom to the cellar here below was as cleverly crafted into the wall here as it was above. The bricks in the door were perfectly aligned with those in the surrounding walls, giving nothing away.

His wife's possible activities worried him more and more. Each day, she was the epitome of competence and dignity as she managed the saloon, finding tasks that kept her busy and at a distance from him. She was incredibly reserved during the day, almost as if they were strangers each time they met.

At night, she ceased to fight him—or herself. Yet no matter how deeply he touched her, how intimate they might become, he could not reach through

some very staunch and determined barrier she had
set between them. Upon occasion she smiled. Sometimes he could tease her to a point where she might
actually laugh. Her smile, her laughter, her touch,
all aroused him to a startling point; she was beautiful, he discovered greater sensuality in her each
time he touched her, found himself further lost. But
no matter what climactic peak he might bring her to,
she withdrew immediately after, pulling away from
him on the *inside*, so much so that he could feel it
on the outside, even though she let him hold her. He
couldn't forget the way she had screamed that night
when he had caught her dozing by the window.
When she had seen his face. Almost as if she feared
he meant to slay and scalp her.

Now, he sat in a hard wood chair against the wall
in the corner of the cellar, hidden from view from
the main stairwell by several rows of beer kegs, his
brandy at his side. He had ostensibly spent his first
week of marriage studying every aspect of *his* saloon, his new enterprise. He'd dealt cards at night,
served liquor with Harold, met with the liquor sales-
men, studied beef with Henri, and studied the building—much to his bride's discomfort, he was certain.
He did find a certain pleasure in her fear that he
would discover her precious door. She had no idea,
of course, that he knew much more about the door
than he seemed to know about her. And no matter
how hard she tried to keep the barriers up between
them, she was watching him constantly. She was
afraid. And it scared the absolute hell out of him that
he didn't know why.

Then there was the matter of Cash Weatherly.

He'd been waiting for Weatherly to show up at
the saloon all week and challenge his marriage.
Maybe just try to walk into the bedroom and shoot
him while he was sleeping. He'd been prepared. He

hadn't been there long, but he could size men up
well; he'd learned to do so at an early age, and the
war had taught him that you couldn't go by the
color of a man's uniform—or his skin. Ralph was
serving as his eyes and ears in town and the envi-
rons—including Weatherly's ranch. Timmy and
Jimmy Yeagher were keeping their positions at the
saloon, with one on duty throughout each night. He
wasn't depending on the two of them alone. Last
Monday his old friend Angus Donahue had arrived.
Angus seemed to be a mixture of every race and
creed upon the continent, taking the best from each
one. He was a huge fellow, standing over even Ian's
six-three, built with shoulders that might have
graced a buffalo. His mother had been a pretty maroon out of New Orleans, his father had been a dis-
placed Cherokee, and Angus had grown up
attending one of the special Indian schools near Ian's
hometown in Georgia. Angus had been older, maybe
five years or so, and when his own parents had died,
he'd come to work for Ian's father. He'd gone to war
with Ian, made peace when Ian had made peace.
And now he'd come to Coopersville. He'd taken a
room in the attic of the saloon. Ann was properly
curious about her new boarder. Ian wouldn't tell her
a damned thing about him; he wouldn't even admit
that he knew the massive black man who had come
to town. She could think what she wanted. She was
hiding things. He could hide a few things as well. It
was damned good to have Angus here. Especially in
the late hours of the night. He spent his time watching, always watching. But he had to face it—marriage had made him vulnerable. Ann had made him
vulnerable. From the very start. From the first moment he had heard her voice, then seen her face. The
entanglement was something he had never foreseen.
He had never imagined that a woman could affect

him so deeply. Nothing was as easy as it had once
seemed. He'd gone so long with blinders on, knowing his duty during the war, knowing that he had
to have justice in his life. Now, she was a factor.
What the hell had he thought when he'd married
her?

He'd wanted her; that should have been enough.
Even if he'd forced the issue by having her make
promises to him, even if he'd hurt her and taken
what he couldn't give back, he should have had the
sense to leave it at that. But the temptation to take
what Weatherly wanted had been too great. Maybe
it had been more than that. Maybe he had just
wanted her so damned badly that he'd been willing
to go to any ends to have her. Now she was his—
as much as he could make her so, at any rate. And
everything was subtly different. He could still see
his goals. But he saw them with a new fear. He
didn't want her to get hurt, caught up as she was in
this plan of his. He was passionately possessive of
her, wanting to keep her safe, but he didn't know
what game she was playing herself.

Thank God Angus had come to even up a few of
the odds.

No matter what war he waged with himself, the
scenario was all falling into place.

He felt that he'd waited his lifetime to get here, to
be where he was now. He'd planned it carefully,
meaning to cross the man at every available opportunity. To force every issue until Weatherly was
ready to lose his mind, and then, only then, create
the challenge that would bring them both out to the
streets for a gunfight.

When it came to it, he wouldn't shoot him clean.
First, a shot to one kneecap, then the other. And then
shot after shot into him, never giving him a mortal
wound until he stood right over him. Until he could

look down at him and Weatherly could stare back up at Ian and scream out, "Why, boy?"

Then he could tell him. "Death is your sentence for the murder of innocence, beauty, life, dreams. For murder, you bastard, for murder in the most heinous and cruel manner. Murder, murder, murder, murder. This is retribution, you pile of cow dung and horse piss. Now, another ear, maybe your eyes. No matter what I do to you, it won't be enough!"

Ian realized that his hands were shaking slightly. He took another swig of the brandy and then tensed. The ground floor door to the cellar had swung open. He could hear the sounds of revelry from the saloon, the piano music, the clink of coins upon the tables, the laughter of men and women.

The door closed and he narrowed his eyes, rising silently to lean against the wall, still hidden from view himself but able to see who had come down the stairs.

It was Ann, followed by Dulcie. She hurried down to the area where the wine bottles were racked, Dulcie on her heels. "However are you going to manage?" Dulcie demanded.

"I don't know," Ann said flatly, finding a bottle and handing it to Dulcie.

"The barn raising for Grainger is going to last all day. And we're all going to be there—"

"That will be good. Grainger needs a new barn."

"But then—"

"Dulcie, will you please not worry and let me think? And quit quizzing me. Someone will hear you!"

Ann looked around the cellar even as she spoke but seemed satisfied that they were alone.

"You scare me, Ann."

"Dulcie—"

"All right, all right!"

"Get that bottle, right there. See it?"

"Yes, I see it."

"Joey is back tonight."

"Yes," Dulcie said softly.

"To see you."

"Hmm."

"What's the matter?"

"Nothing."

"I thought you enjoyed him."

"I do. Too much."

"But Dulcie, Joey cares about you—"

"Right. The rich rancher and the whore."

"Oh, Dulcie! You always told me you wanted to do just what you were doing—"

"And I do!" Dulcie said fiercely. "I have my reasons and you know them."

"Oh, Dulcie!" Ann repeated miserably. "But if you really care about him so much—"

"What? Should I kiss him? Make love to him? Whisper in the dark?"

"Stranger things have happened, Dulcie!" Ann told her softly.

"Right, and when he finds out—"

"He never will."

"Ann, *someday*—"

"Dulcie, he never will."

"Ann, things might unravel here quickly. I'm telling you, you're making a big mistake. Your husband—"

"Dulcie, quit."

"Your husband will throttle you if someone else doesn't!" Dulcie warned.

"I can manage him!" Ann insisted. "I can. Come on, we've got to get back upstairs with these quickly or else I'll have a brawl in the saloon."

They hurried back up the stairs. Ian watched them go, stroking his jaw, gritting his teeth.

The temptation, of course, was to go after them. Drag them both back to the basement and throttle Ann here and now and find out just what she was up to. Except that it wouldn't work. She wouldn't tell him anything.

He had to catch her. At what? He didn't know, but he was damned determined to find out.

Tonight. When they were alone. Maybe there was a way. If he could just control his temper. Somehow challenge her. Unnerve her. Umm. It would be wonderful if he could seduce the truth from her. Whisper his questions hotly against her flesh, hear the answers whispered huskily in return. . . .

Indeed, it would be nice. It was just damned unlikely.

He'd still challenge her. Because he might not get the truth out of her, but he would make certain of one thing.

She'd find out she wasn't going to *manage* him. Not in any way, shape, or form. Ever.

Ann stood by the piano listening to Aaron play, ruing the fact that her life had suddenly gotten so very complicated. Not only was she walking upon eggshells in her own home and place of business, now she was worried about Dulcie.

She hadn't foreseen this happening, but Dulcie had fallen in love with Joey Weatherly. And Dulcie, who had given her just about everything she needed to carry out her plan to ruin Weatherly, was suffering because every piece of information Joey gave Dulcie, Dulcie gave to Ann.

Dulcie wouldn't fail her, Ann knew that. Joey had told them what they needed to know this week, and if Ann took pleasure in anything, it was in the strain that was beginning to show in Cash Weatherly's empire. His big "guns" were paid well and would always be around, but some of his cowboys were beginning to grumble. Cash was slow in paying them; he was having to let some of his boys go. That was a triumph in itself.

But now . . .

"You can let me go alone, you know," Aaron said.

"What?"

"Tomorrow."

She shook her head. "No, don't be absurd. It's a two-man job."

"You are a woman," he reminded her.

"Fine. It's a two-person job," she retorted.

"Annie—"

"Aaron, you can't go alone! If anything were to happen to you I'd want to die myself."

"Ann, my God, what do you think I feel? I can't believe that we've taken this scheme this far! How long do you think we're going to be able to go on before someone fires back and hits one of us?"

"That's why it's a two-man job. You know I can knock the eyes out of a fly, Aaron. I—"

"Your husband's watching," he warned her suddenly.

He was. She bit lightly into her lower lip, staring across the room. Ian was seated at one of the tables, playing cards. The handsomely dressed attorney, Ralph Reninger, was at his left side, the extraordinary new arrival, Angus Donahue, was on his right. She had the sudden, uneasy feeling that they were conspiring about something. Rounding out her husband's table were the Yeagher twins, Timmy and Jimmy, whom she'd always liked. She'd hired them. They were *her* employees and had been loyal to her. But she knew that they were Ian's men now; they had instinctively turned to him as some sort of pillar of strength.

So there, she thought, sat her husband's gang. For-

midable. Ralph was slim, almost dandified, yet he
retained a strong masculinity despite his apparel.
The twins were able-bodied young cowboys, both
tall and well-built, and well acquainted with the
harsh, unwritten rules of the West. Then there was
Angus, towering in his stature, striking with coffee-
colored skin and hard bone structure, awesome in
the sheer power of his build. And beside him, her
husband. Ian McShane, who was somehow the most
frightening man in the group. For though his build
was leaner than that of Angus, she knew better than
anyone how well toned every muscle was within his
body, how quickly he could move, and with what
startling grace and speed. She had yet to discover
what black secrets lay behind his dark eyes, but she
knew his mind was as honed as his body, as sharp
as his eyes, as quick as his movements. When he
watched her, as he watched now, she felt afraid. She
was playing with fire. He hadn't discovered what
she was up to yet because she hadn't given him anything to discover since the day of their marriage. She
hadn't crossed him because he hadn't left her with
the will to do so. Tonight would be like all the other
nights she'd spent since they'd married. She would
begin with the will to be impassive; he would
breathe a whisper against her lips, invade her body,
touch her soul. And she wouldn't be able to turn
away until the tempest had claimed them both. Then
she would wonder what it might have been like had
her life been different, had she not been ruled by this
great purpose, had she dared not turn away from
him. She wanted to whisper in the darkness, pour
out her soul to him, and yet she could not, and
should not, if she could help it. He had married her
for his own ends, none of which he seemed willing
to share with her. He had come to town with his
own purpose in mind; he had seen what he had

wanted and seized it all, and she was only part and parcel of that package.

Joey Weatherly, smiling his charming smile, sauntered over to Ian's table. The cardplayers made room for him. Ian watched Joey strangely, Ann thought. But then, it was quite obvious that Ian bore his own malice toward Cash Weatherly. Maybe his good friend Ralph had told him that Weatherly was a putrid bloodsucker who had ruined half the ranchers in the vicinity. In fact, Ian's assurance that their marriage would infuriate Cash had seemed as much a reason for him to marry her as it had been for her to marry him. But Ian welcomed Joey Weatherly to the table with the flash of a smile that startlingly seemed to squeeze around her heart and cause it to slam against her chest. He could be so forbidding, so tense, so hard with his cleanly lined features, bronzed skin, and fathomless ebony eyes. His smile altered that hardness. It gave his features a compelling, very masculine charm and sensuality. He had seduced her easily enough, she determined, and wondered just how many women had come before her.

And with a pang of jealousy, she wondered just how many might follow.

He had married her.

But what would that really mean to him in the future?

Thoughts of the future suddenly reminded her about the day to come and her worries.

She would do what she must. There had to be a way.

Ian was watching her again. She felt his eyes as if he had somehow known she was planning something. He suddenly crooked a finger at her, beckoning her to the table. No, she thought, meeting his eyes. *Commanding* her to the table seemed to be more like it. She shook her head, pointing to the bar as if there was something she needed to do there.

She hurried from the piano to the bar, only to feel him tap her on the back when she arrived there.

She spun around quickly, but discovered that he was at her side, leaning his elbow upon the bar, watching her, and not where she had thought he would be. He stared at her gravely. "Come join us— my love," he said.

"But I've things to do—"

"Nothing that will not keep."

His fingers closed around her wrist. Other than attempting to free herself from his grasp—which she did not think he would allow her to do at this moment—she had no choice but to follow him to the table.

There were no empty chairs at the table other than Ian's. Dulcie had come over, and was perched on the edge of Joey's chair. Ian sat, dragging her down on his lap. Ralph welcomed her with a smile, Angus with a nod, the twins with the respect due nobility, and Joey stood until she was seated. "Welcome, welcome, to the loveliest and fairest in all the realm."

"Thank you," she murmured. Ian had a lock around her middle as he picked up the cards. She felt acutely uncomfortable seated on his lap, as if she were a saloon girl. It wasn't as if she had ever thought any the less of her friends for what they did for a living, it was just that she was used to running the place, being in charge.

But there was something about Ian's putting her in this uncharacteristic position . . .

Of course! He meant to take her off guard, to discomfit her. She didn't attempt to move, but sat stiffly where he had brought her.

"My deal?" Ian said. His arms around her, his hands still moved deftly upon the cards that lay on

the table. "There are several lush and lovely ladies
in this vicinity, Joe Weatherly," he reminded lightly.
He flashed one of his winning smiles at Dulcie, who
smiled gratefully in return.

"I do agree wholeheartedly!" Joey said, lifting his
glass of whiskey. Around the table, the others did
likewise. Ann had no glass; it didn't seem to matter.
Ian's was pressed into her hands as he lifted the bottle to his own lips.

"Annie, I've never seen you drink whiskey—"
Joey began.

"Oh, I'll bet my lovely wife drinks whatever fits
her fancy at the moment," Ian interrupted. "Cards,
gentlemen?"

"One. One good one," Ralph told him, and the
play went around the table.

"You two going to try to keep the place open and
attend the barn raising tomorrow?" Joey asked,
studying his cards.

"Yeah, I imagine so," Ian said.

"It will be difficult," Jimmy Yeagher said.

"We'll manage," Ann murmured, wishing she
wasn't so aware of her husband's every movement
and of how strange and tense he seemed tonight.
"Harold will stay here," she murmured. "And
Cocoa and some of the other workers. We will manage."

"Ann is sure she can manage just about anything," Ian said. She shifted uncomfortably. His
arms tightened around her.

"It's going to be something for the town to manage, I reckon," Joey said. "Some of the payrolls are
coming in by stage. Sheriff will have his hands full,
what with the outlaw activity in the region lately."

"Well, those with work of their own will be coming back to town when they need to do so. With the
stages in, we'll have more work here—" Ann began.

"But Cocoa is the most efficient woman I've ever come across," Ian said. "We won't need to worry, will we, my love?"

"Well, it is our place, my love," she grated in return.

"Fold," Ralph said.

Jimmy and Timmy dropped their cards as well.

"Angus? You and Joey calling me?"

Angus studied his cards and shook his head. "I'll call you, keep you an honest man," Joey said lightly.

Joey laid out three queens and two jacks. "Impressive," Ian told him.

"But?" Joey said with a smile.

Ian shrugged. He laid out three kings and two aces. Joey didn't seem to mind. He laughed softly. "Luck seems to be with you," he said.

"Sometimes," Ian agreed. "Sometimes we make our own luck."

"Be careful, Annie," Joey said with a laugh. "This man knows when to play his cards, don't you think, Dulcie?"

"Yes." Perched on the corner of Joey's chair, she had been very quiet. Now, she suddenly came to life. "Annie, he knows!" she insisted.

"How wonderful that he is such a good card-player," she said firmly, staring at Dulcie. But Dulcie's expression still seemed to give away something, and Ian's arm remained locked very tightly around her.

Thankfully, a moment later, Harold had a problem with the cash drawer.

"Annie can fix that with a touch," Jimmy Yeagher said with pride. And thankfully, she was able to escape Ian's hold and see to the register. Yet when she was done, she saw that Ian was gone. The game continued, but he was gone, and she was uneasy.

She waited, watching for him, until the saloon had

mostly cleared out. Dulcie, Cocoa, and Ginger had all gone upstairs—alone or accompanied, she wasn't sure. Only a few lone cowhands remained at the bar, and Harold had things well under control. Aaron ceased playing and came to stand beside her at the bar.

"You look like hell."

"Thank you."

"All right, for a beautiful woman you look like hell. Go upstairs and get some sleep. All right, you remain a newlywed. Go upstairs, make your husband happy, and then get some sleep."

She flushed. "I'd like to hog-tie my husband in a closet," she murmured wearily.

"Sounds exotic," Aaron teased. Then his smile faded. "Annie, give it up, for tomorrow, at least."

"We're so close!"

He sighed. "All right, we'll be ready." He lowered his voice, even though the saloon was almost empty. "I won't go to the barn raising at all. Everything will be ready in our stables. Just give me the word, and don't think of doing anything alone, promise?"

"I promise, if you do."

He nodded, and went on up. She waved at Harold, who acknowledged that she was going up. Poor Harold, she thought. He looked worried, too.

She wondered where Ian might be as she walked up the stairs and entered her room, then discovered him where she had least expected him.

He was already in bed, sitting up, his back against the headboard, his muscular chest bronze in the firelight, very dark against the whiteness of the sheets, his eyes like obsidian fires as he watched her.

She couldn't retreat from the room; she had to move into it. "You're here already," she murmured, pausing before her dressing table, annoyed that her fingers seemed to shake as she pulled the pins from her hair.

"Yes, I'm here already," he agreed in a tone that did little to still her unease.

She finished with the pins and started to brush her hair, suddenly unable to disrobe when she could see the reflection of him looking at her in the dressing table mirror.

"It's incredibly late, Ann!" he snapped suddenly.

Her lashes fell against her cheeks. "This is a saloon. Hours do tend to run late."

"But we've a busy day ahead of us tomorrow, don't we?" he demanded.

The barn raising. He had to be talking about the barn raising.

She had given up wearing the black mourning gowns she had worn in memory of Eddie after she had married Ian, but the majority of her clothing was chaste and prim. Today she had worn a deep forest green dress with a collarbone neckline and small bustle. The hooks were in the back and she found herself having difficulty with them. She nearly wrenched them from the satin garment herself, she was in such a hurry to get to sleep.

And not talk.

She struggled with the hooks, then jumped when she felt him behind her, his touch not in the least gentle. "Having trouble *managing* a few hooks, my love? How amazing, for I had thought you capable of managing anything at all."

"I can manage just fine!" she assured him, trying to draw away. Except that he held her fast, and he had swiftly and deftly undone the annoying little fasteners that had refused to comply with her own efforts. He pulled the gown from her head, leaving it in a pool on the floor. To her surprise, he made no further attempt to help her disrobe, but walked

to the windows, pulling back the heavy velvet draperies to stare down at the street.

The moon was full now, illuminating the town
with its soft otherworldly light. Against it, Ian's
body seemed to glint like copper. She nervously
drew her eyes from him, shedding her chemise and
corset, petticoats, pantalettes, shoes, and stockings.
He'd made her so nervous that she plucked a white
nightgown from her dressing screen and started to
slide it over her head.

But he was back, having moved quickly, almost
soundlessly like a whisper in the night, and he
reached for the garment, his jaw set and hard.

"What's this?"

"I thought—"

"There isn't much to this relationship, but I can't
see backtracking on what we do have."

"Fine," she said stiffly, releasing the garment to
him. He infuriated her, towering over her, completely at ease with his nudity in the moonlight. She
didn't know what it was that he wanted from her,
why he was so tense, like a cat in the night, prowl-
ing, ready to pounce upon some prey. Angrily, she
said, "If you're unhappy, you've yourself to blame.
You insisted on marriage—"

"Yes, I did, didn't I? But when I insisted, I was
dead honest with you. No rules."

"And what rules have I tried to enforce? What is
it that you haven't gotten?"

"You."

She felt herself shaking, stepping back from him.
"I don't know what you mean," she lied. "I'm standing here in what was once my own room with you.
In a week, it has become as much yours as mine. I
am standing naked with a naked man, something I
had not done before our marriage. I don't fight
you—"

"And you don't come to me."

"Maybe I can't!" she whispered. "But I don't fight you—"

"You do!" he exclaimed angrily. "You turn away, you raise huge barriers between us."

"I don't—"

"Then tell me about yourself, Ann," he demanded, his hands on his hips, staring at her.

She lowered her head quickly, taking a deep breath. Damn him! He had unnerved her.

"What do you want to know?"

"What you're up to and why."

"I'm not up to anything."

"Tell me about Eddie."

She shook her head again. "Surely, there's nothing I could tell you that you haven't surmised by now. He was a good man. He had his weaknesses, he had his strengths."

"Did he know what you were up to? Better yet, did you share any of your past with him? Did you share all of your activities with him?"

"Stop it!" she cried out. "I'm not up to anything!" she lied, shaking. "There was nothing to tell him. He knew my parents were dead, had been dead. They were killed, and I don't want to talk about it, it hurts to talk about it, all right?"

"Ann—" He started to take hold of her shoulders; she tried to elude him, wrenching back. But he didn't intend to let her go.

"Let go!" she insisted.

"Ann, stop!" he said harshly. "The past is long over, and I can't let you use it against me!"

"There is nothing else I can do!" she cried. She tried to shake him off again, but his hold upon her tightened. She trembled, gritting her teeth. He held her so close. Her naked flesh brushed his. How was it possible to be so angry, so upset, and still feel such strange hot sensations simply because his body touched hers?

"Please—" she began.

"All right, no more questions about the past. Tonight, at least. Look at me!"

She blinked furiously, then raised her eyes to his. "What?" she demanded.

"Listen then, and listen well, my love. You may manage your saloon. And you may have managed many things very well in your life. But you will not manage me, do you understand?"

"What?" she gasped. It was as if he had heard her talking to Dulcie tonight in the cellar. Hadn't she said almost exactly the same thing to Dulcie tonight? *I can manage him!*

"You will not manage me!" he repeated furiously, his hold on her like a vise. Had he heard? she wondered. How? They had been alone in the cellar!

Frightened, she tried to wrench free from him. "You can force a wife," she cried out. "You can force your way in here, you can shake me, beat me, tear out my hair, demand to have me—but there are things you can never make me give, things I never will give, things that are no part of you!"

"You are part of me."

"Only what I choose to give! And I don't care to give you a bloody thing tonight!" she lashed out, still struggling to escape him.

"Oh, you don't?"

"No, I don't!"

Suddenly he freed her wrists, but before she could make use of her freedom, she found herself being lifted, then flung down upon the bed. And he was looming over her, his body crouched tight atop hers, his face so very near hers that she could tell from the fiery expression in his dark eyes that his anger had not abated; it had grown. It was like a fire that had been doused with kerosene, blazing all the more hotly.

"Then I'll take what it is I do have the power to force from you!" he breathed against her lips.

"Bastard! You will not—"

"Oh, but this is what I can take!"

"Force!"

"Have!" he insisted.

She tried to twist from him to no avail. His kiss was hard, and rough, bruising her lips. She tasted salt and blood. His hands were blunt and demanding upon her, thrusting apart her thighs.

She wanted to be just as angry, furious, hurt. For once, she did want to fight him. Yet the same anger that fueled him had given something to her. She was furious. She wanted to lash out. But there was a sweetly wild, haunting, wicked tempo thundering throughout her. She wanted *him*.

His mouth broke away from hers. She felt his whisper against the dampness of her lips, husky, soft, almost like raw silk despite his anger. His eyes burned their coal fire straight into her heart and being.

"Do you deny me this?"

"Ian—"

"Do you deny me this?"

"Damn you."

"Do you deny me this?"

She closed her eyes. "No!" She formed the word. She was certain she never really said it aloud. Yet it was all the reply he needed. She cried out at his rough entry, yet not from pain. To her dismay she found herself clinging to him, riding the storm of rage and fury that had so filled him. Yet when she would have reached a jagged peak, he suddenly refused to allow her to do so, withdrawing, and then . . .

Beginning to make love to her. He was not much more gentle than he had been, yet the things he did aroused and awakened her to a new and abandoned awareness. His hands were everywhere upon her, followed by his lips, his teeth, his mouth, the wicked thrust of his tongue, the stroke of his fingers again. She heard wild, panting, urging whispers, heard her own voice, words she hadn't imagined coming from her lips, cries, pleas. She touched him in return. Everywhere. Felt the wild life pulsing in his sex, stroked, touched, tasted. She felt that she had implored forever, that she could no longer bear the exquisite torture and agonizing pleasure. Then he was suddenly with her again, filling her until she thought she would split, yet she had never felt anything so sweet, so volatile, or so good in all her life. When the sensations climaxed at last, they were so strong that the night, the moon, the earth, the world, all seemed to explode. And even then, as the minutes ticked by, as the night returned, she shook again and again, tremors of sensation continuing to spill inside of her. She was at first acutely aware of him within her still, his powerful body racked with the same tremors, then she was only aware of his warmth as she seemed to fall slowly back to the reality of their room, the white sheets on the bed, the clock that ticked from the mantel, the silver spill of moonlight that came in from the slight parting of the velvet draperies from where he had held them before.

She still couldn't talk; she wanted to be held. She remembered standing by the piano, thinking that tonight would be the same as all of the other nights. And though it had started off with such anger, it would be the same, yet sweeter. For she longed to turn into his arms. To be held. Maybe that would satisfy him.

But she'd never know, for he lay beside her, still for just a matter of seconds. Then he exploded with a sharp curse and rose from the bed. Quickly he threw on pants and a shirt.

And left her.

And she lay alone.

Twelve

*T*he day began badly.

The barn raising had been set for the crack of dawn, which meant that anyone who planned to attend had to get up and out to Grainger's place while it was still dark. Ann had barely slept.

McShane hadn't returned until early in the morning, when he had come in to wake her and dress. She knew he'd slept elsewhere because she hadn't really been asleep when he had come in, she had simply been lying in bed, her eyes closed, weary from tossing and turning.

They rode in the wagon to Grainger's along with Dulcie, the Yeagher twins, and Angus Donahue. They were among the first of the townfolk to arrive, and while Ann and Dulcie began to set up coffee and breakfast for those who would be arriving and working, the men joined Grainger and set to work studying the plans for the barn and going through all the materials that had been donated for its construction.

By nine, a number of men had arrived, Sheriff Bickford among them. The support beams were all in place, and amazingly, the building had already begun to take shape.

A number of the town's good wives had arrived

as well. They were civil to Ann and Dulcie, but talked about them behind their backs, whispering loud enough for them to hear. Ann ignored them. Upon occasion, Dulcie managed to twist a few knives into the self-righteously condemning hearts of the ladies, asking Mrs. Tarleton if the bruise on Mr. Tarleton's left hip was healing up all right and suggesting to Mrs. Dumphries that Mr. Dumphries might come home more often if Mrs. Dumphries could manage to be just a bit more of a *brazen, scarlet woman* herself. She suggested to Mrs. Hennessey, the wife of the town's bank president, that Mr. Hennessey might just quit snoring for her as well if she gently nudged him in the ribs and rolled him over.

"Behave," Ann warned Dulcie softly as she came behind the food table to stand beside Dulcie and pour herself more coffee. She smiled at a very disgruntled Mrs. Hennessey, who was still staring openmouthed at Dulcie. "Mrs. Hennessey, Henri prepared these scones very specially this morning, please do try one."

Mrs. Hennessey managed to close her mouth. She didn't take a scone. "Hmmph!" she muttered, her fingers tight around her coffee tin, and she swung her back on them both.

"Now every man in town is going to be in trouble with his wife, Dulcie. These poor fellows won't be allowed back in the saloon for weeks—maybe never. Did you have to tell her that you'd slept with her husband?"

"Oh, I've never slept with her husband," Dulcie said, waving a hand in the air.

"But the—"

"She's a nasty witch! She was whispering that whores like us shouldn't be allowed among good people like them. Which may be true for me, but—"

"Oh, Dulcie!" Ann murmured unhappily. "Dulcie, you've got to get out of the business. It was fine while it was what you wanted, but you've been miserable lately."

"I'm not miserable. I'm—I'm tired. And it was what I wanted for a while. It just seemed to make sense to make a lot of money doing what had been forced on me for nothing once."

"If you're tired of what you're doing, it's time to stop."

Dulcie shook her head. "You need me."

"You can work in the kitchen, you can serve in the saloon. You don't need to—"

"But I get my information by being with people," Dulcie said softly.

"We can get it another way. Dulcie—"

"Look who's here," Dulcie interrupted suddenly.

Ann turned. Joey Weatherly had arrived with his sister, Meg. She was a very pretty young woman of about twenty with sable brown hair and wide amber eyes. When Joey helped her down from the wagon, she flashed him a smile of thanks and then hurried to where Grainger stood beside the rising structure of his new barn, speaking to him softly and earnestly. Ann watched Grainger as he listened to her and was glad to see that he took her hand, nodded, and seemed to accept everything that she was saying. Meg was innocent of wrongdoing, just as Joey was, Ann was certain. At first it had bothered her to realize that she *liked* a couple of Weatherly's children. Such a monster couldn't have created decent human beings. But he had. It seemed he had taught his two older sons his corrupt ways, but somehow Joey and Meg had grown up with a sense of right and wrong. But there was one big difference between the siblings. From comments he had made, it seemed Joey saw the evil in his father. Meg did not.

And now it sometimes bothered Ann that she had spent years of her life in the pursuit of taking revenge upon a man—when doing so was going to hurt that man's daughter.

"We expected Joey, didn't we?" Ann murmured.

"And maybe Meg as well. I'm sure Meg just gave Grainger her father's excuses. What do you think?"

"Probably," Ann agreed.

"Well, it would be a bit much if Weatherly actually showed up here."

"Indeed, it would."

"He might have shown up—he does have the arrogance for such a thing—but he's going to be waiting for his payroll to come in. Maybe he should get it this time," Dulcie said unhappily.

Ann shook her head. "I can't stop now!" she said vehemently.

"But you have a husband—one right here, right now. Whatever were you thinking when you agreed to marry? Not just any man, but one every bit as mysterious as you can be yourself, frightening as hell since it seems he can see everything with those dark eyes of his. He'll catch up with you sooner or later, if you're not careful."

"I had to marry him. I needed protection."

"Wise choice. Now you need more—from him?" Dulcie commented dryly.

Ann glared at her, assuring her that she didn't appreciate the sarcasm. "Yes, but I did manage to hide my clothing and six-shooters."

"At what price?"

"What do you mean, what price?" Ann demanded with exasperation. "It's not . . . so terrible, being married to him," she murmured, surprised at the blush that colored her cheeks.

"I'll just bet it's not," Dulcie agreed dryly, watching her. "But that's just it—you've sold your soul and you don't even know it yet."

"I haven't sold anything. He's got his own reasons for being here and I have a feeling that when he's done with whatever he needs to do for those reasons, he'll just move on. I believe I might even get everything back—"

"Except your soul, of course," Dulcie interrupted.

"I gave up my soul a long time ago, when I started all this," she murmured.

"You're wrong," Dulcie told her. "You're wrong, and you don't realize it, because you haven't really done anything that terrible yet. You've played Robin Hood, stealing from the truly evil Mr. Weatherly and sending all that you dare of *his* gold to charity for war widows and orphans."

"Dulcie, I hope that if I do get caught, you manage to explain it to the sheriff that way before they hang me."

"I don't think I'll have a chance," Dulcie said morosely. "If you get caught, Weatherly will take care of you before the sheriff has a chance to. That is, of course, unless your husband gets a hold of you first—and then you just may not need to worry about the other two at all."

"Dulcie, quit, please! This isn't like you. You've supported me, you've helped me, you've saved me, you've—"

"I've changed. The stakes are different now."

"How? Weatherly hasn't changed. The past hasn't changed."

"But you have a future now."

Ann shook her head, biting into her lower lip. Dulcie was wrong; she was in love with Joey Weatherly and so she had suddenly turned into a dreamer. Ann's soul was long gone, and no matter what games she might play in her heart and mind, she couldn't turn away from the course she had charted for herself. It was too late, Cash was too evil, and if she went down in a blaze of fire, she would bring him with her. McShane couldn't change that. He could do many things, he could try to coerce, claim, and command her, but he couldn't change the past, or the fact that she had to keep on with her vow to bring Weatherly down.

Nor could she ever allow her own volatile feelings to change her intent. Ever. Not her anger, not the passion McShane awoke within her.

"I've got to go soon!" she insisted in a soft whisper to Dulcie.

"What's Mr. McShane going to say when he notices Mrs. McShane gone?" Dulcie demanded.

"I'll leave at the right time."

"Maybe you've given Weatherly enough trouble—"

"I'll never give him enough trouble. I have to take this all the way, Dulcie. If not, what have I been doing all this time? When will there ever be justice?"

"Is there coffee, my love?"

Ann felt the blood drain from her cheeks. She spun around. Ian stood right behind her. The day was warm. He had stripped off his shirt. His torso seemed almost brown, glimmering with a sheen of sweat beneath the sun, the muscles within it taut and cleanly defined. His eyes were shaded by the rim of his hat, giving her no clue as to whether he had heard any of her words.

"Coffee, Dulcie?" she gasped out.

"I think we need to make more," Dulcie said. "We should do that now. Yes, we should do that now. It will just be a minute."

"I'll bring you a cup as soon as it's brewed," Ann managed to assure him.

He offered her a strange smile, his eyes narrowed.

"Do that, my love," he told her, and returned to work.

When the new pot of coffee had finished perking, Ann looked at the barn again. It had more than taken shape. The support beams were all up and men were even atop the rafters, working on the roof.

"I think it's time I ride back to the saloon," Ann told Dulcie. It was time, because Ian McShane was one of the men on the roof. She hoped he wouldn't notice for some time that she had left.

"You're still going?" Dulcie said.

"Yes!"

"Well, I don't think you need to bring him the coffee anymore," Dulcie told her.

"Why?"

"Look."

She shaded her eyes with her hand against the sun and looked for McShane again. He was up on the highest beam, but he was smiling down, laughing, his hands on his hips. Below him stood Meg Weatherly. She was laughing, looking up at McShane, and offering him a tall glass of lemonade.

"I thought she wanted that for herself," Dulcie murmured. "She was so nice to me when she came for it."

"She is nice," Ann said quickly.

"McShane seems to think so."

"Good. He'll be occupied!" Ann snapped.

"You're not bothered at all."

"No!" Ann lied. She was bothered. She didn't know why. It was just that Meg was so sweet and innocent. Even if she was Weatherly's child. She'd been properly raised. She was soft, feminine, extremely pretty. She didn't frequent saloons. She was the kind of young woman who would make some lucky man a perfect wife.

And McShane seemed to appreciate everything about her.

"I have to go," Ann insisted. And turning, she started to leave.

"Ann, wait! What do I say—"

"That I went to see that things are going smoothly at the saloon."

"And if he rides after you?"

"Then I'll have ridden back here while he was doing so. Dulcie! He may not even notice I've gone. Keep your distance from him as long as you can. Now I'm going! Just do your best!"

Dulcie had never appeared more miserable. But Ann knew she had to go. Aaron would be waiting, worrying by now.

"Dulcie!"

"All right."

"You'll manage?"

"I'll manage."

It was strange. He'd had his eye on her all the damned day—until the arrival of Joey and Meg Weatherly.

Ian wondered what he had expected. The sins of the father should have been apparent somehow in all the children. But Meg was captivating, introducing herself in a most polite and gentle manner, welcoming him to town, congratulating him on his marriage. She brought him lemonade, and he swung down from the rafters to accept it from her, learning something about their home situation. She was still deeply grieved by the loss of her mother, she kept house for her father and brothers. She worried constantly about her father.

"He's just so determined to create an empire out here. He should have been a king. I've heard that he'll be a great politician one day, perhaps leading us into statehood."

"Perhaps," Ian told her, trying to keep his own emotions regarding such a possibility out of his voice.

He glanced up at the sun, then drew out his pocket watch, determined to keep track of the time. The stagecoach with Weatherly's payroll was due in—such things were supposed to be kept quiet but the information had been bandied about by the customers in the saloon as if what they discussed was no more important than flies buzzing around flowers.

Anyone who was interested could find out when this stage was coming in.

"So where's your father today?" he asked Meg.

"Looking after his cowhands; it's Saturday, last Saturday of the month."

Payday. So was Weatherly going to be out riding, waiting for his payroll coach to come in? Ian wondered. Or had he still not realized that his youngest son seemed to be feeding every piece of his business to hungry sharks feeding somewhere in the saloon?

He didn't know, but he saw Ralph watching him from across an expanse of dirt; Angus Donahue was also waiting for his cue.

He excused himself to Meg, then looked around for his wife.

And it was only then that he realized she had disappeared.

He approached Dulcie, who remained behind the food table, preparing plates for the men with a pleasant smile, determinedly ignoring the genteel ladies of the town, who seemed equally determined to let everyone know that women in Dulcie's line of work didn't really belong among them. Odd how they didn't seem to mind that he owned the saloon. But biased as it might be, a man seemed to have the right to such pursuits while a woman did not.

"Dulcie, you're alone?" he asked.

She had been preparing a plate of food for Grainger, who had worked like a son-of-a-gun himself. She nearly jumped sky-high. She quickly regained her composure, offering him one of her laziest, most sensual smiles. "Alone, sugar? Why, I'm just about never alone."

"Dulcie, where is she?"

"Who?"

"Ann."

"Ann . . . why, she was here just a few moments ago—"

"No, she wasn't."

"Well, she intended to ride back just to make sure that everything was going smoothly at the saloon. You knew she was going to do that, right?" Dulcie said very innocently.

"You'll lie through your teeth for her, won't you?"

"McShane, you know I think the world of you myself, but you are getting downright insulting here—"

"Never mind, Dulcie. I won't get the truth out of you on anything, will I?"

"I try always to tell the truth—"

"Trying and doing are two different things, aren't they?"

"Ian—"

"Why is she sometimes afraid of me?" he demanded suddenly, wondering what he might gain by abruptly changing the subject. He still couldn't forget the terrified way she had looked up into his face the time he had awoken her.

"Afraid of you?" Dulcie repeated. "She's—not."

"Yes, she is."

"Not really—"

"Once when she was dozing I woke her and she stared at me as if I were about to scalp her."

Dulcie gasped softly, giving away much more than she had intended. "I—er—I have work to do back here," she stuttered out, trying to elude him.

He quickly leapt over the table, caught her arm, and swung her back with a grim smile.

"Scalping. That brought something to mind, I believe."

Dulcie had turned white. She looked away, then she looked back at him. "Maybe she was dreaming."

"About what?" he demanded with a frown.

"It isn't my place—" she began, trying to look away again.

"Dulcie!"

She let out a long sigh, then met his gaze. And then her words spilled out in a rush. "She was a prisoner of the Pawnees for several years."

He let her go abruptly. "What?"

"Ann had been taken prisoner, she lived among them for several years. I—"

"You what?" he persisted.

Dulcie lowered her head again. "It's where we met." She looked up at him, her eyes blazing. "She saved my life when we were both captives. Twice. So, yes, I'll—" She broke off, biting into her lower lip. "Yes! I'll do anything in the world for Ann. She's my best friend, she's like my sister. We endured so much together, you must understand . . . "

She might have said something else; he wasn't sure. He felt ill. Perhaps that explained her fear, part of it, at any rate. She must despise Indians—any Indians, it might not matter what tribe or nation. Maybe any time that she looked into his face all that she saw was the telltale Sioux blood.

"Ian, please, you mustn't tell her that I said anything, you mustn't let her know. I know that she'll

tell you about it—I, I—think I know that she will,
when she has things right in her own mind. Ian,
please—''

He didn't know how he would have responded to
her then because his attention was suddenly di-
verted. ''McShane!'' It was Angus. ''McShane,'' Angus repeated. He spoke softly so that Dulcie couldn't
hear his words. ''Ralph has the horses. We've got to
ride out. Sheriff Bickford's already started out to see
about the stage coming in. We need to be there,
don't you think?''

Ian still stared at Dulcie for a moment. ''Yeah,'' he
told Angus. ''You're right. Dulcie, I'll see you later.
When you find Ann, maybe you can find a way to
hold on to her. Or else I'm going to have to find a
way. She may like yours a lot better.'' He tipped his
hat to Dulcie, then hurried away with Angus.

Hell! Just how long had Ann been gone? Ian wondered.

And where had she gone?

He didn't like the answer that crept along his
spine.

Ann took the wagon back to the saloon, walked
through it slowly so that the few customers within
could vouch for her presence there, then tore up to
her room for her men's apparel and guns. She didn't
change in her room, but headed down to the cellar
and out to the stable to do so. She'd determined after
her discussion with Dulcie today to move her garb
and weapons here. If they were discovered, at least
they wouldn't be discovered among her personal
property. Between the far back stall and the tack
room behind it there was a storage compartment
easily hidden by a few stacks of hay. It was a tight
fit, yet large enough for her to duck into and change.
When she was done, she hurried out back where

Aaron was waiting in his duster and hat, a kerchief covering the lower half of his face.

"You're very late. They'll be almost to town when we reach them," he warned her.

"We'll get them right off the bluffs. We won't be able to take a chest of coins—"

"We'll fill the saddlebags," Aaron told her. He patted the bags before him and pointed to those on the roan she was riding. "One of us does plan ahead."

She smirked at him, then pulled her kerchief up over her nose. They slipped out of town the back way, then rode hard to come up atop the bluffs where they could watch for the stagecoach that carried Weatherly's payroll.

They had barely come to the vantage point where Ann could best disarm the guard when they heard the coach coming around on the trail. She drew a gun quickly, taking aim just as the coach, manned by a driver and a guard, came around the bend to appear below them. She forced herself to calm her beating heart and make her shot a sure one.

Perfect. She caught the guard's rifle mid-barrel. It exploded and flew from his hands. He started to stand in sheer surprise, then—as the frightened driver panicked and lashed the horses to a faster speed—he did a flip into the dirt at the wagon's side.

"Sweet Jesu! What luck!" Ann cried. "Come on!"

They raced down after the stagecoach, their horses' hooves sliding in the slanting trail of dirt and scrub that took them down into the valley trail, kicking up a haze of dust to cover them. They quickly caught up with the careening coach, both shooting into the air to warn the driver to pull up his conveyance. At last, the white-haired and heavily bearded fellow pulled to a stop, shaking. He didn't even try to reach for a weapon as he watched the two of them approach him.

"You two holding up the stage?" he asked.

"Indeed, sir," Aaron said, inflecting the words with a proper English accent. "And we've little time for talk today, I'm afraid. We're in a hurry."

"You ain't goin'ta hurt me?" the driver said. "I told them, and I told them, they needed more than one guard. They just keep thinking that one trained man should be able to shoot up the two bandits known to be robbing the countryside, but they never want to realize there just ain't no law in the West, no real law, no one to help. Sure, they'll hang you if they catch you, but at this rate—"

"Sir, we've no desire to hurt you, but we'll have to shortly if you don't manage to hand down the payroll chest very quickly," Ann said, deepening her voice to a husky whisper and feigning a rich English accent to match Aaron's. "We'll be on our way."

"Hold it!" someone cried suddenly.

Ann spun quickly on her horse, amazed to see that a young man had come from the stagecoach. He had apparently managed to open the door and take the leap down quickly and quietly, since the step had not been lowered. He wore wire-framed glasses, was bone thin, blond-haired—and shaking like a rabbit. But he was holding a small silver-and-bone pistol, which instantly drew Ann's attention if the young man did not himself.

She sized him up quickly and directed her gun at him, leaving Aaron to watch the guard.

"Drop it!" she snapped.

He did so with amazing speed.

"Oh, Anthony!" came a feminine cry, and a young woman suddenly threw open the door and fell from the stage. She was a pretty young thing with deep red hair and enormous blue eyes. Ann felt Aaron move behind her—instinctively ready to be a gentleman and help the fallen girl from the dirt. But the young man—Anthony, so it seemed—was quick to help her up, smoothing the dust from her cheeks and skirt.

"Are you quite all right, Annabella?" Anthony demanded.

"Yes, yes, so clumsy of me—"

"Excuse me!" Ann bellowed, almost forgetting to lower her voice and maintain her accent. "But this *is* a holdup."

Annabella took a look at both of them and then suddenly let out a bloodcurdling scream. "Oh, help, oh God, rape, murder, pillage, slaughter—"

"Wait—!" Aaron began.

"Oh, God, oh, help, help, help—"

She was shrieking. Anthony was trying to calm her. Ann couldn't take any more. She leapt down from her horse and approached the young woman and slapped her across the cheeks. Annabella went dead still, staring at her with watering eyes and such a look of terror that Ann felt a twinge of guilt. "I'm sorry, but you're giving me a splitting headache! Now, there's going to be no slaughter, no murder, no rape."

Annabella inhaled on a shaky breath. "No murder—no rape?" Her lashes beat furiously against her cheeks. Ann shook her head in confusion, wondering if Annabella wasn't just a little bit disappointed.

"We've just come for the payroll," Ann said.

"Oh!" Annabella breathed.

"Here it is!"

The driver—to whom she'd barely given the least attention in the last few minutes—had crawled atop the stage to toss down the chest with the gold.

"Thank you," Ann told him. Still training her gun on the three of them, she backed toward the chest.

With a flick of her wrist she took aim and blew off the lock, then lowered herself to it. "The saddle-bags," she told Aaron.

Aaron dismounted from his horse, throwing both sets of saddlebags to Ann. While she started to load them with the gold, Aaron approached the two delicate young stage passengers. They clung to one another.

"We just came for the gold," he repeated impatiently.

"No blood!" Annabella breathed.

"I detest the sight of it!" Aaron told her. He reached for the locket about the girl's chest.

"Oh, please, don't steal it! It's all we've got left from our mother."

"Your mother?" Aaron asked.

"Yes, our parents passed away. We've come out west to homestead now. We've so very little. Steal anything—but not the locket, please," Anthony said.

"We don't steal from homesteaders," Aaron told him. He aimed his gun up at the driver. "Back in your seat, old-timer," he warned. "You're going to want to get these two safely into town, right?"

The driver scurried back to his seat. "Hurry there, the guard will probably be limping along any minute now," Aaron told Ann.

She gave him a withering glance over the kerchief tied to just below her eyes. She was doing the work; unbelievably, he was still staring at Annabelle.

"Let's go!" she told Aaron as she finished.

"Good luck homesteading!" Aaron told the pair. By then, Ann had the saddlebags thrown back up atop their horses. She leapt up on her own. Aaron leapt up beside her.

Just in time.

There were horses coming. A number of horses. Ann could feel the movement of them coming first—

then she could see the riders just over the rise where she had been waiting for the stagecoach.

She didn't need to say a word to Aaron. They spun their own horses around and started to ride, hard. She didn't dare look his way; this was the first time they had ever come so close to having the law on top of them.

Yet even as they raced, Aaron cried out to her. "It's the sheriff!"

"Run!"

"They'll catch us."

"He can't ride as well as we can."

"He isn't alone."

"No one in town can ride as well—"

"McShane is with him, Annie!" Aaron cried.

She was so startled she might have toppled from her horse. And she had been so confident. She knew the ground here better than anyone; she knew how to slip back into town when she needed to go there, she knew how to ride out to the buttes and cliffs and disappear into the rocks. She had chosen her horses for their absolute speed at short distances, *but she had never counted on McShane pursuing her*. His horse would be just as fast.

"Annie, you've got to shoot!" Aaron shouted to her.

"Kill him?" she demanded, astonished.

"Of course not! Graze his horse!" Aaron replied.

What if she missed? What if her aim wasn't so perfect at this distance and speed?

"Annie!" Aaron shouted.

She let her mare fly along beside Aaron's mount with a free rein and twisted in the saddle. Looking back, she missed a beat when she saw that Aaron was right.

McShane was hot on their trail. His horse might have been a descendant of the winged Pegasus, it was racing so quickly behind them. She paused, loath to hit the magnificent creature.

"Ann, our necks are at stake!" Aaron called.

More than their necks. McShane was about to draw his pistol, she realized. She knew how fast he was. He could kill her. She could kill him.

She realized incredulously that he wasn't shooting. He meant to take them alive. He could have fired; he could have shot her seconds ago. He had chosen not to.

But he was closing the distance between them fast.

No more time. She fired into the dirt directly in front of McShane's flying horse. The dirt exploded into the animal's nose and eyes. To Ann's relief, the magnificent horse reared and flailed the air.

McShane didn't fall, but held tight, steadying the horse. Yet while he controlled his mount, the sheriff came around him on his white gelding. Ann fired again, this time knowing she was going to have to take a drastic measure. She grazed the sheriff's shoulder, forcing him to fly down from his mount. McShane had to stop his own flight then, or else ride over the fallen sheriff. McShane reined in, stopping for Bickford, and Ann and Aaron were on their way at a breakneck speed.

They circled out of town until dusk, holing up at a ramshackle hut on some dusty, sage-speckled land Eddie had once tried to homestead. They buried their stolen gold, trying to determine how they were going to manage to use it to buy Grainger new stock. Aaron talked Ann into letting him return to town for her clothing and a fresh horse, so she could then go on back to Grainger's place rather than to the saloon.

The hour she waited for him was hell. When he came back, she changed quickly into the clothing she had worn at the barn raising, all the while listening to his excitement and amusement while he told her what had gone on in town.

"That lovely young brother and sister duo raved about us!" he exclaimed. "They told everyone we're polite thieves. We should never be hanged—"

"And I'm sure the sheriff agreed!" Ann said testily.

"He's fine, by the way," Aaron assured Ann. "You gave him a flesh wound, nothing more."

"Thank God. But we were too close today. Aaron, we were holding up a stage, not going a-courting!"

"Pardon me, cousin! You are the mastermind behind our criminal activities and you were the one who was late!"

"I have a husband to watch out for—"

"Who nearly caught you today, Ann," Aaron said, soberingly.

"Nearly. But he didn't. And we got the gold. Weatherly's cowhands will be furious, and he must be running just a little bit dry on the guns he hires as well!"

"So when does it end, Annie?"

"Soon," she whispered. "Soon, I promise!"

"When?" he demanded. "Are you really going to be able to go up to him one day and shoot him in cold blood?"

"Aaron, you weren't there! You can't really know what it was like, what he did."

"But I know you."

"I've got to get back to Grainger's quickly," she told him. "We'll talk about the future later. I still have to get through today!"

"All right, Ann," Aaron said wearily. He studied her unhappily. "But I am worried about you."

"Our danger is the same."

"You're a woman."

"Aaron, that doesn't make any difference—"

"But it does!" he told her, lifting a hand when she would have argued more. "We're doing this for a cause, cousin, and I see that cause. But we came close to hanging today, and I wonder if we aren't risking too much."

"Aaron—"

"You can win arguments too easily, Annie, so I won't argue with you now."

"You had fun today!" she accused him.

He grinned. "Yeah, I did. But I'm still willing to quit while we're both still alive. Maybe McShane can change things."

"No one can change the past!" she assured him passionately, remembering her own thoughts earlier in the day.

"Let's get to Grainger's," Aaron said.

They rode back out to discover that the barn had been completed and that Dulcie was trying very hard to keep a calm front while panicking. She told Ann in a single breath just how terrified she had been when McShane had left, and how relieved she had been when riders had come back to Grainger's from town to inform them all excitedly that the stage had been robbed, the passengers were safe—and the money was gone.

"Ann, this is getting terrifying—" Dulcie began.

"Hush!" Ann begged her. "Let's go back together now. I promise, we'll discuss it all soon."

It was late when the wagon reached the stables. Cocoa came rushing out to greet them. "Sugar, he's really wondering where you are!" she told Ann.

"Cocoa, has he been downstairs since he's been back?"

"Yes, why?" Cocoa demanded.

"I'll slip up the back way. I'll say that I came here and was resting."

"Go, then!" Dulcie told her. "Before he realizes

that the wagon is back and comes out to see if you're on it."

She nodded and leapt from the wagon and raced into the cellar. She tore up the stairs and threw open the hidden door—

And nearly tumbled back down the stairs.

He was there. McShane. Leaning against the wall beside the door, his arms crossed over his chest, waiting for her.

"Well, well, my love! Welcome home!" he told her, his voice deep and husky and full of barely leashed anger.

Instinct caused her to turn, ready to flee back down the stairs.

"I think not!" he said softly.

And he was right. She had moved quickly, but so had he, his fingers threading into her hair. She cried out, his hold eased, but it was too late. His hands fell to her shoulders and she was spun around to meet the coal-dark and glittering fury and challenge in his eyes.

"I think not, my love!" he repeated.

And she was dragged inexorably into his arms and into the room.

The hidden door closed with an ominous click of finality behind her.

Thirteen

*H*aving given Ann what warning she could, Cocoa decided to skirt around to the front of the building and come back in through the front doors. She wasn't expecting to find Angus Donahue seated on the railing, chewing on a long blade of grass in the moonlight, watching, waiting.

He was always watching, Cocoa thought, a quiet yet indomitable presence at all times due to his sheer size. Bullets could cut down any man, Cocoa well knew. But there was much more to Angus Donahue than bulk. She'd never seen him pull a gun, and she was sure he was a careful man—even in the West, the passions that had ignited the recently ended war still simmered, and there were plenty of vengeful folks ready to string up a black man for just about any infraction of any rule. But she knew just as surely that Angus wasn't a coward, either. He was an intelligent, educated black man, still a rarity these days. The Emancipation Proclamation had supposedly brought freedom to folks of color; Cocoa believed with all her heart that freedom was something that they were still going to be fighting for in the years to come and that the fight was going to be a long one. And if it was ever to be won, guns and knives weren't going to do it, education was going to be the weapon.

She liked Angus well enough—liked him a lot, actually. But he was always *watching*, waiting to catch Ann or any of Ann's old friends in some act. No one was going to get caught because of her.

"Well, big man," she said flatly, standing dead still rather than trying to slip on by him, "just what are you waiting for?"

"Not waitin' for anything," he told her. He lifted a hand to the night sky. "Just watching the moon."

"Umm," Cocoa murmured, and she did start to walk by him.

"You made a wrong call this time," he said softly after her.

She paused, spinning around. "What are you talking about?"

He shrugged. "McShane knows about the secret stairs and false doors."

She arched a brow at him. If she'd learned anything in life, it was how to keep a poker face. "So?"

"You're all up to something dangerous."

"Mr. Donahue, we didn't build the saloon, you know. Ann and Eddie McCastle bought the place off a speculator who wanted to move back east."

"But that door came in handy, didn't it? Folks could swear that Annie McCastle had just gone upstairs, that she was in her own room in the saloon, when things were happening elsewhere, right?"

"I don't know what you mean."

"Sure you do."

She shook her head. "You go ahead and suspect all you think you need to suspect, Mr. Donahue. There's nothing you're going to get from me."

"Unless I decide to come up and see you sometime?" he inquired politely.

"Maybe. Depends on my mood," Cocoa said coolly.

He smiled, rising. "I won't be up to see you. Now, on the other hand, you're welcome to come up and see me. But once you see me, you won't be seeing anyone else."

Cocoa backed away from him, surprised, amused, challenged, and—to her vast astonishment—excited.

She lifted her chin. "No one tells me what to do. Not anymore."

"There's telling, and then there's telling," he said softly, a curiously gentle light in his dark eyes.

She was startled to feel the sting of tears at the back of her eyes. "There was a war," she reminded him. "Black folks are free now. I'm free. I'll never be anything else."

"I don't ever want anyone who is anything else," he told her.

"I . . . I need to think about things!" she said, slipping by him. She hurried into the saloon and strode to the bar, asked Harold for a brandy and sipped it quickly. She felt a warmth at her side and turned, immediately aware that Angus had followed her in. He was smiling. He tipped his hat to her and ordered a beer. He managed to stand a little closer to her. "You're just trying to seduce me from keeping my mind on my work," he told her.

"Me?" she inquired haughtily. "Mr. Donahue, I believe you're trying to seduce me from being a good and loyal employee. And just what is your work, by the way?"

"Peacekeeper," he told her.

She looked him up and down. "Peacekeeper. A fine fellow like you, a black man who sounds as if he walked right out of one of the white man's fancy eastern schools."

"Miss Cocoa, it seems you're the more interesting

of the two of us. You just told me you'd been a slave, and for a slave, woman, you seem to have a mighty fine command of the white man's language just the same.''

She smiled. Then she lifted her glass to him and spoke with just a shade of irony in her voice. ''My mother, so I was told, might have been the descendant of a Nubian princess. So the story went. Black or no, she was reputed to have been a great beauty, and she must have been, because she came to the attention of my father—the bastard who owned the plantation where he copulated and procreated where he would. Needless to say, the act never did spawn any paternal feelings within the man, but incest was not among his many sins, so rather than make mistresses of his own daughters, he sold us at very good prices to the highest bidders among his friends. I lived with an Irish flutist, a pompous politician, a mathematician, and the young scholarly son of a neighboring plantation owner, who was mainly responsible for my education. Poor Mr. Lincoln might have freed us on paper a few years back, but it took the end of the war to make it fact. Not that I had to go quite that long,'' she murmured. She lifted her chin. ''But I didn't go quite that long because I happened to be for sale in a small Texas town when Eddie came through town with Annie, who was horrified by the steel chain around my neck. She made Eddie buy me, Eddie turned around and freed me, and I followed Eddie, Annie, and Dulcie out here. Now you think about it. You can talk to me, taunt me, quiz me, impale me, and I am never going to tell you anything about that woman she doesn't want you to know, understand?''

To Cocoa's astonishment, he smiled, a smile that was tender, gentle, and not at all the response she'd expected to her challenge. He reached out, brushing her cheek with the big pad of his thumb. "You're just like a cactus, baby. All those thorns! But out in the desert, the juice can be mighty sweet."

"What happens when you're not in the desert?"

"Then you have to pick through the thorns because cactus can be a delicacy no matter where you might happen to be."

Cocoa laughed. The sound, to her own ears, was husky, sweet, sensual. Real. It was him. She didn't think that she'd ever felt this way with anyone, and she hadn't thought that she could. She'd been convinced that she'd seen the world, known every kind of man there could be. And she had endured a million kind of lessons. Bitter ones from her father; painful ones from the young scholar who'd had a cruel streak when his mind hadn't been on his books. Or perhaps he'd learned a few of his cruelties from his books—he'd had enough of them, and illustrated at that. She'd been sorry for the gentle flutist. There had been men who had taken her too roughly, men who had needed to be taken instead. Men who had beaten her, men who had craved her. But since she had come here, she'd had only the men she had chosen to take. Nice cowboys. Fast in the saddle, a lot of them. Men like Joey Weatherly. Charming. Quick to laugh, quick to pay, quick to leave. She'd known all kinds of men.

But never in her life had she just laughed this way with a man. Never had a man made her feel so good, and he had barely touched her.

"Is Cocoa your real name?" he asked her.

She nodded. "The only one I know. And how about you? Angus Donahue?"

"Don't I look Irish to you?"

She started to laugh again, softly. Scar walked up behind her. He wasn't a bad old cowboy. "Cocoa, want to, uh, talk?" he asked her.

Angus arched a brow at her, and she wondered just exactly what he had meant when he'd said *Once you see me* . . .

This was her livelihood. Not that Annie would ever throw her out on the streets, but . . .

"Cocoa, you coming to see me?" Angus asked very softly. He smiled again. That tender smile that was full of challenge. She had thought that she'd learned everything, but it seemed as if he meant to teach her things she had never dreamed of. His teasing words couldn't matter all that much; she wasn't exactly marrying him or anything . . .

"Scar, honey, I'm busy at the moment," she said sweetly.

"Scar, sir, she's busy for life," Angus corrected. He swept her up into his arms and started for the stairs. Startled, Cocoa stared into his eyes and started to laugh. Good Lord, but he was a handsome hunk of a man. She'd been doing too much talking. She had to find out a few things about him.

Things like . . .

He was strong, very strong. He carried her so easily. His face was strikingly handsome; his bearing and speech were so dignified, his eyes were full of pride. He hadn't ever been anyone's slave, or had he? She wanted to know. She wanted to know everything about him, everything.

He'd taken a small room in the attic. There wasn't much in it. A bed—thankfully, a fine, big one—a chest of drawers, a washstand, a lamp table. Her own room was much nicer, but . . .

This was different.

This was his. His duster hung on a hook, a few books were scattered on chairs. His shaving mug and razor sat atop the chest of drawers. She saw little things that told her something about him. And she was suddenly so hungry for that knowledge.

"Angus—" she began. "What about you—"

"Kiss me, Cocoa. None of it will matter."

She lifted her chin, laughing. "I've kissed dozens of men, Angus Donahue. That's not going to sway me from any talk!"

But he laid her down on the bed and leaned over her, the bulk of his body seeming to encompass hers. He kissed her, and he tasted of whiskey and leather, and she set her hand upon his cheek, testing the texture of it, marveling at the strength and warmth within him, and the gentle way he managed to touch her all the same. She wanted to know so much. . . .

"Angus," she whispered against his lips.

"Yes?"

"I . . ."

She pressed her mouth to his again. Felt his arm encircling her. Felt him bear down against her. Felt her clothing begin to melt away.

"Angus, I want to . . . "

His hands were upon her. Huge hands with brown fingers, slightly lighter than her own flesh. His palms, his fingertips, were slightly calloused. Rough, gentle, rough, tender against her flesh. Playing over her breast. Teasing the dark, dusky rouge of her nipple. Different, so very different. She moaned softly.

"I want . . . "

"Yes?" he whispered.

"I want . . . "

It was all she could murmur, all that she could think.

"I want, I want, I want . . . "

She wanted what it was that she was miraculously getting. She wanted what was so . . . different.

And somewhere within it all, she finally understood. Ah, yes, she'd been so jaded; she'd done it all, had every kind of man. She'd been touched again and again . . .

She had never made love before. And that was what he did. Made love to her. With every whisper, every gesture.

Every passing moment . . .

"Ian, you can just let go of me!" Ann finally managed to grate out. She'd been scrambling frantically for words for the longest time, it seemed, staring into his eyes, feeling the bite of his fingers on her arms.

"I don't think so."

"Why?" She had to quit shaking. If only he hadn't startled her so by being there; if only she'd had the smallest warning.

"Where have you been?"

"At a barn raising with you."

He shook his head. "Try again."

"I came back here—"

"So why were you sneaking up the back stairs?"

"I wasn't sneaking—"

"Oh, God, yes you were. And you've been using that staircase to come and go from this place since you took it over, am I right?"

"It's a staircase! That's all—"

"Amazing! You chose not to share it with me!"

"I don't remember choosing to share—"

"Ah, but you did! You only do what you choose to do, remember? You chose to marry me!"

She went still. She hadn't seen him this angry yet, in control, but just barely, lashing back at her so quickly she was beginning to feel as if her knees were made of dissipating muck. She had to get herself under control, he knew nothing at all except that there was a stairway here, and that was it!

Or was it? *Why hadn't he fired at her today?*

"It's been an ungodly long day—"

"Indeed, I am waiting to hear just how long."

"Well, you will have to wait a very long time because—" She broke off with a startled cry because he had wrenched her close to him with such sudden vehemence. His fingers threaded into her hair on either side of her head, his palms pressing against her skull.

"What do I have to do to make you understand you are playing a dangerous game here?"

"I am playing no games!" she shrieked, slamming her fists against his chest. "I am playing no games!"

She was up, off her feet, flying it seemed. She landed hard upon her bed and she rebounded quickly, frightened by the violence in him. But he had not followed her. His back was to her, straight and stiff as a poker, broad shoulders taut and squared. He swore explosively, then spun on her, striding toward her with swift, menacing steps.

"No!" she screamed, so unnerved by his mood that she responded with pure panic, leaping back against the bed.

To her surprise, he went dead still. His bronzed face was suddenly ashen, and his fingers clenched into fists at his sides. "Damn you!" he all but whispered. He turned again.

And without looking back, walked out of the room.

Ann exhaled on a long shaky breath, fighting a sudden rise of tears.

She closed her eyes, wishing that things could be different. Wishing that she didn't feel the pain the day had wrought upon her soul.

She had no choice but to follow the path she had created for herself!

When she closed her eyes, she could bring back the past. She could recall the last day she had seen her family alive. Her father had awakened, and since she hadn't opened her eyes, he hadn't realized that she was awake. He leaned over her just rousing her mother, his big hand splayed out upon her abdomen, rounded by the second child they all awaited with such sweet hope and pleasure.

"You're beautiful," he'd whispered.

Ann had heard her mother's soft chuckle. "I'm huge and cumbersome."

"But beautiful."

"You're beautiful, too, Joshua. Do you know that? You really are a beautiful man, inside and out. And I'm so sorry for being such a worrywort. I was awful to you, wasn't I? Nagging at you constantly after we'd both made our decisions to move when we did. We could have been further on our way if I'd just been willing to travel alone when some of the others dropped out of our party—"

"Jenny, it's fine. It was no good traveling alone. We'll be safer now, with a larger party."

"What time is it? We need to hurry! We don't dare slow those nice people down after they were kind enough to accept us into their group—"

"Jenny, it's all right! They're glad to have us, and we've plenty of time. Calm down! I want to make it to our western home before my son is born."

"We could have another daughter."

"And I will be delighted. My one little minx is such a pleasure and a beauty—and I'll bet she's listening right now, isn't she?" he teased suddenly, raising his voice.

"Minx, Pa?"

"Minx it is! But come here, give your old folks a big hug, and we'll get on our way!"

It was to be her last hug from either of them. It would be the last time she would feel the movement of promised life within her mother's stomach, tenderly touch the brother or sister who would never know what it was really like to live, to breathe fresh air, feel the sunlight . . .

Even as she thought it, the scene in her mind's eye shifted again.

She heard the barrage of gunfire. Saw her mother go down. She heard her father, screaming her name, reaching out to her.

Falling, dying . . .

Then she was running herself, ready for death, but hell-bent on revenge. There was the awful pain exploding in her own head . . .

Nearly dying.

Living.

Wanting to die.

Surviving because it was a fight. Learning to want to live again because she owed a debt to those who had died.

Ann's eyes flew open. Tears were streaming down her cheeks and she wiped them away. She couldn't bear the memories. At the moment, she had to bear them. They were her strength. No matter what danger she fell into, no matter how hard things became, she had to go on.

Oh, God, no matter how angry Ian was with her, how disappointed he might be in her. No matter how he turned away from her.

She rolled over, pressing her pounding head into the pillows. *There had been good!* But amidst all of the pain and cruelty, there had been good, she reminded herself. Cloud Walker had been a good man. He had cared for her so deeply. He had given her so much. He had never really understood her determination to learn to shoot with precision, but he had been the one to teach her about her guns. He had patiently taken her out day after day, humoring her desire at first, taking pride in her as his teaching brought out her natural talent for accuracy in her aim. She wondered if he had known that she had loved him in return.

And then there had been Eddie. She could still see his dear, grizzled face, white-whiskered, ruddy, smiling, when he'd come to the Pawnee camp, when he'd come for her. "Poor orphaned lass, needin' a home now among her own kind. Ah, and such a lovely wee thing!" he'd said, seeing her first in the camp. He'd stretched out his arms to her, his heart in his eyes. "Don't cry for nothin' now, dear child! Eddie's here, and I'll not let anyone hurt ye now, I'm promisin' that, I am. We've not much between us but lots of heart and gumption, eh, lass? We'll make do, that we will!"

Eddie had been good. So very good. Offering her so much love—and then letting her dictate his life. The only time he'd ever failed her had been . . .

Gambling.

Oh, Eddie, I forgive you! she thought. I miss you. You were so often my strength because you knew the truth about how desperately I wanted to kill a man, and you still loved me! Eddie, I wish you were here!

Eddie wasn't there. She had lost him, and she had lost Cloud Walker, just as she had lost her family.

Now she had a husband. But she was losing him, too, because she simply wasn't able to hold on to him. Even if she had come to need him. Love him.

The past wouldn't allow her to do so.

She bit into her lip, determined to stop the tears that were flowing silently down her cheeks again. But they would not stop.

She realized that even though she cried for her past, she cried for her future as well.

Cash Weatherly looked into the blue eyes of his oldest son, Carl. His palm fell flat upon the mantel with a startling thud, then slammed against his son's cheek with such force that he drew blood. "We lost the payroll, son. Those damned fools sent it out from the city with one stinking guard, and you weren't there when the stagecoach approached this wretched town!"

Carl Weatherly took a step back from his father, wiping the blood from his split lip with the back of his hand. Something inside him churned sickly. "It wasn't my fault! I was working on the books like you told me—"

"Don't back talk me, son! Don't back talk me! Not one of us fools seems able to know where a stage is and when it's coming in but those damned thieves can catch it!"

"Pa, you didn't tell us—"

"What are you, stupid?" Cash seethed with disgust, then raised his hands to heaven. "Maybe I can't fault the company. My own cattle payment goes out with two of my best men—"

"But you can fault me, right, Pa?" Carl said.

Cash's hand whipped out again with a staggering speed. Carl wasn't quick enough to avoid the blow. The older man raised his hand in a fist before his son, shaking it. "All these years, all this work! It's for you, boy. You and your brothers. With the good Lord's help I did His bidding throughout a bloody war, took the spoils of that war, and made an empire here. Now, because of the incompetence of those around me, I am being robbed blind!"

Carl, weary of being struck, refrained from the words that slipped just to the edge of his tongue. *Maybe the good Lord wasn't quite so pleased with Cash Weatherly as Cash Weatherly might like to think. Maybe the good Lord thought that the spoils of war had been wrongly taken, just as so much of their cattle was wrongly taken, and their property wrongly taken.*

"You're the oldest, boy, you fought hard in that war," Cash told him.

Jenson, across the room, wanting to defend his older brother somehow, spoke up. "We all fought hard in the war, Pa. Even Joey."

"Where the hell is Joey? That boy is never around the house anymore."

"I think he's back in town, Pa," Meg said, coming into the large ranch home's grand parlor to set coffee and brandy on a table. Like Jenson, she was sorry for Carl. Their father just wanted his oldest boy to be like him, no, to be him, so it seemed. And poor Carl had spent his life doing his father's errands, his father's bidding, trying to please him. Somehow, their father just couldn't be pleased. Then there were all of these robberies, and such strange things happening, like Grainger's place being burned down.

"He's in that damned saloon!" Cash swore.

"Maybe," Jenson, a paler version of Carl, agreed quickly. Anything at the moment to get the old boy off his tantrum. Next thing, he'd be thrashing the fire poker around at all of them, spouting it was God's right for a man to chastise his children.

"It should have been mine," Cash muttered suddenly. He seemed to have forgotten Carl; forgotten even the fact that he had lost his entire payroll to thieves. He wandered to the heavily stuffed leather sofa before the massive hearth and sank into it. "It should have been mine!" he roared, slamming his fists against the leather now. "Except for that renegade Reb bastard, it would have been mine."

"Pa," Meg said uneasily, "the place always belonged to Eddie and Ann McCastle. And if Eddie hadn't gambled—"

"But Eddie did gamble," Cash said in a low voice. "And then Eddie died. And it should have been mine. And the—" He broke off suddenly, staring at his daughter. "Go upstairs, Meg. Go on upstairs, it's late."

"But Pa—"

"Go!" he ordered.

Meg came to stand behind him, planting a kiss on top of his head. He gazed at her with his very pale blue eyes, searching out her face. "You go on up."

"Fine. Carl, Jenson, you come soon, too, promise?"

"Right, Meg," Jenson agreed.

Carl was having trouble talking. His jaw was swelling from his father's blows.

Cash watched his daughter disappear up the grand stairway he'd built into the house. He waited until her door closed, then he stared into the burning fire before him.

"It should have been mine, and that damned yellow-haired vixen should have been mine as well! And if that half-breed bastard hadn't showed up when he did, I could have danced right in, swept her out in the night, and no one would have been the wiser as to how she came to be with me. She'd have made up for the cattle gold stolen that day."

His strike against the leather of the sofa that time was so hard it made his sons flinch. Carl was glad his father had struck the sofa and not his face.

"Did you hear me? The *whore* should have been mine!"

"Pa, what would you want with her?" Jenson said. "It's not like you might have married her the way the Reb did—"

"She was meant to be mine."

"Pa, now, Joey knows the place and he says she was Eddie's daughter, that she was never one of the girls, she was always ladylike, working the bar, singing, never going upstairs with any of the men. Maybe she's not at all what you thought—"

"Evil!" Cash muttered.

"But, Pa—"

"Evil. She latches onto a man, makes him think he needs her. Well, if he gets his hands on her once, then he'll know. He'll be able to wash those hands off her, shake her from his mind."

"Pa—" Jenson said. "She's married to that Reb."

"That's one Reb that needs to rot in hell. By God, that's it, I didn't finish my job with those slaveholding demons of the devil's dominions!"

He stood again suddenly, looking around the room wildly.

"Pa, this ain't like you!" Jenson said uneasily.

Cash arched a brow at his son and breathed in and out deeply. "You're right, boy. You're right. We've had setbacks; we've had failures. And I'll be damned if there isn't someone out there trying to bring me to ruin! But I have ridden at the head of God's own forces of glory. I've ridden against slave-beating Confederates, pagan redmen, and the dregs of the West. And you know what, boys? I ain't going to be beaten by two-bit bandits and some cocky half-red Reb boy running from the fall of the South! The Reb, boys, is going down, down to the devil's dominion where he belongs. And that blond bitch of Satan is going to rue the day she didn't fall on her knees and beg my mercy."

Jenson glanced uneasily at Carl. Cash was a careful and cunning man. Even when he explained things to them. They deserved the land, they worked the land, they were God-fearing white men reaching out to fulfill a manifest destiny for the country. Men like Grainger needed to be burned out; they were weak. They were bad for the country. The mines they had seized now belonged to the strong; they were creating an empire.

But there was something about this . . .

"She's a witch!" Cash swore suddenly. "Things have been going right to hell since she came here with her smooth voice and her nose in the air and those eyes of hers that just seem to heat the blood inside a man."

"Now, Pa—" Carl tried.

"Boy, you obey me!" Cash snapped. "Before God, if thine own eye offend ye, pluck it out! You listen to me and listen good. There's something evil in that saloon and I'm going to root it out! You're with me, boy, or you're my enemy!"

Carl Weatherly suddenly rubbed his hands together.

There was blood on them. Lots of blood. Blood from his face. The blood of others that would never wash away. He hadn't ridden with his father often during the war, but the few times he had had been enough. He'd half killed a miner in the night, and he'd been with the party that had shot down a reluctant neighbor. All in his father's service. But then, it had always been that way. You were with him—

Or he killed you. It didn't matter that you were his own blood.

Now Cash wanted the woman. He had wanted her. A long time. Obsessively.

Cash had been on a set course all of his life. Now he was just a little more hair-trigger over that course.

"There's going to be a way to trap them all," Cash said softly. "All of them. Whatever is going on is going on in that saloon."

"Pa, don't forget, the sheriff thinks you're a good man, a victim in all this, a war hero—"

"The sheriff is right," Cash snapped. "And his

opinion isn't going to change any. This has gone on long enough. I'm going to catch the thieves who've been robbing me blind and see that they're hanged for it. And I'm going to get me that Reb and the girl, too, when I do it, and if I don't kill the Reb right off, I'll see that he hangs, and if the girl doesn't die right away, well then maybe she will learn to change her ways and bow down before me. But it's going to happen, boys. The trap is going to be set into motion, and I don't care who all else goes down with it, you understand?"

"Yes, Pa," Jenson said.

"Carl?"

"Yeah, Pa."

"Don't nobody breathe a word to Joey. I don't want to slip a noose around my own blood if I don't have to."

Carl and Jenson nodded, both wondering if Cash would even let Joey hang. He seemed to have a soft spot for his youngest son—the one who somehow managed to keep a distance from him.

Yet even as they wondered about Joey, they looked at one another, both suddenly certain that he wouldn't hesitate to shoot them both down.

"Come here, close, and listen," Cash commanded, entirely in control again, his eyes flashing, his mind turning. "Listen to what I've got to say; this has to work exactly. You know—" He paused suddenly.

"What is it, Pa?" Jenson asked.

"Strange, I just had a feeling. Like I'd seen that half-breed Reb somewhere before."

"Maybe all half-breeds look alike, Pa. There's enough of the poor bastards in the West."

"Maybe." Cash stared into the flames. "Maybe. And maybe it won't matter none when he's gone straight to hell. Still . . . Never mind, let's get on with this. Listen, listen well! He's going down, and I'm going to be a senator when the territory becomes a state."

"But, Pa—" Jenson tried.

"Son, this is the land of opportunity. And I mean to seize opportunity."

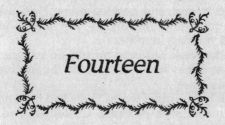

Fourteen

Ann stared up at the ceiling of her bedroom, wondering why she couldn't sleep tonight, amazed by the misery that seemed to weigh her down.

It had been a week since Ian had argued with her furiously, thrown her down—and walked out on her. Never to return. At least so far.

The week had passed quickly enough.

But it had been torture nonetheless. She'd seen him by day, like a familiar stranger. She'd watched him talk with others, laugh with others. She'd felt the painful curl of what she now knew was jealousy creeping through her, taking root in her heart, and still she had never thought that he was, perhaps, sleeping elsewhere. Maybe she didn't want to believe it; maybe she was painfully naive. The worst had been when she had seen him over at the dry goods store, out on the walkway, talking with Meg Weatherly. Meg had been all smiles, all enthusiasm. And he had been . . .

Flirtatious, she told herself. He'd smiled back at Meg, complimenting her, making her laugh in return.

Ann groaned and tossed and pulled her pillow over her head. A week! He'd touched her as he'd brushed by her, and nothing more. He'd asked no more questions, demanded no more answers. Wanted nothing from her. . . .

Yes, the week had been torture. So strange. It was almost as if they were waiting, and the waiting made everyone tense.

It had been a quiet week. There had been no burnings, no robberies. Nothing. Customers had come, played their cards, swallowed their whiskey, and gone home.

Joey had spent time in the saloon. Dulcie had kept him company, but she had been subdued each time she sat with him, talked with him.

Cocoa had been quiet. Incredibly quiet. In fact, she was barely visible.

McShane had been . . .

Distant. Gone often during the day, and at night, she didn't know where he went either. She'd stayed up as long as she could each and every night, but eventually she'd fallen asleep. Sometimes, he must have come to the room at night; he kept his clothes there, and he did change them. She saw him in the saloon at night, dealing poker hands, watching what was going on with those intense eyes of his.

Thursday night had brought a large delegation from Circle Z, Weatherly's massive ranch, but though there had been more gunslingers than cowboys in the group, it had remained a quiet night despite the tension. McShane had taken the measure of each man who had arrived, Ann was certain. There had been ten in the group; Carl and Jenson Weatherly along with the others, including Bad Bull Marlin, who'd gained a reputation during the war with his guerrilla tactics for the abolitionist factions. Then there was Tyler Grissom, a gunfighter out of Kansas City, and Josh Mason, who had supposedly taken down a band of ex-Reb outlaws just outside of Houston at the war's end. They were a dangerous group, but there hadn't been any trouble. Not even when Cocoa had pulled away from one of them, making an excuse when he would have walked her upstairs.

She'd known where McShane had been that night. He'd stayed downstairs. Angus had sat up with him, along with Ralph, and the twins had maintained posts out on the porch. Ann had tried to talk to Ian before he sat down for his watch, but he hadn't even admitted to her that his gang of five was on the lookout for Weatherly's gunslingers. He'd been as curt with her as he'd been all week, and if she hadn't left when she did, she was certain that he might have exploded.

As he had tonight. She'd stayed downstairs very late, watched while the cowboys came and left, watched as Bad Bull Marlin came again in Carl Weatherly's company, just sitting there smiling his way through a poker game where he lost far more often than he won. Then one of the men had asked Dulcie if he might talk privately with Ann and Dulcie had run straight to McShane. When Ann had started across the room in all innocence to talk with the strange cowboy, she'd found herself wrenched halfway back across the room, in McShane's fierce hold as he drew her toward the stairway.

"What are you doing—" she began angrily. She was ready to have it out with him, ready to fight. Anything, anything that would let her touch him again, draw a reaction from him again, break the awful tension and silence.

"Get upstairs."

"Why?"

"It's safer."

"Safer? What are you expecting?"

"Nothing. But I want you upstairs."

"Listen, McShane, I do own forty percent—"

He swore, drowning out her words. He didn't sweep her romantically off her feet; he threw her over his shoulder and all but clumped up the stairs with her, then threw her down on her bed. She'd leapt up like a tigress, flying across the room as he left, slamming her fists into his back.

He spun on her, his eyes narrowed. "Don't even think about talking to any strange men down there, do you hear me?"

"I was only going to talk—"

"Who the hell knows what's going on?"

"I know that I was only going to talk. Maybe—"

"Maybe what?"

Maybe she would have found something out about what was going on at the Weatherly ranch. What had happened when Cash hadn't paid his cowboys all the money that was due? How could he afford to hire these wretched men from other places?

"Nothing."

"Maybe you would have preferred his company to mine? A nice handsome white boy?"

She struck out at him but he reached out and caught her wrist, coal fire in his eyes. And he plucked her up and threw her back, and when she tried to rise, he pressed her down again, and when she struggled, he straddled her, pinning her where she lay. She met the fire and the anger in his eyes, and still she felt herself trembling, wanting him. Missing the warmth he'd brought her at night. She ached so badly. Both to be touched and to be cherished. Oh, God, she needed her freedom from him so badly. She tried to move, and then thought that he was going to curl his fingers around her throat and thrust her down again.

"Half-breed bastard!" she'd cried out, fighting tears. "Am I your prisoner here?"

"For the next hour. Sweet Jesu, Ann, it's night!

You've the precious sanctity of your room returned to you. Go to sleep!"

"But—"

"Damn you, leave it be!" he thundered. His hold on her was so tight she nearly cried out. He seemed to realize he was all but crushing her and released her.

"McShane—"

"What?" he snapped.

She bit her lip. She'd been about to tell him that she could probably outshoot every man in the saloon.

"Go!" she breathed. "Go!"

He obliged her.

An hour, he had told her. Well, an hour had come and gone. She tossed on the bed again, trying to tell herself for the thousandth time that she should be relieved that McShane had walked out when he had. And since their argument a week ago, he hadn't plagued her anymore with questions she couldn't answer. She should just be so damned pleased with herself. He would leave her be.

But she wasn't relieved and she wasn't pleased, she was miserable. She just kept seeing his face in her mind's eyes, seeing the strange fire and fury in his eyes and wondering what lived within his own heart and mind. She'd been lying awake every night for a week. She just wasn't going to do it anymore.

"You're mad!" she told herself aloud.

And maybe she was. But she got up and walked to her bedroom door and listened. It was quiet below. She couldn't hear the clink of a single glass. She looked at the clock on her dresser and saw that it was nearly five in the morning. Even the hardiest of her patrons had finished talking about one another and everything else in town and gone home for what remained of the night.

After all, it was now the Sabbath day.

Barefoot, in her white nightgown, she slipped out into the hallway. Dulcie's door was closed, as was Cocoa's. For an awful moment she wondered if her husband hadn't wanted to be behind one of those doors, then she forced herself to move on toward the main stairway.

She tread down it very quietly.

The saloon was at rest.

The glasses had been washed and hung; the bar was wiped down, the tables were clean, the floors had been swept, the spittoons had been rolled out for a washing in the morning. The piano sat empty. In the hearth that ran half the length of the far wall, a dying fire just barely burned.

And there was Ian, sitting before it. She walked very softly behind him, thinking that perhaps he slept. But she hadn't come very far before he asked, "Annie, what are you doing down here? I told you to stay upstairs."

She went still, then she walked around in front of him. He was eased back in his chair at an angle, held there by one of the support beams. He hadn't been drinking, just watching the fire. He pushed back his hat, his dark hair framing the contours of his face. Ann felt a strange tightening within her, longing to reach out, to touch his face, to curl into his lap. Distance from him was exactly what she needed; yet the distance hurt.

"You said for an hour."

"I said to go to sleep."

"I couldn't. I had to come to . . . see where you were," she told him.

"Well, you've seen," he said quietly.

She waited a moment, then asked, "Why?"

"Why what?"

"Why do you keep—staying away?"

He stared at her curiously. Then he sighed, easing the chair down, staring harder into the flames. "So that I don't throttle you," he said. "So that I don't want to hold you or shake you. So that I don't become frustrated and try to drag information out of you. So that I don't lose my temper."

"You lose your temper all the time," she reminded him. "It never bothered you before—last Saturday."

He glanced at her, then hesitated a minute. Then he spoke very softly. "Lots of things bother me," he reminded her. "It bothered me when you screamed that day I woke you when you had fallen asleep in the chair. You'd seen me. You'd seen my face. So, now sometimes I stay away so that you don't look at me with such horror because you see the face of a Sioux."

"What?" she gasped, astonished and confused.

"Sioux," he repeated. "Remember, you did call me a half-breed just a while ago."

"You accused me of much worse! I was angry; I just threw out any words that came into my mind," she whispered.

He stared at her. "But I understand. Dulcie told me you'd been a captive of the Pawnee for several years. I know something about the Pawnee, and some of their practices can make the greatest warriors among my grandfather's people seem tame in comparison."

"Oh, God!" she gasped. "You think that—"

"Ann, if I'd known your aversion to red blood and the reasons, I'd not have forced this marriage on you. No matter what my determinations."

She didn't realize that she had moved; she must have. She was still so angry with him, so lost and so confused, but it didn't matter. She was down on her knees before his chair, her palms resting on his thighs, staring searchingly into his eyes. "My God, I don't believe this!"

"Ann, I definitely resemble my grandfather in some ways. I can see where you might wake with nightmares—"

"No!" she told him. "I—no. You don't cause me to wake with nightmares."

"You were a prisoner, right? Dulcie told me the truth."

She nodded. "Yes, yes, I was a captive and so was Dulcie. For more than four years. And poor Dulcie, oh, God! It was horrible for Dulcie. They killed everyone where she'd been living; they nearly killed her. But I wasn't badly treated—I mean, I saw horrible things, but I—" She gave up for a minute, at a loss to explain herself. He was watching her so intently. His hands covered hers then, his fingers taut. She was glad to be touching him again. She suddenly wanted to explain. She drew in a deep breath. "Actually, I'd seen worse than what the Pawnee had done by the time I was with them—"

"Where?"

"What?"

"Where? What happened to you? You said that you had seen worse than what the Pawnee had done. What happened, Ann?"

She swallowed hard. She hadn't realized how much of herself she might give away if she wasn't careful. She didn't want to fight, but she didn't dare tell him too much about the truth.

"I was . . . your usual captive," she lied quickly. Then she didn't have to lie. "My parents were killed."

"I'm sorry," he told her. His words were deep. Heartfelt. She swallowed again and nodded quickly. "The Pawnee could be cruel and very fierce, but when I had been among them for a very short time,

I learned that white soldiers had just come into their village. The white soldiers had slaughtered their women and children. I'd been hurt when they found me—"

"When they found you?"

"When they took me," she corrected herself quickly. "I had been knocked unconscious—I came to in time to see them raze a settlement and I was terrified at first. But I came under the protection of a war chief's son. Cloud Walker. He was a very fierce warrior, but a very good man. He made the others think that he slept with me to make certain I wouldn't be captured by the warriors in a neighboring village to be sacrificed in one of their ceremonies—"

"The morning star ceremony," he murmured.

She nodded again, moistening her lips. "The morning star ceremony. When I saw it, it was so horrible! But even then I knew that it was a religious rite to them."

"Tell me more about this Cloud Walker."

She shrugged again, then smiled. "I was afraid; I hated them all. Then I learned more about them; I lived with them. I met Pawnees I liked and Pawnees I didn't like. Cloud Walker was unique. He pretended that I was with him at night, but all he did was hold me. He was waiting for me to grow up. When the awful brave who had seized Dulcie was killed, she came under his protection as well. His sister taught me Pawnee ways and looked after me. They were both good to me; I didn't suffer at their hands, my only pain was in seeing the slaughter of others. I was young when I was taken; in a way, I grew up among them. You feel the same way about them as you would about anyone else. You care, you feel anger. In that time you have to laugh, and you have to feel some warmth. In the end, I knew them.

Their culture was different, but they were people just the same. Some were wise, some were foolish. But I wasn't—'' She broke off.

"Wasn't what?"

"I wasn't afraid of all Indians after I left the Pawnee, just the hostile ones."

"You saw my face, and you screamed."

"Because I'd been remembering, dreaming. Dreams can be so real. I was startled. But I don't—"

"Don't what?"

"I don't hate or fear what you are!" she whispered.

He was silent a moment.

"How did you come to settle in Coopersville? Why didn't Cloud Walker make you his wife? It sounds as if you cared for him."

She smiled. "I did. I suppose that I loved him in a way, but I felt like his little sister. Besides, he wound up involved with another white captive."

"Dulcie?"

She nodded.

"But then?"

"He caught a fever. And when he was dying, he asked his father to see that I was returned to the whites. Soon after that, Eddie McCastle came along to trade with the Pawnee, and he promised to look after me as if I were his own. And Eddie did just that. Except that I wasn't very young anymore by that time—I was nearly eighteen—and Eddie needed looking after almost as much as I did. And we had Dulcie, and the whole wide West before us—" She broke off. She couldn't go any further. She couldn't begin to explain now how she could never have hated the Pawnee the way she had learned to hate a certain white man.

"Come here," he said softly, drawing her up onto

his lap. She curled there very comfortably. His fingers smoothed her hair. It was free, golden in the firelight, falling long over her shoulders and onto her lap and seeming to entwine them together. "I'm glad you haven't an aversion to Indians in general," he said. "But you do have your share of bad memories. You did scream that night when you woke and saw my face."

"I told you—I was dreaming," she admitted. "For a moment there, the fear had rushed back. Ian, remember *your* dream. You know how bad a nightmare can be. But I swear to you—"

"I believe you."

"McShane?"

"Yes."

"You remind me of Cloud Walker." She smiled a little awkwardly. "A fierce warrior; a good man."

His jaw twisted slightly. "What makes you think I'm a good man?" he asked.

She shrugged. "I know it. Inside."

"Don't believe in me too deeply, Annie," he warned softly. "Not as a good man, at any rate. A fierce one, maybe. Fierce enough, I hope, to wage this battle with you. I will win, Ann. I will force you out of danger. If you'd only tell me—"

She shook her head, pressing her fingers against his lips. "I've told you everything that I'm going to tell you tonight. Except maybe . . ."

"Except?" he demanded, arching a brow high.

"Except that I do find you to be much more than tolerable," she said, surprised that she was blushing as she spoke.

"How much more?"

"Well, very tolerable."

"More than that," he insisted.

"Endurable?"

"More."

"Umm—pleasant."

"A meal is pleasant!" he said indignantly.

"Well, you're . . . "

"What?" he demanded.

"Exciting," she whispered.

"This is getting interesting. Do go on."

"You're pushing," she warned.

"Always push for what you want. Go on."

"You're . . . "

"Yes?"

"The most incredible sensation I've ever felt," she told him honestly.

A groan sounded from his throat, hoarse, husky. His arms tightened around her. He rose, his eyes locked with hers. His footsteps were swift as he brought her up the stairs and back to their room.

He pushed open the door, pressed it closed with his back. He stood her before the fire, lifting her chin to kiss her lips, then backing away. He set his fingers upon the tiny buttons of her long white gown, grew impatient, ripped a few, and drew the gown down from her shoulders to a white pool around her feet. His arms around her, he slipped to his knees before her, his head against the silky flesh of her stomach, holding her close for a moment. Her hands fell to his hair, stroking it, feeling the texture of it. For long moments she was amazed by the absolute tenderness with which he held her, so gentle, so lulling.

So swiftly changed. The most subtle movement of his head, the stroke of his hand, the thrust of his thumb, the wickedly sweet pressure of his lips, teeth, and tongue, unerringly intimate, confident of the very nub and heart of desire within her. Hot honeyeyed liquid seemed to sweep through her limbs, her veins, her muscles until all of her was a cauldron, and she could stand no more. She cried out, nearly falling. But he wouldn't let her go.

"No, no, my love," he whispered against her flesh. "More than tolerable . . ."

"Dear God!" she exclaimed, thinking she could bear no more of the hunger, the longing, and the aching that was so exquisitely sweet, so completely intimate, the way that he touched her, the wetness, the heat, the fire . . .

"Ian!"

She tried to escape, but she was drawn back. The world itself seemed to explode into shards of fire that burst around her and ripped through her. She was barely aware that she was down upon the rug, then keenly aware of the weight and force of his body, of the knifing fullness of his own searing brand of heat now driving within her, filling her, so that it all began again, the hunger, the searching, the desperate desiring. His body was one sleek ripple of fluid muscle and motion. His rhythm was hard and demanding, sweeping her along again at the breakneck speed of a storm, holding her, forcing her higher and higher. The blaze was an inferno; she was drenched with it, golden in its light, all but melded to him. Then again, the roar within her, the violent explosion of all the wild sweet hungers, and the fire was a sweet blaze of glory that wrapped around her and within her, burned to a blue light, ebbed in a rocketing series of tremors and smaller climaxes until she lay still again, her hair damp and entangled around his sleek, glistening shoulders and chest. They lay still for some time, then she rested her head upon his shoulder.

"The most incredible sensation I've ever felt," she whispered softly.

He rolled off of her suddenly, his dark eyes intense as he looked into hers. "God, yes!" he repeated vehemently. "The most incredible sensation. The most incredible." His arms encircled her, drawing her close to him. He fell silent. The fire in the hearth continued to crackle softly.

Now the silence, Ann thought, as she remembered the questions he had already asked, the answers she couldn't give. She let her fingers fall upon his hands where they lay around her. She held them tight. She longed to speak.

There was nothing she could say. He didn't know; he couldn't understand.

Her eyes closed. She was so very tired. And physically so sated. He was back with her. His warmth remained with her. His arms were around her. She was wrong to feel so elated. Her life would have been easier and less dangerous had she let the barriers rise higher and higher between them. But regardless of whether or not she'd been wrong to reveal so much of her past to him, she was content tonight. She could feel his chin on her head. His heat, the security of his hold about her. She felt herself begin to drift.

Yet even as she did so, she knew that he lay awake.

And wondered, and worried. She could feel the tension creeping back into him, the distance between them growing despite their physical closeness.

And the fear and dismay crept into her. *What if he caught her? What could she do? How could she stop?*

And the answer was painfully simple. It wasn't just for herself. It was for those she had loved, for the other innocents slaughtered. She was close now and she couldn't stop, she couldn't, she had lived most of her life for this, she had survived for this. And now, she couldn't stop. *She could not. Could not.*

No matter what the cost.

Fifteen

"**S**ir, this is a mighty fine saloon you're running here, but what kind of a whorehouse is it when all the girls in it keep gittin' hitched?" Scar demanded.

"Pardon?" Ian said. He was just coming down the stairs. God, he hadn't gotten a lot of sleep last night, but it had been a good night. Sweet Jesu, he'd not trade it for the world. The time he'd kept away from her had been torture. It had made her coming to him last night all the sweeter. She'd been everything he might have imagined and more; she'd opened to him, let him in. Sexually. It wasn't all that he wanted, but on one level, it sure as hell beat all else.

"I'm sorry, what now?" he repeated to Scar.

"Cocoa!" Scar announced.

"What about Cocoa?" Ian asked, and raised a brow when he saw her standing near the bar next to Angus. It was Sunday morning, and the bar was quiet. Dulcie was sipping coffee and talking with Harold, Ginger was standing by Aaron, who was playing the piano softly. He could hear Henri singing in the kitchen and talking with one of the maids. Likewise, the Yeagher twins were conversing from their rockers out on the porch where they had sat guard through half the night—Ian didn't really believe that Cash Weatherly would come charging the saloon, but then he was determined not to take chances. At the moment, Scar was the only one in or near the place who might be considered a customer, and he was actually much more of a fixture, Ian had decided.

"What about Cocoa?" he queried.

"Marriage!" Scar said with dismay.

"Well, I—" Cocoa began.

"She's marrying me," Angus announced. "Cocoa has consented to be my wife. She's marrying me right after the Sunday service; the Reverend has already agreed."

"Can he do that with our Cocoa?" Scar demanded.

"Well, Scar, seems if she agrees to it, he certainly can."

"Well, what kind of whorehouse is this?" Scar complained again.

"Maybe it will just have to be a saloon," Ian said.

"Everybody gettin' married!" Scar said again with disgust.

"I'm not!" Ginger volunteered. She leaned atop the piano then with a sigh, watching while Aaron ran his fingers over the keys. "Well, no one's asked me as of yet, anyway!" she murmured.

"Nor me, sweetie," Dulcie murmured. "Coffee, McShane?"

"Coffee sounds good," he said, staring at Angus and Cocoa with a smile as he walked by them.

"Married?" he said politely. "Don't you think you're moving a bit fast?"

"We're slow—seeing as who we've both been working for," Angus told him.

"Hmm. Maybe you've a point there," Ian acknowledged. "Does Ann know about this yet?"

Cocoa shook her head. "I didn't know myself until a half hour ago."

"Well, hell! This calls for champagne," Ian said. "Harold, we've got some back there."

"It's Sunday morning," Harold reminded him.

"And we'll be drinking to a godly blessing, my good man."

Harold grinned and headed to the cellar for the champagne. Ann came down the stairs then. There was a touch of hesitance in her eyes when they brushed his. He smiled. Her lashes fell over her cheeks, and she smiled as well.

"Champagne!" Harold called, coming up the steps.

She glanced at Ian, frowning. He laughed, thinking she was afraid he might have shared their evening with the lot of them.

"There's going to be a wedding, Annie," he said.

Her brow shot up. "Who is getting married?"

"Cocoa," Dulcie supplied.

"Cocoa and—Angus!" she gasped. "Oh, my God, I didn't even know, I didn't suspect—"

"Well, you all are just damned stupid then!" Scar exploded with a shake of his head. "Cocoa ain't shown a lick of interest in another fellow all week. She's barely been generous enough with her time to bring a thirsty fellow a beer. She's been all wrapped up with this fellow you brought in, Mr. McShane."

"Sorry, Scar," Ian said politely, amusement flickering in his eyes.

"Next thing you know it will be Dulcie. Then Ginger there. Then what will you have?"

"I guess a restaurant and bar," Ian told him.

Scar snorted, and started for the door.

"Don't you want some champagne?" Ian called after him.

"Champagne ain't what I came fer!" Scar called back, still disgruntled.

Ginger convulsed into a fit of laughter. Dulcie poured the champagne, and then helped Harold pass the glasses around. "Cheers!" she said, clinking her glass with Ian's. He watched her, knowing she was genuinely happy for Cocoa but genuinely miserable herself. She deserved more, he thought.

Ann was hugging Cocoa. "My God, what a surprise."

"I'm still astounded," Cocoa agreed. Ann drank down a glass of champagne in one swallow. Dulcie quickly refilled it.

"The deed isn't accomplished yet, my love," Ian warned her. "We have the ceremony to get through."

"And you're our witnesses," Angus informed her.

Ann nodded. "My God, what a surprise," she repeated.

"What a surprise, and what a change!" Dulcie said. "What are the two of you going to do now?"

"Well, I think we need to stay on here a while longer. Maybe when we're done—"

"Done with what?" Ann asked sharply.

Angus looked at her, then glanced too quickly at Ian and then back at her. "When we're just done here, that's all. When the time is right to move on, we'll move on. Cocoa wants to set up a school for Negro children. I want to homestead, have a little ranch of my own. Ian's got a claim to some land further west in the territory which would seem to be a good place to settle down. Start a new life."

"It sounds wonderful," Dulcie said. "My congratulations to you both." She strode to Cocoa, hugged her, then kissed Angus on the cheek.

"What land?" Ann asked, staring suspiciously at Angus. Angus wasn't going to answer her, she realized, and she turned her level gaze on Ian.

"You've claims further west?" she asked politely.

He shrugged. "My family had claims," he told her.

"So why come to Coopersville?"

"Because I have business here in Coopersville."

"What business?"

"I own controlling interest in a saloon here, remember?" he asked impatiently.

"But why buy that interest here when you already had a good claim elsewhere?"

"Because the business opportunity came up here in Coopersville," he said firmly. "And that land will still be mine whenever I get around to claiming it. Annie, Cocoa and Angus want to get married," he reminded her.

Aaron cleared his throat. "We'd best be getting to the church, shouldn't we?" he asked the group politely.

"Yes! The service will be starting, and we need to keep the good Reverend happy with us all," Ian said. He slipped the champagne glass Ann had been holding from her fingers and set it on the bar. He took her arm, leading her toward the door, beckoning the others to follow.

"I didn't even know she *liked* him," Ann said very softly as they led the group from the saloon to the dusty street along past the cemetery and on to the church.

"You didn't particularly like me when you married me."

"I'm still not sure you like me," she responded sweetly, and he laughed. Then she lowered her voice. "But quite seriously, I don't know a thing about this man—"

"Well, you're not the one marrying him. Cocoa is."

"But Cocoa is—"

"A grown-up woman who can make her own choices in life. I'm sure she's been around and knows how to judge a man."

"But I don't know—"

"But I do know him, almost better than I know myself," Ian said firmly. "And I'll even be so good as to tell you about him later."

"Really?" she asked politely. "And are you going to tell me something about yourself as well?"

"If you can manage to be very well behaved throughout the ceremony, perhaps."

When they arrived at the church, they all filed in, among the last to arrive for the Sunday service. Everyone in Coopersville attended church. In fact, the church and the saloon were the two most popular establishments in town, the church winning out on Sundays by a mile. The good folks of the town took the front pews, the bankers and their wives, the shop-keepers and their sons and daughters. The ranchers were right behind them, except for the Weatherlys, who had obtained the entire stretch of the front row due to their illustrious position—Cash Weatherly had donated the funds to build the church. His name was on the two front pews.

Cowhands and drifters filled in the pews behind the ranchers—with the ladies from McCastle's finding a place in the last pew.

After Fanny Bickford, the sheriff's long-jawed spinster daughter, opened the service with a rousing hymn, the Reverend Eldridge came to his pulpit and welcomed the congregation.

"Another Sunday, another blessed day we of Coopersville share here at Saint Agnes. My friends, when the service is finished today, I welcome you all to stay for a very special occasion which I will share with you when the time is right!"

"Tell us, Reverend!" a cowhand shouted out, but Reverend Eldridge was not ready to share his information.

"Patience is a virtue, my good fellow!" he replied, and motioned to Fanny, and she began to sing again.

It was a long service. Sunday was Reverend Eldridge's one day to shine, to seize the opportunity to make them sit and reflect upon their sins for as long as possible. Today, he sermonized with feeling and conviction about how Jesus had stopped the people from stoning a whore, telling the people that the one among them *without* sin should throw the first stone. He talked about the change the Lord had brought about in Mary Magdalene, how all God's children were lost sheep, some of them black sheep, and how God was happy to back any of his sheep at any time and just about any way that he could.

"Cocoa is a black sheep, all right," Dulcie murmured beside Ann.

"Shh!" Ann murmured sternly.

Ian, at her side, was laughing. She couldn't feel quite as amused as they were; she could feel the congregation turning to stare at them again and again.

Finally, the service ended. And Reverend Eldridge stood before his pulpit to make his announcement.

"Friends, I am pleased to say that we are going to celebrate another marriage in this town!"

"Who, Reverend, who?" Fanny called from the piano. Her long, drawn face was dreamy. Poor Fanny, Ann thought, she would have so liked for it to be her. If only the right cowhand would come along.

"Oh, we are truly blessed!" the Reverend said, lifting his hands upward to heaven. "We bring in a lost sheep among our fold with this blessed wedding! Today, we are marrying Cocoa Cariou to Angus Donahue!"

There was dead silence for a minute, then someone groaned.

"Cocoa's getting *married*?" a cowhand asked.

"Hush up, have you seen the size of the fellow she's marrying?" a second cowman asked.

There was a nervous spurt of laughter among the men, and even tittering from a few of the women.

But then a man stood.

"You're going to marry a black whore and a darky drifter right here in the *white* church, Reverend?" It was the oldest of the Weatherly boys. Carl. His words didn't sound mean, just concerned.

Ian was starting to rise. Ann clutched his hand, trying to draw him back. She didn't mind him defending his friend; she wanted to slap Carl for Cocoa's sake. But she didn't think that their interference was going to be necessary now.

"There ain't no darky church in the town, they've got to be married out of this church!" Scar chimed out indignantly.

"I am the ministry of the Lord in this community, Mr. Weatherly," the Reverend replied respectfully. "It is my duty before God's eyes to see to the welfare of His children here, no matter what their shape or color, sir. Those who wish to remain in the church for the celebration of marriage please do so and all others are free to leave. Mr. Weatherly, our country has just come out of a long, bloody, and painful conflict granting freedom to persons of color. You fought hard in that war, sir, just as your father fought hard with the abolitionists. How can you not celebrate this freedom now?"

Carl appeared startled by the Reverend's words.

"Reverend, we can't be celebrating the likes of this!" Cash stated. "This is a good, God-fearing town where we're wrestling with the demons of lawlessness as it is! What's to celebrate in the union of a harlot and a drifter bringing evil down on us together now?" he demanded.

Ann shot up. "If there's evil in this town, it comes from the hearts of certain men!" she cried out.

Ian caught hold of her arm, jerking her back down to her pew.

"Let me go—" she began.

"Shut up and sit," he commanded.

"But—"

"But sit!"

She couldn't fight his hold, it was firm. But he sat her down, then rose himself. "Reverend, if Mr. Weatherly does not care to join in celebrating this joyous occasion, it's surely his God-given right to vacate the premises along with all those others who agree with him. We're all free people here. Cocoa and Angus are free to wed. And Mr. Weatherly is free to leave."

Reverend Eldridge sighed. "Indeed, good people, if you'll make your choices . . . "

"You, sir!" Cash stated suddenly, his voice ringing, "have come to run a devil's den in this town, and have no right running the affairs of decent folk."

"And you, sir, have been a guest frequently enough in the devil's den I have come to run," Ian responded quickly. "A place that hosts an excellent menu and fair games, where even stagecoach travelers pause to refresh themselves. One that I think even the good wives in our town approve of, and thank upon occasion for getting their husbands out of their hair for a spell. Ladies, am I right?"

Ann was amazed at her husband's ability not just to dominate but also to charm. He smiled dazzlingly as he looked around the church, drawing soft, feminine laughter along with a huskier male variety.

"There's trouble in this town!" Cash roared, unamused by it all himself. He pointed a finger, like an avenging angel, at Ian.

"Indeed, sir, there is!" Ian agreed, his voice carrying powerfully once again.

Reverend Eldridge cleared his throat. "There's to be no trouble. Those who would remain are most heartily invited to do so. Those who don't, for the love of their Lord, please leave quietly now."

And then there was a shuffling. A few of the parishioners did rise to leave—the Weatherlys first among them, Cash rising and drawing Meg up along with him. Carl, Jenson, and the rest of their party rose in his wake.

"Joseph!" Cash snapped to his youngest son.

But Joey just looked up at his father with a lazy smile. "Think I'll stay, Pa. I know the bride a bit and I'd like to wish her well."

"Oh, yeah, he knows the bride a bit, all right!" Jenson snickered.

It looked as if Angus might take a step toward him, but Jenson saw Angus, and while he didn't exactly back down, he did start moving quickly toward the aisle.

Cash looked as if he were about to explode; his face turned so brilliant a shade of red that his pale eyes appeared almost cobalt against his flesh. But Joey wasn't looking at him; his hat in his hand, he was watching the altar, waiting politely for the marriage ceremony to begin. Cash held his temper strictly in control, striding past his youngest son with his daughter in tow and his two older sons grimly by his side.

He paused in the middle of the aisle on his way out. "Remember who funded this place, Reverend," he said quietly.

"By our Lord, I do, and I thank you still with all my heart!" Eldridge said.

Cash turned, and as he did so, his eyes lit on Ann.

She almost jumped back. He'd looked at her before. Talked to her before, but she'd always been careful to keep a good distance away from him. She'd hid behind Eddie when they'd bought the saloon, she'd been quiet as a mouse when he had visited himself. She'd listened, and she'd gone about her dead-set plan of vengeance, drawing as little attention to herself as possible. She'd never done anything openly to draw his animosity.

Until today. Or maybe it had been the night that Ian McShane had arrived, when he'd kept Cash from coming near her, when he'd told Cash that he'd taken the saloon—and Ann.

Maybe it had been the words she'd hurled at him a few moments ago. But it didn't matter how she had drawn his animosity. She had done it. He stared at her with such a strange look of fury and vengeance and hatred that she felt as if she could shrink right into her pew.

And then he smiled. The strangest smile. As if there were a promise to go with that smile.

She barely breathed. She glanced up at Ian, but he hadn't seen Cash go out. He was standing, talking to Angus, ready to walk down the aisle to stand up for his friend.

She'd imagined it, she told herself. And if she hadn't, so what. *What did it matter how he looked at her?*

It didn't. But it scared her. She gave herself a shake and stood, catching Cocoa's arm so she could walk down the aisle with her. She squeezed her friend's arm. "Cocoa, I'm sorry."

"For what?"

"That some folks can be so cruel."

"Ignorant. Honey, you forget. I was born a slave. I know there are white folks who will never think 'darkies' should be in the same place with them. Then there are just folks like you." She flashed Ann a quick smile and gave her a quicker hug, then suddenly grew very grave. "Ann, this happened so fast, I'm not sure I knew what I was doing at first, and I'm not sure I know what I'm doing now. But I'm leaving you in trouble." She lowered her voice still further. "Dulcie's spending her time with Joey, but something is suddenly very different, Joey doesn't seem to know what's going on at the ranch, he doesn't name names or dates or places. I'm not going to be able to give you what you need anymore—"

"Cocoa, are you in love with this man?"

"Oh, my God, yes!" Cocoa's dark eyes widened. She had always been beautiful, but she was more so today. She was radiant, just the way a bride was supposed to be. "He has a very quiet strength to him, all the confidence in the world. And I've known so many men, I thought I couldn't feel anymore, but he made me feel. He loves me no matter what or where I've been, and he can see the future without the past. Oh, God, yes, I love him with all my heart, Annie!"

"Cocoa, my God, that's more than most people will ever have in a lifetime! Don't you even think about worrying about anything else—"

"But Annie, what will you do?"

"I'll keep doing my best!" she whispered softly.

"Ann, have you thought that perhaps you should quit this vendetta, leave it, and go on? Everything has changed, you've been playing with fire since Ian came to town. If he catches you and discovers what you've done—"

"Cocoa, please quit worrying about all this! You're about to get married. Let's go down the aisle!"

Cocoa squeezed her hand. "I won't be leaving, you know. I'll be here until . . ."

"Until?"

Cocoa shook her head. "I don't know. But we're all waiting, aren't we? I'll just be here . . . until." She hesitated. "Until we've destroyed Cash Weatherly," she added on a bare whisper.

With that, she must have seen her lover's face down the aisle, because she tugged on Ann's hand, definitely in a hurry herself.

Watching them before the Reverend, Ann smiled slowly to herself, amazed that she hadn't seen what had happened right beneath her nose. They were so obviously and so deeply in love.

She felt Ian watching her through the ceremony, felt a rush of warmth bring a sweep of color to her cheeks. This seemed so very different from their own hasty marriage. It *was* very different. Yet standing in the church now, she suddenly found it hard to remember life before he had come. His presence was such a strong one. And more than ever, she was torn. He made every move she made so unbelievably difficult, and everything in her life that had worked so well and so steadily was changing. Cocoa had always been the stalwart one, but Cocoa was in love. And even in her quest for vengeance, Ann had never wanted that quest to allow her to hurt anyone else. Cocoa had an *entire life* ahead of her now. The dreams she had woven could be fulfilled. But as Angus's wife, Cocoa had to take on a new role, even if she was determined to stay until they had destroyed Cash Weatherly.

Dulcie had changed as well, and Ann loved Dulcie dearly and with all her heart, they had endured so much together. Dulcie knew her as no one else could, and she would have given anything to see Dulcie married at last. But Dulcie's present misery wasn't something Ann could alleviate anyway; she could only allow her to do as she chose and hope for the best. Ginger was completely innocent of what they had been up to at McCastle's during all this time, which left Harold to listen at the bar and Aaron to discover what he could by playing his tunes so softly that the secrets of others might be heard above them. Then there was her own role in the events, which had become incredibly difficult since Ian had arrived, but which she had determined she could not relinquish. Bringing her back to where she had begun. Ian's presence here. It had changed everything. Dulcie had changed when he had come, Cocoa had met Angus because he had come. And she had become Ann McShane, a wife in ways she had never imagined. She wanted him gone while she craved his presence. She wanted to be held even when she knew she had to slip away. Things had happened so quickly, yet so subtly, and she hadn't begun to understand the tug of emotions at first, but here, standing in the church, she really began to understand the impact of what she was feeling. She was falling in love, even when she knew that she was playing with fire. And it was frightening, something she needed to fight, even when she wanted to lay down her arms. Her marriage was just part of the waiting, part of the "until." Yet where did it really end, and what game was it that Ian played, for he played one as surely as she did herself?

"My friends," Eldridge announced suddenly, "I give you Mr. and Mrs. Donahue!"

Sweet Lord, it was done. Eldridge had been droning away, and she, a witness to the marriage, had been watching without seeing, listening without hearing. To vows. To vows she had made herself not so very long ago.

Angus gave his bride a sound kiss while those remaining in the congregation applauded. Smiling happily, the bride and groom started down the aisle together. Ian offered Ann his arm. She accepted it and then they started down the aisle together, following Angus and Cocoa.

Outside, Ian raised his voice, inviting everyone back to the saloon to celebrate. There seemed to be an overwhelming agreement from the townfolk who had witnessed the ceremony—including those good wives who had decided to stay. When they came into the saloon, Ian went to work behind the bar with Harold while Ann did duty in the kitchen. She was just rubbing her hands on a hastily donned apron when she heard a clicking sound behind her from the kitchen door. She turned around to see that Ian was there, a bottle of champagne in his hand. "Let's have a picnic," he suggested.

"A picnic?" she inquired. "You halfway broke my arm in the church when I had something to say—"

"I nowhere near broke your arm!" he protested.

"You dragged me down."

"You were shouting without thinking."

"I had a right—"

"I had something to say myself. And besides, you're not getting into any pitched battles with Weatherly when I'm there to prevent it."

"But I—"

"You're not, and I won't let you."

"But I should go on a picnic with you even though you think you've the right to behave like a dictator."

"I've a right to protect my wife."

"Ian, I am capable, I speak well—"

"Ann, let's get out of here for a while."

She stared at him with her eyes wide, her brows arched. "Ian, we've a wedding party going on here—"

"And it will go on just fine without us. I've the

wine, grab up a loaf of bread, cheese perhaps—has he any roasted chickens or the like?''

"I—'' she said, staring at him blankly. It seemed incredible after the tension of the week that Ian was standing there coaxing her out on a picnic. He had a subtle smile worked into his handsome features, his hat was pulled low over one eye, and though he still seemed just as dominating a presence as he had from that first day when she had seen him as a silhouette in the doorway, he was both roguish and very charming as well. She should still be telling him to go right to hell.

"I'll—uh—find a chicken,'' she said.

"Meet me out front.''

He closed the door and she heard his footfalls on the wooden porch as he walked around to the front.

Sixteen

Ann stared after him a while, shaking her head, still a little angry, yet smiling. What was she doing?

She wasn't at all sure.

She quickly wrenched off her apron and plucked a basket down from a shelf, found a roasted chicken, a square of cheese, and a loaf of Henri's fresh-baked bread. With her food wrapped in checked linen napkins and placed in the basket, she slipped out the back herself and hurried around to the front of the saloon.

She paused, because Ralph Reninger was standing there beside Ian; they had been deep in conversation.

"Good day, Annie," Ralph told her politely, lifting his hat.

She forced a smile to her lips.

"Ralph, are you joining us?"

"No, thank you. I'm just feeling the breeze out here. It's a fine day."

"Umm," she murmured. Unlikely. Ralph was outside watching.

"Come on, my love," Ian murmured, catching her hand.

"Are we taking the wagon—"

"Just old Joe," he told her, referring to his bay.

"But—"

"We'll be gone a few hours, Ralph," Ian said. He quickly walked Ann to his horse, lifting her atop Joe and then leaping up behind her. He raised a hand to Ralph, then turned Joe to head northward out of town. They trotted down the dusty street until they reached the end of it and then Ian nudged his horse's flanks and they cantered across the brush-covered plain to an old Indian trail that led through an outcropping of cliffs and buttes to a narrow stream by which the dry terrain changed subtly to something almost green. The bank of the stream was mostly sod and the scrub grass thicker. Downed logs seemed like chairs set before the crystal, slow-flowing water, and the cliffs that rose behind them blocked out the sun, providing a shade that was cooled still further by the soft flow of the breeze.

Ian helped Ann down, leaving Joe to his own resources as he walked her to one of the logs, made a dashing bow, and set her down on the soft ground before it so that the log might be a backrest for her. He opened the bottle of champagne, then hesitated, a frown knit into his brow.

"Glasses," he told her. "I'm afraid I'm remiss at picnics."

She smiled, reached for the bottle, and took a long sip from it. "Not so remiss. You knew the one perfect spot in the area. No matter how dry it may be, this stream always runs fairly deeply. No matter how fierce the sun, the air is always cool because of the cover of the cliff."

He sat beside her and took the champagne bottle as she offered it. Ann allowed her head to fall to his shoulder. She closed her eyes and felt the soft caress of the breeze with its hint of dampness to it. The earth around her was fragrant. It felt good to be here.

"So tell me about Angus," she said.

"He's been a good friend for a long time."

"Through the war?"

"Yes."

"So you were a Reb, right?"

"Why, what were you?"

"A prisoner of the Pawnee," she reminded him.

"Not through the entire war."

"By the time Eddie McCastle came, the war itself was a very distant thing from me."

"So you don't hate Rebs?"

She shook her head. "I suppose I might have been one. Of course, those days before it all began seem so very long ago now. A decade. A lifetime."

"Where did you come from?" he quizzed her.

"Originally?" She smiled. "My mother's family were from Savannah, and my father's folks were from Richmond. But my father had been working with a law firm in Saint Louis when they decided that they wanted to come further west. I loved Saint Louis back then. So much hustle and bustle, always! But honestly, I don't remember much about my life there. It was so long ago. The war did seem to go on forever."

"Umm. Forever. I know, I agree. I lived it," he murmured.

"I'm sorry!" she said quickly.

"It was a sorry waste of time and life," he agreed. "And it's over, and people everywhere are sorry and grieving, but it's time—" He broke off suddenly.

"It's time?" she said.

"To move on," he said very softly. He took a long swig of the champagne. "Well, it should be time to move on," he added. He stroked his fingers idly through her hair. He shifted, drawing her down so that she lay comfortably in the cool breeze, her head on his lap, her hair free and flowing over it. "The most amazing thing about your face, Ann, is all that it combines! Such wisdom in those eyes, such character in your chin. And such a strange innocence about it all, as if you know—as if you've learned— all the tricks of the world and yet . . . "

"And yet?"

"Are as pure as the driven snow," he murmured.

"I was, once," she reminded him.

He smiled. "Strange indeed, if only I knew what secrets lurked behind those eyes to create the wisdom within the beauty!"

"And what of you?" she asked softly.

"What of me?"

"Let's start with Angus. You were about to tell me about him."

"I've known him most of my life. He is Cherokee and maroon and was a student at a special reservation school near my home when I was growing up."

"Where?" she demanded.

He smiled slowly, looking down at her. "Southwestern South Carolina," he told her.

"But you said that you were Sioux—"

"Lakota Sioux, through my grandfather. My mother's father. My grandmother was white, but she had been taken in by my grandfather's tribe. She was found alive in a farmhouse, her parents weren't killed in an attack, they both died of a fever and she would have died soon too if a hunting party hadn't gone in and found her toddling around the house alone. She grew up Sioux and married my grandfather, but they were trading heavily with the whites by then, and my grandmother's English was very good. My mother was raised with the Sioux, but her mother taught her the English language and American ways. She probably would have stayed with the Sioux all her life quite happily, but then she met my father. He had been a surveyor with the United States government heading northwest out of Saint Louis. When my father returned home to South Carolina to settle the estate when his father died, my mother went with him, with her family's blessings. My grandfather is a great man—I believe you would think so if you met him. He is a fierce man; he was a strong and powerful warrior in his youth and he has fought the white man often. But he admired my father and could see that his daughter loved him very much. I haven't been able to see much of him in the last few years—"

"The war?"

"The war," he agreed, and shrugged. It seemed for a minute as if he might say more, but he paused again before continuing in his earlier vein. "Back to Angus. When his folks died, mine took him in. He stayed behind when—when my father traveled again. He rode to war with me, and, luckily, he rode away from the war with me as well."

"He was never—"

"A slave? No. He was born a free man."

"Cocoa wasn't born free," Ann murmured. "Freedom means so much to her."

"Her children will be free."

"Sometimes," Ann murmured, "I think I like it here because it is easier to be free."

"Maybe it is. The land is wild and raw and free."

"And lawless sometimes," she murmured.

"With Sheriff Bickford?" he said, a teasing light in his eyes.

She grinned. "The sheriff is a good man."

Ian grunted. "But you're not so fond of having him around."

"I like him just fine."

"As long as he's not asking questions in the saloon."

"Are you fond of him questioning you?"

"I have answers for any questions he might have."

"And you have Ralph on the porch of the saloon now for a reason, right? Angus is the usual guard, but you can't ask a man for too much of his attention on his wedding night?"

"I believe that Angus has spent a few other nights this past week in the pursuit of his newly taken bride."

"You've been watching."

He shrugged. "I've had to."

"Why?"

"Because I know the likes of some of the men Weatherly's brought in because of all the money that's been robbed from his enterprises lately. Bad Bull Marlin is as dangerous as they come."

"I heard he was in the war."

Ian hesitated. "The roughest part of it. He was with the troops out of Kansas from the beginning of the trouble in the West, before the war started. He served with honor, all right. Not that any of it had anything to do with goodness. Nothing in the Kansas and Missouri arena of war had any moral or ethics. Long before the war broke out, the abolitionists and the slaveholders were fighting. I know this sounds strange from an ex-Rebel soldier, but I am truly glad slavery has ended. But that doesn't make any of what happened—especially in Missouri— right. Men were just wantonly killing one another. The Northern sympathizers, the Jayhawkers or Red-Legs, as they came to be called for the uniform they adapted, killed the Bushwhackers, or the pro-Southern side. The bastards out of the abolitionist side—John Brown's followers—savagely murdered men who stood against them. The men who fought back—many of whom joined up with Quantrill and his raiders later—were just as bad. They went in and killed innocents just as viciously. All in the name of God and their causes!"

He sounded bitter. Ann suddenly felt very tense herself, more curious about him than ever.

"You—didn't fight with Quantrill?" she asked.

He shook his head. "No, I didn't, but I almost did."

"I thought you said you were from South Carolina?"

"I am from South Carolina. But I'd been traveling with my family before the war broke out. I was in an area where I'd had the misfortune to see a lot of what was going on. I might have joined up with Quantrill, being—" He hesitated a second. "Being a Southerner," he finished. "But—" He shrugged and smiled. "I was with my grandfather when war was actually declared. He said that no man could do something when he didn't believe in what he was doing. I knew it was wrong to murder innocents in order to avenge the murder of innocents. Not that war was right outside of the Kansas and Missouri theater—no matter what, it's hard to make shooting down a man with a different view an honorable thing. But I discovered that I did need to take a side, and because of my past, my side had to be Southern. I wound up in the cavalry, fighting for John Hunt Morgan, a man I respected and admired. I'm good with landscape and terrain, thanks to my father and good instincts—my grandfather told me I could thank him for the good instincts. I was a scout. I stayed with it to the end, even after Morgan died, and even after I knew the South was going to lose."

"And then—?"

"Now I'm here."

"But—"

"Now I'm here."

"Keeping guard on the saloon. And you're not going to tell me—"

"Obviously, I keep someone on guard at the saloon. It's a smart precaution in a lawless land, and there are some frightening people around, that is all. You're the one who is not going to tell me anything until I find a way to threaten—or seduce—it out of you."

She had to smile. She shook her head. "You will not seduce anything out of me."

"Even when I'm more than tolerable?"

She shook her head.

"But you are admitting that there *is* something to be seduced out of you," he stated.

She sighed.

"I never admitted anything—" she began. But it didn't seem that it mattered at the moment. He set the champagne aside and bent down and kissed her. The feeling was magical.

"But you will," he whispered against her lips.

"I'll not," she breathed back.

"I'll find you out."

"No . . ."

His lips touched hers again. The breeze seemed to rush by, exceptionally cool and fragrant and sweet. She could hear the delicate, almost imperceptible sound of the water moving, feel its coolness. He shifted down to the ground beside her, taking her into his arms.

"Know what we've never done?" he asked her.

She shook her head.

"Played."

"Played?"

He smiled. And kissed her. "Played. Like making love in the daylight by a stream in the shadows of a cliff. Like making love in the stream."

"Out here?" she said, barely breathing.

"We haven't any streams or cliffs *in* the saloon," he reminded her.

She touched his face, running her finger down the hard plane of his cheek.

"Here?" she whispered again.

"Here," he said, and started to kiss her. On her lips, her eyelids. Her cheeks. Her throat. . . .

It was different than ever before. Softer. Cooler. Passion flared, sweet flames burned, but the breeze remained so gently cool, the earth seemed a cushion beneath them. Shadows and light touched them, the world itself was all around them, yet they had never seemed more alone. He coaxed her into nakedness, into the water. It was crisply cold; he was vibrant fire against it. He took her in the water, and at the water's edge. The water had felt like ice. He entered her, and the fire spread throughout her body and perhaps into the water itself. They laughed, they touched, kissed, played. Made love again.

At length, they lay with one another on the grassy bank, warmed by one another. Ann, her head resting on his chest, smiled and stretched.

"A picnic . . . ?" she queried.

"A feast," he teased in turn. He sighed then. "Watch the sun in the sky," he told her.

She shifted against him and did so. The sun was a red half-orb crested on the horizon. It seemed to be moving very swiftly, almost as if it were falling out of the sky. All around it, the world was lit up in shades of orange and yellow and bursts of fiery red. The colors seemed to stretch forever.

"It's very beautiful."

"Odd, isn't it?" he murmured. He eased her down and rose, naked still against the cliff and rock and somehow very powerful for it. "We've rattlesnakes and gunslingers, hard earth and rock—and the beauty of such a sun to conquer it all. It's a strange world."

Ann sat up, hugging her knees to her chest. She felt a trembling inside her, thinking of the years gone by. So much that had been good had faded from her life. She had tried to hold on to it, like worn pictures within her mind. She had fought so hard in the recent past that she had seldom paused to see the good, to feel it, yet like the sun on the prairie, it surrounded her. She had good friends, Cocoa, Dulcie, Harold, dear Aaron, and others. There had been Eddie, gentle, kind, willing to do so much for others, so happy in the simple joys of life, a drink, a song, a game played well.

Now there was Ian. A stranger still in many ways, an enigma. A force which had infuriated her. A man with whom she had fallen in love. Sweet Jesu, maybe she should just tell him the truth. He seemed to have his own arguments with Cash Weatherly. Maybe he would understand.

That she had robbed stagecoaches? *Did he already know? Is that why he hadn't shot at her when he'd had the opportunity?*

She shivered against the growing coolness of the day.

"A strange world," she agreed.

He came to her, drew her to her feet. She shivered again slightly.

"What is it?"

"I'm—growing cold, I think," she whispered.

He smoothed back her hair, watching her eyes. "The night is coming. It's time to go back." He smiled. "I will always warm you. The best that I can."

"You are warm," she whispered. "You are fire."

He grinned. "A strange world. On a night like this, life itself within that world is so very precious."

"Life—is always precious."

"Ah, but there were times when I thought I could give mine easily ... for honor, for justice, even for a cause at times. Sometimes, I didn't even believe in all the cause stood for; I just knew that I was fighting the enemy. I don't think I realized again, until I came here with you tonight, just how precious life can still be."

She smiled, putting her arms around his neck, leaning against his chest. Her words were muffled against the sleek flesh there. "I didn't know so very much until you came."

He held her for a moment there. The breeze rose, whispering around them.

"Umm, I do like to teach well," he teased softly.

She nodded, frightened suddenly by the closeness between them. God knew what she might be whispering soon.

She pulled away from him. "I can't believe I'm standing naked in full view of—"

"Of—?" he inquired with amusement.

She was already plucking up her discarded clothing, struggling back into it. He helped her with her dress, still naked, still at ease.

"There isn't a soul for miles around," he assured her.

"What if someone else is on a picnic?" she demanded.

He laughed huskily, and gave her no more argument, but dressed quickly himself.

When they were both dressed and presentable, he set her atop Joe, and they headed back for the saloon. Ann rode behind him this time, her head resting upon his back. She was tired, smiling, content.

Ralph was still on the porch when they returned. "Word with you, Ian," he said.

Ian lifted Ann down. "Go on in, Annie," he told her, frowning as he looked at Ralph.

"What happened?" she demanded, staring at Ralph.

"Nothing that I know of, Ann," he said innocently. "It's been a busy day, nothing more."

"Busy?"

"Lots of people in and out."

"But nothing happened?"

"Ann, nothing that I know about," Ralph said.

"But you want to talk with Ian."

"Ann, will you please go on in!" Ian snapped.

She bit into her lower lip. He could be charming and seductive. He could also snap out orders with unwavering determination.

If anything had happened, Ralph wasn't going to tell her. "Yes," she said icily. "Thank you, Ian, I will just go on in!" She walked past both men and into the saloon, looking around.

Nothing, it seemed, had happened. Ann went straight to the bar and to Harold, who filled her in on the afternoon. A raucous crowd had followed Cocoa and Angus up the stairs a few hours back, and the newlyweds had accepted a certain amount of the play. Then Angus had firmly sent them all back down, and the saloon had continued to do business. The hands had come from Weatherly's in the afternoon, including his new hired guns. Everything else had been business as usual.

"So Weatherly's whole crew was in?" Ann asked.

"A lot of them. Not Cash himself. Carl and Jenson were in—but not Joey, come to think of it. In fact, I think I heard someone say that Joey was driving his sister somewhere on a visit."

"But the new boys were in?"

He nodded. "Bad Bull Marlin. Tyler Grissom, Josh Mason. All three of them. They played cards, they

raised toasts to the newlyweds, they were damned
well behaved."

"Amazing. We shouldn't have left."

"Ann, if there had been a hint of trouble, one of
the Yeagher boys was ready to ride after you."

"But we were gone."

"Not that far."

"How would they have found us?"

"McShane left word as to where you'd be."

Her brows flew up. So McShane had left word.
And they might have both been discovered in the
water or on the bank, in the very act of . . .

A radiant color must have suffused her cheeks because even steadfast Harold was suddenly very
amused. "Annie, you two are married, right?"

"Yes, thank you, Harold."

"He's a careful man, your McShane knows what
he's doing."

"Careful," she murmured. "It's just that things
can happen so very fast here."

"Ann," Harold whispered, " 'things' haven't
happened here. They've happened to the ranchers,
to the miners. They've happened to Cash Weatherly's stagecoaches and wagons. What's happened
here?"

"McShane has happened here!" she whispered
back.

"Annie—"

"Never mind, Harold," she murmured.

"You should be grateful, you know. A man to take
care of you."

"Harold, I was taking care of myself just fine!"

"Annie . . . " he began, then smiled. He shook his
head. "Annie, you know what? We can all use someone to take care of us a little, men and women alike.
Maybe you've both found that."

"Harold—" she said, then broke off. "I don't

know. Maybe you're right. But right now, I think it would have been nice if I'd been warned that one of the Yeagher twins just might be riding out after us."

"Might have spoiled the day," Harold suggested. He had a twinkle in his eye. There was going to be no arguing with him this evening, either.

"Harold . . . "

"Yes?"

"Oh, never mind."

She thanked him again for his information and sauntered over to Aaron, who told her the same. "But I don't like the looks of things lately, Annie," Aaron managed to tell her softly.

"How?"

"All week, everyone's been watching. Your husband, his men. Waiting. And there are changes at Weatherly's. These new guns of his coming in here . . . "

"All we can do is wait," Ann murmured. "We don't have anything right now."

"And I'm glad," Aaron admitted.

"Aaron, you don't have to be involved—"

"Ann, I'm no coward, and you know it. My concern remains with you. Maybe you've taken things as far as you can take them."

"Aaron, there has to be more, there has to be a way to make everyone see what he has done—"

"Then maybe you need to think more about what you really want to accomplish in the end. So far, we've stolen money—and made him furious."

"If he can't pay his people, he'll lose his power. And he'll eventually lose his ranch."

"Eventually. Ann, we've been lucky so far, but how far do you think we can go?"

"I don't know!" she whispered. "I don't know. But I can't lose sight of what he's done!"

"You can't lose sight of your own life, Ann. Can't you see it, you've got one now!"

"Aaron, I—" She broke off, then frowned, seeing Ginger creating a pathway through the tables to reach her.

"Annie, Dulcie wants to see you," Ginger said, panting slightly as she reached her at last.

"What about?"

"I don't know. She's upstairs. I was passing her door and she asked me to send you up as soon as I saw you. That was a little while ago."

"Hmm. I'd better get up there," Ann said. "Did she say that anything was wrong?"

"No, no. She didn't come out or anything, she just asked me to send you up as soon as I saw you."

Ann nodded. "I'm on my way. Thank you, Ginger."

She left Aaron and the piano, noting that Ian had not come in yet. And strange, but it seemed that Weatherly's boys had already gone—she couldn't see any of them anywhere in the place, not at the card tables, not at the bar.

She hurried up the stairs to Dulcie's door. She tapped. "Dulcie?"

No answer. She tapped again. "Dulcie?"

Still, no answer. She pushed the door open. The room was dark; no lamp had been lit in here. A window remained open, allowing in just a touch of the moonlight.

"Dulcie?" she murmured again.

That time, she heard a groan. From the bed. She rushed to it. "Dulcie!"

She looked down at her friend, choked . . . gasped . . .

And a scream rose to her throat.

Seventeen

"*D*ulcie!" Ann cried, sitting on the bed beside her, reaching out to touch a portion of her unbattered right cheek. The left side of Dulcie's face was swollen; her eye was a closed slit amidst mottled purple skin. Tears stung Ann's eyes. "Dulcie, what happened, who did this to you? Sweet Jesu, Dulcie, no one knows about this downstairs, you didn't tell Ginger, whoever did this—"

"Wait, please wait!" Dulcie managed to whisper. "It's not so bad as it looks. The pain is subsiding—"

"You need cold water, a cool piece of raw meat—"

"There's water, there," Dulcie said, lying back.

Ann instantly rang out a cloth in the water, dampened it again, and laid it over Dulcie's face. Anxiously she sat by her side again, smoothing back her hair. "Dulcie, what happened? I didn't think you were—seeing men anymore. Who did you have up here, and what happened? Please, Dulcie, tell me, we can't let him get away with this—"

"Beating a whore?" she whispered. "What? Will they hang him?"

"I'll hang him!" Ann promised.

Dulcie shook her head. "You've got to listen to

me, you can't go off wildly, you have to heed what
I'm saying, Ann. Cocoa was out of it, I had to try
to find out why so many of Weatherly's men were
milling around in here, why the new guns he's
hired . . . "

"Dulcie, what did you do?" Ann whispered.

"Bad Bull Marlin," she whispered, and winced.

Ann leapt up. "Bad Bull Marlin? I'll get the sheriff,
I'll get every man I know out there—"

"And you'll get them all shot up!" Dulcie warned
her.

Ann sank back down, shaking, knowing that Dulcie was right. Dulcie had stayed here, hiding her
pain, because she hadn't been about to allow anyone
to run off half-cocked to avenge her in any way.

"There's more," Dulcie whispered. "He talked
about the war, about what a good job he'd done for
the right and the mighty in the Northern army
against some of Quantrill's Rebel guerrillas. He said
he halfway won the war himself, that the legitimate
army was in awe of his tactics and abilities, that he
about settled the bushwhacker/jayhawker war all on
his own."

"None of them had the right to claim a part of any
legitimate army!" Ann said bitterly. She'd been a
prisoner through most of the war; she'd been with
Eddie, who'd wanted no part of it, heading through
the West. But she knew all about the way the conflict
had begun, and she'd even learned about John
Brown. Some had called him a martyr after the war.
A saint down from heaven who'd had the calling to
fight against slavery. Well, slavery had been wrong,
but it hadn't made John Brown right, or a saint. Before he'd ever headed to Harpers Ferry, West Virginia, John Brown had used his own brand of justice
out on the Kansas and Missouri border. He'd made
himself judge and jury, murdering men in cold

blood. And he'd taught others to do the same, just as Quantrill had used his deadly tactics against the Northern raiders who had been spurred to their own action by such fanatical leaders as John Brown. The Pawnee had a far greater understanding of justice than these men who had canonized themselves and determined to exterminate those with whom they disagreed.

A chill raced through her. The men involved in the savage guerrilla attacks in the Kansas and Missouri arena before and during the war had no consciences, she was convinced. Dulcie was lucky to have been merely beaten, and not left dead.

"Ann, he fought with Cash during the war. Do you think—?"

"Oh, God, I don't know!" Ann returned.

She started to rise. "Annie, listen to me, don't go getting crazy on my account! I would have hidden from you as well except that I did learn something. I think sweet little Meg mentioned that she'd seen horses and riders at the old shack out beneath the overhang of the cliffs, the one you've used so often. And Cash is convinced the robbers *have* used the place to stash the gold they'd been stealing. He's planning on getting together a group of his boys tomorrow morning to rip apart the old shack right down to the floorboards. You do have most of the money out there, don't you?"

Ann knotted her fingers into fists. "I've moved a lot of it, but yes, there's still a fair amount at the shack."

"You've got to get Aaron and get out there tonight. If Cash manages to retrieve everything that you've stolen, then all of the risks you've taken so far haven't been for anything."

"Dulcie, something has to be done about this, about what has been done to you!"

"Ann! They don't arrest men for getting rough with whores, they just don't do it."

"It's not right—"

"Oh, Annie! There's so much that isn't right, but not being right doesn't always change things." She caught Ann's hands. "You've got to promise me that you won't go doing anything! You've seen a lot out here, the same as me. When men get emotional, they lose the edge. You're fighting your own war just the same, and you can't go running off furious because of me, you'll risk everything."

"What do you think is going to happen when Ian McShane sees you?" Ann demanded softly.

Dulcie shook her head. "He isn't going to see me like this. I'll stay in late tomorrow. If you can just get me a piece of raw meat, most of this will be down in no time. Then—then I'll lie. It won't be something that I haven't done before."

"Dulcie, you're going to promise me that this is it, that you're not taking risks anymore. I don't want you even thinking about creatures like Bad Bull Marlin again, do you understand?" She gritted her teeth, feeling ill. Dulcie had done this for her. She couldn't let it go on any longer. Once, Dulcie had playfully flirted with and seduced her information out of Joey. And Joey would never have done something like this. The game had changed. It might get worse. She had promised herself that she would never let the innocent get hurt, and Dulcie had borne enough pain for a lifetime. "Dulcie, no more risks like this, ever!"

"Ann," Dulcie moaned, "you're not paying attention. You have to go and get the gold."

"Oh, Dulcie!" she whispered suddenly, hugging her friend carefully but fiercely. "Dulcie, why did he do this to you?"

"I was trying to find out what he was doing

around here, why Cash had hired in so many new guns. And he was being such a horse's arse, telling me that half the folks he knew needed killing, that Cash Weatherly said you were nothing but a beautiful witch and you deserved what you might someday get, and that someday just might come with Ian in the dust and you on your back just where you ought to be, paying for being so superior all this time. He'd meant for you to get your comeuppance when Eddie died, but McShane got in his way, and now McShane sure as hell deserves his comeuppance. He had something foul to say about everyone, and he called Joey the runt of a good man's litter, a coward and a weakling.''

"Oh, Dulcie—"

"So I started to laugh."

"Laugh?"

Dulcie sighed with impatience. "Annie, you always were the most unbelievable innocent, but you're married now! *When he took his pants off*, I laughed. I told him I sure hoped *he* was the runt of the litter, because if he wasn't, then his brothers wouldn't even have a part from which to pee."

"Dulcie, Bad Bull Marlin is dangerous. You should have held your tongue with him!" Ann said. Dulcie had always been ready to fight—whether it was prudent or not. Ann felt a hot stinging sensation at the back of her eyes. She couldn't bear to see Dulcie so cruelly injured. "Dulcie, was it worth it? Taunting him that way? He hurt you so badly—"

"Oh, yes, it was worth it! Honey, I learned pain from some experts, remember? My first years with the Pawnee were hell. If you hadn't stepped in twice, Annie, I'd be dead now. This is nothing. I owe you so much—"

"Dulcie, you don't owe me anything! If you could

even imagine that you'd ever had debt to me, you've repaid it a thousand times over!"

"Ann, are you crying? Quit now, you've got to go get the gold dug up before Cash Weatherly gets it all back. Ann, we can't let him get it back. We worked too hard to get it from him. Go, please!"

Ann stood quickly. "Ian will be up here. He'll be up here looking for me."

"You were never afraid of him before," Dulcie reminded her.

"I'm not afraid of him," Ann whispered. "I'm just afraid of what he'll find out, of what he'll do if he thinks I'm a common outlaw."

"You could explain the truth."

She shook her head. "He still wouldn't understand what I've done."

"Make this your last move then—"

"I can't do that either!" Ann breathed.

"You can think about it all later. Right now, you've got to get that gold. Ann, please don't let this have happened for nothing!"

"I won't. And I must get away but it will take a little time. And you don't dare let him see you. Someone will have to say something about you as well—"

"Pretend that I'm with Joey," Dulcie said quietly. "Everyone will know I want to be left alone for hours."

"Joey took his sister somewhere, I heard."

"Well, we'll say that he came back," Dulcie said simply.

"And I—"

"Ann, where is that deliciously cunning mind of yours? Think of something. Move quickly! The night is still very young. Annie, you and Aaron must hurry and move the gold and be back before anyone knows you're gone."

Ann knew that she had to do it, absolutely had to do it. But now she felt so uneasy for some reason, so afraid. But she couldn't let Weatherly get it back, she'd been stealing from him for too long, she had taken too many risks. And he could hire even more men like Bad Bull Marlin and stack the deck so badly that she'd never be able to fight him anymore.

"Annie!"

"Yes, I'm going."

Ann took a deep breath, nodded at Dulcie, then turned and swiftly fled the room, closing the door carefully behind her before hurrying down the stairs. Thank God for small miracles—Ian remained outside with Ralph. She slipped into the kitchen, sneaking a slice of beef out of the rack of meat Henri was beginning to prepare for the evening.

She ran the meat back up. Dulcie thanked her and pressed the meat to her face, rising even as Ann protested.

"I've got to lock my door. I can't have anyone wandering in here," Dulcie reminded Ann.

"All right, but get back in bed. Stay down and keep that meat on your eye. Sweet Jesu, I can say that you're with Joey, but what will happen when Henri, Harold—the twins!—Scar, and Ian see you tomorrow? They'll think that Joey—"

"I'll have made up a story by then. Ann, the gold!"

"Going!" Ann whispered, and fled once again. On the way down the stairs, she prayed that Ian would have remained outside.

He had.

She breathed a sigh of relief and sauntered first to the piano. "We've got to go."

"Where?"

"To the shack. Weatherly is going to dig there in the morning. Dulcie got the information."

"Ann, it's a tricky time—"

"Aaron, I know!"

"I'll get Ginger over here and meet you out back."

She slipped away from him. He finished playing the ballad he had begun. She heard the piano music cease as she moved up to the bar, beckoning to Harold. "If someone wants Dulcie, she's busy for the evening."

"She's been busy most of the week," Harold said, then frowned, "though she was sauntering around the customers earlier."

"Well, her favorite customer is back," Ann said. It hurt to lie to Harold, but she didn't want anyone seeing Dulcie in her present condition. Her first instinct had been to rush out and beat Bad Bull Marlin to a bloody pulp with her own fists. Harold would get himself killed beyond a doubt if he were to tackle Marlin in Dulcie's defense.

Then she added softly, "I'm going out."

"Ann! How will I cover tonight? He's just brought you home, where could you be?"

"Tell him I'm angry because his good friend Ralph never seems to be able to talk in front of me. Tell him that I seemed a little bit upset and that I went for a walk."

"Oh, God," Harold groaned.

"Harold, it's necessary!" she hissed fiercely.

Harold looked sick. There was no help for it. And she didn't have any more time. She was pushing things as it was.

She slipped away from the bar, returning upstairs, and leaving the saloon through the hidden door and secret stairs. Aaron, dependable as always, was ready in back with their horses.

"I just need to change," she told him, tearing down to the last stall, digging into the storage compartment, and finding her masculine apparel and kerchief. She stuffed her dress and petticoats, stockings and church flats into the storage bin, and raced back to Aaron. She mounted beside him, and they quietly slipped out of town, moving under the cover of darkness. Once out of town, the moonlight guided them along the trail to the shack they had come to know so very well over the past year.

"You're quiet, cousin," Ann commented nervously as they rode.

He shrugged. "I'm nervous tonight."

Ann didn't want to admit that she was nervous as well. "I think you're just unhappy because you know we can't possibly come across another Annabella this evening."

He smiled suddenly.

"Annabella is still in town," he told her.

"Is she?"

He was still grinning. "She and her brother have been in the saloon for lunch a few times . . . before you've managed to rise," he told her with a smile and a shake of his head. "Ah, the life of a married lady of leisure!"

"I'm not so terribly sure one gets to run a saloon and remain a lady. Aaron," she said, looking over her shoulder, changing the subject, "we need to hurry now and get the gold—"

"Where will we move it to?"

"We'll bring it back with us," she said.

"To the saloon?"

"Where else?"

"Wonderful. When it's found, we'll hang!"

"Where else can we go?"

"How about one of the deserted mine shafts?"

"Good idea."

The shack lay ahead of them. They both nudged their horses and cantered on to it. They'd worked together long and well, and didn't need to speak to one another as they dismounted and hurried in, ripping up a loose floorboard of the ramshackle dwelling to find the leather bags of gold beneath.

"We can't carry all this," Aaron warned.

"We'll take what our horses can carry and flood the hole with dirt. Maybe they'll miss the remaining gold when they come to find it anyway."

Ann had finished in the shack and was loading her saddlebags when she sensed a rumbling in the earth. She stood dead still. Aaron remained inside, filling the hole with dirt.

"Aaron!" she cried, thundering his name, rushing to the door to call him out. "Aaron, riders are coming *now*. Come on!"

He raced out, following her as she rushed to her mount. They leaped atop their horses almost simultaneously, starting around in the opposite direction from the sound of the hoofbeats. They were just clearing the shack and the cliff that rose behind it when they saw the riders coming after them.

There were ten to twelve men on horseback, riding hard in the shadowy darkness illuminated somewhat by the moon's glow. The men reined in their horses in front of the shack; then someone started roaring out that the thieves were getting away. The earth began to thunder and shake again as half of the group started riding again, coming after Aaron and Ann.

"Move!" Aaron warned, slamming his heels against his horse's flanks. Ann did likewise.

"Can you see any of them? Who are they?" Ann called out.

"Weatherly's men."

"Did you see Cash?"

"No. I saw Tyler Grissom and Josh Mason at the lead."

"Bad Bull Marlin?"

"No. Ann, what difference does it make who is after us?"

"It's not the sheriff—or Ian?"

"No!" he cried.

"And you didn't see Bad Bull Marlin?"

"No! Annie, don't talk, ride!"

They raced across the dry earth at a breakneck speed, leaning close to their horses' necks.

"There's at least six of them riding after us!" Ann cried out.

"The butte! It's our only chance," he returned.

The butte. He meant to race up the incline to the plateau, then career down the slope to the far left edge of it. It was a chance. They were both exceptional riders. They might lose a few of the others in the dust.

"Right!" Ann shouted to him, and took the lead. She urged her horse up the incline, leaning into the animal's neck. Aaron was right behind her.

The riders gained on them, but then found themselves losing ground as they struggled up the sandy path.

Ann and Aaron crested the top and raced across the expanse of it, reining in just in time to slow their mounts for the reckless plunge down the opposite side.

The hoofbeats followed them. The earth seemed to tremble; thunder might have filled the air, and the air itself might have been as thick as lead. Fear filled Ann. She had been unnerved from the beginning tonight. *There had been a reason, so it seemed.* She had been in tight spots before. She couldn't afford to be afraid.

She stopped the rush of terror that had been sweeping over her. She could be her own undoing, if she wasn't careful. Ann managed to concentrate on riding alone. There was nothing else she could do for the first tricky moments. If her horse stumbled, if she lost her seat, she was surely dead, for these men would shoot her before asking her the first question.

But she and her horse managed the slope, and Aaron came down behind her flawlessly. In a matter of seconds, they heard cursing as the men followed. They heard a cry as one horse faltered and sent its rider flying. Another fell. Someone else swore, and held back.

"Two of them coming!" Aaron warned.

She heard a shot sizzle past her ear and she lowered herself for another reckless gallop across the dusty earth. Sweet Jesu, but they were close! She drew her gun and turned to take aim. She thought the rider behind her was Tyler Grissom; she could tell by his hat. She fired. Again she heard a burst of furious cursing as one of the riders' horses shrieked, reared—and sent its master flying into the dust.

"His horse is down. You've taken him out of the chase. Only one to go!" Aaron cried to her against the ever-pounding thunder of their own horses' hooves.

She turned again, taking aim at the fellow who was closing in on them in the night. Josh Mason— Weatherly had hired men who could ride hard and shoot with expertise. If she didn't stop him, she and Aaron would be the dead ones.

The moonlight kept them from total darkness and her eyesight was excellent, but still, because of the speed with which they raced, it was difficult to find her mark. She narrowed her eyes, steadied her hand, and fired. She saw that she'd hit his right shoulder.

A cry sounded from the rider, who then cursed and floundered. A second cry sounded and she realized it had come from herself.

"Annie?" Aaron shouted.

She couldn't answer him at first. It had been amazing. She had felt a burning, searing pain in her left side, right along the rear of her rib cage. Then the pain had seemed to dull and disappear. It came again and she realized the horrible truth. She had been shot.

"So just what the hell is going on?" Ian demanded of Ralph. "What is he doing, bringing in all these men? The likes of which I know well enough, with their brand of warfare. Cash Weatherly's people crowd the saloon, but there's no trouble, they just come and enjoy a whiskey like fine, upstanding citizens, then move on."

Ralph cleared his throat. "History will surely tell that the likes of the fanatical Northerners on the Kansas and Missouri border were just as heinous in their behavior as Quantrill and his men, but at the moment, Ian, not enough time has passed since the war, which the North did win. These fellows Weatherly has brought in are considered fine, upstanding citizens. Sheriff Bickford does not believe that Cash Weatherly might have had anything to do with Grainger's misfortunes. Take a good look at the way things appear, Ian, and Cash Weatherly is a sorely trod upon man, a rancher of conviction, almost a war hero to some, who has been robbed of his hard-earned profits by heathen outlaws."

Ralph walked the length of the porch in front of the saloon, rubbing his jaw.

"Cash Weatherly is an upstanding citizen—so it appears. So he can't just come in here and shoot the place up and all of us as well. He doesn't want to hang, become an outlaw himself, or go to jail. He wants the territory to become a state, and he wants to be a senator. So just what the hell is he doing in here?"

"Trying to unnerve you?"

Ian shook his head. "No."

"We are on edge!" Ralph reminded him.

Ian paced. "He knows there is something going on in the saloon relating to him."

Ralph frowned and sighed. "The outlaws are working from the saloon, right?"

Ian nodded.

"And your wife knows it."

"My wife is the damned ringmaster of it!" he grated out.

"Now, Ian, you don't know that—"

"I know it's ending," Ian said. He drew in a deep breath. "It's the only answer here. And I believe that Cash has these men coming in here to try and spread false information. He knows his every movement has been traced through this place. How better to trap a thief than to send him—or her—an invitation to steal?"

"Ian, you can't judge too hastily—"

"There's nothing hasty here. I've been watching since I came. Why the hell is she doing this? Hell, why am I asking you?" He slammed his fist against the rail, and paused, gritting his teeth hard as he remembered the afternoon. Remembered his wife. Her smile. The light in her eyes when she laughed, the cobalt smokiness that came to them when she was roused to passion. He had wanted a wife; he hadn't thought that he could fall in love. He had intended to seduce a response from Ann, and he had discovered himself aroused to a fever of emotions instead. It didn't matter. She'd been playing with fire long enough. He had to stop her.

"Showdown!" he told Ralph softly, straightening his shoulders and stiffening his spine.

* * *

"Ann!" Aaron cried to her. "What in God's name is it?"

"It's—nothing!" she called back to him.

They couldn't stop now, they couldn't stop here. They had to disappear, get to the abandoned mine shaft Aaron had mentioned, stash the gold, and get away before more of Cash Weatherly's riders found their trail and came after them.

She was all right, she told herself. She knew that she was all right. The bullet hadn't lodged within her; she would know if it had. She would feel the terrible pain.

"You shouted—"

"I was afraid for a minute. Startled. Aaron, you know where you're going. Take the lead."

Aaron did so. Twenty minutes of hard riding brought them down to the riverbed, into the water, across it, and to one of the abandoned claims. Ann didn't try to dismount, though she wouldn't allow Aaron to see that she'd been hit. She handed him her saddlebags.

"Think it's safe here?"

"I think that we don't dare take it back to the saloon. And I can't possibly send any of it to charity funds right now. It would be too dangerous, someone would surely grow suspicious that we had so much gold when so much gold just happened to be missing."

"I know. Aaron?"

"What?"

"You're sure you didn't see Bad Bull among the men?"

"Ann, I'm positive. Why?"

"Aaron, do you think that we might have been set up? Maybe Cash Weatherly thinks that some of his trouble is coming from the saloon and he sent Bad Bull Marlin in to throw out information, hoping that someone would act on it and when that someone acted, he would be waiting and watching, ready to pounce.''

"It's possible, Annie."

"Marlin told Dulcie that Cash would be digging up the shack in the morning—yet we came out here tonight, and Cash's men were right on our tails."

"Maybe tonight was a setup."

"And we fell for it."

"There's one good point."

"What's that?"

"They mean to use the gold to trap us. They didn't think we'd move the gold."

She smiled. "You're right." She hesitated. "Of course, it may be less gold than they think. We have managed to give some of our ill-gotten gain away. And I lost the wagon that night. To whoever killed the man who was about to shoot me down."

"Yeah, and that still concerns the hell out of me," Aaron murmured. "Not that he saved you, but that we have no idea what was going on."

A pain surged through Ann. She couldn't reply right away. She held very stiff, biting into her lower lip so that he wouldn't see the agony in her face. "It worries me too," she managed to whisper.

"That gold is probably long gone now."

"Yes."

"In another territory, maybe. Or down in Mexico."

"Maybe," she breathed.

"Well, the gold we have will be down the shaft for now," he told her.

With the saddlebags in his hands, he disappeared. Ann bent over, clenching down murderously hard on her lip to keep from shrieking out with the pain. They had to get back. Oh, God, they had to get back quickly.

She could feel the blood trickling down her side.

* * *

"All right, Harold, where is she?"

"In the kitchen perhaps?" Harold suggested brightly.

Ian shook his head. "I've been in the kitchen, Harold. Where is she?"

Harold inhaled and exhaled. "All right, she was upset. Says you and Ralph have all manner of secrets, and you less than politely keep them from her. I imagine that she doesn't want to see you, that she's walking somewhere perhaps. Perhaps she's gone to see a friend."

"Oh, yeah, like maybe she's dropping in on the Reverend's daughter?" Ian said sarcastically.

Harold didn't hear the sarcasm. "Well, now, you never do know. Things seem to be changing here. We might just become the meeting place for the church group any time here, huh?" he said hopefully.

"Harold, where is my wife?"

"Ian, for the love of God—"

"Fine, I'll ask Dulcie."

"Now, McShane, Dulcie's—er, she's gone on upstairs. I believe she's with Joey Weatherly, and if I'm not mistaken, they do both enjoy—"

"Joey Weatherly?" Ian said with a frown.

"Yes, sir!"

"Joey wasn't here before."

"Well, now, I didn't see him myself, but—"

"Thanks, Harold."

He took the stairs two at a time and quickly gave his room a glance. His wife wasn't in it.

He walked down the hallway and pounded on Dulcie's door. "Dulcie, it's Ian, let me in."

"Ian!" she cried out after a minute. "Why, sugar, I'm just not ready to receive at the moment, didn't they tell you that I was busy?"

"Dulcie, you can open the damned door or I'll break it."

"Now, Ian—"

"Open the damned door."

"Ian, be a gentleman."

He threw his shoulder against the door. Another heavy slam and he'd break the bolt.

"Wait!" came a gasp.

He stood in the hallway. The door opened. The room was dark. The drapes were closed; she had just snuffed out her lamp. He could smell the oil.

"Dulcie what the hell is going on here?" he demanded.

"Why, Ian—"

There was something wrong. Really wrong. He caught hold of her arm and drew her out into the hallway.

He looked at her face and his jaw tightened. "Who did this?"

"Ian, please—"

"Who did it?"

"Ian, come on now, please, I can't tell you—"

"You have to tell me."

"I can't, I'm afraid—"

"Dulcie, who did it?" he roared. "Who?"

"Ian—"

"Dulcie, tell me!"

"Bad Bull Marlin," she whispered at last.

"Did Ann go after him? Tell me, did Ann go after him?"

"No!" Dulcie cried out. "Ian, Ann is fine, she's just—she's upset with you. She'll be all right, she's just somewhere thinking. Please, Ian, you can't make something out of this, you can't—"

"And what the hell were you doing with Bad Bull Marlin?"

"I—" She paused. "Ian, I—this is what I do. Bad

Bull came in here and you know me. I said things.
I teased him. He wasn't up to it. So—''

Ian spun around; there had been movement behind him.

Joey Weatherly had really and truly showed up at
last. He stood perhaps twenty feet behind Ian, halfway up the stairs. He must have seen Dulcie's face.

For his own handsome features were as pale as
ash. He turned and went running down the stairs,
across the saloon.

''Joey!'' Ian shouted.

''Oh, God!'' Dulcie shrieked. ''Ian, please, for
the love of God, you've got to go after him, stop
him! Joey isn't a killer. If he goes after Bad Bull
Marlin—''

Dulcie hadn't needed to say a word. He was already racing down the stairs. He had to catch Joey;
Dulcie was right. Joey would challenge Bad Bull, try
to shoot him down. And Bad Bull was fast as lightning.

Joey had to know that. It seemed that Joey didn't
care. He felt that he had to make his stand.

But no one in town could best Bad Bull Marlin;
since the war, he'd been a professional gunfighter.
No one could take him on, except someone else who
was ready for a gunfight.

Ian himself.

And a gunfight between the two of them would
be close.

It would set things into motion, surely. Either one
of Weatherly's guns would kill him, or he would kill
one of Weatherly's guns, and Ian knew he couldn't
possibly afford to die right now.

But somehow, the end was beginning.

Ian burst out onto the street.

And a shot rang out.

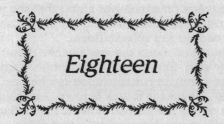

Eighteen

Ann could barely sit up anymore. They had ridden so hard she feared they were killing the poor horses. They had to ride back just as hard, and slip back into the saloon. And quickly.

Where was Ian now? she wondered. Still with Ralph? Or looking for her? What was she going to do? Feign sleep? Perhaps tonight she would get away with it. She had to get away with it. Perhaps she should be angry herself, telling him she was weary of all his secrets and being sent away. She would have to do something, or else he would realize she was injured. God, what kind of story could she invent to explain this wound?

A sudden, stabbing pain shot through her and she clutched her side. Stickiness surged over her fingers. She was bleeding badly, she realized. Just how seriously was she injured?

"All done!" Aaron said softly, reappearing from the mine shaft in the moonlight. "We'll take the river back as far as we can. They'll never be able to trace us that way."

"You're right," she agreed, talking through clenched teeth.

She was barely aware of the ride back to town; it took all of her strength and energy to remain on her horse. Several times she was afraid that she was going to black out, but she bit into her cheeks, shocking herself back to full consciousness.

Aaron talked along the way but she didn't hear a word he said. She clutched her saddle, desperately trying to maintain her seat upon her horse.

At last, they made it back to town. Ann could hear activity on the main street. Voices, men talking. But thankfully, Aaron knew what he was doing and they rode slowly and silently through the back way to the stables behind the saloon. Aaron dismounted from his horse and turned to her, whispering impatiently.

"Ann, come on. We're back. Let's not get caught at this stage!"

"Aaron, I—"

"Annie, what's wrong? Annie?"

She swallowed hard. Her fingers felt like ice as she gripped the saddle. "Help me."

He swore and hurried forward, helping her when she slipped from her saddle and down into his arms. "Annie, oh, my God—"

Joey walked down the street, firing. Following quickly in his wake, Ian saw beneath the flaming street torches that Bad Bull Marlin had been standing, leaning against one of the columns, at the sheriff's office. Bull had been lighting a cheroot. Joey was a good enough shot to cause him to drop the cheroot quickly, along with his matches.

"Joey!" Ian said.

Joey spun around. His jaw remained locked hard; a pulse ticked rampantly at his throat. "He had no right to do it. Sweet Jesu—"

"Joey, you can't—"

"Don't you go telling me there isn't any reason to defend a whore. Don't you go telling me that!"

"I wasn't about to tell you that," Ian assured him.

"He hurt her!"

"Yes, but Joey—"

"Hey, kid, I ain't got no argument with you!" Bull shouted out. "Son of bitch, your old man don't want you dead, boy—"

"This isn't for my father, you lousy, murdering bastard! It has nothing to do with my father. This is for Dulcie!"

"The whore?" Bad Bull said incredulously. He was a man who lived up to his name. His shoulders and arms were as thick as oak stumps. His head looked oddly small atop his massive shoulders.

"The *woman*," Ian said with a wealth of quiet dignity.

"Boy—hell!" Bad Bull swore.

Joey started to raise his gun again. Bull was ready to jump down from the planked sidewalk to the street, ready to draw his gun.

Joey wouldn't stand a chance in hell. Ian hadn't managed to explain that to him, and if he had managed to do so, it might not have done any good.

Ian came right behind Joey before Joey could get off another shot. There was also no way to explain to Joey now that they were drawing an audience on the street, that everyone would have to admit—once Bad Bull had gunned him down dead—that Bad Bull hadn't had much choice in the matter, Joey had come out of the saloon shooting.

Joey was just about the last man in the town who deserved to be dead.

Ian swiftly, efficiently, brought the butt of his own Colt crashing down on Joey's head. Joey never fired another shot. He fell to the dirt without a whimper.

Bad Bull was in the street then, grinning. "Glad you got the kid out of the way, McShane. It's you and me now, ain't it?"

"Seems that way."

It seemed, as well, that they had taken their positions in the street. Ian could hear windows and doors opening, then closing again. The townfolk wanted to see what was going on—they didn't want to be a part of it. Gunfights tended to be accurate unto death, but just in case, no one wanted to be the recipient of a stray bullet.

"Heard you were one of them Rebel heroes, huh, McShane?" Bad Bull taunted. "Should have died in the war, maybe."

"Heard you were one of them red-legged murdering bastards during the war," Ian replied. "Damned sad you weren't killed in the war, but then that's all right, we can correct the matter right here."

"It'll be corrected. And when I'm done with you, there's another whore in that place who's going to get a beating. But then, I won't be touching your pretty little widow. Weatherly will be having her all to himself. For a time. Well, all right, maybe I will touch her just a little bit before I hand her on over to the boss man. He's paying me good, but then, the victor is the one to take the spoils, huh, and I think I'll have to consider myself the victor here first. She's just such a damned tempting piece!"

"You're not going to be touching anything," Ian assured him. "If I was ready to send you to hell before, you can guarantee the thought of you ever touching my wife will help me get you there all the faster."

"Can't wait to feel that ivory flesh, see it all naked, McShane!" Bad Bull taunted.

"Be damned hard to see when you're burning for eternity," Ian responded. They were pretty equally matched; each knew it. Each sought a way to make the other so angry he would lose control.

Bad Bull laughed suddenly. "Breathe your last, you spawn of Satan, bastard half-breed Reb boy.

This is going to be a pleasure. I wasn't expecting to get to kill you tonight, but that's all right, tonight will be just fine."

"You ready to meet your maker?" Ian asked him, and smiled.

Bad Bull took his stance, hands out by his guns. "I'm ready to send you to yours, McShane."

"Let God decide," Ian replied, his guns in his belt now, his hands at the ready.

"Draw!" Bad Bull roared.

Split seconds ticked by. Their eyes remained locked on one another. Another split second.

They drew.

And the sound of gunfire exploded on the street again.

"Aaron, please don't panic on me—"

"You're bleeding to death and I'm not supposed to panic?" he demanded sharply.

"No!" she whispered frantically. "It's not that bad; I was just nicked."

"Don't tell me that—let me see the wound."

"It's not bad. Just help me get my things, quickly. I'll change, I'll go in. Dulcie or Cocoa will help me stop the bleeding. Then I'll be fine."

"Ann, you're covered in blood!"

"Wounds bleed!" she insisted.

"Never again," he swore.

"Aaron—" She broke off, listening. They had come into town the back way, skirting Main Street, and in the stables in the far rear of the saloon property, they could hear little of the activities of the town itself, but Ann was suddenly convinced she heard gunfire.

"Did you hear a shot?" she asked Aaron.

"I didn't hear anything."

"You weren't listening then. I'm sure I heard a shot. Or shots being fired."

"Ann, the only shot you need to worry about right now is the one that's going to kill you!" he said impatiently.

"But—"

"We've been fools, we've even ignored the close calls we've had. I shouldn't have allowed things to come to this. Never again, Ann! My God, we've got to see how badly you're hurt."

"It's not bad, Aaron, honestly. And damn you, listen."

He obligingly remained quiet as several seconds ticked by, but they heard nothing else.

"No gunfire, and we haven't any time. If this wound weren't serious, there wouldn't be so much blood, Annie!" he told her. He helped her pull off her duster, then ripped the buttons off her shirt to pull it away to see the damage. She stood still, gritting her teeth, while he wiped away the blood with his kerchief. "My God, I can't even try to treat this out here—"

"Aaron, I can take care of it, please, I swear to you!"

"You can't just leave this—" He broke off, shaking his head, his handsome features drawn and tense. "I'll get your petticoat and rip it up for a bandage. Come on, you've got to sit before you fall." He led her to a bale of hay, then disappeared into the back stall to retrieve her dress and petticoat. He brought them back to her, ripping up pieces of petticoat as he came. "Stand, Annie. Let me bind this. If Dulcie thinks there's any danger at all, we're going to call the doctor."

"We can't call the doctor! I'll be hanged if anyone discovers what I was up to. We'll be hanged. We can't take that chance, Aaron."

"Well, Ann, I am damned sorry, but I will not just let you die! You're going to have to think of a story, we'll think of a story, but we may need the doctor. We can say that I shot you accidentally, something—"

"I don't dare say that!"

"Why? Your husband will kill me?"

"Aaron—!"

"It doesn't matter, we'll have to do something."

"Let Dulcie decide how bad it is first, please? I can think of something, I can say that I shot myself—"

"At that angle?"

"Aaron, you can't be a part of this!"

"Then, Ann, you've got to think of a better story, and think of it fast."

"We ran into a party of Apaches."

"What were we doing out riding together?"

She shook her head. "I don't know. I went out riding, you were worried—" She broke off, wincing.

"We've got to take care of this or the excuses won't matter, you'll be dead."

She didn't protest; she braced herself against him as he wound the petticoat into a bandage around her midriff. "This wound has to be cleaned well."

"Aaron, I have no death wish. I'll get Cocoa to come to my room and she—"

"Cocoa is a newlywed, Ann, remember? She's going to be with her husband and any man or woman in his or her right mind would wonder what was so important at this hour of the night that you would call a bride from her groom!"

"Then Dulcie will help me. Come on, Aaron, we've got to get back in there."

"All right!" he grated out. He finished wrapping her rib cage. She turned her back to him and he pulled away her tattered shirt and then slipped her dress over her head.

"One second!" she told him, nearly crying out again when she stooped to shed her guns, trousers, and boots. "Take all of this and hide it quickly."

Aaron did so, taking her guns and clothing back to the last stall, then returning. She was leaning against the hay. She pushed herself back up again. "I'm all right—"

"You look like death."

"Thank you."

"Ann—"

"Please, Aaron, just help me get this on. We must get back inside before someone realizes that we've been gone!"

He sighed. "Come closer so that I can manage these ridiculous little hooks," he told her.

Ann inched back and around. Then she gasped. An awful gasp. An intake of breath that brought burning, searing, ungodly pain to her.

Yet she was barely aware of it, she was so frozen with horror and dismay.

They weren't alone in the stables. She didn't know when he had come in; she hadn't heard the slightest whisper of movement, the hint of a footstep.

But *he* had come. Ian had come. He was inside the front door, leaning against the door frame. Watching her. With Aaron. Even though they stood in nothing more than moonlight, she could see his eyes. They were alive with cold fury. An anger unlike anything she had ever imagined before.

"Ian," she breathed.

"My love," he replied derisively, his black gaze flickering to Aaron.

"McShane—" Aaron began.

"Get your hands off my wife!" Ian said. The words weren't loud. They were deep. They were filled with the abject, deadly fury that blazed so menacingly within his eyes.

Aaron's hands fell. He stepped away.

"McShane—"

Ann gasped again as Ian drew one of his Colts. He was unbelievably fast. His movement was so swift it tricked the eye.

"Ian, no!" she cried out.

"No?" he repeated. "You know, I am getting sick and tired of killing. In the war you kill your enemy. In the West, the only difference is finding out just who your enemy is. And I'll be damned if I ever thought it was going to be the piano player—and my own wife."

"Ian—" Ann tried again.

"But you're right. I'd never actually planned to be a gunslinger; things just turned out that way. And I've no damned desire in the world to shoot Aaron. I'm just going to rip his heart out by hand and then I'll get to you!" he stated, his voice touched by such a loathing that she felt as if her skin crawled on the inside. He stared at the gun in his hand, then shoved it back into his holster.

"What an ass I've been!" he said, a bitter smile twisted into his lips. "And you son of a bitch!" He charged Aaron.

Ian had no more than taken one step toward Aaron when Ann flew into motion.

"No, no, you are an ass!" she gasped, rushing forward to block him from reaching her cousin. "He came after me, that's all. Quite frankly I was furious with you, I didn't want to see you, I went riding out to get away. Harold will tell you, and—"

"Dulcie would tell me, too, of course. Except that she's occupied with Joey Weatherly."

Ann exhaled. Thank God, it seemed he had believed the story about Dulcie if nothing else.

"Aaron is absolutely innocent!" she stated. "Of anything. Of everything, I mean."

"Ann, you can't fight my battles—" Aaron began. "This is my battle."

She cried out; even as they had spoken, Ian had come forward the last few steps to touch her, his copper features tense and hard in the moonlight and shadows, his fingers reaching out and grabbing her hair with a speed that defied even that of his draw.

"Get away from him!" Ian grated out, drawing her from Aaron. She was in absolute terror that he would kill Aaron. Her cousin surely was no coward, and he was a man who could defend himself. But not against Ian. Somewhere in Ian's life, he had become absolutely lethal, so honed and trained, so swift and smooth, that she was certain he could easily kill with his bare hands.

"Ian, you don't understand."

"Understand? Hell, it seems I have been slow to understand! The two of you have been so close since I've been here, whispering, talking at that piano. You always made beautiful music together. So this is the affair. And you say that I don't understand. You've both been missing for hours and I find him dressing you in the stables? Just what is it that I don't understand?" Ian asked. His voice was still low, and so deep it terrified her.

He drew her face close to his, then suddenly thrust her away. The pain stabbed through her again, but he had turned back to Aaron. He was like a mountain lion, tensed, poised, ready to leap down from the cliff upon his prey—and rip out its throat.

"No! You don't understand!" she cried again, pitching herself at him, slamming her fists into his shoulder and back until he turned to her. "You don't understand, you—"

He caught her wrists, his fingers merciless. She

couldn't seem to inhale, and when she did, the pain was staggering. She tried to pull free but it was futile, it caused an even greater anguish to sweep through her. "Let go of me, you stupid, senseless fool—" She broke off. She'd moved too much. The pain seemed to be impaling her, robbing her of all ability to draw in air. The moonlight was fading. She blinked furiously.

"Then what the hell is going on?" Ian demanded furiously, catching her against him, shaking her. Her teeth seemed to rattle. She saw stars.

And she saw his arm. The upper sleeve of his shirt, just below his shoulder, was covered in crimson.

"Your arm—" she gasped. "I *did* hear gunfire."

"Never mind my arm. The gunfire is over. I want to know what the hell is going on here between the two of you."

"There's nothing, before God, I swear it!" Aaron cried out. "Let her alone, I beg of you, you don't know what you're doing!" He reached for Ian's shoulder. Ian swung around with a menacing and lethal manner. Ann drew on her last reserves of strength, clinging to her husband again.

"Ian, no!" she shrieked.

"It's no affair!" Aaron told him quickly. "Sweet Jesu, no affair, I swear it. She's my cousin."

"Cousin?"

Ian's startled gaze snapped from Ann to Aaron.

Aaron exhaled on a long, miserable breath.

"Aaron, no more, please—" Ann began.

"What the hell is going on?" Ian roared. "He's your cousin, and a damned close cousin if he's dressing you in the stables!"

The sound was so loud, then all sound seemed to be fading.

"Ann, you've got to tell him—" Aaron began.

"No!" Ann insisted again, but to no avail.

"Sweet Jesu, Annie!" Aaron exclaimed. "This can go no further."

"What can go no further?" Ian demanded. The quiet in his voice was gone at last; the words seemed to echo and thunder throughout the confines of the stables, which somehow seemed suddenly very tight.

"Aaron!"

"What will you do? Hide for weeks?" Aaron challenged her.

"If one of you doesn't tell me what in hell is going on I swear to God I will make you do so," Ian promised. Ann no longer had to cling to him to keep him from Aaron. She had his full attention again. She felt the bite of his fingers around the flesh of her arms. It was good. It kept her from feeling the horrible sting against her ribs.

"Ann?" he demanded. There was a chill in his voice now. Wrapped around the fury and the heat.

Ann couldn't answer.

"Ann!" He pulled her tighter against him. His eyes were a dark blaze against the tension that drew his features taut.

Aaron swore softly to her with a groan. "You'll drop down dead in a minute, Annie, it's over, you can't take it any further." He came to them, trying to take Ann by the shoulders, to release her from Ian's punishing hold.

"I'll thank you to stop—" Ian began.

"You've got to let her go!" Aaron demanded. "Give her over to me—"

"The hell I will, enough!"

"Let her go!" Aaron insisted.

"Wait—" Ann began, but it seemed that Aaron had lost his senses. Her fault. She should have given in already; they had no choice!

Aaron took a swing at Ian.

"Aaron!" Ann cried, but her cry, as well, was too late. Ian easily ducked Aaron's swing, and it was almost as if he had been waiting for it. His fury was so great, he was waiting for any chance to strike out.

And he did.

Before Ann quite knew what was going on, Aaron was down in the dust on the floor and Ian was atop him, getting ready to slam him in the jaw.

"No!" she shrieked out, finding her voice at last. She jumped upon Ian with the fullness of her body and what was left of her strength, beating against his back, clawing at his arm. He was like steel, unmovable. Almost entirely unaware that she was there. "Ian!" she grated, rising and throwing herself at him with all of her force again, and this time managing to unbalance them both, catapulting him from Aaron's body.

She brought them both down hard upon the hay-strewn floor.

She didn't know if the fall, or the pain, completely sucked her breath away. She had been on top; she was suddenly on the bottom. And she couldn't help herself anymore, she cried out with the pain, frantically trying to push Ian from her.

Aaron scrambled over to Ian's side. "McShane, she's got to have help!" he pleaded. "She's been shot," he said swiftly.

"Shot!"

Ann heard Ian rasp out the word. Tears were stinging her eyes. It hurt so badly. Aaron was talking, but she couldn't hear him. She could still see Ian balanced atop her, staring into her eyes, his own wide and startled. Sound was fading away. The image of his face seemed to waver before her. Pale moonlight dimmed still further.

She was clutching his arm. She realized that it was

damp. Sticky, just like her side. Her own eyes widened as she tried to focus upon him. She'd seen the dark crimson on his shirt before, now it was sinking into her mind that the substance upon his arm was blood.

"You—" she began.

But a sharp pain stabbed through her, then began to turn into a strange numbness.

She had clung so fiercely to consciousness, but now the blackness was beginning to overwhelm her.

Mercifully . . .

"Annie!"

She wasn't aware that he leapt off of her, reaching down for her. She never felt it when he lifted her into his arms, nor did she see the look of anguish and fear that replaced the fury in his eyes.

She didn't even hear the agony in his voice as he cried her name again.

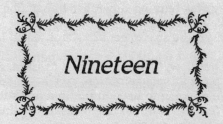

Nineteen

In the hours that followed, Ann wished that she might have remained completely unconscious, but unfortunately, she did not.

She was painfully aware of too much that happened.

There was light, lamplight. She was up in her room, in her own bed. Aaron was with her, as well as Dulcie—and Ian. Aaron was holding the lamp close to her flesh, Dulcie was wiping up the blood at her torn side—and Ian was digging into her flesh.

"Ian, you're sure—" Dulcie was saying.

"I pulled enough bullets out of men in the war. I'm sure. Dulcie, get a hold of her so that she doesn't move on me now. If I get a clean grip on it, I'll have it."

The next seconds were awful. She felt as if she were being knifed clean through her body. She started to scream with the pain, but Aaron was suddenly by her face, shushing her with a tender but determined touch. "You can't cry out, you can't cry out, Annie!"

"Give her some of the whiskey," she heard Ian say.

Aaron dragged her up, tilted her head, and then

329

whiskey was burning down her throat. She started to choke and cough.

"Will you be able to get it?" Aaron asked Ian anxiously.

"It's out now," Ian said simply. "Dulcie, give me a new piece of sponge; Aaron, give her more whiskey. We're going to have to put in a few stitches."

She felt the burn of the whiskey again. Then, thankfully, she passed out once again.

A little while later, she managed to open her eyes. Everything was spinning. The pain in her side was down to a dull burn.

Aaron was by her side, bathing her forehead with a washcloth.

"Aaron?" she whispered with dry lips.

"It's all right."

"Where's—Ian?"

"Downstairs."

"Dulcie?" she croaked.

"With Joey."

She shook her head. "No, no. We made that up—"

"She's really with Joey now. He was hurt. Ian—"

"Ian hurt Joey?" she gasped.

"Annie . . ."

His reply faded away. She tried to listen, but she couldn't hear anymore. The effort to see him, to listen, to understand, had all been too much. The misty blackness rose around her and swallowed her.

Aaron stood on the porch unhappily while Ian McShane stared at him with his impaling, merciless dark eyes, his arms crossed over his chest, pure demand and anger tightening the rigid muscles of his body as he waited.

Dulcie was back with Ann. They had all watched

her carefully through the night. McShane knew something about medicine. It seemed he'd been part of an elite unit during the war, that he'd ridden with a physician and had assisted that physician any time his men had gotten shot or wounded. Aaron could well imagine that a full four years of watching men struck by bullets, swords, and shrapnel come beneath the knife had certainly taught him something.

Aaron's admiration for the man had grown throughout the night; once McShane had realized his wife was injured, he hadn't asked any questions that didn't pertain exactly to the injury.

It was apparent, of course, that McShane assumed Ann had been shot while involved in illegal pursuits—McShane didn't want to bring in a doctor unless it was necessary. He had been quick to bring Ann to their room, quicker still to give clear, quiet commands to him and Dulcie to get Ann undressed, to hold the lamp, to bring clean water, to let him assess the damage. "She's in so much pain because the bullet is still lodged in her flesh. Thankfully, it missed the rib—and the lung," he had said almost tonelessly. He'd had a ball retriever in a small medical chest he carried along with his belongings. He'd hesitated only a second, his fingers had trembled only once. Then he'd moved with speed and unerring efficiency to remove the bullet from Ann's body and sew up the gash that had remained.

Even then, he'd refrained from questions. And he hadn't mentioned the bloodstain on his own arm. He'd bandaged Ann's wound carefully, helped Dulcie slip a nightgown over her head, then set to keeping her brow cool. "We've got to keep her from developing a fever. If we can do that, we're home free."

Ian had stayed with Ann himself until daylight had broken. Then he'd left Aaron with her.

Now Dulcie was with her.

And it was time for questions again.

"You can start at the beginning," Ian said wearily. "You are really her cousin?"

Aaron nodded. "Our mothers were sisters."

"You were taken by the Pawnee too?"

"No. Ann's folks were heading west with her before the war. Her mother was quite a letter writer, so we'd followed their progress along the way, we knew who they were meeting, what they were seeing politically and geographically." He hesitated a minute. "Before they left, she was more like my sister. We were both only children, we played together. We were going to grow up to be a great musical act, which, of course, our parents frowned upon at the time. Not a proper vocation for well-raised children."

"So you opened a saloon?" Ian murmured.

"Well, life doesn't turn out quite the way we expect it to," Aaron said with a shrug.

"Why didn't Ann just tell me you were cousins?" Ian demanded.

Aaron shrugged uncomfortably. "I don't know."

"Maybe she thought I'd see her illegal activities too clearly if I knew the connection?"

Aaron held very still, determined to maintain his dignity. He was in a difficult position because, of course, he had been taking part in illegal activities, yet he couldn't explain his part in those activities to McShane because he considered it Ann's place to do so.

"Ian, you can outdraw me, and that's a fact, and you probably are capable of ripping my heart out of my chest, but I'm begging you, please talk to Annie."

"I intend to. If she lives."

Aaron's heart slammed into his ribs. "But you said—"

"I said I think that she's in the clear. The wound is far from healed. We've got to prevent an infection from setting in."

"Perhaps you should be worried about yourself," Aaron pointed out. Ian was still wearing the shirt with the bloodied arm.

"This? It's a scratch. Bad Bull wasn't quite as good as I'd thought."

"Wasn't? Then he's—"

"Dead," Ian said quietly. "And Sheriff Bickford is breathing fire at me, talking about arresting me."

"You shot down Bad Bull?"

"Well, it wasn't exactly what I had intended for the evening, but it was the way things came about. Joey—who was supposed to have been with Dulcie—happened to be behind me when I insisted on seeing her. Joey wanted the honor of shooting Bad Bull."

"But Joey—"

"Wouldn't have made it. I stepped in," Ian said simply. "Let's get back to you and Ann and your family history."

"It's simple, really. Word came back to my mother that there had been a terrible massacre. My aunt and uncle had been found dead, but since there was no sign of Ann's body at the scene, we hoped that she might be alive. Stories circulated; an army scout heard that a girl fitting Ann's description was living among the Pawnee. For a time, the army kept searching for Ann. They spent a few hard years searching, but then the war broke out." He shrugged. They both knew what had happened when the war broke out. Most troops had been called back east to fight. There weren't many soldiers left to deal with the Indians. "My mother died of a fever in 1861, my father died at First Manassas. I was wounded right after and given a discharge. I had promised both my parents and myself that when I was able, I'd find Ann. I was no good to the army then—there were still plenty of able-bodied young men at the time—so I came out to Saint Louis in 1862 and met up with Eddie McCastle. He was trapping then, meeting with any number of the Indian tribes, and he'd heard about a young, blond white woman being kept by the Pawnee. It wasn't long after we'd talked that he met up with Cloud Walker's tribe, and it was right after Cloud Walker had died, so blessedly, my quest was not a long and painful one, even though I'd not seen Ann in years by that time. But I'd lost everyone else, finding Ann was all that I had left in life. It was the same for Ann. She'd been taken from everyone she loved, but after Eddie went in and brought her back from the Pawnee, she created a strange new family. There was this little group of us, and all that we had was one another. We came out here and Eddie bought the saloon and Annie put it all together. She had Dulcie and Cocoa and they found Ginger right away, and she had me to play the piano. Henri had been working in the finest restaurants back east in Baltimore, but after the war he'd gotten into a knife skirmish with a soldier still in uniform. The soldier was killed. Henri said he'd been defending one of the Reb serving boys just back from the war. Ann believed him. Back east, I suppose Henri is wanted somewhere. Out here, he's worth his weight in gold. Cooking like his is hard to come by out in the wilds, as you know.''

"So Henri is a murderer—and you and Ann are a pair of outlaws. He's wanted back east—and the two of you are wanted by the sheriff right across the street.''

"The sheriff knows nothing about us."

"Whoever shot Ann might know he struck his target."

"We weren't seen, or caught. And we aren't really outlaws—"

"No?"

Aaron hesitated. The rest of this needed to come from Ann herself.

"We aren't responsible for all of the gold that has disappeared in the area," he said.

"That doesn't matter. You two are guilty of armed robbery. They can hang you in the blink of an eye."

"They can't prove that we're guilty."

"They can get mighty suspicious if the wrong people were to realize that Ann is recovering from a gunshot wound."

Aaron was silent for a moment.

"It is over for you," Ian told him.

Aaron nodded. "I know."

"I should let them hang you. What kind of a fool notion of yours was it to drag Ann into your robberies?"

Aaron was so startled that his brows flew up. A smile curled his lip, then he lowered his head quickly, trying to hide the telltale surprise on his face. McShane didn't know Ann quite that well yet. Not if he thought that anyone could drag her into something if she didn't want to be a part of it.

"It's over," Aaron said. "We were wrong."

He looked up. McShane was staring at him. "So Ann dragged you into *her* scheme?"

"McShane—"

"Never mind, I knew it from the beginning."

"You can't just condemn her, because you don't know—" Aaron began, then cut himself off. There was nowhere for him to go. Whatever else Ann wanted to tell him had to be up to her. "You don't understand," he said.

Ian swore with impatience. "I'm trying damned hard to understand."

Aaron stood straight, squaring his shoulders. "There's nothing else I can tell you. I can swear to God, beyond death and further, that Ann and I are like brother and sister, first cousins, good friends, nothing more. I know that as a wife, she has been completely loyal to you—even if she did marry you for strange reasons. I'll—I'll understand if you want me out of the saloon, but you've no reason to despise Ann—or even me—for sins that have never been committed."

He was startled to see that McShane was wearing a rueful smile. He was leaning against the wall of the saloon, his shoulders touching it, one booted foot up against it as he stared out at the day. Then his eyes focused on Ian. "Other than the fact that you are both notorious bandits?"

Aaron sighed.

"And where's the gold now?"

"Down a mine shaft. Most of what we took, at any rate. I told you. Ann held up a wagon one night that was stolen from her before she ever got her hands on it."

"You were risking your lives all along!" Ian snapped, suddenly furious again.

"Yes."

"You should have stopped her."

"I couldn't stop her. Maybe you can."

"There's no maybe to it," Ian guaranteed him. "She's stopped."

When Ann awoke again, Dulcie was sitting by the side of her bed, frowning over a book. Dulcie looked a hundred times better. The swelling in her face was gone. Only the blue tinge of a few bruises remained.

"Dulcie?" Ann murmured.

"Annie, you're back with us!" Dulcie said happily.

Ann's head was spinning. She felt as if she had been living at the center of a twister. Snatches of memory, visions, rushed to her mind. She wasn't quite certain what had been real and what had been a dream. But she was afraid. And one of the visions that remained foremost in her mind was that of Ian and Aaron, ready to tear one another apart.

"Dulcie is . . . it's true, we were caught, right?" she whispered.

Dulcie nodded unhappily. She stood, rinsing out the washcloth at Ann's side, cooling and cleansing her face with it as she talked, then offering Ann a long sip of water from the glass and pitcher that sat on the stand as well. "Annie, perhaps you can't see it yet, but thank God! That bullet was inside of you. None of us would have known what to do. We'd have had to get the doctor, and who knows what he would have done with the information that you'd been shot? Annie, you were dealing with a murdering bastard on one end and the law on the other. Nothing could have come out right."

Her throat was dry. "Aaron?" she asked painfully.

"Aaron is fine. He wasn't hit by any bullets," Dulcie said frowning.

"No, but Ian . . . "

"Oh. Aaron and Ian are together now."

"What happened? How did Ian find us? He said that you were with Joey, so he hadn't seen you—"

"I was with Joey when he said that I was with Joey."

"I thought that we were saying that you were with Joey so that Ian wouldn't see you."

"It didn't work that way. By the time Ian found you, I had to be with Joey. He wasn't in very good shape by the time Ian finished with him—"

"Oh, my God, then what is he doing to Aaron? And dear Lord! What did he do to Joey?"

"What did he do to Joey?"

Ann's head snapped around as she suddenly heard Ian speak, repeating the question, his voice deep and angry. He had come into the room, so damned quiet she hadn't heard him. He stood just inside the doorway, his arms crossed over his chest, the door still open behind him. She instinctively inched back against the headboard of the bed, staring his way, wishing for the moment that she hadn't regained consciousness. It hurt to move, but now the pain was merely annoying, not agonizing, as it had been before. She felt stiff, and disheveled, and totally at a disadvantage.

"Ann—" Dulcie began nervously.

"Dulcie, I think maybe Ann and I should discuss this ourselves," Ian said.

"Oh, amen!" Dulcie breathed, heading swiftly for the door. "That's the best idea I've ever heard!"

"Dulcie, wait, it might be a good idea if—" Ann began, but too late. Dulcie had disappeared out the door.

And Ian closed it.

He walked across the room toward the bed, his arms still crossed over his chest. His eyes had never seemed blacker. Colder. Harder.

There seemed nothing to do but go on the offensive.

"What did you do to Joey?" she demanded, bracing herself for whatever might come.

"I knocked him out with the butt of my gun."

"Why?" Ann demanded. "What could Joey possibly have done to you?"

"Not a damned thing," he told her.

"Then you had no right—"

"Don't tell me about my rights, Ann." He took a seat at the foot of the bed, staring at her. "Because I have a few things that I'm going to tell you."

She inhaled, aware that he was trying to keep his distance from her. She could only vaguely remember the night before. His hands, his fingers, moving over her, tender upon the wound, gentle and sure even as he dislodged the bullet from her flesh. Bathing the blood away, bandaging her, dressing her. His touch had been so gentle, so very different from the way he was treating her now.

"How could you hurt Joey?" she asked, but did it more softly.

"Joey is fine. But you might have died, Ann. And for what? A few handfuls of gold? What is it that you don't have that you think you're going to be able to buy?"

There was contempt and disdain in his voice.

"Nothing. Not a damned thing," she told him coolly, her eyes narrowing.

"You're done, Ann."

She didn't reply. He stood up and leaned over then so that she caught her breath, his face was so close to hers.

"You're done, Ann!"

She exhaled on a long breath, furious, frightened. She might have explained, except it seemed that there was a massive wall that had risen between them. She couldn't touch it; she could feel it.

"If you're so damned self-righteous, why don't you just turn us over to the sheriff?"

"My concern has nothing to do with self-righteousness."

"Then—"

"You just got yourself shot, you little idiot. Lots worse could have happened a dozen times. You were asking for it. I knew the day the stagecoach

was held up that the outlaws were coming from
somewhere in the saloon, and I knew damned well
you had something to do with it. I had a clean shot
that day, Ann. I could have taken you down."

"So why didn't you?"

"Because I was afraid it might be you."

She didn't dare breathe.

"You are done!" he repeated violently. His arms,
stretched around either side of her face and braced
against the headboard, trembled slightly with the vehemence of his words. She saw his shirtsleeve, dark-
ened, crimson with dried blood.

She cried out softly. "Ian, you—"

"It's a nick, no more."

"Your sleeve is nearly black with dried blood. It
can't be a nick—"

She broke off because he had pushed away from
the bed, wrenched at the buttons, and ripped off his
shirt. She stretched forward, unaware that she had
ceased to breathe and that her heart was thundering.
There was a narrow black slash across the top of his
arm. It was an ugly wound, but neither too long nor
too deep. She lay back again, inhaling deeply, her
heartbeat easing again.

"But what happened?" she whispered. Oh, God,
when had he been wounded? Hadn't she seen the
blood on him last night? Before he had nearly pum-
meled Aaron. Where was Aaron now, and in God's
name, what had happened to Joey?

"Oh, God, Ian, Joey—"

"Joey is going to be just fine."

She was trembling. "I don't care what you have
to say to me. Joey didn't do anything to you. You'd
no right to hurt him. And you have no right to—to
hurt Aaron, to hold anything against him. Anything
that he's done, he's done because I asked him to do
it. Don't you dare even think of hurting him. You

can't even begin to think about turning him in to any of the authorities, you—"

She broke off. He was standing by the bed bare-chested, the bloodied shirt now on the floor. His muscles seemed to gleam a wicked shade of copper, his fists clenching and unclenching at his side.

"I haven't touched your precious Aaron," he assured her. "Come to think of it, at the moment, I have a hell of a lot more respect for him than I do for you."

He strode across the room to the dresser where a drawer now housed some of his clothing. He wrenched it open, found a clean shirt, and slammed it shut. He turned around on her. "Let's get this straight now. For the next few days, you don't even leave this room. We'll say you've caught a cold and you just don't feel up to coming down. I mean it, Ann. You don't leave the room. If you so much as put a toe out that door, none of us will need to worry about the sheriff hanging you because I'll strangle you myself."

With those final words, he swung around, heading for the door.

"Damn you! You don't understand!" she cried after him.

He paused, his hand on the doorknob. He turned back to her slowly.

"Well, I'm just waiting to understand."

She swallowed hard, wishing he didn't seem quite so distant, so hard. He had the Sioux ability to clear his features of all emotion except the cold fire in his eyes.

"You will never understand!" she charged him.

"Maybe not," he told her. "But so help me God, Ann, I will be in control here. And that is something you had best understand!"

He turned again, opening the door, leaving her. Slamming the door behind him.

She lay back down, shaking, and very weary again. She had barely set her head down before there was a knock on her door. Not Ian, she decided, and she was right. When she beckoned the knocker to enter, it was Henri. He had come with his own cure for her—chicken soup.

Even Henri seemed to think she was suffering from a cold. He tried to cheer her, assuring her that his chicken soup would make her well in no time. It was delicious soup. She was famished. He bid her to eat slowly and carefully and she managed to do so. When he was gone, she lay back down again, warmed by the soup, still shivering with worry.

Despite that, she fell asleep again.

Sometime, when it was dark, she woke again. There was someone by her bed and she almost cried out. But enough pale moonlight was filtering into her room, and she realized that it was Ian. He was in his pants, shirtless and bootless, watching her in the night. Groggy, she spoke to him. "It must be late. I'm sorry, I'm taking all the room. Are you coming to sleep?"

He shook his head. "I'm on the daybed."

For a moment, his hand touched her forehead. "No fever," he murmured, and walked away from her in the darkness. She heard him stretch out on the daybed.

"You know you really don't understand," she told him.

"I told you, I'm waiting to do so."

"You might have some faith in me."

"Ah, the way that you have faith in me?" he queried.

"What faith can I give you? I only know what I see and hear."

"How amazing. That's exactly what I seem to have to go on myself."

She bit into her lower lip. "Ian—"

"Go to sleep, Ann," he told her impatiently.

She would never sleep again, she thought, but eventually she did.

When she opened her eyes again, it was daylight. She imagined that it must be Tuesday morning. She woke feeling so much better. She blinked hard, and saw that Dulcie was by her bed.

"Good morning. How are you?" Dulcie asked anxiously, the bruises on her face having faded almost completely.

"Fine."

"Well, you're not fine, you've got a bullet wound, but you do look much better."

"Than what?"

"Yesterday, you looked like death."

"Thanks."

"Look what I have for you," Dulcie said cheerfully, ignoring the sarcasm in Ann's voice. She moved aside. The hip bath was filled with steaming water. It looked wonderful, like the nicest thing Ann had seen in years.

"How did you—"

"It was easy. Ian built a fire up here and we had the kitchen staff just bring up buckets of cold water to be heated. No one had to come in here that way— they left the buckets at the door and I brought them in."

"Thank you," Ann said.

"Let me help you up. You may not be strong enough."

To Ann's dismay, she wasn't very strong, but she did rise with Dulcie's help, and she managed to shed her nightgown that way too.

"What about the bandages?"

"I'm to take them off. And you're not to scrub the wound; though Ian says the water will not hurt it. We'll salve it with sulfur and cocoa butter when you're done and rewrap it." Dulcie took the bandages off. "Annie, it's really not too bad at all anymore. Can you see?"

The wound was in her side, but she could see it clearly enough. The bullet had made a slash across her ribs and must have imbedded in the flesh just beneath them. She had missed death by a matter of inches or seconds. She was stitched along the slash, neatly, tightly. The flesh around the wound seemed healthy; there was no sign of infection.

"It's beautiful!" Dulcie said, pleased.

Ann arched a brow. She wasn't sure *beautiful* was the right word for the wound, but she was grateful that it seemed to be healing well.

"Come on, into the tub with you," Dulcie said.

Ann crawled in, delighted that the water was so warm. It rushed around her, cleansed her. She ducked her hair back into it, then plowed down face forward to feel it wash around her. It stung the wound slightly at first, then felt good against it. She didn't think that anything had ever felt so good as the warm bath at this time.

Except being with Ian.

Something she didn't dare think about now.

She lifted her head from the water and eased against the back of the tub. "Thank you, Dulcie. This is wonderful."

"It gets better," Dulcie said, handing her a cup. "Tea with lots of cream and sugar."

Ann accepted the tea. "Thanks again," she told Dulcie. "It's wonderful, and you look wonderful, too."

Dulcie smiled. "I told you I was going to be all right."

Ann leaned forward in the tub. "Dulcie, I'm just so worried—" she began.

A tapping on the door interrupted her. "Excuse me," Dulcie said, and went to answer it, going out and closing the door behind her.

Ann leaned back, setting her tea on Dulcie's nearby chair. There was a movement next to her. Dulcie was back, she thought. She opened her eyes.

Ian.

His hair was growing longer, she realized. Still dead straight and almost black, it fell past his collar now, a handsome frame for the hard contours of his face and unfathomable dark eyes. She couldn't tell how much hostility remained in the way that he looked at her, but she instantly felt defensive. She curled into herself at his arrival, staring up at him.

"Let's see how you're doing," he told her.

She felt ridiculously ill at ease. "I'm fine."

"Get up, Ann."

"I'm fine."

He swore. Then he reached for her, lifting her from the water with a tick of impatience, standing her before the fireplace, where a few dying embers still burned. She hugged her arms to her chest, naked and glistening and uncomfortable.

He reached for her towel, blotting the moisture from her face, her shoulders, and then her side. She trembled all the while.

"Does it hurt you?" he asked her with a frown.

"No. It's sore. It doesn't hurt anymore. It's starting to itch."

"Good," he murmured. "Stand still."

She did so, not knowing why, but unable to do anything else. He strode from her to the bedside table, returning with a yellowish salve which he spread across the wound.

"Sulfur?" she asked.

"And other ingredients. Grandfather's concoction. It served me well throughout the war."

"It's working well," she said stiffly. It seemed the closest she could come to a thank-you for the moment.

He nodded, then returned with linen bandaging. She stood very still, her heart thundering, while he lifted her arms to wind the bandage around her rib cage. He finished, expertly tying it off at her other side. He held away from her for a second, then she felt herself grow very warm, trembling all over again because his eyes were raking over her flesh, naked except for his own handiwork upon it.

He touched her cheek. "You shouldn't have been marred, Annie. Nothing should have touched you!" He said the words fiercely, angrily. She swallowed hard.

"It was my risk, my flesh—"

"No more!" he told her. He opened his mouth, about to say more, but a tapping came on the door again. He swore, wrapping the towel around Ann, heading for the door.

She heard a whispering. Then she recognized Dulcie's voice and the words, "Ian, he insists! You've got to come down and talk to him."

The door closed. Ian didn't come back.

She'd been told not to leave the room, and she did stand there for a few minutes, shivering, debating what to do.

She was bandaged; she was clean. She felt strong. And something was going on downstairs and she had to know what.

She hesitated a second longer, remembering Ian's threats, but then she marched to her drawers and wardrobe. She eschewed any type of corset but slipped into a cotton shift and calico day dress, one that hung comfortably about her. She set her feet into black slippers, brushed out her still-damp hair, and hurried to her door. She opened it. No one was in the hallway, and she could hear a number of voices coming from downstairs.

She walked to the staircase, and paused.

Ian was by the bar, along with Cash Weatherly, Carl, Jenson—and Sheriff Bickford. Ralph Reninger stood just behind Ian, and Angus was behind Ralph.

"Well, now, McShane," Sheriff Bickford was saying, "Mr. Weatherly here is charging you with murder!" he stated firmly.

Ann threw the back of her hand against her mouth to keep from crying out. Murder?

"It was a gunfight, fair and square," Ian said calmly. "And half the town saw it."

"Dueling ain't legal—"

"I didn't choose to duel," Ian said.

"By the laws of the territory—" Sheriff Bickford began.

"By the laws of the territory," someone suddenly interrupted, and Ann saw Joey Weatherly sauntering forward from where he had apparently been standing by the piano, "perhaps I should be the one arrested."

"Shut your mouth, son!" Cash snapped.

"The truth is that I was the one who ran after Bad Bull, I was the one who fired the first shots," Joey said, ignoring his father. "Mr. McShane here gave me one damned good headache because he knew I didn't have a prayer in the world of outshooting Bad Bull Marlin. McShane did outshoot him, but it was a fight Bad Bull wanted. Remember the good book, Sheriff. 'He who lives by the sword, dies by the sword.' Bad Bull lived by his guns, and he died shot down on our street. He got off his own shot. McShane was grazed in the arm. It was fair, Sheriff Bickford, and that's that."

"I'm afraid that I would have to refuse to allow you to arrest my client on such a charge, Sheriff," Ralph Reninger was saying.

"There is no damned possible charge!" someone else added impatiently.

Aaron. He, too, walked over from the piano and stood next to Joey. He appeared to be in perfect health.

Ann gripped the railing. She felt weak, and like a fool, and a frightened one at that. Ian had never hurt Joey; he had saved Joey's life. And he hadn't done a thing to Aaron.

"Well, now, McShane, this is a law-abiding town here!" Bickford said with a sigh. "Mr. Weatherly, seems like there isn't a charge here, sir, none that will stick, none that can be tried. Good day to you all," he said. And he tipped his hat and left the saloon.

There was silence as he left. Then Cash Weatherly looked at McShane. "This isn't the end of it, McShane. You will pay for the murder you've done!"

"Yeah? Well, sir, I've a similar opinion. You will pay for the murder you've done," Ian said.

Cash turned, his face mottled and furious, and started out, his elder sons and a few of his men following behind him. He stopped in front of Joey, looking as if he were ready to suffer an apoplexy at any second. He pointed a bony finger at his son.

"You! You are no longer flesh of my flesh! You are not of me, you have no home, no family. You are a bastard from hell's spawn that I rip from my flesh and being."

He spat on the floor and started walking out again.

"Well, thank the good Lord for that!" Joey exclaimed.

Cash spun around. From where she stood, Ann could see what the others could not.

"Ian, he's drawing his gun!" she shouted down.

The sound of clicking as guns were drawn and readied filled the lower floor of the saloon.

Then there were long seconds when everyone just stared at everyone else, Cash with his gun leveled at his son, Ian with his gun leveled at Cash.

"It seems we've come to a draw," Cash said, holstering his piece once again. "The next time I take aim at you, boy, I'll be pulling the trigger," he told his son.

Then he started out of the saloon again, his men in his wake.

When he was gone, a joyous cry went up, followed by laughter. Harold threw out glasses, Cocoa came from the kitchen to hug Angus, Dulcie rushed to Joey Weatherly, and he lifted her from her feet, spinning her around.

Ian looked up, staring at Ann where she stood at the top of the stairs. The expression in his eyes was as enigmatic as ever.

He pushed away from the bar and started for the stairs.

And to her own surprise, Ann met his gaze.

Then she spun and made a beeline back to her own room.

Twenty

She was barely back into the room before Ian burst through the door, slamming it closed behind him, leaning against it.

"I thought I told you to stay in here."

"Why didn't you tell me what had happened?"

"You were told to stay in here!"

"It—it will make matters worse if it seems that I'm hiding," Ann said quickly.

"And what happens if that suddenly bleeds through the bandages and your clothes?"

"It's not going to, it's already healing. Ian, why didn't you tell me what had happened?"

"When?" he demanded. "When I discovered you bleeding all over the stables, or when you were only half conscious when I pulled the bullet from your flesh?"

"You killed Bad Bull."

"Well, in my mind, it was preferable to being killed myself."

She was trembling, wishing she had some way to thank him for Joey. It was impossible because he hadn't forgiven her for a single thing and his features were so grim, bronzed skin stretched tight against the rigid structure of his face.

"You killed him—before he could kill Joey?"

He shrugged, arms crossed over his chest. "I would have had to have gone after him, no matter what. I never quite got that chance because Joey saw Dulcie and went off half-cocked."

"So you knocked Joey out."

"Yeah, so I knocked Joey out."

"And Bad Bull got you in the arm, but you got him—"

"Straight through the heart."

She swallowed and nodded. "You could have just told me. There's been plenty of time since I was bleeding all over the floor and since you took the bullet out."

"What could I have told you? You'd already made all your assumptions."

"Well, I had just watched you nearly tear Aaron limb from limb!" she defended herself.

"I think I had a little provocation there."

"You weren't willing to listen—"

"I'd heard enough lies."

"Ian, you've no right—"

"No right?" He exclaimed the two words with such vehemence that Ann was afraid the whole building might shake apart. She backed away from him, teeth gritting, as he came into the room, long strides bringing him closer and closer to her. "Let's see, you haven't been lying to me from the minute I stepped into this saloon?"

"What did you expect?" she cried in return. "You didn't just come in, you barged in. You demanded whatever you could possibly take, what would make you think any of us should offer more than you already had your hands on!"

"What did I expect? Umm. Well, now, I thought I was marrying a whore who turned out to be the virgin queen of the outlaws. Stealing gold from stages and wagons, terrorizing a man who could chew her up and spit her out like tobacco if he got wind of what she was up to!"

"I have managed fine."

"You've nearly been killed twice and if Sheriff Bickford discovers your little dress-up activities, you'll be hanged. That's hardly fine."

"You don't understand—"

"That again. Pray, do enlighten me?"

"Go to hell!"

"I'm telling you again, Ann, don't leave this room until that wound is well on its way to being healed. No, better yet. Don't leave this room until you've got my permission to do so."

"Your permission—"

"My next step will be to tie you to the bed. And you'll be there so tightly it would take Dulcie and Cocoa a week to find a way to let you loose."

He turned to leave her.

"You might just have offered me a bit of faith!" she cried after him.

He went still; still and straight, his back to her. He spun around slowly. "Like the faith you offered me? Regarding Joey?"

She felt a little as if something had been sucked out of her. "Thank you for Joey," she managed to say stiffly. "And Dulcie."

He shook his head. "You don't need to thank me on either account. What I did I did for them."

He turned again and left her, and she didn't see him for the rest of the day.

Nor did he come that night. Ann knew, because she lay awake most of it waiting. When she did sleep, she dreamed. Broken snatches of images came to her in her sleep. She could see herself running, she could hear gunfire. She could remember trying to shoot, and not really knowing how to do so. Take the gun, aim, fire. There was so much gunfire around her! But she couldn't aim, and she couldn't pull the trigger, and she knew that horror awaited her because she could not do so. . . .

She saw the Pawnee face above her own. Cloud Walker's face. She heard the war cries. . . .

Saw *his* face. Ian's. She tried to reach out and touch it. She wanted to cry out to be held. She couldn't find her voice, she couldn't cry out, she couldn't beg him to come for her.

She needed him to do so. Because there were footsteps behind her again, and when she turned now, she would know who was coming. A monster wearing a man's face. A monster who had rained death and destruction upon so many. A monster who was coming to finish what he had once begun. . . .

She finally slept deeply, awakening to Dulcie's cheerful face. "Tea, some of Henri's absolutely delicious scones—and he says you must eat heartily—and another bath. I've been in so many times to see you, but you've been sleeping so soundly and so late. Things are getting lively below, though, so I want to make sure that you're all right up here before it gets much busier—the men are so little help these days, on guard the way they are. But don't you worry about anything, you have nothing to worry about. Of course, you're going to be absolutely fine. You know, Ian is really so remarkably smart. Between the things he knows about medicine because of the war and all the earth medicine his grandfather taught him, he can heal almost anything."

"He's just the wonder of the modern world," Ann murmured.

"He told me that fighting men have known a long time that bits and pieces of fabric can cause tremendous infection in wounds. That's why the Indians fight naked half the time—they know that a wound encrusted with clothing will putrefy when a wound on naked flesh will not. He said he saw lots of men heal during the war when they kept their wounds clean and freshly bandaged. He really could have been a doctor himself."

"If he weren't so busy with other things," Ann murmured. She bit into a scone. It was absolutely delicious. She felt fine, very hungry. And she was going to be consigned to another day in her room.

If Dulcie heard the twist of bitterness in Ann's voice, she gave no sign. "Isn't it wonderful, too?" she said wistfully, sitting at the end of Ann's bed. "Cocoa is so happy. Can you really imagine Cocoa married? To such a very fine man."

"Yes, it's wonderful," Ann agreed.

Dulcie smiled and spoke very softly. "Joey is here, Ann. He can't go home, you know."

"Yes, I know."

Even as Ann spoke, there was a tap on the door and Joey stuck his head into the room. "Hi, stranger!" he said to Ann. "We miss you downstairs, you know."

"Well, you can come in and visit," she told him.

He stepped in and seated himself next to Dulcie. "You look like you're feeling a lot better."

"Yes, definitely," she said, realizing that Joey believed she was suffering from an influenza. "I should be down soon," she told him. "And—welcome to you, of course. I understand you've taken up residency with us."

He shrugged, offering Dulcie one of his charming, rueful smiles. "I was here all the time anyway. Of course, now I'm going to have to see about obtaining some kind of full-time work."

"I heard what you said to your father, Joey. Thank you. I'm sorry for the pain you must be feeling."

Joey shook his head. "If I feel any pain, it's only for Meg. She's a good kid, and doesn't deserve to spend

her life beneath his power. As to my father ..." He
hesitated, his eyes darkening. "I hate him. I think that
if he didn't actually kill my mother, he surely hastened
her into her grave. Besides, you know, your husband
did save my life."

"Because you were trying to defend Dulcie."

"Because I was a fool," Dulcie said softly.

"No," Ann told them both firmly, "because Bad
Bull Marlin was a vicious man, and that's the end of
it. Joey, again, we're glad you're with us."

Dulcie stood suddenly. "Joey, I guess we should
leave Annie alone—she has a fine steaming bath
which is going to grow cold."

"And there's a lot of commotion going on downstairs."

"What's going on?" Ann asked, silently swearing
against Ian and wondering if she dared defy his orders to go and see for herself. What could he do to
her? He wouldn't really dare tie her to the bed,
would he?

Joey glanced over at Dulcie, then shrugged. "Lot
of cowhands are in. Poker games all over."

"Sheriff Bickford has been called out of town—"

"Maybe she shouldn't know that, Dulcie," Joey
suggested mildly.

"Oh! But I've always told Ann everything—"

"Ann isn't feeling well," Joey reminded her.

"Right," Dulcie murmured. She gave Ann a kiss
on the cheek. "You go on along, I'll be right there,"
she told Joey.

He nodded. "Feel better, Annie."

"Thanks," she said, then looked to Dulcie, hoping
for more information.

"Take the bandages off while you bathe; Ian will
be along to help you wrap back up, though hopefully you should be improving nicely." She gave

Ann another swift kiss on the cheek, and departed with Joey.

Ann rose the second they were gone. She didn't approach her temptingly steaming bath, but washed her face in cool water from the pitcher on her washstand. Still in her nightgown, she determined to get just a peek of what was going on downstairs. Barefoot, she silently moved along the balcony and then ducked down, holding on to the rail.

It was very busy. Aaron wasn't even playing the piano; he was with Harold handing out beers and whiskey from behind the bar. The dealers were all at their tables, and Henri was even out of the kitchen, serving food.

There were all manner of cowhands in—all manner of cowhands from Cash Weatherly's Circle Z. Bad Bull Marlin might be dead, but Josh Mason and Tyler Grissom were in attendance at the saloon, engaged in card games. Mason was a slim fellow in his late twenties with nearly yellow, snakelike eyes. Grissom was older, maybe closing in on fifty, rugged in his appearance, a handsome man with a strange spark to his eyes. He'd done well in the Kansas and Missouri theater of war, so Ann had heard, killing Indians and Southerners with like disdain, heedless of their gender or ages.

Mason and Grissom would certainly want revenge for Bad Bull, Ann thought, yet by all appearances, the play downstairs was just as smooth as silk. There were at least another twenty men in from Belle Vista, but none of them as talented at gunplay as the two remaining professionals Weatherly had brought in.

Ann searched out their own people. Through the slatted swinging doors, she could see that Angus was on guard in the front. Ralph Reninger was at the bar, and the Yeagher twins were both seated at card tables. Scar, who had adopted the place as his own rather than ever officially being hired, was seated atop the piano, keeping a brooding eye on all events.

Cocoa was serving drinks. Not a man out there— all of them aware of the size and strength of her new husband—touched so much as her skirt as she moved among them.

Ann frowned, aware then that she didn't see Ian.

Yet even as the thought filled her mind, a booted foot landed light by her side, right where she crouched by the rail. She looked up. A great, long way, so it seemed.

She barely met his black eyes before she was strangling down a cry of surprise and outrage as he dragged her up, yet lifted her carefully into his arms, aware, no matter what his temper, of her injury. They both remained silent until he had taken her back into her room and closed the door firmly with a foot, then both of them spoke at once.

"I was just trying to see—"

"I warned you what would happen—"

"I *needed* to see what was going on—"

"If you weren't injured already I'd be tempted to cause some severe pain to your backside."

"I'm really so much better—"

"Good, then it won't matter if you learn a few lessons from the width of my palm."

"Oh, you wouldn't dare."

"Tempt me again?"

"You dictating son of a bitch—" she began, then broke off with a cry of alarm because he'd set her down on the bed and was in the act of stripping off her gown. "Wait, wait!" she gasped, struggling to hold on to the material, struggling to protect her backside, amazed and outraged that he would attempt some violence against her. "Wait! Wait! I am still injured—"

And she was naked and he was straddled over her, black eyes pouring into hers.

"Yes, and I'm just getting ready to place you into that place because of that injury."

"Oh!" she breathed, then furiously tried to writhe from his hold and push him from her. "You, you— bastard! You like to make a fool out of me, you—"

"Ann, stop it, you are healing nicely and you're going to rehurt yourself if you're not careful."

She lay still, swallowing hard. He crawled off her and reached out his hands for hers. She hesitated, then took them, and he drew her to her feet, his fingers brushing her flesh as he unwound his bandaging. He nodded as he did so. "You'd almost never know it. I can clip out the stitches in a few days."

"Then I don't have to stay up here."

"Oh, you're going to stay up here today. Tied to the bed."

"You wouldn't."

"You can't seem to learn to listen."

She didn't get a chance to respond to that because he had swept her up into his arms again. She was startled by the impact of the sudden desire that lashed through her with his intimate touch, his hands upon her, his dark eyes still locked with her. Her lashes fell. It seemed so incredible that she hadn't even known what such a sensation could be until he had come into her life. And now it was enwrapped with so many emotions. The hunger was wistful as well as aching. Jealousy stirred in her heart as she wondered where he slept when he did not do so with her. Anger burned within her although with the sheer desire to be touched.

He didn't hold her long, but set her into the tub. He hunkered down by her side and she cast him an evil glare.

"Doesn't the water keep the wound damp and keep it from healing?" she demanded.

"I thought you loved a bath."

"I do. But—"

"In my experience, wounds heal more quickly with water and proper sulfur ointment and bandaging."

"An old Indian taught you that?"

"An impressive Yankee surgeon who was our prisoner for a while until we traded him for one of our own men."

She changed the subject abruptly. "Where were you last night?" she asked him.

To her surprise, he hesitated. "Cash Weatherly's place."

She gasped. "Why? How?"

He shrugged. "I needed to see the layout of it. Cash and his boys were out; Meg sent me an invitation."

Meg. Ann looked down quickly, amazed by the strength of the pain and jealousy that ripped through her. Meg. Sweet Meg, Joey's favorite little darling, so just and fair and fine in her dealings with others that Cocoa and Dulcie had always liked her as much as Ann did. Meg, pretty, just, pure—and not, in Ian's mind, an outlaw who held up stages and endangered innocent lives for the love of gold.

"You went to spend the evening with Meg at Circle Z?" she said incredulously.

"Yeah."

"You're a saloon owner!" she whispered.

He shrugged.

"A—married man," she reminded him coolly.

"Umm," he said noncommittally.

She hugged her arms to her chest, amazed to feel a little bit as if she was dying. In about two seconds she would explode and go clawing for his eyes—

and lose any pretense at dignity she might have ever had.

"Could you please get the hell away from me?" she asked. His eyes narrowed instantly, but before he could reply, they heard his name called from outside the door.

"Ian!" It was Joey's voice. "Ian, Angus has asked to see you outside. Now." There was a note of urgency to his voice.

Ian stood quickly, but before he left, he leveled a finger down at her. "Last warning, Ann. You leave this room again, I'll tie you to the bed. I'll be back to take care of your wound."

"I'll take care of it myself; don't come back!" she replied.

"I mean what I say," he warned her, and he was gone before she could reply again.

She sat in the tub, feeling the water grow very cold around her. She wanted to cry, and she wanted to hit something, anything. No, she wanted to hit Ian. She didn't want to hurt the way that she hurt, she wanted to go back to the day when he had first come, when she had known that he was dangerous. When she had made a partnership with him while wishing that he would keep his distance. She didn't want to care about him, want him. Be in love with him. It hurt so badly.

She hadn't managed to move and the water had grown quite cold when she heard her door open and close. She gripped the tub, her lashes downcast, knowing that he was back. What did she do? Demand to know what happened between him and Meg? Tell him that she couldn't bear to be near him if he wanted another woman? Cling to her anger, convince him that she hated him?

"Umm. My, my, my. Well, I do see what the boss is after!" she heard.

She stared at the door, her lashes flying upward. She was so stunned at first to see that Josh Mason had come into her room with his yellow eyes sealed upon her that it took her long seconds to inhale for a scream.

His eyes were snakelike, as well as his movements. She had barely managed to get out a gasp and come to her feet before he was upon her. His one hand covered her mouth and half smothered her while a weak sound choked out of her. She felt his other hand upon her naked, wet flesh, lifting her from the tub. She struggled insanely, horrified to feel him touching her all over while his clamp over her mouth and nose started to steal all air from her lungs. Stars spun before her but she kept fighting, kicking, hitting, getting in some good strikes as he was forced to keep his hold upon her mouth to stop her from screaming. She landed suddenly upon her bed; he was trying to wrap her within the covers. She managed to kick him in the groin. He groaned in agony, but quickly gained control and cut off the sound of his own voice. His hand released from her mouth, but even as she desperately drew breath, it came cracking across her cheek, stunning her. He started throwing the covers over her again and she managed to leap up, heading for her door. Oh, God, if only she still had her guns in here! But they were out in the storage compartment in the stables, and . . .

His hands were in her hair, drawing her back. She managed to get out something of a scream before he wrenched her back and threw her down. "Bitch. Let's have a go of it here and now, while that half-breed of yours deals with the problems downstairs. No one will believe what you say to them about me. A married whore ain't gonna be nobody's sweet innocent. Go ahead, try screaming again. Try it."

She did try it. His hand landed against her face again so hard that the room blackened. For a second she ceased to struggle, fighting desperately to come back from a wall of darkness. He was crawling over her, forcing her legs apart. He was filth; he was scum. He was a trained murderer who had been hired by the man who had destroyed what should have been her life. His breath was heavy with whiskey, his eyes were like death, he resembled so very much a rattler. She struggled, trying to scream, only to find her breath cut off again by the force of his hand. She pounded at him while he wedged his weight between her thighs and fumbled with his belt and the buttons on his pants.

"We've got just a little bit of time. Be nice to me, maybe I can make things go a little easier once you get where you're going."

She bit his hand. She managed to scream.

Her door burst open and Ian was standing there. The hand fell from her mouth and she started to shriek and scream, pounding at Josh Mason once again. Ian was across the room in a matter of seconds, wrenching Mason from atop her, slamming his fist into the man's face with a force that landed with an audible crunching. It was Mason's turn to shriek out with pain as his nose broke. He fell to the ground and rolled. "Get up!" Ian roared.

Mason started to do so. His gun belt had fallen by his side and he reached for his pistol in a whiplash movement. Ann heard herself scream again, and she heard the explosion of a shot.

To her relief and horror, she saw a crimson stain stretch itself out across Mason's shirt. The man's gun went slipping from his fingers, sliding across the hardwood floor. He went pitching downward himself, dead.

Ian gave him little thought, turning instantly to

Ann. She was shaking furiously. She clung to him but he pressed her away from him, searching out her form. "Did he hurt you? Are you all right?"

"Yes—"

"You're bleeding again, your stitches have ripped open. We'll have to take care of it—" he began, but he broke off suddenly because there were footsteps coming quickly toward them, a lot of them.

Ian swept up Ann's bedcovers, wrapping her quickly in them. The door burst open. Angus was there along with half the saloon, so it seemed. And it was apparent just what had been going on. Most of Cash's men had come in today to have the effect of sheer numbers. Maybe Josh Mason had been supposed to kidnap her while the others created a diversion. That was surely why Ian had been called away, why she had been alone.

And all hell was breaking loose now.

"He's shot down another man!" one of Weatherly's cowhands called out.

"Murderer!" another man shouted.

"He pays now!" declared another.

A shot was fired into the air. Angus had fired the shot, and for a moment there was silence.

"There's no murder here!" Ian cried out. "This bastard nearly raped my wife, then tried to kill me."

"The whore seduced him up here so that you could kill him!" someone cried in return.

Ann saw Ian's face go white; the pulse at his throat ticked furiously. "There's no chance of that!" Ian declared.

"Get the hell out of here!" Angus roared. "Or I will start shooting."

"I don't think so," someone suddenly announced. The crowd started splitting toward the hallway. There was the third of Weatherly's newly hired guns, Tyler Grissom, older, more mature. Good with his guns—and his wits.

He had Cocoa against him, his knife against her throat.

"You put that gun down, boy," Grissom announced, "or I slice up this bitch, you got it?"

"You injure her," Angus declared, "and you'll die sliced up bit by bit, screaming for me to let it come to an end quickly."

"I take her with me, and you'll have some trouble getting to her. I've got at least thirty men in this place. You're outnumbered badly."

"The sheriff will hang you!" Ann cried furiously.

But Grissom was staring at Ian. "You come on out. You come on out quietly and the woman goes free. And I take all of my men out of the saloon."

"Get them out now," Ian said.

"We all go. Come on, nice and slow."

Angus pointed at him. "You're a dead man."

"The law is on my side, boy. Ian McShane has just committed his second murder. And he's going to hang for it."

"You're a dead man," Angus repeated.

"Don't let him get away with this, McShane!" Cocoa called out. "Let him cut me, let him get himself hanged—"

"Get out of this room," Ian said.

Ann followed behind as they started from the room. Then there was a greater pandemonium. Ian drew at the speed of light, shooting Tyler Grissom in the shoulder. Grissom shouted and lost his gun and Cocoa, but there was such an upheaval that Ann lost all sight of Ian. A complete brawl broke out with men fighting everywhere. She saw Angus tangling five men, Ian shooting and then throwing down his guns to take on the men with his fists, fighting all the way down the stairs. Aaron was in the fight, the

dealers were in the fight. Harold cracked a whiskey
bottle over a man's head, Ralph Reninger was in on
it all as well.

Ann tried to follow, to grasp the covers to her, to
help somehow, to find Ian. She lost him in the melee.
Suddenly, Dulcie was upon her.

"They've got him outside. He brought down at
least seven men, but they've got him outside.
They're going to lynch him!"

In panic, Ann started racing for the door.

"No!" Dulcie shrieked toward her. "They'll stop
you, they'll hang you right along with him."

Ann paused, and realized Dulcie's wisdom. "Get
my guns!" she commanded.

She raced back up the stairs herself. She didn't
blink an eye as she jumped over the dead man who
lay in his own blood on her floor. She burst through
her windows to the balcony porch and stared searchingly down the street. They had slung a rope over a
tree and they were dragging Ian down the street.
Someone else was leading a horse to the tree.

Ian had taken down his share of the men. Fallen
bodies littered the street on the path toward the
rope. Some men half rose, groaning; some lay still.
But Tyler Grissom now had his pistol placed
squarely against Ian's throat and four men were
leading him along.

Dulcie came flying in behind Ann, handing over
her gun belt. "Shoot them! Shoot them all!" Dulcie
commanded.

"I can't just shoot them all."

"You've got to stop this."

"I know! That's why I have to concentrate on freeing Ian rather than shooting them all!"

"Ann, they've got him."

"Dulcie, we need every advantage."

"Ann, I'm so scared. You've got to start shooting,

killing if you have to. Grissom needs to die!"

"Ian first!" Ann breathed. Her covers fell away as she lifted her arm and took very careful aim. She waited. Waited until they had dragged him up and placed the rope around his neck. Even then, he was fighting, kicking one of them with such strength that he screamed out, falling to the side.

The rope was around him; his hands were bound at his back. Ann inhaled and took careful aim.

Tyler Grissom was talking. "We hereby condemn you to death, you Rebel half-breed, for the cold-blooded murder of two good men. We—"

Ian told him succinctly what he could do with himself.

"Hang him!" Grissom shouted.

That was it; Ann's cue. Someone started to slam a hand against the rump of the horse. The horse whinnied in a shrieking protest and began to race.

Ann fired.

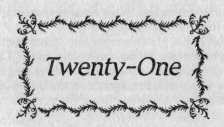

Twenty-One

*T*he rope tightened. . . .

But Ann's shot had been clean, her aim had been perfect, snapping the rope in two. Every eye from the street below came riveting up in astonishment to stare at the naked woman shooting from her balcony.

Ian took advantage of the situation, struggling up. He'd freed his hands and taken a gun from the man next to him. He began shooting, his shots going up into the air. Shouts and screams rose in the street, men began to scatter everywhere. Tyler Grissom, the orchestrator of all that had happened, turned to disappear into the crowd. Ian caught him by the collar. He turned and tried to shoot Ian, but Ian struck him in the jaw and the man went down.

Cash Weatherly's men were scattering. Disappearing. She couldn't see many of them at all in the melee down below. The other men were out from the saloon, Angus and Ralph, the twins, Scar, Aaron, Harold. Ralph bent to drag up the downed Grissom. "We ought to hang him!" Ralph declared.

Others in the street took up the cry. "Hang him— he caused the trouble!"

There seemed to be an angry throb picking up

among the townsfolk who remained in the street. "Hang him!" came another cry.

"Damn it, no!" Ian shouted out. "There will be no more lynch mobs in the street. No more! Get him locked up at the sheriff's office, and let that be it!"

There was a sudden silence in the streets as men realized a sense of shame. In a matter of seconds, the street was quiet and emptying.

Dulcie gripped Ann. Ann realized only then that Dulcie had already wrapped Ann's bedclothing around her once again. "Let's get in!" Dulcie cried.

She drew Ann into the room. By then, Ann was shaking. With Dulcie's help she sat at the foot of the bed, just staring now at Josh Mason's body. Dulcie wrapped her in the bedcovers again, hugging her. "It's going to be all right, Annie. It's going to be all right."

It was. They heard a slamming against the door and looked up. Dusty, bruised, bleeding in a half dozen places, Ian stood there, his battered friends at his sides, Ralph, Angus, the twins, Harold, Joey, others from the saloon.

Ann stood. She and Ian stared at one another. Ian's eyes fell to Josh Mason's body. "Angus, would you—"

Angus started forward. "We'll get this and the other refuse out of the saloon."

He hiked up the body. "Mighty fine shootin'," he told Ann.

"Thanks," she murmured.

"Dulcie?" Joey said, reaching out a hand to her.

Dulcie slipped out, taking Joey's hand. A moment later, the others were gone, and she was standing with Ian alone.

"You saved my life," he told her.

She shrugged. "You saved mine." She kept trembling. He was still a moment, then he walked across the room to her, sweeping her off her feet with an agonized groan, holding her against him as he sat upon the bed, drawing her closer.

"We beat them," she said.

He was quiet. "We held them at bay, at best," he said after a moment. "They'll be back."

"Sheriff Bickford—"

"Sheriff Bickford is a well-meaning man, even an intelligent man, who refuses to see evil in Weatherly. To him, Cash Weatherly is a rancher sorely beset by outlaws."

"But he can prevent more of what happened today."

"Maybe," Ian said with a shrug. "And maybe we'll be in worse trouble once he returns."

"How? Why?"

"Well, let's see. Half the town saw you naked this morning."

"I had no time, I lost the covers—"

"And I thought you were exceptionally beautiful. You looked like an avenging angel up on that balcony. I'm just wondering if anyone was close enough to see the wound in your side and to start wondering how it came to be there."

"It's nearly healed."

"It's broken open and there is dried blood on you."

"There was so much going on—who would have paid attention to my side?"

"Well, there were other parts of you to pay attention to, I admit."

"That's not what I mean. You were firing in the street, people were screaming—"

"I hope that you're right."

There was something in his voice that disturbed her. A note that was slightly condemning.

Umm . . . yes, condemning. Because she had gone after Cash as a thief, an outlaw.

She struggled from his hold, standing, trying to draw the covers around her regally. He didn't seem to realize for the moment that he had offended her; he was deep in thought. But then he looked up at her. "Let me see how the wound is doing, if we're going to have to put in a few more stitches."

"You're bleeding from a dozen places," she reminded him, drawing the covers more tightly around her.

"Surface scratches."

"I'm fine. I know that I'm fine," she protested again. But his hands were firmly on the covers, which were gone before she knew it, and he was picking her up to lay her on the bed. His touch was gentle enough but not at all sensual. "Salve and a bandage," he murmured. "It really has healed well."

She was silent as he worked upon her, looking anywhere but into his eyes. When he was done, she quickly found her feet and then drew a thin cotton shift from her wardrobe. When she had slipped it on, she found that he was watching her curiously.

"I knew you were an outlaw," he told her quietly, "but I'd no idea that you could shoot so well."

She shrugged. "Yes, I'm very good."

"Come over here," he told her.

She hesitated, still feeling half naked and very vulnerable to his questions and his eyes.

"Annie, please."

She came over to stand before him.

He hesitated. "Did your father teach you to shoot so well?"

Ann hesitated, gritting her teeth together. "No. Want to take off your shirt and let me try to treat a few of those surface wounds?"

"There's nothing that bad," he told her.

He was watching her so probingly. "Humor me, allow me to treat you," she insisted, desperately needing something to do.

He pulled off his shirt. A number of the gashes on his body were fairly long or deep. She brought fresh water from her ewer to the bedside table along with a clean washcloth from her drawer and began dabbing at the wounds. "We need to make sure no fabric adheres to them," she said. "Fabric can cause infections."

He arched a brow to her, but remained silent until he cried, "Ouch!"

"It's not that bad."

"I need a whiskey."

"I don't keep any up here, so you'll have to do without. And you've enough scars to indicate a few previous injuries, so be a man about these as well."

"You are ruthless, you know," he told her, black eyes looking up at her.

"Where do you keep that magical yellow sulfur salve of yours?" she asked him.

He indicated his side of the bed, where he had left the salve after treating her. Ann went for the salve and returned to him, generously rubbing the stuff into all of his wounds. It felt good to touch him, good to feel the tension and ripple of his muscles, the sleek, hot smoothness of his flesh.

"Weatherly really seems to hate you," Ann said.

"He does."

"Maybe he's blaming you for the robberies."

Ian shook his head, glancing up at her with an arched brow. "He was being robbed long before I arrived on the scene."

"But you hate him, too," Ann said. She hesitated, set the salve down, and backed away from him. "You knew him when you came here. You knew him the first night we met. You weren't just defending me when you insisted to him that night that I was busy. In fact, I think you bought out Eddie's debts just because you hated him so much. Why?"

"I didn't buy out Eddie's debts because I hated Weatherly—though I would have with greater relish had I known he wanted the place. I bought out Eddie's debts so that I could come here and stay with a reason for being in town."

"You married me because you hated him."

"You married me because you hated him," he reminded her.

"Why do you hate him so much?" she persisted.

Ian inhaled for a moment, staring at her. Then he expelled the breath.

"Because he's the most wretched murderer I've come across in all my life. And, naturally, because he's gunning for me as hard as he possibly can."

"But—"

"Who knows? Maybe he is aware that I have part of his gold."

"What?" Ann demanded, backing away.

He stared at her, jaw slightly twisted with irony. "I have part of his gold—not the main supply you and Aaron have been removing from his wagons and stagecoaches all this time. I have the cattle payment. I think you were trying to steal it alone, and you were nearly killed that night."

"That was you? Firing when I was on the butte?" she demanded furiously.

"I saved your life that night," he reminded her sternly. "I didn't even know it was you at the time, I was only aware that something was going on and it was all happening from the saloon."

"But you stole the gold."

"You stole the gold. I merely kept it. And I kept it for a reason."

"How dare you condemn me—"

"I just told you, I stole it for a reason!"

"What reason?" Ann whispered.

"Weatherly slaughtered my family."

She felt as if the air had been sucked out of her. She sat on the foot of the bed, even as he rose, pacing toward the fireplace, staring down at the dead ashes as if a fire still burned in the hearth and he could draw warmth from it.

"He killed your family?" she said, scarcely breathing, not believing what she was hearing.

"My family, and at least two dozen other people, men, women, and children. He killed them, and he left me for dead. He'd thought he'd killed me. He just failed."

"McShane," Ann said, enunciating clearly, swallowing hard. "What happened? Tell me!"

He shrugged. "It was before the war even began. Well, before it was declared and begun back east. When things started getting nasty across the Kansas and Missouri border. The abolitionists, John Brown and his kind, started claiming that the slaveholders were causing the trouble; the slaveholders claimed it was the abolitionists. Who knows where the violence really started; I heard from good men on both sides that John Brown really believed that he had a right to kill in the Lord's name to free the slaves. But he, and others on both sides, just went out and savagely murdered those who didn't agree with them." He sighed. "John Brown did become a legend; the country did run with blood! But Brown was a murderer, plain and simple. He took the law into his own hands when he came after folks who owned slaves. He cut them down without judge or jury, and who knows, perhaps at this point it is only God who can sort out the good men from the bad in the travesty." He inhaled again. "John Brown wanted to stop the spread of slavery when he came into Missouri. But a lot of men—on both sides—just took advantage of the situation." Again, he hesitated. "Cash Weatherly used the situation to create an empire. He went after Southerners who were seeking to homestead a new world, and he killed them—in the name of God—and then stole their belongings. My father had decided to come west. He had gathered together a very small party of wagons, but he was a known Southern sympathizer, even if he didn't own slaves himself. We'd come through a town with Weatherly in it and met up with him at a saloon, the men just slaking their thirst while getting their wagons ready. My father tried to make a case for states' rights; Weatherly claimed there was no such thing as states' rights, there were just a bunch of sadistic men who found power in owning other men. My father could be very academic and he tried to explain that it was a difficulty that had been around since Jefferson had drafted the Declaration of Independence. He'd wanted to outlaw slavery then, but there was a massive matter of the economy. My father tried to explain that only rich men could afford slaves, and that mostly poor men would wind up fighting a war over them. The conversation began to turn, Pa decided it was time to get out of town. Well, we left town." He closed his eyes, opened them, still staring at the dead ashes. "I can still see the dust cloud coming. I can feel the earth tremble from their horses. In my dreams, I can see my father die over and over, I can watch my mother fall."

"You were on the trail?" Ann breathed, frozen as she stared at him.

He nodded. He lifted his hands. "We were a small party. Cash Weatherly came after us with ten men. We put up a fight, the women fought, the children fought. Because once he came after us, we knew that he intended murder. If anyone would have surrendered, he would have shot us down on our knees. I saw old Rufus die even while he was trying to drag me away from the corpses of my parents. Then there was a little girl. They rode her down. She tried to shoot, but missed. They struck her down with a rifle butt. They killed everyone. Every man, woman, and child. Even the unborn perished in their mothers' wombs." He stopped talking suddenly, staring at Ann. She was snow-white, bent over where she sat.

"Ann, my God, damn you, what the hell is wrong?"

She was laughing.

"Sweet Jesu, Ann—" he began angrily.

But she leapt up and suddenly threw herself at him, tears streaming down her face as she beat her fists against his chest, still laughing even as she cried. "You fool!"

"Damn it, what the hell—" he began, trying to get a hold on her, trying to gain control.

"Oh, you absolute fool! You've been condemning me for all that I've done, when you're here doing the same thing."

"I'm here for revenge," he told her angrily, grappling hard to catch her hands and stop the wild, abandoned flailing she was aiming so vehemently his way. She had snapped, he thought. He had never seen her so wild, never seen her cry. He caught her wrists at last, his eyes black and furious, and he struggled to hold her still. "I haven't come to steal from the man, I've come to destroy him. I've come to avenge the deaths of all those people. By God, I survived the war just living to find Cash Weatherly and destroy him! Ann, sweet Lord, what the hell—"

He finally had her. She was panting, gasping for each breath, but her wrists were locked in his grip and she was drawn to him so that she could do him no more harm. She was shaking rampantly.

"That's why I've been stealing from him!" she exclaimed wildly.

"Because you hate him."

"I loathe him."

"But don't you understand? I owe him for a dozen lives—"

"Sweet Jesu, don't you understand? What do you think?" Ann cried. "Damn you, can't you see the same emotion in others? I followed Cash Weatherly as soon as I was free. I came to destroy him because *I was the girl!*"

"What girl?"

"Don't you understand yet? I was the girl in your party!"

"What?" he demanded, incredulous.

"You said there was a girl. She tried to shoot one of them and missed. They slammed her head with a rifle butt. Ian! I was that girl."

"That girl couldn't be alive! They cracked her head in!" he whispered. "She was dead when the Pawnee came. Everyone was dead."

Ann started to laugh. Her laughter scared her; she couldn't control it. "No, I should have died, but I didn't die. I was the girl! Oh, God!" She was going to start laughing again hysterically, uncontrollably. "We'd never met, you and I hadn't met, because my parents and some friends of theirs had just joined the party the night before. They were so excited, so pleased, because so many members of their original group had dropped out, they'd found the rigors of the Conestoga wagons and the trail just too much, and they'd thought we'd be safer traveling with a larger party. Cash slaughtered my family that day. My father, my mother—and the baby she carried. I wanted to be dead as well, but I wasn't. Oh, my

God, you knew I was a prisoner of the Pawnee—"

"And I'd thought that the Pawnee had slaughtered your family. You led me to believe that the Pawnee had killed them!"

"I couldn't take a chance on letting you know what had really happened when I was trying to keep you from knowing that I was involved in illegal activities. My sweet Jesus, I don't understand. *I* don't remember *you* being with the Pawnee. I was unconscious when they took me. When I came to, they were attacking a settlement, further down the trail. It was where they captured Dulcie. If you survived the massacre, you would have to have been taken by the Pawnee as well—"

"I survived, and I *was* taken by the Pawnee," he said quietly. "I lived then, spared by them, because I was wearing one of my grandfather's amulets and they knew that I was Sioux. I had been injured, and I was drifting in and out of consciousness as well when the Pawnee came, but they were interested in me for a reason—I could be valuable to them. We were from different tribes, but sign language on the plains is such that most tribes can understand one another and I knew a little of their tongue. I was taken immediately from the site of the massacre by two of the Pawnee warriors who knew I could be traded for people of their own who had been taken by the Sioux." He grew very quiet, and shook his head again, as if he still couldn't fully comprehend what he was hearing. "I thought that I was the only one who had survived. The only one. Oh, my God."

His hold upon her eased. He pulled her into his arms. Ann was still shaking, still half laughing, half crying.

"It can't be!" Ian whispered.

"He killed everyone," she said.

"But us," he said incredulously.

"It was horrible. So horrible. I wanted him dead so badly and I was powerless."

"So was I, Ann. He shot me. Grazed my skull. I thought that I was dead."

"It's amazing that we survived."

"Thank God."

"And we're here now."

"All three of us are here," Ian added with a touch of bitterness.

"He just killed everyone."

"I know. Ann, please—"

She pulled away from him, her eyes wide. "That's why I learned to shoot so well. I swore that I would never miss again when it mattered. I swore it. I practiced it when I was with the Pawnee. Cloud Walker taught me first with his hunting rifle."

"God, Ann! Why didn't I know, why didn't I recognize you. There were no McCastles in our party of travelers—" he began, then broke off with a groan. "That was Eddie's name," he said.

"I took his name when he took me in. To the Indians, Eddie had adopted me. And I didn't know if Cash had ever known my family name."

"Probably not. He doesn't seem to know me. He may wonder. And he may even have a strange feeling that he should recognize me. But it was a long time ago now. Nearly ten years."

Ann started to laugh again. She was clinging to him because she was afraid that she was going to fall. "All this time, I didn't think I could make you understand—"

"I didn't understand. I thought you were a greedy little petty thief," he admitted. He took her face between his hands, lifted it, very gently kissed her lips. "I'm sorry, Ann. So sorry."

"We've wanted the same thing."

"For all the same reasons." Dear God, life had

been the same for her. She'd survived the Pawnee, and survived them well. And after all the years, she'd still known why she'd been living all that time.

Revenge. Against the man who had taken everything that she had once had.

Ian had followed Cash easily enough once the war was over. And oddly enough, he'd never felt the bitterness over the war itself. They'd lost. Well, it might have been God's will, it might have been history. Slavery was wrong, and even if it had brought a proud people to their knees and left the nation strewn with blood, it might have been something that had been ordained.

But not Cash's way. Cash had used the slavery question, he had used men's emotions, to do murder for his own pleasure and gain. That seemed a crime greater than any other, the motive making the slaughter even more tragic and chilling.

"Annie, I will get him," he promised her softly. "I always knew I would."

"I said that *I'll* get him, Annie," he told her firmly.

"We'll get him," she murmured.

No. He wasn't going to argue with her right now. Holding on to her was too precious at the moment. Touching the golden blond silk of her hair, feeling her warmth beneath the thin shift. She'd seduced him without meaning to do so, entangled his soul without knowing.

And now this new bond.

She meant too much to him. She was life; she was everything worth living for. She was beautiful and brave, and hurt in a way that desperately needed healing, and he knew he'd die a thousand times over before letting anything happen to her again, ever.

He chose not to argue with her for the moment. He groaned softly, lifting her chin. He kissed her lips again with tenderness and poignancy. His lips

brushed her throat. He kneeled before her, drawing
her against him, his head resting against her abdomen. She cried out softly, her fingers moving into
his hair.

He had just meant to hold her ...

But he wanted her. Wanted her with a new, longing hunger, with an aching. Needed to touch her,
feel her, breathe with her, be one with her. The thin
cotton shift she wore did nothing to conceal her
warmth, fragrance, or the evocative softness of her
flesh.

He rose quickly, swallowing hard. "You're hurt,"
he reminded her huskily.

"Not so hurt as I will be if you leave me!" she
cried to him.

"Annie," he groaned.

"Please ... " Her whisper touched his earlobe
along with the tantalizing brush of her tongue and
teeth. He held dead still, willing himself to remember that she was recovering from a bullet wound and
that she had been through a rough time.

"Ian!"

His name was a whisper, a caress against the flesh
of his throat. Her lips pressed against his pulse, the
rise of her breasts crushed against his chest. She
came off her toes and began rubbing against his
groin.

He groaned again, trying to ease from her. Her
fingers raked lightly over his chest, nails touching
flesh with the most subtle caress. Then her hands
slipped beneath the waistband of his pants, her lips
touched upon the breadth of his chest, feathering,
playing, licking. Her fingers moved upon the buttons of his fly with amazing subtlety. She shoved
down his waistband even as she moved lower
against him, her kiss and the flick of her tongue
moving wickedly against his flesh.

"Ann . . ."

Her name was a groan, a protest, a plea. His hands ran over the golden length of her hair while wild, riveting sensation burst into him. It became such exotic pleasure it was pain, the sweetest agony. He grated his teeth together, crying out her name again, plucking her from the floor. He pressed her to the bed, so hungry for the taste of her that he caressed her breasts through the thin cotton of her shift, his teeth moving over the peaks of her nipples, his lips moving lower against her, his tongue now as ruthless and wicked against her flesh, finding her through the shield of the fabric, creating an agonizing and erotic friction. She writhed, she tossed, she dug her fingers into his hair. She cried out his name. He wrenched the shift by the hem, pulling it over her head, pressing his lips to her naked flesh and at last parting her thighs, plunging between them, withdrawing, plunging again, until he was so deeply inside of her he felt he touched her soul at last, so aroused that his muscles convulsed with the force of his desire. He locked her within his arms and let the force of the sudden hunger between them sweep them away. Sweat broke out upon them, beaded, made them sleek. He moved with rhythmic, increasing speed, aware of each brush of her flesh, aware he was entangled in her hair, aware of her, of her body, inside and out. Aware when she strained and arched and writhed against him, screamed out unintelligible words, burst around him with a liquid warmth . . .

Seconds later, he climaxed violently himself, spilling back the sweet searing warmth . . . again . . . again. Yet even as the magnitude of pleasure seized him, his arms were around her. Passion became tenderness. He filled her completely at last and drew her against him, softly smoothing back her hair.

He bolted up suddenly then. "My God, your wound—"

"Is all right, I swear it!"

She twisted to the side, showing him the bandages, the fact that she hadn't bled or torn the stitches.

He eased back, exhaling.

"Now you—you're a mess," she teased. Her eyes alight, innocent still somehow, such a beautiful, trusting blue.

He swallowed, stretching a hand atop his pillow.

She curled up against him. "Ian, we will get him, really get him. I know that we will. I swear by God, we will! Ian, now that we're together, nothing can stop us," she whispered.

He didn't answer. He pulled her closer.

Cash Weatherly sat in one of the huge leather-upholstered chairs before his fireplace, fingers splayed tautly over the heavily stuffed arms.

"You say he was *nearly* hanged."

Cash sighed, glancing over at Jenson.

"Nearly. We did everything right, Pa. Tyler did everything right. It was all laid out just the way you wanted it. It was just that McShane was shot free."

"And who shot him free?" Cash demanded incredulously, eyes narrowed.

"She did, Pa. Annie McCastle."

"Annie McShane," Jenson reminded them.

Cash looked at both boys. "You're sure? It takes some mighty fine shooting to snap a hanging rope like that."

"Pa, she come out on the second-floor balcony porch thing of hers right outside her bedroom and she fired her gun and snapped the rope," Jenson said.

"Stark naked," Carl told him.

"Josh Mason had been up there, ready to take her

out, when McShane burst in on him. Josh was deader than desert sand by the time Tyler Grissom got up there, so he used it against McShane. The whole saloon turned into one big brawl, and McShane was dragged out on the street. There was a rope around his neck and he was seated on a horse. Then Tyler slaps the horse, and there's the shot. McShane should have been dead, instead, he's free, and everyone is staring up to the saloon where she's standing, just like some warrior queen."

"Stark naked," Carl repeated. "She's one pretty woman, Pa."

"Like the devil's own," Cash muttered.

"Yeah, Mason must have thought so. The fool died over her rather than getting out of there."

"Anyway, Pa, she fires this shot, McShane is free, and he's got someone's gun, and he's shooting up the street so that every man who had been with us is running like a rabbit. Then the mob shifts, and they want to hang Tyler, but McShane won't let them do it—so Tyler is in jail."

"So let me see, McShane was *almost* hanged—but he's alive and well and kicking. Josh is dead, and Tyler is in jail. Know what that proves to me, boys?"

"What, Pa?" Carl asked warily.

"It means that no matter what I've tried to teach those around me, I've wound up with incompetent fools. I can't quite reckon what it is with McShane and Annie, but something about them isn't quite right, there's something I should know. And you know what else it means?"

"What, Pa?" It was Jenson's turn to ask the question.

"It means," Cash said, pointing a finger at his son as he narrowed his eyes. "It means I'm going after McShane to kill him next. It means I'll be going after Ann *myself* to see that I bring her in. It means you're

going to ride with me, my boys, and so help me, by
the Lord above, you'll turn this time. Because I won't
fail. Listen up, and try to pay better heed to me now.
I'm going to get them, and by God, I'll do it swiftly
and without mercy!"

Carl glanced at Jenson. Their father was so intense, and so relishing the idea of murder.

It was frightening.

Even to them.

"Annie, I love you."

He said the words too late. She was curled to his
side, tender as a kitten. Her breath came in an easy
flow and ebb, her lips were softly parted, her lashes
fell softly over her cheeks.

"Annie, I love you," he repeated anyway, smoothing a wild tangle of blond hair from her face. "I
love you, and it has changed the stakes so very
much. . . ."

He drew her closer to him, just needing to feel her
warmth and softness, to hold her, cherish her.

It was so damned odd. All of these years, he had
been living for revenge. He had done his duty in the
war, but he had survived the fighting for revenge.
Justice was on his side; if ever a man needed killing,
it was Cash Weatherly. And still, things were suddenly different. Because of Annie.

He still wanted revenge.

But he wanted to live. And more than that, he
wanted her to live. He wanted to believe in a future,
to have a future, to move deeper into the untamed
West. He wanted to hold her like this for all of his
life. And for the life of him, he didn't want to leave
her. He didn't want her at risk. He didn't want to
take chances with her in any possible way. He didn't
want Cash Weatherly anywhere near her.

He was so close to that which he had sought with

such a vengeance all those years—revenge. He'd been determined, he'd never faltered. It wasn't that he hadn't felt fear at times; he'd just ignored it.

But now, he suddenly knew what it was to be afraid. Because he loved her so much that the emotion was deeper than any he had ever known—even the hatred.

He couldn't stop now. . . .

But something was gnawing at him, deeply. Fear. Cash Weatherly wouldn't stop now. He wanted Ian dead, and he wanted Annie and the saloon. And if he didn't know it already, he would soon discover that Annie had been robbing him blind, and when he found that out . . .

A deep shudder ripped through Ian. He knew Cash Weatherly. Knew the man's ruthlessness; knew his absolute lack of conscience and his total disregard for human life.

His arms tightened around her even as he realized that he was going to have to let her go. Of course, it wasn't going to be easy getting her out of here. She wasn't going to want to go.

She was going to have to.

Bound and gagged, hating him all the while, she was going to have to go.

There was no other way out of it.

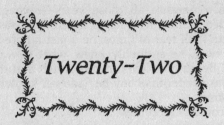

Twenty-Two

Ann awoke feeling happier than she could ever remember being. He knew the truth. He knew the truth, and he understood, better than anyone else in the world could understand. *He had been there.* Seen the horses, the gunfire, heard the earth, the cacophony, seen the death. Felt the helplessness, the rage, the pain, the anguish. It was open and out between them, and they both still remained alive and almost perfectly well.

As she opened her eyes, she realized that he was awake as well, that he had been awake. He was up on an elbow, staring pensively down at her, a slight furrow in his dark brow. It disappeared as she caught him studying her, and a handsome smile curved his lips. Despite the intimacy they had now so often shared, she suddenly felt shy with him. It made no sense. Or maybe it did. Once upon a time she had tried to deny even to herself the way that she felt about him. Once upon a time there had been no future. Now there was.

"What?" she asked him.

He shook his head and arched a dark brow.

"What are you thinking? Why are you staring at me so?"

A white smile slashed across his dark features. He

shook his head again. "I'm not staring; I'm watching."

"Watching?"

He nodded, then reached out a hand and brushed his knuckles over her cheek. "Watching the sun come in to touch your hair. It seems like spun gold, trailing then over your flesh. I'm watching your face, the way that you breathe, the way your lips part. And it makes me shake just a little inside because it's all so incredible, and because I'm so grateful that you're here, beside me. *Alive.*"

She caught the hand against her cheek and drew it to her heart. "Very much alive," she whispered.

His hand against the heartbeat nuzzled there between the softness of her breasts and he leaned over and kissed her lips lightly. Again. There was something both passionate and tender in the touch that seemed to stir every emotion within her. Time and fate seemed to have played such a strange trick upon them, but this morning it didn't seem to matter. Nothing outside of the room seemed to matter then, nothing outside of *them.* She felt the sleek, wired heat of him, the warmth and rise of his desire. Her arms rose around him welcomingly and she shuddered fiercely as she felt the movement of his kiss and caress. Every touch seemed so light now, so tender, and yet so provocative. At first she barely dared move, barely breathed. By the slender streaks of light that filtered through the draped windows, slim refractions where dust motes danced and gleamed, he made love to her. Manipulated and turned her, as if eager to kiss, caress, and know each inch of her. Seared a slow trail of kisses from her nape to the tail of her spine, turned again, seared her anew. The dust continued to dance upon rays of light. The sun rose higher. She was unaware. When at last the volatile seizures of climax had seized and released her, she lay in his arms, newly amazed that anything so tender could be passionate, that such sweet yet violent passion could end with such a gentle and loving touch upon her.

She did love him. So much. The wonder of it caused her to tremble inside again, and she almost let the words describing her feelings come tumbling from her lips. She held them back, yet in his arms she thought of the little and varied things about him that she did love so very much. The texture of his hair, the color of it. The sound of his voice, the depth of it when he spoke her name. His eyes, the way he stood, the way he squared his shoulders. Even the way he looked at her when he was angry, the way his height and the breadth of his shoulders seemed to fill a doorway when he stood within it. His passion, his intensity and his integrity. His belief in right and wrong. His need for . . .

A cold shiver swept through her.

Revenge.

It was what she wanted, right? She would never let it go, never forgive Cash Weatherly. But she bit into her lower lip suddenly and knew that no matter how sweet it was to lie here, no matter how she loved him, she knew why the words couldn't come right now. There was something here that wasn't finished, and perhaps there could be no future until it was. She thought perhaps that he shared her feelings, for he was quiet as he held her, and she was certain that he was holding his own thoughts on the matter to himself—no matter how tenderly he might hold her.

"Where do we go from here?" she asked him softly.

He was saved from making a reply because there was suddenly an urgent tapping on their door. Ian instantly drew up the sheets. Dulcie popped her head in without waiting for a reply.

"Ian, Sheriff Bickford is downstairs," she said nervously.

"Dulcie, that was to be expected," he told her. "I'll be right down."

"Maybe you should go out through the window and run away somewhere," Dulcie said, her eyes wide and miserable.

"Maybe she's right," Ann said. It hadn't occurred to her that Ian could still be in danger, but Bickford could be a stickler, and self-defense or not, Ian had killed another man.

"Ladies, I will not run when I was wronged," Ian said firmly. "Tell Sheriff Bickford that I'll be right down, Dulcie."

Dulcie still stood there, staring miserably at them both.

"Dulcie," he said with a patient sigh, "I know that male anatomy holds no shocks or surprises for you, but if you don't mind . . . "

"Oh! Oh!" Dulcie said. She swung around and left them. Ian rose instantly, poured water from the ewer to wash, then dug clean clothing from his drawers, dressing quickly in a crisp white cotton shirt and denim pants. Ann found herself following worriedly after him.

"Ian, are you sure—"

"Ann, I'm going to be all right. Trust me on this." He gave her a kiss and left her.

Ann washed and dressed quickly herself, then hurried downstairs as well. But by the time she reached the main room, both Ian and Sheriff Bickford were gone.

She rushed to the bar, where Dulcie and Aaron stood talking with Harold.

"What happened?" she demanded worriedly.

But Harold shook his head. "Nothing, really. I swear it. Bickford just asked him to come to the jail and make a statement. That's it, clean and simple. Ian said that he was pleased to oblige, and that he'd be right back."

"They ought to be arresting Cash!" Ann murmured unhappily.

"Ann, you let him manage all this. He knows what he's doing."

"That's right, little lady!"

Ann swung around. There was another newcomer to town standing at the bar. He was a tall fellow, probably almost as tall as Ian. But this man had light, reddish hair and sharp green eyes. He wore black, with a low-browed hat and a heavy gun belt.

At the moment, he was politely sipping a whiskey, but from the moment he addressed her, she knew that he was dangerous.

"Your man knows what he's doing."

"Sir, I don't recall soliciting an opinion from you," Ann murmured, and started to move away.

"Those Sioux boys, they know what they're doing!" the man called out.

Despite herself, Ann stopped and turned back. He lifted his glass to her. "Heard tell you were a prisoner of the Pawnee. So you know Indians." He shook his head. "Boy, I could tell you a pretty piece about the Sioux! Happened in Minnesota, right in August of 1862, right in the middle of the War of the Southern Rebellion, taking good army boys out of the fighting where they were needed against the Rebs. Eight hundred men, women, and children lost their lives. It wasn't a pretty picture. The savages raided homes. They told the white women they weren't going to hurt them or their children and just waited for the folks to start walking to shoot them in the backs. They were government Sioux,

Mrs. McShane, Injuns taking annuity money from the United States, but when they got riled up, that didn't matter none."

Ann felt her temper rising. She was about to comment when Harold stepped into the conversation.

"I heard about the incident," Harold said, calmly drying a glass. "It was a bad time, a bad time. The white folks had taken the best land and put the Indians in a difficult position. They couldn't hunt, they couldn't farm the land well. The war made it hard for the government to pay the promised annuities. The traders on the reservation refused to give the Indians credit. It was a hard situation all way round."

The darkly clad stranger at the bar smiled wickedly with bad teeth. "Don't matter none what you want to say. The red savages hacked to pieces men, women, and children. Sioux savages, Mrs. McShane. No better than the wretches who held you captive."

"Well, sir, I bear no hatred for the Pawnee. And as for the Sioux—"

"As for the Sioux," Ian's voice suddenly boomed, "they are not all guilty of these depravities, any more so, sir, than all Northern white men are guilty of the murders that took place in Missouri before the war officially broke out."

Ann felt her heart thundering in her throat. Ian had come back quickly. It was what she had wanted, except that she hadn't wanted him here, now, challenging another man. Maybe it wouldn't be the same. This man wasn't attacking her.

No, he was going straight for Ian's throat.

Please, God, Ian, don't let him taunt you! she prayed silently.

The stranger's smile broadened.

"We're talking about savages here—friend."

"White men can be damned savage," Ian stated.

"Well now, seems to me that the South seemed to take it to heart that she could do what she wanted and thumb her nose at the government. There were people keeping other people in chains. Seems that it might be right that those people should pay with their lives."

"If you've come in here to cause trouble," Ann said quickly, "it isn't going to happen. The war is over."

The stranger leaned against the bar, still smiling broadly. "The Indian wars ain't over," he assured them.

"Well, a man with Sioux blood in his veins owns this place, stranger, so if you've a problem with that, you'd best leave it now, don't you think?" Ann demanded angrily.

"Fighting his battle for him?" the stranger demanded.

"Trying to save your miserable life!" Ann snapped back quickly.

"Well, I—" the stranger began, then broke off. Ann saw that Sheriff Bickford was standing right behind Ian. She let out an inaudible sigh of relief.

"There's going to be no more trouble in this town!" Bickford swore, striding on into the saloon. "No more, do you hear me, sir?"

The stranger kept smiling, and he swallowed down his whiskey. "No trouble, Sheriff!" he said politely. "I've come to see that there is no more trouble. To let this half-breed know that he can't attack the likes of Cash Weatherly's men and think he's going to win. You see, McShane, we outnumbered you from the start. You think you can shoot men down and shoot men down and that will be the end of it. Well, it won't. Because there's dozens of us out there willing to spend our lives chasing after Rebel boys like you. Just be aware, sir. We're out there." He tipped his hat to Ian and walked toward the sheriff. "Just making sure I can protect my boss, a good man like Cash Weatherly. You coming, Johnny?"

Johnny?

Ann swung around. Rising from one of the back tables was Johnny Durango. He still wore a sling, and his right hand—his gun hand, dangled brokenly from it. Johnny Durango smiled at Ann and stopped before Ian. He lifted his mangled hand and offered up another smile. "I got me some friends now, half-breed" he hissed softly, then followed the newcomer from the place.

To Ian's credit, he remained dead-still despite the provocation.

"No trouble in my town!" Sheriff Bickford announced.

The newcomer and Johnny Durango laughed as they went for their horses.

Ann watched them go and then sniffed loudly, staring at Sheriff Bickford as he walked on into the saloon with Ian. "You questioned Ian and didn't arrest Cash Weatherly!" she stated incredulously.

"Annie—" Ian began.

"Ian—"

"Ann, dammit!" Sheriff Bickford interrupted. "You're waging a personal fight with this man, but you've got to see it the way that it is. Cash Weatherly is a wealthy and influential man in this town. He has been heavily assaulted by outlaws, all but robbed blind!"

"He hires outlaws."

"He hires gunmen." Bickford sighed again. "Most ranchers are having to hire gunmen these days, young lady. Because of the go—gosh-darned outlaws running rampant and stealing everyone blind!"

"They nearly hanged Ian!" Ann said indignantly.

"Ann, would you leave it be?" Ian demanded.

"But—?"

"Ann, please." His voice was grating. Ann felt tears stinging her eyes. He didn't want her defending him.

"This has to stop!" she said.

"It's going to," Ian told her softly. He was angry, aggravated with her. She knew him well enough to know that. But he still came to her side and slipped an arm around her. He kissed her forehead. "I'm starving. So is Sheriff Bickford. Would you be so good as to see what Henri can whip up for the three of us? I'll get us some wine."

For the three of them . . . they were, at least, going to have her join them for lunch. She nodded stiffly and headed into the kitchen.

As soon as she was gone Ian looked to Sheriff Bickford miserably. "Do you see my problem?"

Even as he spoke, Doc Dylan came into the saloon, frowning as he approached Ian.

"Do you have the laudanum?" Ian asked.

"I do. The exact dosage I prescribe for your intentions, though I admit, I don't feel quite right about this—"

"Annie needs a break from this place," Ian said flatly. Dulcie had come up behind him. "Am I right?" he asked softly.

Dulcie nodded nervously. "She needs to get away, definitely."

"And something *is* going on," Ian said.

"All the more reason I should stay—" Sheriff Bickford began.

"I beg you, sir! You must go with Annie, you are all the protection I will have for her. And we must keep the fact that she is leaving secret. Dulcie will help calm her temper once she awakes and you'll be far away and nearly ready to come back yourself by then. Sheriff, I beg this of you! I can keep my temper

with these fellows, but you know how women are—
volatile little creatures. Wild things. If you want law
and order here, you've just got to help me."

"What happens if she insists on coming back?"
Sheriff Bickford demanded.

Ian couldn't tell him that he expected the showdown to be over by that time.

"Dulcie will take over, I promise," Ian said.

Ann came back through the kitchen doorway with
a large silver tray. Ian quickly went to help her with
it. "Fried chicken," she announced. "I hope you will
all enjoy it?" she asked.

"Indeed!" Sheriff Bickford said happily.

Ann set the plates, napkins, and silver on the table. She started to turn around to go for the wine,
but a smiling Harold was at the table even as Ian
seated her. "A fine and aged white, perfect with
chicken!" he announced, serving the wine as the
men were seated. "Well, drink up?" he encouraged.

Ann lifted her glass along with the others. Sipped
her wine. Tasted her chicken. She was glad that
Sheriff Bickford was there with them—she did want
the law on her side. But it seemed equally clear that
she was never going to be able to admit that she had
lifted most of Cash's gold from him, no matter what
else she was able to prove.

She was too nervous to be hungry so she sipped
her wine instead. She decided to go about things
another way. "Sheriff, you are aware that there is
definitely some hostility toward us coming from
Cash Weatherly, aren't you?"

"Perhaps, perhaps," Bickford murmured.

"More wine, my love?" Ian inquired.

"You weren't here, you didn't see. Ian was very
nearly killed."

"But you valiantly came to his rescue. The whole
town is talking about it," the sheriff said.

"The whole town is relishing it," Ian murmured. "And their memories of my wife's unclad body."

"Ian—" she began. She blinked. She was suddenly so tired. And it didn't seem to matter. She giggled suddenly. "It must have been funny."

"I wasn't that amused."

"Ian—"

"Grateful, my love. You did save my life. But I don't appreciate the fact that so many men are now coveting my wife."

She started to giggle again. "Well you had thought at the beginning that all those men actually knew your wife!"

"It won't be long now," Ann heard someone say. She blinked. Doc Dylan was standing by their table. She hadn't remembered seeing him before. Yes, he'd been by the bar, talking to Harold. Now he was in back of Ian. Ian was staring at her, Bickford was staring at her. Dulcie was staring at her.

"It knocked me out all night!" Dulcie whispered.

Ann struggled to rise, staring furiously at her husband. "What's going on, what are you doing?" she demanded. She couldn't seem to stand. She was slurring her words. She was going to fall.

He was up, catching her. She longed to slap him, scratch at his eyes. She was slipping, fading in and out. But she was aware enough to know that he had drugged her.

"Bastard!" she hissed to him. He was carrying her. She could feel his arms around her. Bands of steel. She couldn't fight, she couldn't even move. Or cry. Why had he betrayed her like this?

Why? Because he wanted her gone. Out of danger. He wanted to do the fighting himself. If necessary, he wanted to do the dying himself.

She tried to reach for his face, touched his cheek.

"No!" she said, forming the word. "I'll never forgive you for this!"

"But you'll *live* to hate me!" he whispered to her.

Then he kissed her. Kissed her eyelids, her forehead, her lips. Kissed her tenderly, gently, passionately. She couldn't fight him at all. She was losing all awareness.

"I love you, Annie."

A velvet night was racing in upon her. "Let me stay, let me help you! Please . . ."

"Dear God, I love you, Ann."

She heard no more, felt no more. Not the jolting of the stagecoach as they started out. Not Dulcie's gentle touch as Ann passed out on her lap. She heard no more. Not even Sheriff Bickford's sighing words.

"There's that Johnny Durango again. Slinking around the stables."

"Did he see us?" Dulcie asked worriedly.

"Well, he saw me, but I'm supposed to be traveling out to pick up my daughter today. No surprise there. Now you relax there, Miss Dulcie. The law is riding with you today!"

Dulcie wished she had more faith in the law.

"All right, she's gone now," Aaron said, seated at one of the saloon's round tables along with Ian, Ralph, Angus, Joey Weatherly, and the Yeagher twins. Harold was holding down the bar. They were just waiting for Scar, who had been sent to ride a discreet distance behind the stagecoach, just to make sure that it began its journey in safety. "So what are you going to do now that Ann is no longer within Cash's reach?"

"Showdown," Ian said.

"Showdown?" Angus demanded. He snorted. "Ian, there's still only so many of us—"

"When did that ever hurt during the war?" Ian asked wryly.

Angus grinned. "Ian, still—"

"I'm going to ask Cash to meet me. I'm going to see if he's willing to meet man to man."

"It's not going to happen."

"Right. But at least I think I'll be able to draw his fire here by nightfall. We'll have the rest of the ladies out, and we'll be prepared. I think we can appreciably lower his numbers."

"Bickford is going to be furious," Ralph said morosely. "He doesn't want trouble, and you're inviting a mass battle."

"There's no help for it," Ian said.

"You may hang yet," Ralph warned.

"We'll cross that bridge later. For the moment—"

He broke off suddenly. Scar had arrived at last. He stood in the doorway, then staggered and fell to the floor.

Ann awoke in a daze and stared up at Dulcie. She knew what had happened, and she was still furious with Ian. "Where are we?" she asked. Her tongue was dry.

"Not far enough away from Coopersville," Dulcie said unhappily.

"Annie, now, you just get some sleep!"

The words came from Sheriff Bickford. He was across from her on this unholy journey. She felt ill. The smell of leather seemed to be overwhelming. Dirt and dust, kicked up by the wheels, seemed to invade the whole of the coach.

"But—"

"Annie!" Dulcie whispered. "Don't you see, Ian couldn't hope to fight Cash if he was constantly guarding you against the man's trying to kidnap you!"

"But I can fight!" Ann whispered back.

"Young ladies, now—" Bickford began, but his words were cut off suddenly by the sound of a scream from above them.

The driver! Ann thought. The stagecoach driver!

Her fears were fully realized when something heavy careened from the top of the wagon. She dragged herself up to look out the window. They were swiftly speeding by a fallen body.

"Dear God!" Dulcie cried.

"There's a driver and a guard and me!" Bickford said angrily. "This may be those damned stage-coach-robbing outlaws after us here—"

He broke off. He too had been staring out the window, drawing his gun, taking aim.

He slumped back into the stagecoach. Ann gasped, seeing a burst of red streaming down his temple. "Oh my God!" she cried, ripping out her hem to create a bandage and slamming across the wildly careening coach to dab at his forehead. His gun had fallen. "Dulcie, get over here and help the sheriff so that I can get in a few shots!"

"You can't even hold the gun right now!" Dulcie wailed.

"Dulcie!"

The stagecoach was slowing down. It teetered as someone catapulted himself from a horse to the coach. Ann got hold of one of the sheriff's guns just as the coach pulled to a halt. She aimed at the door as the step to it was lowered and the door itself was thrown open.

Cash Weatherly was there himself. Faded blue eyes hostile and icy upon her, weathered features merciless, silver and iron hair the same as it had been that first day she had seen him slaughter everyone around her and leave her for dead herself.

He too had a gun cocked and ready to fire.

"Put it down, Annie. I'll kill Dulcie here and now without blinking if you don't do so."

"I'll kill you!" she cried out.

"But Dulcie will be dead as well," he assured her.

Ann hesitated. "I keep my gun. I keep my gun until you let the stagecoach head back. Sheriff Bickford is injured. He may be dying. He may live if he gets help. I'll step from the stagecoach and give you my gun after I see it return over that rise."

Cash smiled. He offered her a hand.

"Annie!" Dulcie cried.

"Dulcie, you've got to get back to the saloon!" Ann told her.

"Ann, don't go with him."

"Annie, come," Cash said politely.

She started out. Dulcie clung to her.

"Dulcie, get back to the saloon."

"You'll be dead before we can reach you!" Dulcie said in tears.

"Oh, no. I intend to keep her alive for a while!" Cash said, smiling wickedly.

Ann tore away and tried to avoid Cash's hand.

"Take it, Annie. You'll be taking a whole lot more of me today. Might as well start with my hand."

She ignored him and jumped from the stagecoach but it didn't do her any good. It was turned back toward town with no driver, Dulcie and the injured sheriff within it.

As Ann watched it head back toward town, she felt Cash's arm curl around her abdomen. He pulled her against him. "The gun now, Annie."

She toyed with the idea of turning it on herself. He must have known. Something struck her temple from behind, and she was falling to the dirt.

Blackness fell all around her.

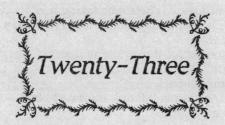

Twenty-Three

"*T*hey took it!" Scar cried out. "They took the wagon. Hell, Ian, I saw it all, but there was nothing I could do. Well, hell, now, wait a minute. I've got the wagon, I caught it coming back. And we need Doc Dylan, Sheriff Bickford's in there hurt, and Dulcie—"

Dulcie burst in behind Scar. "Ian, Cash has taken her! He made her get out—"

"He attacked the damned wagon with the sheriff inside it?" Ian exploded.

Dulcie nodded. For a second, Ian lost all strength. He sank back into his chair, dragging his fingers through his hair, wishing that he could press his own skull hard enough to make it so that it wasn't so.

He felt a hand on his shoulder. "He won't—he won't really hurt her. He wants her too badly."

"Oh, God!" Ian groaned.

"It will hurt you, but you'll still love her, no matter what he does," Aaron breathed.

Ian looked up at them all, shaking his head. "I'd love her no matter what. I'm afraid of what she'll do to *herself* if he—"

"Rapes her," Dulcie supplied.

Ian stood, no longer at a loss, no longer weak. He

stared at Joey. "Where's he taking her?"

"The house, I imagine. He'll feel he knows how to defend it."

He started for the swinging doors.

"Wait!" Angus called out.

Ian turned back.

"We're coming," Ralph informed him.

"It's my fight."

"You've fought for all of us. It's our fight as well."

"It may be suicide—"

"We've been on suicide missions before, right?" Ralph said to Angus.

"Hell, yes!"

"You've got to realize—" Ian began.

"Go!" Dulcie commanded. "Damn you, Ian. She needs you and you need them. Just go!"

"We're going to have to go in with guns blazing," Ralph said. "But we're going to have to be very careful, too. Not only has he taken Ann, but Meg's innocent in all this, Ian. We've got to watch out for Meg."

"Maybe Weatherly has sent her away. Maybe he wanted her off visiting relatives when he brought Ann to the ranch," Angus suggested.

"And maybe he didn't," Ian said. "Joey, what do you think?"

"I don't think he's ever really given a damn about any of us," Joey said angrily. "My sister may very well be there. We'll have to watch out for her. Even so, Ian, we need to move quickly. We need to get going now."

Ian shook his head. "I need just a few more minutes. I've got to see the sheriff."

"Bickford's hurt, Ian—"

"Bickford will understand. He's going to deputize us. I'm going to get my wife back, and I'm going to bring Cash Weatherly down, and I'm going to do it with the full consent of the law he's mocked and flaunted all these years. Or die in the trying!"

She awoke, strangely enough, to softness and comfort. She opened her eyes slowly. There was a handsome mahogany wardrobe to her side, a beautiful cherrywood washstand nearby. There was a rocker upholstered in crimson brocade.

Her head was killing her.

She tried to rise.

Then she saw him. Sitting right by her side on the bed, faded blue eyes calculating.

"He was the kid, wasn't he? That young bronzed boy brought down half my men before the war."

She sat up, inching away from him. "Yeah, he was the kid."

"And you?"

She smiled without humor.

"The other kid."

He arched a brow. It was clear he didn't even remember her. "So you were hating me, and I was coveting you!" He laughed dryly. "Well, you're mine now."

"He'll come for you."

"And he'll be shot down."

"He's tough. He may live."

"It won't make any difference to you. Bitch. In fact, you are the thief who's been stealing from me, right?"

"Everything I could," she said vehemently.

"Ah, such passion. Well, I will have a taste of it!"

He smiled. Ann inched back and tried to leap from the bed. His fingers wound around her wrist. God, he was strong! She tried to wrench free, tried to bite him. His hand came cracking across her face, dazing her. She tried to fight the black that started to whirl before her again. His hands were on her, ripping at her clothing.

"No!" she shrieked out.

He was laughing. Laughing because he was stronger, laughing because he could hurt her. She clawed at him, wriggled, fought. She felt his hands on her leg, felt his weight over her.

"No!" she shrieked, fighting wildly.

"Yes. Yes. Again and again and again. Until you're broken, until you want to die. Until I bring his corpse in here and you stare into his eyes while I hurt you again."

"You are sick, you are evil!"

He smiled. "Yes."

He almost had her. She felt something rip. Felt his touch against the bare flesh of her upper thigh. She bit into his shoulder. He raged, striking at her again. The world began to spin. She was lost. She would want to die . . .

No. She didn't want death. She wanted life! She wanted Ian, to ride with him, be with him. Into the sunset . . .

"Now . . . " Cash grated to her.

But it was then that she heard the gunfire.

They came like a storm. The horses running at full speed and appearing, from a distance, almost like mythical beasts, like creatures racing across clouds. But they didn't ride on clouds, they created that misted field in which they ran, their mighty hooves kicking up earth and dust and dryness and sending it all spiraling into the sky around them. With the setting sun at their backs, they created an extraordinary picture.

And now, Ian was a part of that picture.

He rode with friends who would not leave him, but the fight remained his. He would face a small

army of gunslingers as well as the creature out of
hell it had seemed he'd chased all his life, so he was
glad of the company. He feared for his friends, but
he knew that a man had to do in life as his conscience dictated if he was to lead any kind of a life
at all, and so he had not tried to dissuade them long.
He prayed for them, and he prayed for Ann. He
prayed that she could withstand whatever torment
Cash doled out to her, that she would have faith in
Ian to come for her, faith in her own ability to survive, faith in life itself—and the days that could
stretch before them.

No matter how he prayed, he still saw visions. No
matter what Ann's strength, she couldn't physically
battle strong men when she carried no weapons to
use against them. And if Cash and his men knew or
suspected the truth about her, they might well blame
her for the deaths of some of their own. Maybe that
wouldn't even matter. Cash wanted her, and he
wanted to hurt her. He would rape her without
blinking. And it remained most frightening to Ian to
wonder what desolation and despair she would fall
to herself were Cash to take such action.

He spurred his horse to a greater speed. Their tim-
ing was everything.

They rode hard across the prairie and the plain,
coming at last to the ranch house where Cash
Weatherly ruled. Even as they neared the outer
fence, shots rang out. Ian lifted a hand, bringing his
group of rugged horsemen to a halt. He waved in
either direction, having the men draw up the broken
wagons to provide them with safe cover from which
to shoot. Cash's men had already planted themselves where cover was provided by the house, the
watering trough, a tack room, the outhouse.

She was in the house somewhere. Ann was in
there. All that he had to do was get into the house—

kill Cash Weatherly at long last—and reclaim his wife. That was all. Except that his small party had to get past a good twenty gunmen in order to get near the house.

He remained seated upon his horse, a Colt six-shooter in each of his hands. He had taken down those he could while they were still assuming his party would all be desperately scrambling for cover. Speed, again, was of the essence. He scanned the house and surroundings and started shooting. Before he had emptied the chambers of both Colts his shots had catapulted two men from the roof, sent one bursting from the outhouse to fall down dead ten feet in front of it, and sent another man sprawling out, injured and moaning, upon the porch. He retreated behind one of the wagons to reload his guns and discovered Joey Weatherly reloading his Spencer carbine repeating rifle. Joey grinned grimly up at Ian. "You are one hell of a shot," he said.

"But am I good enough?" he asked, his teeth grating as he forced his hands to remain steady as he reloaded.

Joey nodded briefly, then ducked as a barrage of fire came their way. They saw men scrambling to new positions under that fire.

Ian could see their faces. They were grim faces. Some bearded, some clean-shaven, some young, some aging. Some eyes appeared near dead, some were blazing. Some men just looked wearied, like fellows with a purpose to be done. So much time had gone by since he had first faced Cash Weatherly. So much had changed. So much had stayed the same.

But *he* was different, he knew. He was no longer a boy—he had been baptized in fire by Cash's own hand. Once, Cash had taken everything from him. Now, Cash wanted the woman Ian loved, not to mention Ian's own life. And now, Ian had to win.

He had waited his whole life for this moment, only to realize that he had never really lived. If he was ever to have the chance to do so, he must do more than win. He must win *her* as well. Fate had brought them all back full circle to a dusty plain. Life had been lost beneath the sun, life's blood had watered the plain in crimson. Now it was time to take it all back. To live.

"If you can burst through the doors," Joey said, pointing out double doors with etched glass windows that graced the front of the elegant two-story ranch home, "he'll probably have two men stationed within the front." He hesitated a second. "His room is to the left rear of the house, and he'll be ready to kill her or bargain her life for his own should you make it that far. Be careful if you get past the men at the windows—there will be another two in the kitchen, which is to the right, and God knows how many may be upstairs."

Ian stared down at him. "Thanks, Joey." He shook his head. "You don't have to keep fighting your own father—"

"You know he killed Eddie McCastle as well," he said tonelessly. "He bragged about it to my brothers; I happened to hear. It was so damned easy to make Eddie have an accident. And there was Ann crying over him and Eddie so broken up that he couldn't tell her what had happened. Maybe not just Eddie. I think he killed my mother. I think he put a pillow over her face and snuffed the life out of her because she might have stood in his way. She was beginning to know too much about him." He stared hard at Ian. "You ever see any resemblance to my father in me, McShane, you do me a favor. Shoot me—fast. Promise?"

Ian shook his head. "There is no resemblance, Joey."

Another barrage of fire sent Ian's horse skittering a distance from Joey. Ian calmed the animal. Cash had to know that his house was under fire. He also knew he had it well covered. Was he even concerned with the shooting?

Or was his attention all for his captive? Ian didn't think that he dared wait any longer.

Guns loaded, reins draped over his horse's neck, he gazed over at Joey and the others. The Yeagher twins were crouched down by Joey, along with Scar. Aaron, Ralph, and Angus were across from them behind the second wagon. "Go for the snipers on the roof and at the bedroom windows!" he said to Joey's group. Then he turned to Aaron and his own men. "Get them off the porch and out of the windows— I'm going in."

Angus saluted him; Aaron gave a nod. Joey was already firing. The Yeagher twins and Scar were taking aim.

Ian slammed his heels against his horse's sides and sent the animal leaping forward across the yard. The sheer audacity of the suicidal mission must have given him an advantage, because at first not a bullet was fired his way. His horse's hooves thundered upon the wood of the porch. A fortyish bearded fellow, obviously a war relic, aimed at him from one of the lace-curtained front windows. Ian let loose with a barrage of fire. He was grateful to hear the fellow grunt and the crash of glass as he came through the window.

It was strange. Ian's life had been so filled with warfare. To most men, nothing could have been more painful than the war between the states. But all Ian could remember was that distant prairie. He could see his father's face again, hear the words he had spoken when he had tossed Ian the extra rifle he carried. "Make your shots count, boy!"

Make them count.

He nudged his heels hard into his horse's flanks, urging the animal through the doors. For a moment, his horse balked, then took flight, ramming the doors with their glass-paned windows. Wood shuddered, groaned, and gave; glass cracked, shattered, and seemed to rain down in a myriad of tiny crystals. Sunlight surged into the parlor of the house, illuminating the men coming in from the dining room and the fellow who was just swirling inward from the window.

Make your shots count, boy.

They had to count. One misfire and he was a dead man himself. Decisions made in split seconds. Fire in both directions, aim doesn't have to be perfect, just make sure that they can't fire back. . . .

A barrage again, his right Colt firing away at the men on the stairs, his left taking down the man from the window. Shrieks, groans; the stairway banister cracking as the weight of a man slammed against it. His horse rearing on the wooden floor. Gunfire from without, an eerie silence from within.

Reload!

He did so, just in time. Two more men came in from the dining room, firing even as they entered. He heard the whistle of their bullets along with the click of his horse's hooves against Cash Weatherly's hardwood floors. His horse reared and screamed as a ball ripped by its shoulder. Ian swiftly steadied his aim and fired, losing one man back to the hallway, but seeing the other one fall where he stood without a whimper.

"Steady, boy, steady," he told his horse. "Don't think that one was so bad, it's not in you, boy, it just ripped some hair and flesh and settled into the door frame there. Just a flesh wound, fellow, you're going to be just fine." He nudged his horse and was grateful to realize that the well-trained gelding seemed to believe him. They moved on in past the parlor, past the stairway. They brushed by an occasional table. A fine marble porcelain statuette fell to the floor, shattered. He barely heard the sound. He saw the door to the rear room before him and he tensed, knees tightening hard. His horse knew the command, gathered speed despite the polished hardwood, and rammed hard against the door. Again wood shuddered, groaned, splintered—and gave. Ian burst through the door on horseback, eyes narrowed and swiftly surveying the room, guns leveled.

Cash had known he was coming.

Ian didn't know what fierce struggle Ann had already waged on her own. Her hair was loose, flowing in wild, golden tangles down her back and over her shoulders. One sleeve was nearly ripped from her gown, the skirt was in tatters. She dragged in every breath she took, yet did so carefully, with as little movement as possible.

Because she had been dragged to her knees at Cash's feet. One of his hands sat atop her head, his fingers threaded through her hair. With his right hand he held his pistol with the barrel pressed flush against her temple. Ann had certainly done some struggling, perhaps even some winning. There were long scratches on Weatherly's cheeks, just below his colorless blue eyes.

"How excessively rude, young man. Didn't anyone ever teach you that it was polite to knock?" Cash drawled.

"You all right, Annie?" Ian asked.

Cash smiled. His cold, inhuman smile that didn't touch his pale, nearly colorless blue eyes. "Is she all right? She's on her knees at my feet, boy. You're going to drop those Colts before I blow off her head. Then she may be all right. Your life for hers."

"Don't listen to a word he says!" Ann cried fiercely. "He's like a disease, he was a disease before the war and he wants to be a disease in the West. Ian, you can't let him fool you, you can't be afraid for me, you—"

She broke off with a sharp little cry because Cash had tightened his grip mercilessly on her hair. "How touching! Imagine. She's told me everything, of course. But just think, all of these years gone by, and we're here, together again, the three of us." He shook his head with weary disbelief. "Who'd have imagined that the Pawnees would neglect to finish you off! There's a lesson to be learned here, of course."

"Yeah," Ian said, "always make sure that those you leave for corpses are really dead."

"Indeed, young man, indeed!" Cash agreed, his smile deepening. "Now, sir, you'll throw those Colts to the floor, or watch her brains splatter over my fine wallpaper. I do prefer the first—I am quite fond of this wallpaper."

"Ian, no—" Ann tried again, only to be silenced by another jerk upon her hair. Teeth grating, she stared at Ian, pleading with him with her eyes. *Don't fall for it; he'll kill us both.*

He'd kill her more slowly, of course, Ian knew. Finish what he'd been trying to start with her here, in this room. Do it with Ian's body still lying on the floor. Because there was something ungodly cold about the man. Something evil deep in his soul.

Although Ian was inside the house, he could suddenly feel a breeze. Feel the past coming back. He could hear the riders again. Feel the earth move and tremble. They came closer. The riders were upon them. The dust cloud began to choke them. It became a storm. The ground trembled. The horses that raced so hard cast off droplets of sweat while foam worked around their bits.

Ian could hear the first shot being fired again.

It came from their leader.

His hair was iron gray, his features were weathered and hard, his eyes were a cool blue. It was an oddly striking face, chilling, somehow compelling, strangely ageless. He was one of those who smiled as he rode. Smiled as he took aim, shot.

God, if he did try shooting Cash while Cash held Ann so closely, he would be taking a chance. How *could* he take such a chance with Ann's life? Even if Cash killed Ian, his men had been falling in the battle they'd fought so far. Angus, Ralph, Joey, and the others might prevail, save Annie no matter what happened to Ian. But by *not* shooting he might just be taking a chance as well.

"The Colts, boy!" Cash raged.

It was back again, the past. It was in this room with the three of them. There was sunlight, dust, dirt, sweat, and air. Ian could see it all so clearly around him, ghosts of time gone past. Horses reared, horses fell, men, women, and children tried to take cover behind them. The dust was stirred up so that the air tasted of it along with the acrid smell of gunpowder. The same black powder hung in the air. Ian could feel it hurting his lungs when he tried to inhale. Nothing that could be seen seemed real anymore, the day was so filled with powder and dust.

"The Colts, boy!"

Ian could feel the dust in his mouth. He didn't need to close his eyes to see the blood expanding across his father's shirt. See him clutch his chest, fall.

The old scream rose in his throat. He saw his mother again, in slow, strange motion now, saw her racing to his sprawled pa. She was a beautiful woman. Everyone had always said so. Slim and always laughing, with the face of an angel. One second she was running.

The explosion of a bullet; she was dead.

"Give me the guns!" Cash bellowed.

But the past wouldn't ease its grip. Ian saw the girl again, running. The fellow riding hard behind her, reaching for her, laughing.

"Little young!" someone called.

"He likes 'em that way!"

The girl turned. To the astonishment of the riders, the little caped creature was carrying a pistol. She took aim and fired. She missed, but just barely. She nicked her attacker's ear. Blood spurted from it as the man howled out in pain.

The girl. Annie.

Ian saw what was going to happen next. He just couldn't stop it. He screamed and screamed as he watched, but he couldn't do anything at all. He made it to his feet, but he hadn't even begun to run when the furious rider turned on her, swinging the stock of his rifle hard across the girl's hooded head.

Ian heard the impact. Watched her crumple. He shrieked and screamed and started to run, his rifle empty now, but swinging nonetheless.

"Ian!" Ann shrieked now, pleading.

"The guns!" Weatherly roared.

He saw her eyes. Saw in them her fury, her fear, her pride.

"I love you, Annie," he told her.

She smiled, heedless of Cash Weatherly's cruel touch upon her.

"I love you, Ian."

She enunciated his name and he realized that she was saying far more to him than the words might tell. She loved him—and she had faith in him. In his ability. In the faith that he could pull his trigger, fire—and leave her alive.

"The guns—" Cash started to repeat.

Ian fired.

Twenty-Four

T here were dead men everywhere.

And after all the sharp whips and retorts of gunfire, there was suddenly silence. Joey carefully stood along with Angus, Ralph, Scar, Aaron, and the Yeagher twins. There was no sudden burst of fire now that they were fully visible. Of course not. There were dead men everywhere.

"Did we get them—all?" Joey said with disbelief.

Angus, reloading at his side, shrugged and looked around. "McShane took down a good number, and yeah, it seems we got them all. Lots of food for the buzzards here!" he added softly.

"The house?" Ralph said.

"Yeah, the house," Angus agreed with a heavy heart. He cast his dark, sharp gaze on Aaron and Joey. "There's no cause for you two going on in—"

"Yeah, there is. We've all got to go in," Aaron said.

"No matter what we find," Joey agreed.

"All right, then, we move slowly," Angus directed. "Crescent pattern. Eyes to the left at all times, eyes to the right, eyes behind us. Got it, boys?"

They all nodded and formed the ranks Angus had indicated to approach the house. They moved very slowly and carefully at first, but there was no retort of gunfire to be heard. They reached the porch and the shattered doorway, the dead man hanging from the window.

More bodies littered the parlor. Joey took the lead then, striding hard past the stairway for the rear of the house. They came to another shattered doorway, ragged splinters of wood cast all about them.

The first thing they saw was Ian's horse. The big bay's rump seemed enormous and out of place, blocking off the bedroom. Angus smacked a hand on the horse's rump, directing the fine creature back out of the house.

Joey saw his father.

Cash was slumped down on the ground, his gun still entwined in his fingers, the side of his head painted in red. Dead or alive? Joey wondered. But it didn't matter as long as his father was down, he determined. He didn't even pause to find out if Cash's heart was still beating.

Ian and Ann were to the rear of the room, Ian seated upon the old rocker there, Ann in his lap. They were both dusty, ragged, and worn, but a finer looking couple was not to be found on the face of the earth, Joey was quite certain. They hadn't seemed to have noticed their company as yet.

"Sweet God, I was scared to death!" Ian was saying passionately, his hands on his wife's face, holding her, searching out her eyes.

"You shouldn't have sent me away."

"I shouldn't have."

"You drugged me!"

Ian groaned. "I was trying to save your life."

"I know."

"Forgive me?"

"Love you."

"God, did he hurt you?"

"Not so badly—"

"I was afraid of what you'd do to yourself if he would have—if he would have—"

"I knew that you were coming."

"Dear God!" Ian said, trembling.

"I knew, I knew that you would come!"

"Through hell itself!"

"It was so strange," Ann said. "I didn't know until today that the revenge didn't matter anymore—"

"It was the living that mattered," Ian murmured.

"Justice is needed, justice is important. But to live for revenge and hatred—"

"It's so much better to live for the future. Yet we might never have known that—"

"We didn't know we had a future."

"He might still be alive."

"I don't need to see him dead."

"That's the sheriff's concern."

"If the sheriff lives."

"He belongs to the law."

"Good God, yes!" Ralph interrupted the two at last. "We must have the law!"

Ann and Ian started, looking up. Ann smiled and began to rise.

It was just then that Joey noticed his father. Cash's eyes were open. Faded blue, cold. So close to colorless.

Cash's fingers started to tighten around the butt and trigger of his gun.

Joey realized that he should have checked on his father's heartbeat after all.

He drew his own gun, ready to fire. Cash pushed himself up with inhuman strength and started to turn, determined to kill either Ian or Ann.

Joey started to pull the trigger.

Before he could fire, a shot exploded. Crimson spread out across Cash Weatherly's chest, right at his heart. There was no question as to whether he was alive or dead now.

Startled, they all stared across the room to the shattered door, every last one of them.

Meg stood there, one of her father's old war carbines still smoking in her hands. "He killed my mother, you know." Her voice was steady, but her face was wet with her tears. "And he might as well have killed Carl and Jenson. They weren't really bad; they just tried to be his sons. They're both dead, you know. In the dirt, outside." She suddenly dropped the gun and stepped back.

Ian stood and walked awkwardly to her. He pulled her gently into his arms. "I'm sorry."

"We've got to bury them," Meg said, sobbing.

Ann joined them, taking Meg from Ian and agreeing, "We've got to bury them all." She lifted Meg's chin, smoothed the tears from her cheeks. "We've got to bury them, and then we've got to move on, Meg. We've all got to live *our* lives, and let go of the shadows of the past."

"Amen," Joey agreed softly. "Amen."

The week that followed was a strange time for Ann. She had never known fear as she had known it when she had discovered herself Cash's prisoner. But neither had she ever known love as she had felt it when she saw Ian come crashing through the doorway, defying death to come to her side.

Each moment with Ian now became doubly precious. Their dreams were gems to be shared. Love was an exploration, deepening, expanding. They would always know its value.

At the end of the week that followed the events at Weatherly's ranch, there was a trail of wagons braked in front of McCastle's saloon.

Beyond Ann's and Ian's own situation, it had been

an interesting time. The first part of the week had been filled with burials.

Then had come the weddings. Meg Weatherly had consented to become Mrs. Ralph Reninger.

Dulcie was still walking on clouds, still unable to believe that Joey had insisted on marrying her. He hadn't just asked, he had insisted. No matter what her protests, her fears, her own insistence that he remember all the men who had clouded her life, he had told her firmly that the future was what mattered—and their future was going to be together.

Aaron, swept up in the spirit of love and marriage, had asked Ginger for her hand. He had done so quite eloquently, Ann had thought. He was a handsome young fellow, who had such a way with words.

But to the astonishment of all within the saloon, Ginger had determinedly turned him down.

"Aaron, sad as it may seem, I like what I do. And with all of the rest of you moving on . . . well, I like the saloon. Annie and Ian will let me buy it on time. I intend to become one of the renowned *madams* of the West. I'm going to rename it Ginger's, of course, as soon as I've got the chance. And I will be hiring new girls, naturally, but the Yeagher twins and Scar will be around to help me, even if Harold and Henri are going to move on with you all."

So Ginger didn't marry Aaron, but just when it seemed that he was going to go into a depression over her rejection, Annabella walked in with her brother. *The* Annabella, Ann thought, the gorgeous young creature they had met while holding up her stagecoach. They came for lunch before preparing to head out of town on their own search for the American dream, but wound up staying for more than lunch because Aaron was determined to meet Annabella—as himself, rather than an outlaw.

It was the most amazing thing Ann had ever seen. In a matter of minutes, Annabella's brother had given up trying to join in the conversation, and had joined a card table instead. Annabella and Aaron had their heads lowered together for hours, talking passionately. Soon they were holding hands.

At twilight, they walked to the stables together.

By full nightfall, they announced their engagement.

Within twenty-four hours of being rejected by one woman, Aaron married another.

So Ginger was going to keep the saloon, Scar, the twins, and most of the help. Sheriff Bickford was healing nicely, because Doc Dylan had taken good care of him. The town would live on fine—but the rest of them were going to climb aboard their wagons and move on. Annabella's brother had decided to hold off on their own claims and was accompanying his sister and Aaron. Ian's father had left him thousands of acres in homesteader claims, and all of the claims were good. The land lay farther west, near one of the burgeoning new towns in the Colorado territory, and they were all eager to reach it. Henri was going to open a restaurant, Ralph was going to practice frontier law. Cocoa was eager to open a school for young black children. Joey Weatherly was going to teach them all how to do some cattle ranching.

And Ann and Ian were going to begin to learn to live.

Even though the wound in Ann's side had healed, the week had been a little rough on her. Too much trauma, she thought. Maybe even too much happiness. Joy could be rough on the stomach. But when the wagons were loaded and half the town had come out to wave good-bye—most of the good wives along with their husbands—she realized she needed just another minute in Coopersville.

"Wait a second!" she told Ian, who held the reins to their wagon. "I just need a second."

She leapt down from the wagon and hurried to the cemetery. There were dozens of new graves there now, but she didn't pause by any of them. She went straight to Eddie's grave and set down a wild-flower she had plucked on her way over.

"You were such a good man, Eddie!" she said softly. "You let me boss you all over the place, but you always liked to tell me that I wouldn't find happiness in hatred and revenge. You were right, Eddie, but I'm glad Cash is gone anyway because he was so evil. Oh, Eddie, he even caused your accident, and I didn't know. But you can rest in peace now. I'm sorry to be leaving you, but Ginger is a tough little lady, and she's promised to look after the grave for me. You know, in the end, Eddie, it didn't matter. I mean that the revenge didn't matter. Justice was important, but Ian mattered, more than anything. . . . "

Her voice trailed away. Ian was behind her. His arms slipped around her.

She cleared her throat. "Anyway, Eddie, I wish you could have met him. It's all over at last; we're moving on. We're husband and wife, and very much in love. Isn't that remarkable? And there's something good, Eddie. Out of all this pain and death. There's *life*. It will be a while yet, of course, which is good—we'll be building and all—but we're going to have a baby. At least, I'm pretty certain. No, I'm sure. I—"

"A what?" Ian exploded, swirling her around.

"A baby," Ann told him. "You know, small human creature. Cries quite a bit, wets—"

"A baby?"

"Yeah, a baby." She sighed and added softly, "I may have been the unlikely innocent in this relationship but at least I have always been aware of the possible results of those intimate little moments shared by husband and wife and—"

"A baby!" he exclaimed, and she gasped for breath, she was off her feet so quickly and into his arms. His mouth crushed down upon hers, hard, tender, filled with a million wonderful emotions and all the passion and love she could ever desire. The kiss seemed to last forever, and yet never long enough. But his lips parted from hers, his eyes, with the ebony fire she loved so dearly, continued to burn into her own. "A baby?" he said again.

She nodded.

He smiled, and spoke softly to the grave.

"Rest well, Eddie McCastle. We've got to move on now. A new world, a new life, and *love* await us." He looked back down at Ann. "Ready?" he asked softly.

She returned his dazzling smile.

"Ready," she agreed.

And within moments, they were riding into the sunset.

Together.

Unforgettable Romance from

Shannon Drake

"She knows how to tell a story that captures the imagination"
Romantic Times

KNIGHT OF FIRE
77169-1/$5.99 US/$6.99 Can
With gentle words and sensuous kisses, the steel-eyed Norman invader, Bret D'Anlou, vanquishes beautiful, defiant Princess Allora.

BRIDE OF THE WIND
76353-2/$4.99 US/$5.99 Can

DAMSEL IN DISTRESS
76352-4/$4.99 US/$5.99 Can

Coming Soon

BRANDED HEARTS
77170-5/$5.99 US/$6.99 Can

Buy these books at your local bookstore or use this coupon for ordering:

Mail to: Avon Books, Dept BP, Box 767, Rte 2, Dresden, TN 38225   C
Please send me the book(s) I have checked above.
☐ My check or money order— no cash or CODs please— for $_____is enclosed please add $1.50 to cover postage and handling for each book ordered— Canadian residents add 7% GST).
☐ Charge my VISA/MC Acct#_____Exp Date_____
Minimum credit card order is two books or $6.00 (please add postage and handling charge of 1.50 per book — Canadian residents add 7% GST). For faster service, call 1-800-762-0779. Residents of Tennessee, please call 1-800-633-1607. Prices and numbers are subject to change without notice. Please allow six to eight weeks for delivery.

Name_____
Address_____
City_____State/Zip_____
Telephone No._____   SD 1094

America Loves Lindsey!

The Timeless Romances
of #1 Bestselling Author

KEEPER OF THE HEART	77493-3/$5.99 US/$6.99 Can
THE MAGIC OF YOU	75629-3/$5.99 US/$6.99 Can
ANGEL	75628-5/$5.99 US/$6.99 Can
PRISONER OF MY DESIRE	75627-7/$5.99 US/$6.99 Can
ONCE A PRINCESS	75625-0/$5.99 US/$6.99 Can
WARRIOR'S WOMAN	75301-4/$5.99 US/$6.99 Can
MAN OF MY DREAMS	75626-9/$5.99 US/$6.99 Can
SURRENDER MY LOVE	76256-0/$6.50 US/$7.50 Can
YOU BELONG TO ME	76258-7/$6.50 US/$7.50 Can

Buy these books at your local bookstore or use this coupon for ordering:

Mail to: Avon Books, Dept BP, Box 767, Rte 2, Dresden, TN 38225   C
Please send me the book(s) I have checked above.
❏ My check or money order— no cash or CODs please— for $_____is enclosed
(please add $1.50 to cover postage and handling for each book ordered— Canadian residents
add 7% GST).
❏ Charge my VISA/MC Acct#_____Exp Date_____
Minimum credit card order is two books or $6.00 (please add postage and handling charge of
$1.50 per book — Canadian residents add 7% GST). For faster service, call
1-800-762-0779. Residents of Tennessee, please call 1-800-633-1607. Prices and numbers
are subject to change without notice. Please allow six to eight weeks for delivery.

Name_____
Address_____
City_____State/Zip_____
Telephone No._____   JLA 1094

FREE GIFT OFFER

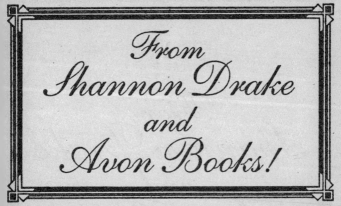

From
Shannon Drake
and
Avon Books!

As our special thank you from Shannon Drake and Avon Books, your purchase of BRANDED HEARTS entitles you to a free picture frame. This lovely gift is the perfect way to display photos of your loved ones at home or in the office. Just fill out the information below and send it in with your proof of purchase of BRANDED HEARTS (cash register receipt) to receive your free frame today!

MAIL TO:
AVON BOOKS, FREE FRAME OFFER
Box 767, Dresden, TN 38225

Offer valid while supplies last. Void where prohibited by law.

Name_____

Address_____

FREE GIFT OFFER

From
Shannon Drake
and
Avon Books!

See other side for details